Digital Book ISBN: 978-1-64873-181-5
Paperback ISBN: 978-1-64873-180-8
Hardcover ISBN: 978-1-64873-179-2

Printed in the United States of America

Published by:
Writer's Publishing House
Prescott, Az 86301

Cover and Interior Design by Creative Artistic Excellence Marketing
Project Management and Book Launch by Creative Artistic
Excellence Marketing creativeartisticexcellence.com

Acknowledgments

The fate of all life, both good and bad is determined by the deeds and actions of all who tread before us, somewhere within the vast spectrum of time.

Branchview – The Portal of Time
–By Brian Jay Nelson

Table of Contents

Chapter One:

The Girl in The Mirror

A bit of normalcy had returned to the Great House of Branchview after months of waging a war against evil. On this beautiful summer morning, the sun casts a warm glow on a part of the Estate Gardens, which fortunately escaped the wrath of the tsunami. Beneath the pergola, a small gathering of the Branchview family watched as a loving couple exchanged their wedding vows. None gave much thought to the fact that they witnessed a truly miraculous event right before their eyes. For on this day, the mighty god Poseidon, who everyone knew as Philip Seagraves, was marrying Tina Lane. The mannequin transformed into a woman by the magic of Charlotte Locke, was the only woman other than Amphitrite, to succeed in capturing his heart and filling it with love. The perfect weather and flower-filled garden setting created a fairy tale type of magic that could rival the most lavish of royal affairs. As the minister closed the ceremony, they kissed, while all in attendance applauded joyfully.

Later, in the Branchview Grand Ballroom, Loraine bustled about in her elegant gown, making sure the servers had everything placed perfectly for the reception. Sharie nervously entered the room and promptly addressed her staff.

"Okay, everyone! It's almost showtime. Let's make this a memorable event for our new couple."

Mrs. Porter ambled up to Loraine with contained excitement. "Are you happy with the way we decorated the room?"

"Yes…" Loraine's answer was cut short when she noticed the reflection of a young woman in one of the massive wall mirrors. The woman was dressed in a modest Victorian style dress, and she had long, braided, beautiful golden blonde hair. She peered into the room from the other side of the mirror with naïve innocence. Her blue eyes searched desperately to every corner of the room.

Loraine watched her for a long hypnotic moment before Mrs. Porter gently tugged at her arm with great concern. "Are you alright, Lori? You look as though you've seen a ghost."

Loraine quickly turned her attention back to Mrs. Porter. "Oh! I'm quite fine, Mrs. Porter." She sighed. "I'm completely caught up in the wonderful magic of the moment. And yes, everything looks marvelous, dear."

Loraine smiled, as a delighted Mrs. Porter turned away, and meticulously carried on with her chores. She strolled closer to the mirror to investigate, but the young woman was now gone.

Sharie approached from behind, as Loraine's eyes wandered to all corners of the massive mirror. "Did my people miss a spot when they were cleaning?"

Loraine was somewhat startled and quickly reacted. "Oh, no! I was simply admiring the fine craftsmanship of the frame around this mirror."

"Trust me! You could live here for an entire lifetime and still be amazed by the small intricacies of this house" She smiled. "We're almost ready here."

"Excellent! I'll tell the others." Loraine paused to glance back at the mirror with a puzzled expression.

Later, as the party began to wind down, and the late day sun streamed through the stained-glass ceiling panels, and the large windows on the west side of the room, the bride and groom gracefully danced across the marble floor within a menagerie of mellow light.

At the end of the dance, Steven took a break from the piano, as the band continued to the next song without him. He strolled across the floor to where Philip and his new bride conversed with his brother, Ezekiel, and his companion Meryl Markopoulis, a striking, dark-haired woman with a commanding presence.

Meryl, who was actually the immortal goddess Metis, glanced at Steven with an approving eye. "I must say. You are an accomplished pianist, Mr. Spencer."

Steven replied with a grateful nod, "Thank you, Ms. Markopoulis. I strive greatly to carry on the musical legacy of my late father."

He paused to glance between the two women, "Would one of you ladies care to dance?"

Tina replied with enthusiasm. "I would love to dance with you, Steven."

Steven gracefully took hold of her hand, and all watched as they began to glide across the floor in a three-step waltz.

Meryl looked to Ezekiel, and Philip with a raised eyebrow. "He's a handsome man, and quite charming I might add."

Ezekiel quipped, "Darling! Are you trying to make me jealous?"

"I don't know. Am I?" She smirked.

Her eyes then wandered across the dance floor, where she caught sight of Loraine. "If you gentlemen would excuse me, I must ask Mrs. Spencer about that lovely dress she's wearing."

As she sashayed in that direction, Philip jokingly raised his glass of wine toward Ezekiel. "Metis is still just as catty as I remembered her being."

"Nevertheless, even after all these centuries, I'm still madly in love with her."

Philip chuckled. "Love is definitely a wonderful thing. It's certainly transformed me."

"So, I see." He gestured toward Tina. "Will she become an immortal like us?"

Philip thought intently for a moment, as he watched with amusement, while Steven twirled Tina around on the tiles. "No! I've decided to give up my immortality to grow old with her, and my new friends here at Branchview. "

Ezekiel was visibly flabbergasted. "That's a steep decision. Are you sure that's what you want?"

Philip answered confidently. "I'm quite certain!" He paused with a sigh. "I've grown tired of watching acquaintances grow old, and die throughout the centuries, while we soldier on, and live perpetually as young men and women.”

“But that’s our purpose.” Ezekiel scoffed. “After all, we are immortal gods.”

Philip shook his head with stubborn indifference. “Amphitrite had the right idea. She gave it all up for love.” He chugged down the last of his wine. “And that’s exactly what I intend to do.”

Ezekiel grunted. “I suppose I have no other choice than to honor your decision.”

Philip grinned as Steven and Tina glided by the two men. “Cheer up brother, it's not as though I’m going to die tomorrow. I plan to live a long, and happy life with that lovely woman dancing out there.”

Across the ballroom, Meryl chatted up a storm while Loraine patiently listened. “… And there’s this marvelous little boutique on the Isle of Rhodes that you have to see to believe.”

Loraine glanced away as she spoke, and she noticed the woman in the mirror was back. She pressed her hands against the mirror, longingly looking through it, and hoping to find a way to pass through.

"Excuse me, Ms. Markopolous. I have something I must urgently attend to. Could we continue this conversation later?"

"Of course! Perhaps over a glass of that yummy wine, your staff is serving"

Loraine answered with a pleasant smile before hurrying toward the mirror. She came to a halt in front of it, making direct eye contact with the young woman, and causing her to react in a cowering manner. The woman shyly clasped her hands in front of her, as she watched Loraine.

Suzy McVea casually strolled up next to Loraine and watched with great curiosity as well. "Who is she?"

Suzy took Loraine totally by surprise. "Who's who?"

Suzy gestured toward the young woman. "There in the mirror, I know you can see her too."

"You can see her?" Loraine inquired.

Suzy rolled her eyes and laughed. "Yeah! You and I are obviously the only ones in the room that can."

Loraine glanced at the other people around them, and noticed that none of them were aware of the woman's presence. "I suppose, like myself, you must possess a sensitive perception for that sort of thing."

The young woman, realizing they could both see her, fled into the landscape within the mirror. Suzy strolled over to investigate further, while Loraine looked at her with astonishment. "How long have you had this ability to see things?"

Suzy sauntered back to Loraine. "I started noticing a change shortly after the tsunami hit. It was as though I became more sensitive to everything around me.

Loraine sighed and lowered her voice. "You mustn't mention this to anyone else. Do you understand?'

Suzy laughed, "Are you kidding? I don't want people to think I've gone plum crazy."

"I can fully assure you that you're not losing your mind."

Tony Freeman approached Suzy from behind and tapped her on the shoulder. "Andrea gave me permission to dance with you."

Suzy accepted his outstretched hand with an amused smile and turned back toward Loraine with a wink. "We'll definitely talk more about this later."

After the long day of celebrating, Steven and Loraine ascended the stairway to retire to their room for the night. Steven paused at the first landing to eye the photo of the stern-faced woman and grunted. "I have no idea which one of my relatives she is, but her face is enough to give anyone nightmares."

Loraine giggled with considerable amusement at his comment. "What a magical day this was." She smiled in reflection and sighed. "Philip and Tina are so much in love."

Steven loosened his tie, almost oblivious to her comment, and also sighed. "I can tell you one thing. I can hardly wait to get out of this tux.

They continued to the top landing, where Steven glanced off to his left. "I've been so busy with the wedding these past few days that I haven't had the time to check out the progress in the East Wing." He glanced back toward Loraine. "Would you like to join me?"

"I'll check it out tomorrow, Steven. I need to check in on Mama Millie and the babies."

"I'll only be a short while. Keep the bed warm for me."

They kissed, and Loraine exited into the North Wing, while Steven continued on, and opened the large double doors of the East Wing. He entered slowly, flicking on the light switch, and the bare bulb hanging from a dangling wire in the ceiling brightly illuminated the room. He pushed aside a plastic tarp, which was suspended from the ceiling, and looked around the empty, unfinished Sitting Room.

As he continued deeper into the Wing, his footsteps echoed loudly as he strolled across the newly laid wood flooring. He came to a sudden halt and listened closely to what appeared to be the chatter of an almost inaudible discussion between a man and a woman. The voices seemed to be coming from another portion of the Wing, and he curiously proceeded down a dark hallway to check it out.

There was a sudden loud noise, and he twirled around quickly with high anxiety. He then laughed to himself when he saw that their cat, Charlotte, had simply knocked a construction bucket off a ledge. The cat meowed loudly, and affectionately brushed against his leg, while he turned his attention back to the voices.

He walked a few steps forward, and paused in front of a set of double doors, just off the hallway. He listened closely, and then looked back down at the cat. "I think I may have found where those voices are coming from, kitty cat.

He swung the doors open, only to find himself confronted with a solid brick wall. The voices immediately ceased at that moment, and the only sound heard was the purring of the cat and the beating of Steven's heart. He ran his hands across the rough-textured brick facing, then gazed around with puzzlement as he mumbled to himself. "What in the hell is going on here?"

He shrugged it off and shut the doors again while continuing to quiz himself. "Why is there a set of doors that lead to nowhere?" He shook his head in wonderment and began to retreat down the hallway. Suddenly, the voices commenced again. "What the…?" He paused momentarily, shaking his head again in disbelief. With a sigh, he continued, choosing to ignore it. "Come on, kitty! Let's call it a night." The cat scurried out the door to the outer hallway as Steven flicked the light switch off, and quietly closed the doors to the Wing.

In the Branchview Grand Ballroom, the light of a late summer full moon peeked through the windows that lined the sides of the high ceiling. It casts its beams directly into the massive wall mirror, revealing the young woman on the other side. She peered longingly into the darkroom, gently running her hand across the surface of her side of the mirror. Much to her surprise, her hand broke through the portal to the other side.

She gingerly stepped forward, placing her entire arm through. She then mustered the courage to go completely through, shielding her eyes against a nearly blinding moonbeam. The young women stepped into the massive room and gazed upward with amazement at the high ceilings.

"It's just as I remember it."

She gracefully whirled around in an imaginary dance, while the moonbeams moved away from the mirror, and eventually from the room altogether. Suddenly, she found herself in total darkness. She anxiously turned to return to the mirror. Running her silk smooth hands across the surface, she quickly realized she was unable to go back through.

Meanwhile, Steven and Loraine were sound asleep in their North Wing bedroom. Loraine suddenly awakened wide-eyed from a dream, and Bumpers also alertly awakened from his perch at the foot of the bed. She quietly got up, put on her robe, and grabbed a flashlight. She paused to whisper to the dog before exiting the room. "You stay put, Bumpers." The dog answered with a slight whimper as she tiptoed by.

Moments later, the giant clock within the Grand Ballroom chimed at 1 am, sending out a bellowing echo that startled the mysterious young woman that sat alone in the darkness of the cavernous room.

While she hunkered in fear upon a bench at the edge of the dance floor, a beam from a flashlight caught her frightened face. Loraine strolled closer, as the terrified woman pointed to the flashlight she was holding. "It's ok, sweetheart. It's only a flashlight. It won't harm you."

The woman shyly replied. "I've never seen such a device."

Loraine paced closer with a perplexed expression. "You're the woman I observed earlier in the mirror. Who are you, and what is your intention for being here?"

She curtsied, timidly toward Loraine. "My name is Emma. Emma Lindstrand."

Loraine smiled warmly. "There's no need to bow to me. I'm far from being royalty"

"You looked so elegant, and pretty in that beautiful gown, you wore earlier. I assumed you were someone of importance."

Loraine curiously sauntered closer. "I detect an accent. Are you Swedish?"

Emma answered with a humble nod. "I arrived here earlier in the summer from Gothenburg. Daniel Branch hired me as a housekeeper."

Loraine responded with disbelief. "Daniel Branch?"

Emma nodded with enthusiasm. "Yes! Is he here?" She paused to glance around for a quick moment. "I know this house very well, but all the faces I noted earlier were so unfamiliar."

Loraine sat down next to Emma and spoke with great seriousness. "You may not be aware of this, but we are living in the year 2019."

Emma placed her hand to her head with great distraught. "Oh my! That must mean I've been…"

"Dead for over a hundred years" Loraine finished her statement for her.

Emma gazed sadly to the floor, and Loraine was moved with great compassion for the ghostly apparition. She carefully tried placing her hand on her shoulder and was surprised when she actually could feel it. "Come now, dear. I will try my best to help you sort things out." Loraine gave her an assuring smile. "My name is Loraine Spencer.

Can you tell me how you entered our time through that mirror?"

They both looked toward the mirror as Emma tried to recant her experience. "It had to have been the moon. It shined so brightly into it, that it nearly blinded me."

"What happened next?" Loraine inquired with great interest.

"I simply stepped through, and into this room. But when I tried to go back, the moonbeams had shifted, and I couldn't return to the other side."

Loraine looked upward with renewed enlightenment. "The moonbeams must've opened the time portal long enough for you to step through. Then when it passed the mirror's direct path, it closed again."

Emma reacted with much nervous anxiety. "Does that mean I can't go back?"

"There's nothing for you to go back to, sweetheart." Loraine breathed an emotional sigh before continuing. "You need to go to the light, and I can help you with that."

Emma stood up and became very emotional. "No! No! I must find my Edward.

Loraine responded inexplicably. "Who is this Edward you speak of?" She asked. "Perhaps I can help you with that as well.

Emma settled back on the bench next to Loraine, and her eyes filled with tears. "Edward Branch! He was my fiancée."

Loraine glanced away momentarily and shrugged cluelessly. "I don't recall seeing his name in the family journals."

"He was a second cousin of the Branch family from Boston. Mr. Branch gave him a job in his company, and he arrived at Branchview around the same time I did." She paused in a moment of fond reflection. "We quickly fell in love."

"What happened to him, Emma?"

"I don't know." She emotionally scanned the room as though searching. "We were dancing over there in the center of the room."

Loraine anxiously gestured for her to continue. "He said there was something he needed to get from his room." She paused for a moment of painful thought. "He left and never returned. That was the last time I ever saw him."

"Do you know where his room was?"

"Yes! He was staying in the East Wing with young Matthew Branch."

"The East Wing?" Loraine rolled her eyes and placed her hand on her forehead with much anxiety. "Oh! Why am I not surprised?" She refocused on Emma. "What happened next?"

Emma emotionally continued while Loraine listened with serious attention. "Days went by, and no one could locate him." She bit her upper lip. "Then this woman who had frequently visited the house sent me a sealed message. She said she might have information on where he had gone." She drew an emotion-filled breath. "She told me to meet her on the cliffs overlooking Lighthouse Point the following evening." Loraine urged her on. "I was waiting there, enjoying the serene view of the ocean when someone forcibly pushed me from behind." She struggled with much pain to continue. "I remember falling toward the rocks below, as if in slow motion. Then everything went black."

Loraine shut her eyes and took a deep, emotional breath. "By chance, was this woman's name Liddy McPherson?"

Emma trembled with pent-up anger. "You know her?"

"I know of her, unfortunately. That woman has been a pariah to this family for centuries."

Loraine looked upward with an anxious sigh, then looked Emma directly in the eyes. "I will try to help you locate Edward's spirit. But then I need to send you both to the light. Do you understand?"

Emma responded with a weak smile and a nod. "Yes! Thank you, Loraine."

Chapter Two:

Into The Portal

In the North Wing, Steven woke to find Loraine missing from the bed. He immediately got up, and put on his robe, while Bumpers stretched, and began to whimper.

"It's okay, fella!" He patted the dog on the head. "You stay here. I'm just going to check on Loraine and the babies."

Steven shined his flashlight to either side of the long wide hallway and made his way to the nursery in the adjacent room. He quietly peeked into the darkroom to see the babies sleeping soundly. Then he ducked back into the hallway, careful not to make any noise that would wake his children.

He tip-toed further down the hallway, aiming his light to the open doors at the entrance to the Wing. "That's odd. Those doors are never open at night." He decided to explore a bit further outside the Wing. "I wonder where Lori went."

As he entered the landing foyer, he directed his light on the entrance foyer below. Just as he prepared to descend the stairs, he paused when he heard two people having a loud, but inaudible argument. His attention quickly shifted to the closed doors of the East Wing. "Oh no! Not this again."

Steven swiftly moved toward the East Wing with much irritation. Once inside, he hurried to the double doors, where the argument between the man and woman had escalated considerably. Without hesitation, he flung the doors open, and much to his surprise, he found a room on the other side. "What the…?"

The voices had now ceased, and no one else was inside the room. He cautiously stepped across the threshold, and toward the center of the room that resembled a rather rustic ambiance, with colonial-type stylings. As he struggled to take it all in, the entrance doors slammed shut behind him. Before he could run to open them, a blinding flash of light filled the room, and an invisible force pulled him backward, causing him to lose all consciousness.

Steven came to his senses, opening his eyes to see that he was no longer in the room. He was flat on his back in a field of tall weeds, and grass. The sky above him was filled with stars, and he also noticed the mellow light of the full moon shining down on the surrounding countryside.

He struggled to get to his feet but found it difficult. "Wow! I feel like an NFL lineman tackled me." He retrieved his flashlight and shined it toward the imposing outline of an enormous, colonial New England-style home. He stumbled to his left, and leaned against a huge boulder rock, desperately trying to regain his breath.

The light revealed several carved markings on the top face of the rock. He sought to interpret the elementary markings, but they made no sense. Totally bewildered, he glanced around, "Where in the hell am I?"

On his way toward the house, Steven decided to stay quiet, and at a safe distance. He observed the adjacent stables where he could hear horses quietly neighing, and stirring in the dark. "This must be someone's farm," he pondered.

He glanced to his right and noticed an enormous entry gate to the property, with a wooden marquee sign. He strolled over, shining his light upward to read it. "No! No! This Can't be possible" His blood ran cold when he saw that the carved letters on the marquee boldly spelled BRANCHVIEW.

A horse in the pasture whinnied, startling an already shocked Steven. He saw a dim light appear in the window of the house, and with anxious desperation, he took off in a fast trot down the rough dirt, and stone driveway. He could feel the sharp stones digging into the sides of the feet. His light flip-flop slippers were definitely not meant for outside running.

As Steven trudged onward, he gazed up at the simple dirt path, leading into a thick canopy of trees. The overwhelming scene caught him off balance. Once under the cover of the trees, his dimming flashlight only illuminated a few short feet, so he slowed to a trot, then paced to a stop. "If I'm where I think I am, this must be the pathway to Lighthouse Point."

A sudden loud rustling in the bushes distracted him, and he ended up falling face-first into the pathway before him. "Oh……" Steven groaned as he struggled to get to his feet, "you little rascal!" A raccoon crossed in front of him, pausing to observe the human with its' glowing red eyes, before it scampered off into the underbrush.

Now exhausted, Steven arrived at the clearing above Lighthouse Point, and he paused to observe the ocean view that he'd grown to love. He noticed a stark difference however. "The Lighthouse! It doesn't even exist yet."

His eyes searched further, and he noticed that a large white gabled house stood at the site of the old Locke Estate ruins. It also had a stable, pasture, and circular driveway, "If this is some crazy dream, I'm ready to wake up any time."

Steven walked to the edge of the point, to find that the staircase was absent. "This definitely won't be easy." After several stumbles, he finally reached the bottom.

In a complete stupor, Steven paced the waters' edge. The incoming tide lapped at his slippers, and the salt stung the abrasions on his feet. In a low, but audible tone, he called out over the waters of the vast Atlantic. "Amphitrite! Poseidon! I need you!"

A haunting sound echoed off the water surface. Steven stood patiently, listening to the sound of the mermaid's chatter. A sudden gust of wind then blew inward, tossing his hair, and nearly knocking his exhausted body over. As he regained his footing, a lone nightbird cawed from above the waters in front of him, revealing two figures emerging from the depths.

Steven waited anxiously as Poseidon and Amphitrite approached with stern expressions, "Am I ever glad to see you two?"

Poseidon twirled his trident, aiming the points at Steven's throat, "Who are you, and why have you summoned us?" he demanded.

Steven desperately announced, "My name is Steven Spencer." He breathed heavily. "I know this sounds crazy, but we were friends in a future time." His eyes darted desperately between the two. "Can you tell me what year it is?"

Poseidon grunted arrogantly, as he pulled back his trident. "Pitiful, drunken fool! It's the year 1697 AD."

Steven reacted only with silent shock at the revelation, as Amphitrite stepped forward, and eyed him up and down. "This man must either be insane, or he's a wizard. Look at those strange clothes he's wearing."

"These are my nightclothes. It's what I was wearing when I disappeared in the future." Steven humbly responded.

Poseidon let loose with a hearty laugh, "Are you saying a mortal man such as yourself is capable of time travel?"

Steven reacted with utter frustration, "It's complicated! I promise I'll explain it later in the best way I can."

Poseidon wielded his trident again and grabbed Steven by the collar of his robe. "I suggest you explain it now."

Steven instinctively reacted to his aggression with a low growl, as his eyes illuminated with a red glow. Both Poseidon and Amphitrite backed away a few steps with surprise. "You must be a demon!" Poseidon barked.

"Surely!" Amphitrite added. "No mere mortal would have such powers to transform like that. Perhaps he came here in a spaceship."

Poseidon gave her a stern glance, while Steven replied with renewed exuberance. "You two know about UFOs?"

Poseidon shook his head defiantly. "We know of no such thing, demon." He readied his trident to strike. "Prepare to die!"

In a last shot of desperation, Steven waved his hands in front of him. "Wait! It was you who granted me the powers to transform into a beast. You were both there in the Secret Cave. It was the year 2019."

Poseidon backed off again, and he and Amphitrite exchanged puzzled expressions. Poseidon turned his attention back toward Steven with much suspicion. "How would you know of the Secret Cave?" No mortals have that knowledge?

Amphitrite glared at Steven with an almost hypnotic stare, while he gave a frustrated sigh, and fell to one knee. "As I told you before, we were friends and allies in a future time. I was granted my powers in the ceremony of the three swords."

Amphitrite snapped out of her trance-like stare. "I sense his heart is pure and that he is telling the truth, Poseidon."

Poseidon eyed Steven with great interest, as he planted his trident in the sand, and offered his hand in helping him to his feet. "What more can you tell us of the future, and why did we grant you these powers?"

"We all fought a battle together on this very beach. Our nemesis was your brother Hades, the dark witch, and the Secret Society."

Both Poseidon and Amphitrite reacted with wide-eyed surprise as Steven continues, "Your other brother Zeus joined us, along with the forces of the parallel world." Steven exhaustingly sighed, "I promise I'll tell you more in a less desperate moment."

Poseidon looked to the horizon, and then back at Steven. "Very well! It'll be dawn soon. We'll take you to the Secret Cave, so you can rest."

Amphitrite eyed Steven keenly, and with an admirable grin. "We must get him some appropriate clothes as well. If he were spotted by any of the locals, they would surely accuse him of being a disciple of the devil."

Chapter Three:

Dreadful Discoveries

Loraine woke up surprisingly early, concerned that Steven was nowhere to be found. As she shuffled through the large doors of the Sitting Room, Ezekiel, Meryl, and Suzy were all conversing over cups of coffee.

Loraine nodded when everyone turned and noticed her. "Good morning, everyone. Have any of you seen Steven this morning?" They all shook their heads cluelessly.

"Have you checked his office?" Ezekiel asked. "Perhaps he's in there writing."

Loraine reacted with much distress. "I already checked in there. Sometime during the night, he must have left our room and never returned to bed."

"I did think it was odd that the coffee wasn't ready this morning," Suzy added. "He's usually up before anyone."

Meryl stood up concerned. "I certainly hope he's alright."

Ezekiel looked to Meryl and rose from his seat as well, "Meryl and I were just preparing to take our morning stroll on the beach. Perhaps we'll find him there."

Loraine responded with visible anxiety. "He left his cell phone on the nightstand, which is very rare. If you do see him, please have him return here right away."

"We certainly will, Lori," Meryl answered.

After Ezekiel and Meryl left, Loraine sat down on the love seat next to Suzy, and spoke in a low voice. "That woman entered the house through the mirror last night."

Suzy sat up straight, and glanced around the room. "She's actually here?"

Loraine answered her with a nervous nod. "Can I count on you to help me with this?"

Suzy cleared her throat as Alan, the construction foreman in the East Wing, peeked into the room. "Excuse the intrusion, Mrs. Spencer. We have a minor issue in the East Wing. He gestured in that direction. "Do you have a few moments?"

Loraine rolled her eyes at Suzy and stood to address the large, burly man. "Yes! Of course, Alan."

Suzy stood as well, and set her coffee cup down on a side table. "I'll tag along if you don't mind. I'm eager to see how things are progressing."

As Loraine and Suzy followed Alan up the stairs, Emma's spirit appeared in the foyer below. She approached, and admired the enormous grandfather clock just as it chimed at 8:30 AM. She paused in a moment of reflection, then gazed toward the stairs with a determined expression.

In the East Wing, Alan led the two women down the hallway to the double doors. "A few of my workers have claimed to hear voices coming from behind these doors. I know from observing the blueprints of the house that a room doesn't exist there."

Eddie, a young carpenter casually listened as he placed new woodwork nearby. "Well then, let's just see what's behind there. Shall we?" Loraine responded.

She pulled the door open, and they were all baffled to see a solid brick wall. "How odd that they would place a doorway here that leads to nowhere," Loraine commented, as Eddie looked up with raised eyebrows.

Alan removed his hat, and cluelessly scratched his head. "The main courtyard is just beyond that wall. Perhaps at one time, they had plans to expand the house."

"As if they could make it any bigger." Suzy laughed.

Alan then pointed to a grated floor vent nearby. "Sometime in the last century, they installed gravity heat. I'm guessing the voices we hear echo through the old vent piping from another part of the house.

"Well then!" Suzy stated jokingly. "I guess we'll have to watch what we say from now on."

Eddie paused from his work and glanced up at Loraine. "If I, were you, I'd remove those doors altogether." He gestured toward them. "That's quality wood, and they'd net a high price from a salvage dealer."

Alan became agitated at his suggestion. "Mrs. Spencer doesn't need you telling her what to do, Eddie."

Eddie stopped what he was doing, and addressed Loraine with a humble nod. "My apologies, Mrs. Spencer. I didn't mean to sound bold."

"Oh! That's alright, I know you were just trying to be helpful."

"What would you like us to do with the doors, Mrs. Spencer?" Alan asked. "We can remove them, and cover the wall without a problem."

Loraine pondered with indecision. "Let's just hold off until my husband returns. I'll let him make that decision."

Just then, Emma's spirit wandered onto the scene and called out with excitement. "Edward!"

Eddie stared in her direction with surprise, and shock. While both Loraine's and Suzy's eyes quickly glanced between the spirit and Eddie. In the awkward moment, the two women subtly nodded with all-knowing expressions.

Alan took notice of Eddie's hangdog expression as he continued to gaze at Emma with awe. "What's wrong with you, Eddie? You look like you just saw a ghost."

Emma vanished from the room, and Suzy whispered inaudibly to Loraine. "He saw her."

Loraine replied with a raised eyebrow, as Eddie stepped out of his brain fog long enough to answer Alan. "Oh! I uh… was trying to remember if I left one of my tools in the truck."

Alan looked to the two women with a shrug, as Eddie swiftly left the room. "He's a good worker, but he can be a bit strange at times." He glanced back toward the doors, "We'll work around those doors until Mr. Spencer makes a decision." Loraine nodded, then gazed toward Suzy with a wide-eyed expression.

In the Secret Cave, Steven wandered in from an adjacent room, rubbing the sleep from his eyes, and only wearing his robe. Amphitrite watched him with calculating eyes from her perch in one of the crystal throne chairs.

He addressed her with a puzzled expression. "I woke up naked! Where are the rest of my clothes?"

Amphitrite smirked as she stood up, and strolled down from the altar. "I removed them while you were sleeping, and burned them."

Steven shook his head in astonishment. "You actually saw me naked?"

"You aren't the first man I've ever seen naked, and you certainly won't be the last." She strolled by him and teasingly tapped his shoulder while sporting a provocative smirk.

Steven's eyes searched the room. "Where is Poseidon?"

Amphitrite settled in another less comfortable chair. "He went to get you some new clothes, and to also find his brother Zeus."

She stood up again and seductively moved closer to Steven, eyeing him with great curiosity. "What was I like in the future?"

"You walked on land under the alias of Dr. Amy Seagraves. You were a psychiatrist."

"A psychiatrist?" she inquired cluelessly.

Steven strolled over to a nearby chair and sat down. "In 2019, that's what they call a doctor that helps people with ailments of the mind." Steven smiled. "I also know that you went by the name of Amanda Green when you were in this area around the year 1897."

Amphitrite was astonished. "And how would you know that?"

Steven leaned forward, and glanced upward at the high crystal ceilings of the cave for a moment, before resuming eye contact with Amphitrite. "You were in love with my great uncle, Matthew Branch." He recanted. "So much in fact, that you were prepared to give up your immortality to be with him."

Amphitrite softened her demeanor and became attentive. "And why didn't I do that?"

Steven paused with sadness, before answering. "Before you two could get married, Matthew was killed by the witch."

"And who was this witch?"

"Her name was Liddy McPherson." Steven sneered at the mention of her name.

Amphitrite stood up in quiet thought, strolled to a nearby table, and poured water from a clay pitcher into a mug. She gestured to Steven. "Would you like one as well?"

"Yes, please! I'm parched."

She poured water into another mug and then strolled over to hand it to him. He quickly took a satisfying sip and reacted with surprise. "That's the finest water I've ever tasted." He declared.

Amphitrite grinned at his reaction. "It's from the artesian well here in the cave. It's the freshest, and most mineral-filled water you could ever find."

She lingered in front of him, running her hand through her shiny red locks of hair, and seductively staring at him with great curiosity. "Do you find me attractive, Steven?"

"I'd be lying if I said no. You're an extremely attractive woman."

Amphitrite slyly grinned, as Steven took another satisfying sip of water. "I find you fascinating as well." She paused. "Would you be interested in having an affair with me?"

Steven choked at the comment, spitting out his water, while Amphitrite couldn't help but be amused by his reaction. "Amphitrite! With all due respect, I'm a happily married man with two twin babies." He took a moment to recompose himself. "Besides, I would never betray my friend by having sex with his wife. It's totally against my morals."

She backed away, impressed by his reaction. "Any lesser man would've fallen into temptation" She grunted and turned away to hide her emotion. "Poseidon would've surely ceased such an opportunity."

"He'll change with time, and so will you. Trust me on that."

Amphitrite gave a subtle, but doubtful chuckle. "I'll fix you some breakfast."

In the future, Loraine stood at the bottom of the stairs with her arms folded firmly in front of her, as the construction workers left the East Wing for the day. She smiled and gestured goodbye to each worker as they left. Her thoughts spilled out in her mind like words on a written page.

Once again, strange events are taking place in the great house of Branchview. Events that will soon center our attention on a mysterious doorway in the East Wing. The coming days will prove to be a training ground for the young Suzy McVea, as she realizes the full potential of the supernatural powers she possesses.

As the last workers filed out the door, Loraine continued to hold a firm vigil, tapping her foot impatiently on the tile flooring.

Eddie finally made his way down the stairs, hauling his heavily cumbersome toolbox. Loraine watched him intently until he reached the bottom foyer. "I was beginning to think you were holding out on me, Edward Branch."

Eddie was taken aback for a moment by her comment but quickly recovered with a slight laugh, as he continued lugging his gear toward the door. "I'm sorry ma'am! You must be mistaken. My name is Eddie Benson."

She waited until he reaches for the door handle. "I know you saw her this morning."

Eddie was taken aback again, and turned with renewed, but cautious curiosity. "Who did I see?"

"Emma! Emma Lindstrand!" She paced closer. "I could see her too. She told me all about how you disappeared without a trace."

Eddie breathed an emotional breath, looking upward with his eyes closed. "I never thought I'd see her precious face again."

Loraine stepped even closer, "Set your gear back down, young man. I think you and I need to have a long talk."

With an emotional sigh, he set his equipment down near the door and followed Loraine into the Sitting Room. Suzy soberly sat waiting as they entered. Loraine placed a throw blanket onto a chair and motioned for Eddie to sit down. "I'm so dirty and dusty. I hope I don't mess anything up."

Loraine proceeded to sit in a nearby chair. "No worry! I can assure you. This is far more important than dirtying up the upholstery."

Eddie turned his attention toward Suzy. "You're Suzy! The waitress down at the Diner."

Loraine diverted his attention and answered for her. "She's seen Emma as well. She's just here to help me sort out what's going on."

Eddie's eyes searched curiously about the room. "Is Emma here now?"

Loraine sighed. "Oh! I'm sure she's lurking around here somewhere. She's nervous about being seen."

Eddie shook his head with visible frustration. "Maybe you two can help me make sense of what happened. I seriously don't know where to begin." His eyes darted between the two women. "I eagerly took this job, hoping I could return to Branchview, and find some answers."

"You can start by telling us everything that happened that night," Loraine stated with an understanding nod.

Eddie hesitated for a long, agonizing moment. "I had already asked Emma to marry me, but I had to wait until I had the money to buy her a ring." He paused with humble embarrassment. "I wasn't independently wealthy as the rest of the Branch's were."

Loraine continued for him. "And you had planned to finally give her that ring in the Grand Corridor that night"

Eddie nodded and continued, "We called it the Grand Ballroom back then. It was a different era." He paused in fond reflection. "Nevertheless, I had left the ring in my room in the East Wing, and went to retrieve it." He drew a deep breath and continued. "When I started back toward the Ballroom, I heard what sounded like a couple having a heated argument."

"Was it behind the double doors?" Suzy inquired.

Eddie nervously nodded yes, and continued. "I opened the doors, and there was an empty room that never existed." Eddie concentrated as he struggled to remember. "I walked in, and the doors slammed shut behind me." He grew increasingly anxious. "Then there was this bright, blinding light."

Loraine impatiently urged him on. "What happened next?"

Eddie continued with great emotion. "I found myself outside in the courtyard, flat on my back, and disoriented."

Suzy leaned forward, and into the conversation. "Eddie! Was there a full moon that night?"

"As a matter of fact, there was a beautiful late summer full moon." He smiled. "I thought it was the perfect night to make our engagement official."

Suzy and Loraine exchanged an anxious glance. "When did you realize you were in a different time?" Loraine probed further.

"Almost immediately. I walked past the window of this Sitting Room and noticed people there that I didn't recognize. They wore strange clothes, and the electric lighting was so different, and more advanced than I had remembered." His eyes grew wider as he continued. "I ran as fast as possible to the town of Lockeport, but everything there was different as well."

"What on earth did you do next?" Suzy asked.

"I was terrified! I stole some clothes from a Salvation Army bin, and did whatever I could to adapt to this new modern world." He paused and painfully continued. "I eventually took on a new identity and started all over. I knew I could never return to my own time."

Loraine and Suzy reacted with great sympathy, but still decided to inquire further. "How long have you actually been in this time, Eddie?" Loraine asked.

"I entered seven years ago, in the year 2012."

Loraine and Suzy were confounded with his story, while Eddie grew impatiently restless. "I'm sorry, but I have to go." As I mentioned, I have a new life now. I met someone, we married, and we have a little girl." Eddie nodded nervously. "They're waiting for me to come home as we speak."

Emma's spirit cried out emotionally from the entryway to the room. "Edward! How could you?" They all stared in her direction with surprise, as the Sitting Room doors slammed shut, and Emma's weeping cries could be heard as she retreated toward the South Wing.

Eddie distressfully placed his hands over his face. "Mrs. Spencer! We have to remove those blasted doors before another innocent person wanders through them."

Loraine shot up from her seat, reacting with equal shock and grief. "We can't do that, Eddie."

Eddie stood up and challenged her with much defiance. "For God's sake! Why not?"

Loraine countered with equal emotion. "Because I fear my husband may have wandered into that room, just as you did." Both Suzy and Eddie reacted in speechless horror at her revelation.

In a distant time, Steven sat patiently waiting, as Poseidon finally returned to the Cave Room, carrying clothes, and supplies. He casually strolled over and set the wrapped parcels on the table in front of Steven. "These should be a bit more appropriate for this century."

Steven nodded with gratitude. "Thank you. I was beginning to think you forgot about me."

Poseidon smiled and glanced around the room. "Where's Amphitrite?"

"She went back to the water, she said she'd return later."

Poseidon sat down on the other side of the table and watched while Steven eyed a small sack, tied around the top, that sat on top of the bundle of clothes. "What's in the bag."

"Those are the gold currency coins you'll need to purchase anything you might need."

"That's a little bag. Are you sure it'll be enough?"

"The presentation of only one of those coins will identify you as a very rich man," Poseidon assuredly stated.

Steven let that comment sink in for a moment and shook his head with a smile. "It wouldn't go too far in 2019," he laughed. "Would it be too much to ask for a cup of coffee as well?"

Poseidon curiously peered across the table. "How do you know about the coffee bean?" He asked. "Not many people outside of Africa know of it."

Steven reacted with utter disbelief. "It's an ordinary drink in the future." He paused with emphasis. "In fact, you and I have had a few interesting conversations over a hot cup of coffee."

"Is that so?" Steven gave him an assuring nod in response, and Poseidon continued, "Well! I can say with certainty that in this time period, you'd either have to travel to Ethiopia or perhaps Austria to enjoy such a beverage."

"Wonderful!" Steven rolled his eyes in disbelief. "I can tell this isn't going to be an easy transition." He sighed. "How should I present myself when I go into town?"

Amphitrite casually sauntered in unnoticed and spoke before Poseidon could answer. "You'll present yourself as my husband, and a member of British royalty.

Chapter Four:

A Desperate Dilemma

Back at Branchview, Loraine had gathered the entire household in the dining room for an evening meeting. As she took her place at the head of the table, she glanced toward Sharie. "I trust you've told the evening staff to allow us the utmost privacy."

"Absolutely!" She assuredly stated. "I also have Sally Lennox watching over the babies in the nursery."

Loraine proceeded with a long, accentuated nod, "As you all know, Steven has turned up missing." She choked with emotion and paused to regain her composure. "Suzy and I have reason to believe he may have entered a time portal that exists in the East Wing."

Everyone gasped with shock, and Meryl spoke up first with much doubt. "What on earth would make you believe that?"

"We met a man who entered that same portal from Branchview's past.

Everyone reacted with shocked surprise once again, and whispers rose between the attendants, as Loraine moved the conversation along. "We also believe the full moon cycle might play a role in the opening and closing of that portal."

Ezekiel responded with an agreeing nod, "That would make sense. The rotation of the earth and the angle of the moon also play a role in what time is entered. "He gauged everyone's reaction. "It's all factored in advanced geometry."

Gerard's interest is peaked with the statement, "I'm quite good at math equations. How can we determine what time Steven may have entered?"

"First, we would have to determine the approximate time he may have entered," Ezekiel replied. "Then we factor in the moons' angle as it shined on that portion of the house, at that particular moment."

Meryl shook her head, "This is all beyond my understanding."

Loraine pondered what was said before she spoke further, "That's all fine! Even though it sounds complicated." She paused. "But once we determine where he is, how can we get him back?"

Ezekiel glanced around the table with all seriousness. "I suppose someone else will have to enter the portal to retrieve him."

Tony Freeman quickly volunteered. "I'll go."

Andrea cradled her pregnant belly and rebuked her husband. "Oh no, you won't, Tony Freeman! I lost you once, and I can't bear the thought of losing you again."

Ezekiel backed Andrea's protest. "She's right! You need to be here for the sake of your wife and child." He reluctantly paused. "Philip and I will go."

"But we don't even know where Philip and Tina are." Loraine protested with anxiety.

Ezekiel moved to calm her with a gesture of his hands. "I know they're honeymooning somewhere in the Mediterranean. They shouldn't be hard for me to track down."

Gerard motioned Ezekiel away from the table, and both men paced a short distance from the rest, speaking in a whisper. "The two of you can't go. There's too much risk that you'll come face to face with your past selves." Gerard reasoned.

Ezekiel gave a reluctant, but agreeing nod. "You do have a valid point there."

"I can go." Gerard eagerly offered.

"Are you out of your mind?" Ezekiel responded in an urgent tone. "You realize that black people were historically not treated well in this country."

Gerard responded with a disappointed sigh. "Unfortunately, you're right about that."

Both men returned to the table, and Mrs. Porter boldly stood up. "I've taken care of Steven since he was a baby." She trembled. "He's like a son to me. I'll go, and bring him back.

"Absolutely not, Mrs. Porter!" Loraine balked. "The journey would be far too hard on a woman of your age, and I couldn't bear the thought of losing you as well."

Millie shot up from her seat next. "Then I shall go! I had the proper training as an MI6 agent, and I could surely endure such a mission."

Loraine also balked at her offer. "No mother! You're way too much of a modern woman. I'm afraid you wouldn't be pleasantly accepted in the past."

Before another word could be said, Suzy bravely stood up. "What about me?" She asked. "I have no family, and no one special in my life." She nodded assuredly. "I can go."

Loraine shook her head with further protest. "No! He's my husband, and even though I'm needed here, I should be the one that goes."

Ezekiel waved his hands to silence and calm the gathering. "We have to consider the possibility that he may not even be in the past." He pauses with emphasis. "For all we know, he could be in the future. If that was the case, whoever went might confront their future self."

"I suppose that eliminates all of us," Millie commented.

Ezekiel paused for a long moment before he glanced with all seriousness at those in attendance who knew his secret. He then reluctantly continued. "Ms. McVea, Mrs. Porter, Mrs. Sandstrom." He nodded to all three women. "There's something that's common knowledge among the others here that I think you should all know." He took a deep breath. "Philip and I aren't exactly who we seem."

All three women countered with puzzled expressions. "We're both immortal gods that you may have read about at one time or the other. I'm Zeus, and Philip is my brother Poseidon."

The women looked absurdly at each other for a moment, before bursting into immense laughter. "And I, my dear friends, am the queen of England." Millie sarcastically quipped.

All three women continued laughing while everyone else remained sober, "That must mean that Ms. Markopolous is Cleopatra." Suzy teased.

"Hardly!" Meryl harshly replied. "I'm actually Zeus's first wife, Metis, and I too am immortal."

Ezekiel simmered with rage, and could not contain it further. With a loud yell, he raised his fist, and an enormous crash of lightning was heard, followed by a flash of light that filled the room. Everyone became silent, and Loraine gingerly stood to further address everyone.

"This is no laughing matter." She paused to glance at the three women. "they're telling the truth. None of them can go back, nor forward in time, because they already exist there."

Everyone else confirmed her statement with a sober, and serious nod. When the truth finally sunk in, Mrs. Porter pointed a bony finger at Ezekiel. "I knew there was something strange about you, and that Mr. Seagraves."

Ezekiel humbly glanced downward at the table. "Now that you know, I can only ask that you fine ladies never speak of this to anyone outside of this room."

"Who in their right mind would ever believe us?" Suzy quipped.

"Hopefully, no one." Ezekiel chuckled as he stood up. "With that in mind, I would request everyone continue to address us by our earth names."

Loraine became agitated and simply had to speak her mind. "We can't just sit here, and wait for Philip and Tina to return. We have to do something."

"I have advanced psychic abilities. Perhaps I could locate Steven in the time spectrum." Meryl offered.

"Perhaps I can help as well." Suzy volunteered.

Ezekiel gave the women a nod of approval. "Excellent idea!" He then addressed everyone else. "I might also have a plan that wouldn't require any of us to enter the portal at all."

"Then please, tell it to us." Gerard impatiently requested.

"For now, I'll just say we'd need to enlist an old friend and ally who has nothing to risk, and everything to gain." He stated with authority. "But before I speak further, I'll need to discuss it with my brother."

"Then I suggest you get right on it," Meryl commanded.

Ezekiel replied with humble, and patient restraint. "Yes, dear!"

On a rustic, 17th Century Street in Lockeport, an elegantly dressed Amphitrite under the alias of Abigail Stuart Spencer strolled proudly with an equally well-dressed Steven. She gripped tight to the arm of her make-believe husband, while commoners, townspeople, and rough-looking sailors keenly eyed the handsome couple. Steven gazed around in amazement at a town he had grown to know so well in the future, but barely recognized now.

"I can't believe how different everything looks. There isn't even one landmark that I recognize from the future town."

Abigail answered in an impressive British accent, as she leaned closer and loudly whispered. "Just don't appear so naïve, darling. She winked. "Just put on your best British accent. We want to be as convincing as possible."

They approached the entrance of an old English-styled pub, and Abigail craned her graceful neck to look in the window. She then looked up at the wood-carved sign hanging above the door and gave an approving nod.

"The Fox and Hound." She looked to Steven for a reaction. "This appears to be a reasonable establishment. Shall we mingle with some locals?"

"Yes, perhaps we might find some palatable food as well."

Steven rushed ahead to open the door, and Abigail sashayed in with a supercilious expression. All activity and conversation seemed to cease, as everyone in the establishment eyed the strange, elegant couple with great curiosity and envy. After what seemed like an eternal few minutes, everyone resumed what they were doing prior, and the two chose a seat at a heavily varnished top table.

The smell of stale beer and cheap cigar smoke prevailed in the air, and Abigail turned her nose up with displeasure. She ran her white-gloved finger across the table-top, then gazed at it with equal disdain. "Not as clean as I'd prefer. But I suppose it's the best this town has to offer."

A buxom wench of a woman with crooked teeth, and heavy cleavage, hurried over to the table. She plopped down two tattered paper menus, and immediately flashed a keen eye toward Steven. "Could I bring you an ale, handsome?"

"I'd prefer to start with a cup of tea. Thank you." Steven replied in his best British accent.

The wench rolled her eyes and looked to Abigail with a fake smile. "And what would the lady prefer?"

"The lady would also prefer a cup of tea, and a tumbler of freshwater."

The wench glanced at both of them with calculating eyes, equally filled with disdain. "Very well! I'll be back with your drinks."

Steven glanced around toward the bar area, where an old man with a Greek fisherman's cap played his concertina with great pleasure. Two drunk sailors danced in a jig, and one caught sight of Abigail. He danced over to the table, ogling her with hypnotic wonder, before loudly proclaiming, and pointing toward her. "It's you, lass! It's really you!"

The music and conversing abruptly stopped. And once again, all eyes were focused on the couple, making them feel uncomfortable. Abigail casually, but somewhat nervously glanced up from her menu, as the sailor continued to point at her. "As God be me witness, this red-haired beauty saved us when our ship went down in the storm." He blessed himself.

The other sailor stumbled over and eyed her over the top of his thick, dirty spectacles. "I'll be blarney! I think ye may be right." The crowd burst out in uncontrollable laughter, while Steven and Abigail exchanged anxious glances.

The poor sailors glanced around, seriously pleading their case. The first sailor balked back at them. "It is true, I tell you." He pointed toward her again. "Her and a host of other sea nymphs pulled us to the surface. This one saved me." He nodded with all seriousness. "I could never forget such a beautiful face."

He goes down to one knee, and bows reverently before Abigail, while she and Steven exchanged a fleeting, wide-eyed glance.

From out of the onlookers, stepped a sharply dressed businessman who looked in his mid-forties. He had a thick mustache that curled at both ends and carried himself like a man of authority. He casually strolled over and pulled the sailor up by his shirt collar. "That'll be enough, sailor." He reached in his pocket, pulled out a shiny coin, and planted it in the palm of the sailor's hand. "Go have another mug of rum, and leave the fine lady alone."

The sailor headed back toward the bar without saying another word. But he couldn't help but turn around for one last look at Abigail. The dignified man turned his full attention back to Abigail, failing to even notice Steven. "My extreme apologies for this man's rudeness." He confidently grinned. "I'd have to agree with him on one matter, however. You possess the beauty one would expect from a goddess of the sea."

Abigail slightly blushed, while Steven and the gentleman exchanged a fleeting glance. He quickly turned his attention back to Abigail, and respectfully bowed his head to her. "My name is Jonathan Locke, and I'd like to welcome you to my fine town."

Abigail acknowledged him with a slight nod. "My name is Abigail Stuart Spencer, and this is my husband, Steven Spencer." She grinned across the table with pursed lips. "We only arrived this morning on the ship from England."

Steven and Jonathan exchanged cordial nods. "You're a lucky man, Mr. Spencer."

He quickly turned his attention back to Abigail with much curiosity. Stuart! You wouldn't happen to be?"

Abigail answers before he can complete his question. "Yes, I would! I am the first cousin of King William III."

Jonathan bursts with exuberance. "I must say. I'm honored to be in the presence of such royalty."

The returning wench rolled her eyes with envy as she set the drinks down, and hurried away again. Jonathan continued to probe with further questions. "May I ask where you'll be staying during the duration of your visit?"

"I believe we'll be staying at the hotel down the street" Steven announced.

"I would hate distinguished individuals like yourselves to take lodging in such a common place," Jonathan stated with much animation. "I would insist you be my houseguests for the duration of your visit."

Steven started to answer, but Abigail purposely beat him to the punch. "How hospitable of you, Mr. Locke. We will gladly accept your invitation."

"Excellent!" He proclaimed. "I'm just leaving for my home now. I shall send one of my carriages for you immediately."

Abigail glanced across the table at Steven with a clever grin, while Jonathan gave another cordial nod, and departed.

Meanwhile, on a residential side street of 21st Century Lockeport, where many houses were under reconstruction from the devastating tsunami, Sandy Benson sat in the closet-sized bathroom of her FEMA trailer. The fair-skinned woman in her mid-twenties casually brushed out her light brown hair while staring into a small propped-up mirror. Her six-year-old daughter Tricia hurried toward her mother from the other room.

Her blonde curls bounced as she scurried with excitement. "Mommy! Mommy! A strange woman just walked into the house."

Sandy glanced to the outer room but saw no one there. "Oh, sweetie! There's no one there. It's all in your imagination."

Sandy resumed brushing her hair, while the little girl remained adamant. "But Mommy! She's here! She's right behind you."

Sandy glanced back at the mirror and saw the angry, jealous face of Emma's spirit peering over her shoulder. She screamed as the mirror shattered, and splinters of glass fell to the floor. Emma disappeared, but Sandy grabbed Tricia's arm and fled from the trailer in horror.

Outside, Eddie was just pulling up in his weathered Chevy pickup truck, as a terrified Sandy fled toward him, followed closely by a much calmer little Tricia. Eddie quickly jumped out of the truck, as Sandy hysterically ran into his embrace.

He kissed her on the forehead and tried desperately to calm her. "Baby! Hey! What's wrong?"

She gazed into his eyes with terror and stuttered. "In the trailer…there was a woman. She watched me as I brushed my hair. She had such anger in her eyes." She sniffled as he held her tight. "Then the mirror completely shattered in front of me."

Eddie stroked her hair as he further tried to calm her. "It's okay, baby! It's all over! He looked her straight in the eyes. "Whoever it was, I'm sure she's long gone."

Tricia stared up at her father, then pointed back toward the trailer. "No! She's not, daddy! She's right there."

Eddie is shocked when he sees Emma's spirit standing outside the front door. She angrily glared at him for a few long moments before subtly vanishing. Eddie was visibly shaken and closely huddled his family. "You and Tricia get into the truck. I'm taking you over to your mother's house. Right now!"

In 1697, an elaborately decorative horse and carriage pulled onto the circular drive of a stately white house atop the cliffs of Lighthouse Point. The uniformed coachman dismounted and opened the carriage door for Abigail and Steven. As they stepped out onto the front walkway, Steven eyed the house with amazement. He leaned over and whispered to Abigail. "This must be the house that burned to the ground in 1897."

Abigail only replied with a subtle nod as Jonathan opened the front door to greet them. "Welcome to Locke Haven. A little slice of heaven by the sea."

"I must say. It's lovely, Mr. Locke," Steven commented.

Jonathan held the door as Steven and Abigail made their way into the foyer of the grand house. They both gazed upward at the high wood-framed ceilings, where the late afternoon sun streamed through an enormous half-moon window.

Jonathan made a welcoming gesture toward the spacious parlor room that adjoined the foyer. "Please make yourself comfortable while I go upstairs, and check on my wife." His expression showed more annoyance than concern. She hasn't been feeling well the past few days."

The couple continued into the room as Jonathan exited up the stairs. The spacious parlor had a massive stone hearth fireplace, an upright harp instrument placed near a corner of the room, and an unusual combination decor of rustic early colonial, and old European design. Steven wasn't impressed by the less than elegant design he surveyed. "I can't say I care much for the decor of this period."

It's also a bit remote from what I'm accustomed to. But I do like that harp," Abigail commented.

They proceeded on and settled onto a firm couch in the center of the room. A little girl around the age of six entered from another area of the house and stood timidly in the entranceway to the room. She had brown hair, tightly braided into ponytails, and an unruffled demeanor.

Abigail took notice of her with a fond smile. "Well! Hello there, little one! You can come in. We are quite friendly."

The little girl shyly paced closer, and Steven tried to ease her apprehension. "I'm Steven and this is my wife, Abigail."

She didn't reply but only peered at Abigail with great curiosity. "You're very pretty."

"Thank you! And you're quite beautiful yourself."

"I guess that makes me the beast in the room" Steven joked.

The little girl giggled, and moved closer, while Steven noticed a stunningly familiar woman enter the room. She looked in her mid-20s, with strawberry blonde hair tied in a tight bun. She carried a tray with a pitcher of water, two drinking glasses, and a plate of appetizers. She set the tray down on the sofa table and displayed a subtle, but melancholy smile.

Steven's jaw dropped when he realized who she actually was. "I see you've met my little Lydia." She paused slightly. "My name is Jenny, and I'm Mr. Locke's housekeeper. I brought you some fresh spring water, and buttered scones to enjoy."

"Thank you so kindly, Jenny. That water is exactly what I needed." Abigail replied with a smile.

Jenny never wavered her expression as she served the two distinguished guests. The little girl stood nearby, soberly observing, and her mother's eyes wandered to her for a moment. "You run along now, Liddy!" Jenny exclaimed while pouring the water. "Mr. and Mrs. Spencer are no doubt tired from their long journey."

Liddy turned, and slowly left the room, dejected, and not saying another word. Abigail tried to remedy the awkwardness. "She's a pleasant little girl."

Jenny only responded with a pleasing smile as she finished serving, and took notice of the calculating stare Steven held on her. "Is there something wrong, Mr. Spencer?"

"No! Not at all." Steven responded with nervous anxiety. "I apologize for staring, but you look remarkably like someone I used to know."

Jenny laughed subtly, hardly changing her expression. She held her hands humbly cupped in front of her as she addressed him. "I can honestly say I've never been to England, and I surely haven't mingled with the royal family. So, I'm confident we've never met." She nodded to Steven with emphasis. "If you'd excuse me, I have dinner to prepare, and we're quite short on staff.

"Of course! We totally understand." Abigail gestured with a nod.

Jenny stood vigil for a moment more as she added. "If you should need anything, simply ring the handbell on that side table."

Without any further word, she swiftly departed the room, while Abigail abruptly turned to Steven with annoyance. "Can you please explain what that little exchange was all about?"

Steven sighed, and lowered his voice. "Remember, I told you about the mother and daughter witches we battled in the year 2019?"

He countered with serious eyes. "Yes! I remember." Abigail also lowered her voice. "Didn't you mention that their last name was McPherson?"

Steven gave a long, accentuated nod. "That woman and her little girl are in fact, those very witches." Abigail reacted with speechless, wide-eyed surprise.

Chapter Five:

An Old Friend Returns

Somewhere over the dark Atlantic waters, Poseidon rode upon the immortal Pegasus. The majestic creature flapped its wings in rhythm as they glided through thick sea fog, and against a strong headwind. Poseidon's thoughts ran through his mind like the memorized lines of a play.

From time to time, as I travel between the two worlds, I'm bluntly reminded of my responsibility as an immortal god. Just yesterday, I was away with my beautiful new wife, on a wonderful honeymoon. Today, I am on a desolate journey to converse with a spirit I seriously thought I'd never see again.

The neighs of Pegasus are heard through the thick fog, as it broke through it, and gracefully landed on the beach at the island of Avalon. Poseidon gently pulled the reins back as they settled to a smooth stop. He dismounted and paused to glance at the first crack of light along the eastern horizon. He lightly patted the beautiful white horse, and Pegasus responded with an affectionate head bump.

He spoke softly to his mystical companion. "You can stay here, and graze on the seagrass. I'll return soon." Almost as though understanding him, Pegasus reared its head back and loudly whinnied.

Poseidon set his sights beyond the beach to the dark tree line in front of him. He trudged through the sand, and deeper into the interior of the island until he saw the lighted torches of the reception party. Magnus marched in front, followed by a host of other spirit warriors. He let out a bellowing laugh when he saw Poseidon, and the two men greeted each other with a brotherly hug. "Poseidon! We expected to be greeting newly arrived spirits. We certainly never expected you."

"I can honestly say I never expected to be here either," Poseidon sighed. "I had to cut my honeymoon short when I received an urgent summons from my brother Zeus."

"Honeymoon!" Magnus laughed heartily. "And how long should we expect this marriage to last?"

"Permanently, I would hope. I'm very much in love."

Magnus patted him on the shoulder. "I'm truly happy for you, my friend. He smiled. "Now! How might we help you?

Poseidon's eyes scanned the congregation of warriors. "I desperately need to see Charlotte Locke. Is she somewhere among you?"

Magnus reacted with unease and glanced toward the other spirits. "She lives on the other side of the island in a secluded area." He shook his head. "None of us are permitted to have contact with her."

"Very well!" Poseidon shrugged. "Just point me the way, and I'll go on my own."

"I'm afraid that's impossible." He stated with much seriousness. "The terms of her sentence require she remain secluded. Any violation of that would anger the Council of Elders."

I'll answer to the Council of Elders." He grunted. "I've been making a habit of that throughout my eternal lifespan."

"Always the rebel." Magnus laughed.

"It really is imperative that I speak to her."

Magnus sighed." Very well! I'll take you to the line of demarcation, but no further." He paused with emphasis. "After that, you're completely on your own."

Magnus continued with an intense stare. "I truly can't guarantee what might happen once you cross that line."

"Well, my dear friend." Poseidon sighed. "I suppose that's something I'll have to find out for myself."

In the Branchview foyer, there was a loud rapid knock on the front door. It repeated just a few seconds later, as Loraine tried to hustle in from the Sitting Room. "Good grief! I'm coming as fast as I can."

She swung the door open in a huff and found an agitated, fidgety Eddie standing there. "Where is she?" he stormed in. "Where's Emma?"

"How should I know?" She rolled her eyes with annoyance. "It's not as though I keep track of her every minute of the day."

Eddie settled himself a bit. "I'm sorry for being a bit on edge." He pleaded with his hands. "Can we talk?"

"Of course!" Loraine quipped. "I am capable of doing that." She motioned for him to follow. "We can talk in the Sitting Room."

He impatiently followed Loraine, and they both settled on the couch. "Now, please tell me what urgency brought you here at such a late hour?"

"Emma's spirit showed up at my house today, and frightened the hell out of my wife."

"Oh, dear!" Loraine placed her hand on her forehead. "I never thought she'd do that."

"Mrs. Spencer!" Eddie sighed. "Emma must understand I still love her. But even if I found my way back through time, she would no longer be there."

"Yes, I know!" Loraine replied with distress. "There wouldn't be any way for her to go forward in time either."

"It's all so damn complicated," Eddie complained.

"The poor child has been wandering aimlessly between two worlds, searching for you, for over a century."

Loraine stated with great sympathy. "All that time, she never knew she was dead, and she couldn't understand what happened to you."

"I'm sorry she had to endure that." Eddie sadly stated.

"This is all Liddy McPherson's fault." Loraine quipped with frustration. "I know she was out to destroy both the Locke and Branch family. But why would she want to harm poor Emma?"

"Out of jealousy, I suppose," Eddie grunted. "Liddy had her eyes set on me from that first day I arrived here at Branchview." He paused with brewing anger. I can assure you, that the feeling wasn't mutual. I never had any attraction for that woman at all."

"That was definitely a wise choice on your part, but a double-edged sword in this case." Loraine huffed.

Eddie replied with much emotion as he recanted his story. "For a while, after I arrived here in the future, I lived among the homeless. That's where I met my wife, Sandy." He paused. "She was a drug addict. I protected her from harm, and helped her overcome her addictions."

"Does Sandy know about your past?"

"She thinks I was an orphan who ran away from a foster home when I was seventeen."

Loraine rolled her eyes in disbelief. "She's your wife, Eddie! Don't you think it's time she knew the truth?"

"How in the world is she ever going to believe a story like that?" Eddie replied with frustration.

"If she loves you, as I'm sure she does, she'll believe you." She paused. "Then I think you should talk to Emma."

"When can I do that?" He anxiously asked. "I just want everything resolved, so we can both move on."

Loraine stared at him with pensive thought. "Give me a little time. I absolutely need to chat with her first."

Simultaneously, in the main Study of the Branchview house, Meryl and Suzy sat across from each other at a small table, attempting to use their psychic abilities to solve another part of the puzzle surrounding Steven's disappearance.

"Are you ready to sharpen those newly discovered abilities of yours?" Meryl grinned.

"I'm not convinced yet, but I'm certainly ready to try."

Meryl opened her hand to reveal a necklace choker with an aquamarine. It was the same one given to Steven from Amphitrite at their initial meeting. "This was given to Steven by Amphitrite. We should pick up on both their vibrations and hopefully locate them within the spectrum of time." She gave a confident wink. "Are you ready to start?"

Suzy answered with a timid nod, and the two women grasped their hands across the table and closed their eyes. They could feel the increasing warmth of the aquamarine stone as they cradled it tightly between their two palms. They both drifted off into a semi-trance and closed their eyes. Suzy's eyelids moved rapidly as she received information, and she reacted anxiously.

"I see Steven!" She exclaimed with excitement. "He's with a woman that looks like Dr. Seagraves." She added with a perplexed expression.

"That's good!" Meryl smiled with an assured nod. "Little did you know, but Dr. Seagraves and Amphitrite were the same person."

Suzy's face showed surprise at the revelation, though she never opened her eyes, and remained centered while Meryl continued to speak. "I can see them with another man." She paused. "It's Poseidon!"

"Philip Seagraves?" Suzy inquired, and Meryl gave her hand a slight squeeze to confirm.

They both weaved and bobbed within their seat as more information came to them. Suzy spoke first with apprehension. "Their wardrobe and surroundings are different." She paused to process things. "It all looks somewhat Colonial in nature."

"I'm definitely picking up that they're in the past," Meryl stated and began speaking audibly to the universal powers. "Spirits of the universe, as we clutch this pendant ever so tightly, give us a series of numbers that may give us an indication of where Steven Spencer might be within the spectrum of time."

They both waited patiently, and in complete silence. "I see a one, followed by a six." Suzy blurted out with exuberance.

"Nine...seven," Meryl added.

With a deep sigh, they released their grip and opened their eyes simultaneously. "1697! Steven is in the year 1697! Suzy exclaimed with great alarm.

Meryl attempted to catch her breath, and eventually regained her composure. "At least we know he's not alone." She assured. "We can be confident that he's in the able company of Poseidon and Amphitrite."

On the island of Avalon, Poseidon hiked through the thick trees, and underbrush as he crossed the line of demarcation, and into the forbidden zone. The skies suddenly darkened above him, and the wind picked up as well. With a flash of bright light, and a deafening crash, lightning struck a large nearby tree, splitting it in two. The tree tumbled down, blocking Poseidon's progress. An immense orb of light appeared and momentarily blinded him. As he struggled to regain his sight, and his composure, Anu, the watcher of the skies, appeared before him.

"Poseidon!" He announced with surprise. "What business do you have in the forbidden zone?" he demanded with both curiosity and vigilant fury.

Poseidon answered with a respectful nod. "I meant no disrespect to the supreme powers, nor you, my friend. But I must speak with Charlotte Locke."

"Did Magnus not explain that she was to have no visitors?"

"Yes, he simply escorted me to the line of demarcation. It was I who decided to cross over."

"What is this urgency that brings you to see her?" Anu stepped closer.

"A mutual friend, Steven Spencer is in great danger."

"I remember this Steven Spencer from the battle." Anu nods.

"He wandered into a time passage that exists at the Branchview Estate, and we must send someone in to bring him back."

"How would Charlotte be able to help with that?" Anu inquisitively probed.

"She's the only one who has nothing to risk, and perhaps the most to gain in bringing him home."

"I see your point." Anu looked away in deep thought. "Charlotte needs all the redemption she can get to make up for all the misery that her evil caused throughout the years. A good deed like that would surely earn her favor in the eyes of the higher council." He glanced toward the woods in front of them and pointed. "Her house is in the clearing, just beyond the tree line," he paused. "I'll take you there, but you must wait until I return with permission from the supreme power."

"I fully understand."

On a night in 1697, Steven impatiently paced within the Locke Estate Foyer dimly lit with candle lanterns. Abigail quietly entered from outside and quickly began to converse in a whisper. "I expected you back hours ago," Steven stated with frustration. "I had to tell Jonathan that you had a headache, and you were napping."

"Poseidon has returned with Zeus." Abigail sighed. "We need to meet at the Secret Cave sometime tomorrow."

"Did you have time to go back to the ocean?" Steven asked with concern.

"I had time to refresh myself earlier. I'll sneak out again after everyone in the household is asleep."

Steven quieted Abigail as voices were heard coming from an adjacent room. His expression turned to enlightened surprise as they both listened. "Those voices!" He whispered. "They're the ones I heard in the time portal just before I entered."

They moved cautiously closer to the closed door, while the voices escalated into a heated argument. "How dare you spurn my advances," Jonathan growled. "If it wasn't for me, you and your little brat would be out in the street. You owe me."

Steven and Abigail reacted with quickened glances to what they heard. "I appreciate all you've done for me since my husband passed away." Jenny expresses emotionally. "But the fact remains I could never love you."

There was a loud sound of a slap that caused them both to wince, followed by the sound of Jenny weeping. Abigail cringed, and could barely contain her anger as she continued listening. "You insolent bitch!" Jonathan roared. "You'll be sorry you ever said that."

Steven and Abigail quickly retreated when they noticed the knob began to turn. As they hid from direct sight, Jenny ran from the room in tears. She paused with embarrassment after noticing the couple standing near the front door. "Is everything alright?" Steven asked with great concern.

"Yes!" Jenny responded. "Please excuse me, Mr. and Mrs. Spencer."

She hurried up the stairs, while Jonathan sauntered into the room, reacting rather sheepishly when he noticed the couple standing there. "Good evening, Mr. and Mrs. Spencer." He cleared his throat. "I thought you two would have surely been turned in for the night."

"It's such a beautiful evening." Abigail declared. "We thought we'd step out for a breath of fresh air."

"With all due respect, that's not a rational decision," Jonathan grunted. "There are several wild animals, and various creatures of the night lurking within the woods."

"Then perhaps we'll reconsider," Steven replied.

Jonathan tried to smooth over the recent event with his guests, as the encounter turned awkward. "I should apologize for what you might have overheard." He paused. It appears you walked in on a heated argument between my servant and me."

Abigail lightly tugged Steven's arm as she led him toward the stairs, simmering with a fit of anger on the verge of exploding. She turned near the base of the stairs, and sternly addressed Jonathan. "We're only guests here Mr. Locke. What takes place between you and your house staff is no concern of ours."

They all exchanged a polite, but uncomfortable gesture toward each other. "We'll see you in the morning,

Mr. Locke," Steven concluded, as he and Abigail ascended the stairs.

Back at the Island of Avalon, Anu led Poseidon to the clearing, where a majestic, white Victorian-style home was nestled in a picturesque setting. The house had first and second-floor porches lined with hanging ferns and adorned with ornate lattice woodwork. "What a beautiful house!" Poseidon proclaimed.

"Quite sufficient for a paradise prison, I suppose," Anu remarked. "I'll leave you here to visit while I obtain permission on your request."

A tropical bird perched on the second-floor porch squawked out a loud warning that visitors had arrived. Anu nodded to Poseidon with a smile, and in a flash of light, and the sound of a harp strum, he departed, leaving Poseidon staring upward at the nervously squawking bird.

A fond smile graced his face as Charlotte exited from the interior, and showed her presence at the porch railing. "Poseidon!" She called out. "You're certainly a sight for sore eyes."

"It's good to see you as well, Charlotte."

"I would've prettied myself up, had I known you were coming?" She fussed with her hair. "The front door is open. Let yourself in, and I'll be down shortly." Poseidon chuckled with amusement as he set his paces toward the house.

At Branchview, Loraine sat at the head of the dining room table for yet another late-night meeting with the recently returned Ezekiel and Tina, as well as Meryl, Suzy, Sharie, Tony, and Andrea. Loraine turned her attention to Sharie first. "Gerard won't be attending?" she inquired.

"He's an assistant coach with the high school football team." She replied. "They had a practice scrimmage in New Haven this evening."

"Really! Ezekiel stated with great interest. "I've grown to be quite fond of American football.

Sharie rolled her eyes. "That husband of mine lives and breathes it." She huffed. "He's a die-hard New England Patriot fan."

"I need to introduce him to Tom Brady sometime." Ezekiel confidently replied.

"You know Tom Brady?" Suzie enthusiastically broke in with wide-eyed surprise.

"Oh yes!" He confidently replied. "We've attended several of the same charity functions."

"His wife is an absolute gem," Meryl added.

Tina naively glanced at each person at the table, feeling lost, and left out of the conversation. "I have absolutely no idea what you're all talking about." She sighed. "I have so much to learn about this world."

Loraine broke in with a frustrated sigh, "Could we all please stick to the subject at hand?" She paused to gather her thoughts. "We've determined Steven is trapped in the year 1697, but he was obviously wise enough to summon Amphitrite and Poseidon."

"How do you know this?" Sharie asked.

"Meryl and I observed him with Philip and Dr. Seagraves," Suzy answered.

"Dr. Seagraves?" she further questioned.

"Her and Amphitrite are one, and the same," Meryl stated in matter-of-fact way, while Sharie reacted with astonishment, and glanced around the table cluelessly.

"Is there anyone else at this table who isn't who they appear to be?"

Tony gave a slight nod. "Some of you might be surprised to know that I'm really Triton, son of Poseidon and Amphitrite."

Suzy also reacted with astonishment at the revelation and flashed a totally perplexed expression toward Andrea. "I never actually told you the whole story," Andrea stated in her own defense. "I'll fill you in on all the details later."

Both Suzy and Sharie were totally flabbergasted, while Tina chimed in next with a sober demeanor. "I was a mannequin at Nordstrom's before Charlotte Locke turned me into a woman."

The women stared at her with further wide-eyed surprise, and it became so quiet in the room at that moment, that a pin drop could've easily been heard.

Ezekiel finally cleared his throat and confirmed the revelation. "For those who didn't know already, I'm afraid that's true as well."

Loraine lost her patience with everyone, "Good grief!" She complained. "Could we please just discuss these matters later?"

Ezekiel motioned for Loraine to settle herself and took control of the conversation. "Lori's right." He stood up to address everyone. "But since Charlotte Locke's name was mentioned, I'll have you all know that Philip is with her on the island of Avalon as we speak."

"He certainly picked a fine time to pay a social visit," Loraine replied with frustration, while Ezekiel pleaded her patience with a gesture of his eyes.

"Let me explain." He paused with emphasis. "No one else at this table would go into that portal without suffering serious repercussions." His eyes wandered to everyone in attendance. "Charlotte, however, is a spirit with the powers of witchcraft. She would be the best choice for bringing Steven back safely."

"How soon can we do this?" Loraine inquired with frustrating anxiety. "Steven is a modern man, stuck in a primitive time. We must bring him home as soon as possible."

"I'm afraid we'll just have to be patient." Ezekiel sighed. Charlotte can't enter the room until the exact moment in the next full moon cycle."

"That's at least three weeks from now," Loraine complained. "What will we do until then?"

"We plan, and make sure everything is perfect," Ezekiel stressed. "If she entered that room at the wrong moment, she could end up somewhere completely different within the spectrum of time." Everyone in the room reacted with expressions of stressful anxiety.

At Charlotte's house in Avalon, she and Poseidon relaxed and casually conversed in large, high back wicker chairs on the upstairs veranda porch. Their iced tea glasses sweated with condensation from the moderate warmth of the afternoon sun.

"This place is delightful, Charlotte." He proclaimed with a pleasant smile. "I'm so delighted to see that you've been treated fairly by the Council of Elders."

"I'm thankful for my surroundings." She stated with a melancholy smile. "But loneliness and isolation can be a terrible sentence to endure."

"I can only imagine," Poseidon answered with absolute sincerity.

Charlotte took a refreshing sip of her tea and looked toward Poseidon with serious thought. "You mentioned Steven entered a time portal at Branchview." She bit at her upper lip with active thought. "By chance, would it have anything to do with the doors in the East Wing?"

"You know about this?" Poseidon inquired with much surprise.

"I know that it's part of the reason Daniel Branch the first sealed off that Wing of the house." She nodded. "You already know the other reasons all too well."

"Can you tell me anything in particular about this imaginary room?" He further probed.

"I only heard rumors about several unfortunate souls that had wandered through those same doors, and were never seen or heard from again."

"My God!" He exclaimed with horror. "There were others?"

Charlotte responded with a matter-of-fact nod and continued. "If I'm permitted to go with you, how do you want me to help?"

"We need someone to enter those doors, and bring Steven back." He stressed. "Since you're already dead in this time, you're the only logical being of choice."

"What if I fail?"

"Then both you and Steven will be lost in the spectrum of time, and everything connected to your past lives will disappear." He sighed. "That might bode well for you in some ways, but not so much for Steven."

Charlotte pondered the situation for a moment, "And what if I can succeed?"

"Then I would suppose your good deed would count greatly toward paying your karmic debt." He paused. "That would be for the Council of Elders, not me to decide."

"I would do anything to redeem my soul for all the evil I caused in my life." She proclaimed passionately. "By all means, count me in."

"Fantastic!" Poseidon exclaimed with a relieving sigh. "Hopefully, Anu will return soon with an answer."

"In the meantime, my good gentleman." She raised her tea glass toward him. "Could I challenge you to a grueling game of backgammon?"

"My dear lady!" He answered with a sly grin. "I most certainly accept your challenge."

Late at night in the Branchview Ballroom Grand Corridor, the large ornate clock chimed at midnight, echoing out, and mingling with the faint chimes of other clocks within the house. Loraine wandered into the enormous darkened room and stood at the center of the dance floor. Though she was alone, she could feel the eyes of Branchview's spirit past watching her every move.

"Emma! I know you're here!" She called out. "Please come talk to me."

Emma paced slowly from the shadows, and into the dim light. Loraine pursed her lips and eyed her in a demeaning fashion. "I know what you did, and you should be ashamed of yourself." She scolded.

"I know I was wrong to be so angry." Emma lamented. "But it's just not fair!"

"What's not fair, Emma?" Loraine lectured. "That Eddie has made a new life for himself, and he's happy?"

Emma shrugged, and Loraine became more sympathetic. "Come, dear! Let's go sit." She sighed. "It's been an exhausting day."

They both strolled from the center of the dance floor and took a seat, side by side, on a bench. "There are many things in this life that aren't fair." Loraine continued. "How do you think I feel, knowing that my husband is lost somewhere in time and may never come back?"

"I know." Emma smiled. "But there's still a chance he will come back. Edward and I will never be together again."

"How do you think Edward feels about that?" Loraine countered. "He loved you very much, and he still does. But after a time, he realized he could no longer live a past that wasn't there anymore." She reasoned. "Now it's time for you to accept that, and move on as well."

Emma pondered the thought for a moment, then erupted in a quick burst of anger. "It's all that Liddy McPherson's fault." She proclaimed. "She ruined our lives."

"I totally agree. She ruined your lives, and those of many others." She paused with compassion. "But I can assure you that Liddy is paying dearly for all the sins she committed." She concluded with a nod. "You need to let it go, sweetheart." She smiled sweetly and whispered. "Go to the light."

Emma reacted with over a hundred years of penned-up emotion. "Can you please do me just one favor, Mrs. Spencer?"

"Please call me Lori." She stated. "And yes, what can I do for you?"

"Can you help me to find my grave?" She pleaded. "I just want to know that someone remembered me."

Loraine was caught off guard by her simple request, and nodded rapidly, while emotional tears began to flow from her eyes. "I'll do just that." She assured. "And I can promise you, that you'll never be forgotten, my dear." The two women emotionally embraced.

Back in time, at the Locke Estate, Steven and Abigail descended the stairs in the early morning hours, as light streamed through the large window of the parlor. Abigail swiftly moved ahead and set eager sight on the upright harp. "I can't contain myself anymore. I must play that harp."

Steven followed her, pacing slowly. "It's too bad they don't have a piano as well." He stated. "I'm sure we could create some beautiful music together."

"What's this piano that you speak of?" Abigail asked with a perplexed expression.

"I'm afraid that instrument hasn't been invented yet." He chuckled. "But it will bring much pleasure to our ears in future times." He added with a smile.

Abigail sat gracefully on the stool behind the harp and gently embraced it. With much delicacy and grace, her fingers danced across the strings, creating a heavenly sound that echoed across the cathedral ceiling. Her face expressed the feeling of every chord played. Steven sat down on the edge of the sleigh couch to listen. He leaned against the arm, closing his eyes, and equally losing himself within the music.

Jenny quietly entered the room, and stood for a time, with her hands humbly cuffed in front of her. She also appeared entranced in a more sorrowful way. Abigail caught a glance at her, and abruptly quit playing. Jenny quickly recovered her composure, as though suddenly snapping back into reality. "Please pardon my intrusion." Jenny bowed. "Mr. Locke wanted me to tell you that he had business in Essex. He won't be returning until late tonight."

Steven stood up, and strolled over to her, showing more concern with the woman before him than for what she had to say. Abigail abandoned the harp and followed with equal concern. "That's a nasty welt you have beneath your eye."

Jenny reacted with embarrassing anxiety. "It's nothing, Mr. Spencer." She trembled. I got up in the dark last night, and walked into the edge of a partially open door. It was a clumsy accident."

"It's quite swollen." Steven examined it closer. "Perhaps you should apply a cold pressing to it."

"Perhaps I'll do that." She nervously answered. "If you'll excuse me, I do need to prepare breakfast. It should be ready shortly." She paused before exiting the room and turned to Abigail timidly. "I must say you play the harp quite well, my lady."

She nodded with respect and hurried from the room, as Steven abruptly turned to Abigail, speaking in an angry, loud whisper. "She didn't walk into that door." He vented. "That pitiful excuse of a man hit her last night."

"I'd have to agree," Abigail responded with equal disdain. "It's becoming apparent that Jenny might not be the evil monster you initially thought."

"There's definitely more to this story than any of us in the future could ever imagine." He added.

Unnoticed by either of them, a frail woman in her early 40s stood in the entranceway of the room, watching.

She had frazzled hair, harrowing distant eyes, and was dressed only in her nightclothes.

She spoke, while Steven and Abigail reacted with anxious surprise. "Excuse me! I could've sworn I heard someone playing my harp."

They strolled over to her, and Abigail reacted with mild embarrassment. "That would've been me." She admitted. "I apologize if my playing disturbed you."

"On the contrary." She replied. "I enjoyed hearing it again. You play it marvelously."

"Thank you," Abigail replied with a warm smile, while the woman looked down at her trembling hands.

"I haven't been able to play in some time." She sadly explained as she glanced toward the harp.

"I'm sorry! You must be Mrs. Locke." Abigail gestured respectfully. "We're Mr. and Mrs. Spencer."

"Oh yes!" she answered with enlightenment. "I'm Merideth Locke. My husband did mention we had guests. But unfortunately, I've been far too ill to greet you."

"We fully understand, Mrs. Branch," Abigail replied.

Merideth grew unsteady and appeared as though she was going to faint. Both Abigail and Steven moved urgently to prevent her from falling. "We must get you over to a chair, Mrs. Locke." Steven urged. "You're far too weak to be standing on your own."

They helped her settle into a comfortable chair. Then Steven alertly retrieved a crocheted throw blanket from nearby and wrapped it snugly around the shivering woman. Abigail placed her hand over Merideth's forehead. "Steven!" She urgently whispered. "This poor woman is burning with fever. We must get her a doctor."

Steven quickly rang the bell on the side table, then continued aiding the sick woman. Within moments, Jenny swiftly entered the room. "Mrs. Locke!" she cried with concern. "What on earth are you doing out of bed?"

"She's a gravely ill woman, Jenny," Steven stated. "Can you take a carriage into town, and summon a doctor?"

"There's a spare carriage in the stable." Jenny nervously replied. "But I'll need some help harnessing the horse."

Young Liddy innocently entered the room while the adults conversed with urgency, and Jenny turned to Abigail.

"Would you mind watching Lydia while I'm gone?" She asked. "The other servants won't be here for another two hours."

"I'll watch over her," Abigail assured her as she looked to the little girl. "She can help me care for Mrs. Locke."

"Is there anyone else who can help us until you get back?" Steven inquired.

"Malcolm Branch and his wife Beatrice." Jenny nervously answered. "They live in the house on the other side of the woods."

"I know where that's at," Steven replied. "I'll go there immediately after I help you with the carriage."

Steven and Jenny swiftly exited with great urgency, and Abigail calmly glanced down at the somber-faced child while attending to Mrs. Locke.

"Would you be a dear, and fetch me some wet clothes?" The little girl anxiously nodded and hurried from the room.

The grandfather clock in the Branchview foyer chimed at 10:30 am. The desperate hours continued to pass as the inhabitants searched for a way to access the portal of time, and bring Steven Spencer back to the future. Their one dim hope demanded approval by the Supreme God, and the Council of Elders.

On this morning in late summer, all anxiously waited for an answer. The front door opened, and Philip Seagraves peeked in, "Hello! Is anyone here?"

He entered the quiet house, and rang the spirit bell near the door, before walking over to the entrance of the Sitting Room, where he looked in to find no one. He turned just as Ezekiel and Meryl were swiftly making their way down the stairs. "Good heavens, brother! We're coming as quickly as possible." He tapped the banister rail with the palm of his hand as he reached the bottom. "You're making enough noise down here to raise the dead."

"That wouldn't be too hard of a task in this house." Philip joked.

All laughed, and the two exchanged a brotherly hug, before Ezekiel's demeanor turned serious. "I take you didn't succeed at bringing Charlotte back."

"On the contrary," Philip replied with a sly grin. "We just wanted to surprise everyone."

He strolled over, opened the door, and Charlotte sauntered in with a grand entrance. "Hello there, handsome!" She addressed Ezekiel with a wink. "I heard you were trying to get the old team back together."

"It's good to see you again, Charlotte." Ezekiel chuckled as he greeted her with a cordial embrace.

Meryl reacted uncomfortably to her greeting, as Ezekiel moved her forward with a light touch to the small of her back. "This is my ex-wife, Meryl Markopolous."

"I prefer the term estranged." She greeted her with a feminine handshake and flashed Ezekiel a cold stare. "After all, we never officially divorced."

Charlotte shared a glance, and a grin with Philip, before the awkward situation was cut short by the entrance of Tina at the top of the stairs. "Philip! I thought I heard…" She froze in mid-sentence when she saw Charlotte.

Charlotte looked up at her with much emotion, as her eyes began to well with tears. "It's okay, my dear!" She assured. "I'm not the terrible witch that you remember."

Tina descended the rest of the way down the stairs and greeted her with a quick hug. "I apologize for my reaction." She paused. "I'm still traumatized by that part of my short life."

"I can fully understand." Charlotte stood back, embracing her shoulders at arm's length. "I can honestly say that out of all the ill-fated deeds I've done in my past, I'll never regret creating you."

"And I can truly say I'm forever grateful for that creation as well," Philip added as he and Tina kissed.

"Shall we all move to the Sitting Room?" Ezekiel suggested. "We have quite a bit of catching up to do."

They all began strolling in that direction, but Philip paused. "Where is everyone?" he asked.

"Lori and Suzy left the house early this morning," Tina answered. "And everyone else is probably off somewhere, taking care of their own business."

"There have been some interesting events taking place here while you've been gone," Meryl commented. "We definitely have to bring you two up to speed."

Philip sighed, and he and Charlotte shared a wide-eyed glance. "We have a few interesting things to tell all of you as well."

Chapter Six:

The Bluebird and The Hand Maiden

In an old section of the Branchview family cemetery, was an assigned portion of land where only hired help with no known family were buried. The last known interment in that plot took place sometime in the 1930s. After that, most hired help opted to have their own houses and a life beyond their workplace. In recent years, the section had been neglected and forgotten. It was a shamble of damaged tombstones, and terribly overgrown with weeds and bramble. On this morning, Loraine and Suzy aimlessly searched this forlorn property for Emma's burial place.

"It's virtually impossible to find anything in all this overgrowth." A frustrated Loraine proclaimed. "I can't believe they let this portion of the cemetery fall into such disrepair."

"Are you sure she's even buried here?" Suzy asked. "We've checked practically every grave marker."

"The Branch family journals recorded this was the site." She glanced around with her hands on her hips. "I can't imagine where else she would be." Loraine cluelessly stated.

They both stood, looking perplexed, and defeated for the moment, until an idea brought an enlightened expression to Loraine's face. "Take my hands Suzy, and center your concentration on Emma." She suggested. "Perhaps her spiritual energy might lead us to the right spot."

They grasped each other's hands, and quietly closed their eyes. After a few moments, Suzy broke the silence. "I'm seeing an old elm tree, with roots uplifting the ground around it." She pondered further. "Also, deep grass, and it's close to the fence line."

Both opened their eyes and looked around. "Over there!" Suzy exclaimed with excitement. "I think that's it."

"It's hard to believe they would've buried someone so close to the fence," Loraine commented. "But we'll check it anyway."

The two women aimlessly kicked around in the deep grass for a time, until Suzy struck something with the tip of her foot, merely a short distance in front of an enormous elm tree. "Ow!" She yelled, holding her throbbing sneakered foot. "I just stumbled onto something."

Loraine hurried over, and they both began pulling aside grass with their gloved hands until finally, an overturned and submerged marker was revealed. "It's partially buried in the ground." A winded Loraine stated. "Let's try to pull it up from this side."

The two women strained with all their might until they finally succeeded in flipping the headstone upright. They vigorously brushed away the caked-on dirt until they could read the weathered engraving.

EMMA LOUISE LINSTRAND
July 28, 1877 – August 15, 1896

The victorious, exhausted duo knelt by the marker with reverent, and solemn sorrow. "The poor child!" Loraine exclaimed. "She died only a little over two weeks after her nineteenth birthday."

"She wasn't even a year older than me," Suzy added with much sadness.

Loraine glanced upward with a distressed sigh, just as a bluebird landed on a branch of the elm tree, tweeting out as though it were talking to them. Loraine smiled emotionally at the sight. "We finally found you, Emma."

In 1697, at the Locke Estate, Steven, Abigail, and Jenny paced impatiently, as they waited for word from the doctor that was upstairs with Merideth Locke. Along with them, but a bit more subdued was Malcolm Branch. He was a distinguished, quiet-mannered man in his early 50s who sat in contemplation on a wooden chair within the foyer.

He looked up from his thoughts long enough to voice his inner impatience. "I wonder what's taking the doctor so long?" He quipped. "I merely wish Jonathan were here."

All conversation suddenly paused as Doctor Webster, a short man in his late 60s with a bushy mustache and thick spectacles, descended the stairs. Right behind him was Beatrice Branch, a stern-faced Puritan woman in her mid-forties, who appeared much older than her actual age. Steven was shocked when he recognized her daunting expression as the same woman in the portrait that hung on the wall of the future Branchview stairway landing.

Dr. Webster breezed by everyone and set his attention on an unsuspecting Jenny. "Ms. McPherson!" He exclaimed. "Am I correct to assume you handle the cooking chores for the household?"

"Yes! That is part of my duties." She firmly answered.

Dr. Webster glanced back at Beatrice, who raised her head in an arrogant, all-knowing manner. He continued to further question Jenny. "Have you also been responsible for taking Mrs. Locke's food to her?"

"No!" Jenny exclaimed with much anxiety. "Mr. Locke insisted on taking the food to his wife."

Dr. Webster stared over the top of his spectacles at Jenny in an intimidating way, and Malcolm grew impatient. "Can you please tell us what's wrong with Mrs. Locke?"

He swung around to aggressively address Malcolm. "Mr. Branch!" He paused. "I can tell you with absolute certainty that Mrs. Locke shows all the indications of arsenic poisoning."

All, except for Dr. Webster and Beatrice, look at each other with expressions of shock. Beatrice set a grim, fixed glare on Jenny, that made Steven's blood run cold when he noticed it.

Jenny immediately proceeded to defend herself. "I can assure you all that I had no part in this." She trembled with anxiety. "Mrs. Locke has always been kind to me and my child."

She held a terrified Liddy, who had just entered the room, securely in front of her. Dr. Webster somewhat changed his demeanor when he saw the frightened child.

"You did say Mr. Locke isn't due back until later tonight?" He asked.

"Yes! He said he would be delayed."

Dr. Webster glanced at everyone with serious thought. "I suggest someone be constantly at her side to administer the medicine I prepared for her."

"I'll stay with her," Beatrice announced, while still holding a cold stare on Jenny.

"Is she going to live?" Malcolm inquired with much concern.

"It would be a miracle, Mr. Branch." Dr. Webster dauntingly replied. "I seriously doubt she'll make it through another night." He pushed his spectacles up the bridge of his nose and continued. "I have no other choice than to involve the sheriff in this matter. He turned and glared sternly at Jenny. "I'd encourage you not to leave the house, Ms. McPherson." He glanced at everyone else. "I would also ask that none of you to mention this to any of the other servants." He paused with emphasis. "They are also considered suspects until proven otherwise."

"I'll do exactly as you say," Jenny replied. "I'll be in my quarters with my daughter if anyone needs me." All quietly watched as the mother and daughter exited the room.

Without changing her hauntingly stern expression, Beatrice turned to ascend the stairs once again. "I'll tend to Mrs. Locke." She concluded, before drifting out of sight, and onto the top landing.

"I'll walk you out, Dr. Webster." Malcolm offered with a sigh.

Before exiting the house, Dr. Webster turned to Steven and Abigail, and bid goodbye. "Mr. and Mrs. Spencer, I hope to see you again, under more pleasant circumstances."

"We can only hope, Dr. Webster," Steven replied.

Everyone's departure left Steven and Abigail alone in the foyer. Steven turned to his surrogate wife with urgency. "They're going to accuse Jenny of doing this." He proclaimed in a loud whisper. "We both know she's innocent."

"I know!" She sighed with equal frustration. "But we can't get involved."

"I couldn't live with my conscience if we didn't." He added.

"Steven!" She held his shoulders at arm's length and peered into his eyes. "If we interfered, that would create disastrous consequences in the future." She reasoned. "We must discuss this issue with Poseidon and Zeus later this evening."

"I see your point," Steven concluded. "We'll wait."

In the Branchview study, Ezekiel, Philip, Gerard, and Charlotte were all gathered around a small table to discuss the plan of sending Charlotte to the year 1697.

"Gerard! With the time frame we gave you, were you able to figure out the correct geometric formula for the angle of the moon?" Ezekiel asked.

"I researched the lunar coordinates, and then measured to where the center of that imaginary room would be in the courtyard," Gerard explained. "I estimated the full light of the moon would've shone on that spot at approximately 1:07 AM on the night Steven disappeared."

"All good!" Philip nodded. "We obviously know what time the portal opened, but how will that help us now?" He waited a few moments for someone to respond before continuing. "We can't just wait until the next full moon to send Charlotte into the portal. There won't be enough time for her to get Steven in that spot before it closes again."

"Philip's right!" Charlotte exclaimed. "I have to go in ahead of time, and find Steven first." She paused. "We also have to remember that hardly anything in 1697 is as it is now."

All paused with visible frustration as they pondered the situation further. Gerard then suddenly slapped the palm of his hand on the table-top with enthusiastic enlightenment.

"I might have a solution." He proclaimed, as everyone turned their full attention toward him. "If I could somehow position a spotlight high enough above the center of the courtyard, perhaps we could simulate the light of a full moon."

"Brilliant!" Philip blurted out with exuberance. "Then we could send Charlotte into the room at the correct geometric period that the portal opens."

"I can estimate it down to a fifteen-minute maximum interval. That will assure us that Charlotte is in the room at that exact moment." Gerard replied.

"That's an immense window," Ezekiel added. "But it just might work."

In the Branchview kitchen, Sharie polished the granite countertops, while Millie attempted to feed smashed peas from a jar to the finicky, and resistant babies as they sat in their high chairs.

"They don't want much to do with these smashed peas, and I can't say I blame them," Millie commented.

"I remember those days all too well." Sharie laughed.

Loraine and Suzy entered from the adjacent shed, covered with dirt and grime from head to toe. "Ah! Don't you dare!" Sharie scolded. "You two need to take off those dirty shoes before you come into my clean kitchen."

"Good grief!" Millie remarked as she eyed the two women. "Have you two been out rolling in the dirt."

"We've been in the old servants' graveyard, looking for a particular tombstone." Loraine groaned as she removed her shoes, and entered the kitchen area.

Suzy followed close behind and rested her hand on Loraine's shoulder. "I'll talk with you all later." She sighed. "I have to get out of these dirty clothes, and get a shower."

"Don't you dare touch anything on your way up the stairs, young lady," Sharie warned as she departed the room.

Millie smiled, continuing to try and spoon-feed the babies, as Loraine moved closer. "How are my precious little angels this afternoon?"

"Don't you dare come near those babies until you've bathed yourself?" Millie quipped indignantly.

"Oh, mother!" Loraine remarked. "It's only dirt and perspiration. It's not as though I have the plague."

"On the contrary, Lori!" She haughtily replied. "You've been wallowing around in a cemetery. There's no telling what sort of vermin might lurk within that dirt."

Sharie listened to the mother and daughter squabble with much amusement as she continued to work. "Oh! Tut, tut!" Loraine concluded with surrender, as she strutted over to Sharie.

"I need you to do an enormous favor for me, Sharie."

Sharie paused from her work and gave her full attention. "I need you to notify the groundskeeper, and have him and his crew clean up that portion of the cemetery as soon as possible."

"I'll contact him immediately, Lori," Sharie replied. "Is there anything else you'd like me to tell him?"

"Yes!" Loraine added with thoughtful emphasis, "tell him there's a gravestone that we dug up, seven paces in front of an old elm tree on the south end of the lot. Have him mark the spot, and bring the stone to the maintenance garage."

"What do you plan to do with it?" Sharie inquired with a perplexed expression.

"I want it cleaned, and restored to its original condition." She stated. "I also plan to have an engraver add a special message onto it."

"Why all the fuss over an old forgotten gravestone?" Millie asked.

"Because the person who is buried there deserves a respectful resting place." She responded with a miffed attitude. "It's the least that we can do."

Charlotte unexpectedly sauntered into the kitchen, breaking the tense exchange between mother and daughter. "I thought I heard familiar voices in here," Charlotte announced.

"Oh, Charlotte! Loraine exclaimed. "I can't begin to tell you how delighted I am to see you."

Charlotte moved closer, but then backed off a bit, "I'd give you a hug, but you're dreadfully filthy, my dear."

"Oh! Let me go get cleaned up." Loraine laughed. "Then we'll have a long chat over a cup of tea."

"And quite a chat we'll have," Charlotte added. "I'll meet you in the Sitting Room."

At the beach, which would later become known as Lighthouse Point. Steven and Abigail made their way toward the Secret Cave Room. They walked on the rocky portion, close to the cliffs, but Abigail still struggled along with her narrow, primitive shoes. "I can't understand how human women can wear these torturous contraptions for an entire day" She complained. "They definitely weren't made to walk on sand or rock."

"Now I know why you prefer magic as your normal mode of transportation." Steven quipped.

She raised her long dress as she struggled over the rough terrain. She lost her balance, falling to one knee, and Steven quickly moved to lift her, steadying her with both hands on her hips.

"We only have a short distance to go. Could I carry you the rest of the way?" He offered.

Abigail gazed at him through dreamy eyes, abruptly pulling him close, and surprising him with a forceful, passionate kiss.

Steven reeled as though getting hit with a knockout punch. "What was that all about?" He demanded.

"Isn't it obvious?" She answered in a frustrated huff. "I'm falling in love with you." She further vented. "If you would only forget about going back to the future, and stay here with me, I would make you a very happy man."

"I'm sorry, Amphitrite!" He glanced upward with a sigh. "If it were under any other circumstances, I might be tempted to say yes." He paused with emotion. "But I'm deeply in love with my wife, and children, and I desperately need to get back to them."

Abigail reacted with devastating disappointment. The awkward moment was short-lived, however, as they were interrupted by the sound of weird chants carrying along with the breeze. The sounds seemed to originate at the south end of the beach. They looked in that direction and saw an immense gathering of people in what little light the dusk was now providing. They all carried torches and were gathered around a huge bonfire. "What is that chilling chant?" Abigail shivered. "It is not a comforting sound at all."

"I don't know what it is, but I've heard it on several occasions in the future," Steven answered. "I can say with certainty it is not associated with anything positive."

Abigail rested against a rock and began to remove her cumbersome high laced shoe boots. "I have to agree it sounds very unpleasant." She commented. "Would you know what those people might be up to?"

"Once again, whatever it is, it can't be good." He answered. "Let's see if we can get a closer look."

Steven helped her stand up, and they began walking toward the congregation. As they get closer, they hunched down behind a huge rock to observe from a safe distance.

The crowd surrounded the bonfire, and their faces were covered with dark hoods and hideous-looking masks. Their repetitive chants grew louder, and more intense, as a masked individual stepped forward, carrying an enormous pig with bound hooves. The robed figure set the squealing pig down, and slowly lifted the mask from his face.

Steven and Abigail were shocked when the light from the bonfire revealed his identity, "That's Jonathan Locke!" Steven exclaimed in a loud whisper.

Jonathan stared downward at the struggling pig with a sinister grin. Then without warning, he wielded a large dagger from beneath his robe and thrust it into the defenseless pig.

Steven and Abigail cringed at the brutality of the sight, as the assembly went into a frenzy. They moved in around the sacrifice, dancing and chanting even louder.

"What demonic, and savage people they are." Abigail proclaimed. "We need to leave this place now."

"I agree," Steven added. I certainly wouldn't want to suffer the same fate as that poor pig."

As early evening fell on the future house of Branchview, most inhabitants were busy carefully preparing their strategy to bring back Steven Spencer. Loraine and Charlotte casually sauntered into the Sitting Room after spending a good part of the day in each other's company. They settled next to each other on the couch for further conversation.

"I can't believe how simple shapeshifting can be, once you've tapped into that part of your consciousness." Loraine marveled.

"With practice, I assure you it will become second nature to you," Charlotte added.

While the two women conversed, Ezekiel, Meryl, and Philip urgently entered the room. "Excuse me, ladies!" Ezekiel announced. "I hate to interrupt, but Meryl has just had a disturbing vision."

Meryl anxiously stepped forward, and both women rose to their feet to eagerly listen. "I saw a vision of a wicked man." She began. "He was laughing, and there was fire all around him."

"Do you have any idea who this man might be?" Charlotte inquired.

Meryl shook her head and continued, "I caught a fleeting glimpse of a large white house on the cliffs overlooking the ocean."

"Could that possibly be the old Locke Estate?" Loraine questioned Charlotte.

"Possibly." She answered. "What else did you see, Meryl?"

"Nothing more." She replied with frustration. "But I did feel a terrible, sickening dread. I fear Steven might indeed be in grave danger."

Loraine emotionally placed her hand on her forehead and closed her eyes, while Charlotte moved quickly to comfort her, "We can't take any chances," Philip stated. "We must send Charlotte into that room tonight."

"As we speak, Gerard and Tony are at the rental facility, obtaining the elevated floodlight we'll need," Ezekiel added.

"Let's see!" Charlotte thought deeply. "How would a lady of fine taste adorn herself in the late seventeenth century?"

She pondered the thought for a few moments more, and then gracefully ran her hands from the top of her head, and down the length of her shapely body. Within seconds, her long raven hair fell into a perfect bundle atop her head, and her modern clothes transformed into a proper, long black dress, with red trim. The finishing touch arrived with the appearance of her narrow, laced boots.

Everyone marveled as they observed the transformation. "You always did prefer black and red." Loraine teased.

"At least my soul isn't black, as it once was," Charlotte replied with a clever smirk.

"We have a little over five hours to prepare." Philip addressed Charlotte with urgency. "I would suggest you rest while myself and the others prepare for the event."

"I'm so glad we have a bit of time." Loraine sighed. "I nearly forgot that I had some other business that I needed to tend to tonight."

Within the Secret Cave Room, Steven, Amphitrite, and Poseidon all sat in solemn ponderance, while Zeus rested in one of the throne chairs, displaying a scowl of displeasure.

"This far-fetched story of all of us in the future is difficult to fathom." Zeus proclaimed. "I'm surprised the world hadn't self-destructed by the year 2019."

"I can assure you it's all true, and we're all still here at that time," Steven replied.

Zeus stood up and strolled from the marble altar to confront Steven, "This personal issue between the Branch and Locke family, and these witches, does not concern us." Zeus maintained. "Why should we become involved?"

"Because over the centuries, this issue grows into a major problem that affects all of us."

Zeus slammed his fist down on the table in front of Steven with boiling anger. His outburst even startled the other two immortals, "All of Europe and the rest of the world are either at war or in serious turmoil." He turned away in a huff. "We have no time to worry about the year 2019."

Steven rolled his eyes in frustration, "Much time will pass between now and the future." He reasoned. "But I can truly say the situations in the world have not changed. They only have a cast of new players."

Poseidon stood briefly, and motioned to calm the conversation, before settling back in his seat to speak, "Zeus and I discussed this situation at length before you two arrived." He paused. "We decided it would not be wise to intervene. It could have drastic repercussions if we somehow altered the future."

"They're right, Steven," Amphitrite added. "If we don't allow events to unfold as they originally did, we will upset the course of fate, and time."

Steven pondered the situation for a moment, "I see your point." He humbly stated. "My only role here should be a casual observer. But, it's still hard to not want to stop a catastrophe before it happens."

"I understand," Zeus assured with a much calmer demeanor. "But our focus should be on getting you back to your own time." He cast a stern eye toward the Mermaid goddess. "Although I'm convinced Amphitrite has different thoughts on that."

Poseidon also casts a hardened glare at his estranged wife, while Steven quickly attempted to quench the tension, "I think she and I have already settled that matter." Amphitrite defiantly looked away in an attempt to conceal her emotions.

In the darkness of the Grand Ballroom/Corridor, a single mounted spotlight went on over the dance floor. The echo of footsteps could be heard as Loraine and Eddie entered the room. Eddie glanced upward at the high ceilings, admiring the ornate craftsmanship. "I'd nearly forgotten how beautiful this room was." He smiled.

Loraine led the way to a padded bench. "Please! Have a seat, Eddie."

They sat down, and Eddie stared dreamily toward the marble dance floor and pointed, "That's where I last saw her in 1897."

Loraine replied with a sympathetic smile, "Did you tell Sandy everything?"

He answered with an emotional nod, "Imagine her surprise when she learned her husband was a 145-year-old man."

Loraine gave a brief chuckle of amusement, while Eddie continued to gaze to all corners of the room. The silence was nearly deafening.

"It's almost like the empty sanctuary of a church. Do you think she'll make an appearance?" He asked.

"She said she would." Loraine sighed.

After a few moments, light footsteps were heard approaching, and Emma shyly stepped forward from the shadows. "I'm here, Edward."

Eddie slowly stood up and paced toward her with great emotion. "Emma! I'm so sorry this all happened."

She lightly placed her hand on the side of his face, and he breathlessly shivered when he felt it. "It wasn't your fault." She sadly stated. "We may have been robbed of our life together, but I'm still pleased you had a second chance."

Eddie shut his eyes and shook his head, "I can't tell you how many times I'd wished I'd never left you here that night."

"It was fate." She assured him with a nod. "Your wife and daughter needed you just as much as I did."

"You must know that I never stopped loving you." He proclaimed. "I simply accepted my fate, and moved on."

Emma forced a smile and glanced toward the dance floor. "Could we have one more dance?"

Eddie managed a nod and took her hand. The couple moved to the center of the floor, where the single spotlight in the ceiling enveloped them.

Loraine watched as the couple gracefully waltzed a few circles. Eddie twirled her around and pulled her in close.

The spirit of Maggic Branch then stepped in from the shadows, and stood watching. "They dance quite well." She stated. Loraine responded with a warm smile toward the little girl.

On the other end of the Grand Corridor, a bright doorway opened, spreading white light into the room. The dancing couple paused and observed for a long moment with amazement.

Emma suddenly ignited in a burst of excitement, "I can see my mother and father waiting on the other side." She cried.

The sight mesmerizes Eddie as Loraine and Maggie strolled up to join them. Maggie slipped her little hand within Emma's and smiled up at her. "Are you ready to go, Emma?" She asked. "We've all been waiting a long time for you."

She glanced downward at the child with great wonder. "Do you and I know each other?"

"I'm Maggie!" She answered. "I used to live here before you arrived. I'd sometimes return, and watch you as you sat in the garden."

Emma gazed off in fond remembrance, "I used to love sitting outside in the gardens, and watching the bluebirds flutter about."

Loraine couldn't help but smile and choked on her emotion as she recalled the bluebird, she saw in the elm tree above Emma's gravesite. "I promise I will always remember you when I see a bluebird, Emma Lindstrand." She declared.

The women exchanged an endearing smile, and Eddie took hold of Emma's other hand and gave it a gentle squeeze, "As will I." He assured. "I also promise I will see you again someday."

"I'll be waiting, as I have since you left this room that night." He leaned in. and kissed her lightly on the cheek, and she did the same to him.

"Goodbye Edward!" She started toward the light, and then turned back momentarily. "Have a happy life."

Maggie soberly looked up at Emma, "We have to go now."

Emma turned back toward Loraine and Eddie with an anxious glance. "Go on, sweetheart!" Loraine urged her on. "It's okay!"

Emma gripped Maggie's little hand tighter and set her eyes ahead to the light. Together they strolled slowly into it. The portal closed once they stepped through, and disappeared with a loud swoosh sound. Loraine and Eddie looked on with stunned, emotional silence.

After a few moments, they awkwardly wiped away their tears and struggled to regain their composures, "I think that went well," Eddie stated.

"At least you both have closure" Loraine concluded.

"Sort of!" Eddie hesitated. "There's one more thing I need to tell you about."

Loraine stared inquisitively at him as he continued, "Just before the time Sandy and I left the homeless camp in 2013, a black woman arrived, and claimed she had traveled through time from 1886." He paused as he recanted the circumstances. "I remember everyone laughed at her and called her crazy Mary."

"Did you ever attempt to talk to her?" Loraine inquired.

"She was rather eccentric, and I never knew how to approach her." He stated with much regret. "Sandy and I were both so anxious to get out of that camp, and move on with our lives." He sighed. "Once we left, we never went back."

"You realize we must find this woman?" She declared with great urgency. "If her story is true, that means the poor soul has been wandering in a strange time for nearly seven years."

Eddie responded with an anxious nod of agreement. "Do you actually believe she may have some sort of connection to Branchview?"

"I don't know." She replied. "I've recently learned there were others who may have wandered into that room other than you and Steven. They were never seen or heard from again."

"Good God!" he proclaimed with much grief. "I never knew that."

Loraine nervously contemplated for a moment, and Eddie was breathless with anxiety, "Sharie, our property manager, knows the history of all the black servants that ever worked at Branchview." She stated. "Perhaps she'll be able to help us with this."

"We need to get right on it," Eddie added.

"Believe me! We will

Chapter Seven:

Charlotte Is Our Only Hope

In the Branchview Courtyard, Gerard stood next to the generator below the elevated light stand. He worked a toggle stick to move the tower, while Philip and Ezekiel charted the exact path that the light needed to shine. "A little bit to the right, Gerard," Ezekiel commanded.

"That should put you right about dead center." Philip rechecked the coordinates. "Perfect!"

Gerard strolled over and joined the two gods. "As long as the breeze doesn't shift the light tower, we should be okay." He remarked.

"I can fix that." Ezekiel confidently stated. He waved his hand, and the air became still.

"I keep forgetting who you two really are." Gerard laughed.

Philip checked his watch, "It's five minutes before 1 AM." He anxiously announced. "Let's hope this works."

"I'll text Lori, and tell her to get Charlotte ready," Ezekiel replied with urgency.

In the Branchview Sitting Room, Sharie, Meryl, and Mrs. Porter nervously paced. They paused when both the mantle and foyer clocks chimed simultaneously at 1 AM. "The suspense is killing me," Sharie remarked. "I wish I knew what was happening."

"The men thought it was best if we stayed here," Meryl added. "But I just feel so helpless."

"They're probably right," Sharie responded. "There's not much we can do." She turned to the other two women. "Perhaps we should just turn in for the night."

"I'm not going anywhere until I know they've succeeded." Mrs. Porter protested.

In the East Wing, Charlotte and Suzy sat anxiously in front of the doors, as Loraine rushed in. "Well! Where have you been all night?" Charlotte asked.

"I had another urgent issue to tend to." Loraine sighed. "Remind me to tell you about it when you get back."

"I hope I get that chance," Charlotte replied.

Tony entered the room and fidgeted nervously. "Has anything happened yet?"

Loraine glanced at her watch, "We're within the fifteen-minute window, but we still haven't heard voices."

Charlotte remained focused directly on the door. "What time is it?"

"It's eleven minutes after one." Suzy replied.

"Oh, dear!" Loraine exclaimed. "If something doesn't happen in the next four minutes, I'm afraid it will all be for naught."

"Shhh!" Charlotte silenced everyone. "I hear something."

Everyone moved cautiously close to the door and listened to the faint voices that grew increasingly louder. Charlotte swung the doors open, the voices ceased, and everyone stared into the empty room with wide-eyed wonder. "Here I go!"

Charlotte bolted into the room, followed immediately by an enormous crash that sounded like thunder, and a blinding flash of light that sent the trio back against the opposing wall. Almost as quick as it arrived, the light receded, and the three picked themselves up from the floor in a stunned daze. The room was no longer there, and only the brick wall stood before them.

They all stood dumbfounded for a few long moments in the aftermath, and the silence was deafening. "Astounding!" Loraine exclaimed breathlessly. "She's gone!"

"The portal gate opened at approximately 1:13 am," Suzy remarked.

"And closed quickly," Tony added.

"Let's just pray Charlotte ended up in the right place," Loraine concluded.

Charlotte opened her eyes to see a night sky filled with stars. She was lying on her back in a field of tall grass and weeds. She struggled to sit upright, and placed her hands to her head in agony. "Oohh! I forgot how bad a headache feels."

She glanced all around her with a perplexed expression. "If this is supposed to be Branchview, it's the furthest thing from the way I remember it."

She fumbled about, but finally managed to get to her feet, and somewhat regained her senses. "Let's see now!" She pondered. "It's in the middle of the night. I assume it's the year 1697. I have no idea where I'm going, and I'm talking to myself." She laughed. "Come on, Charlotte! Pull yourself together."

She sighed and evaluated the situation for a moment. "Perhaps I can get a better perspective of where I'm at from an aerial view."

She flicked her wrist in the air, shape-shifted into a nighthawk, and swiftly flew off into the darkness.

Chapter Eight:

Another Alarming Discovery

The massive grandfather clock chimed at 1:30 AM, and the loud ticking of the pendulum thereafter resembled the sound of a heartbeat within the now silent house.

Suzy had returned to her room and plopped down at the foot of her bed with a sigh. Her thoughts spoke loudly, almost like recited words within her head.

In the aftermath of witnessing Charlotte's disappearance into the portal of time, I find myself reflecting on my own tragedies and losses. I can only imagine the immense sorrow felt by the loved ones of those unfortunate victims who entered into that imaginary room in the East Wing and were never seen or heard from again.

She reflected in sorrow for a few minutes more and sadly shook her head.

"I think it's time to call it a night, Suzy."

In the Sitting Room, Sharie sat in a chair by the picture window and stared out into the darkness. Like everyone else in the house, her foremost concern was whether Charlotte had reached the correct destination and if she and Steven could ever return.

A visibly exhausted Loraine entered the room and interrupted her deep thoughts. "Oh good!" Loraine announced with relief. "I'm glad you're still up, Sharie. There was something I desperately needed to talk to you about."

"Of course! Sharie replied. While gesturing for Loraine to sit down, "I was just waiting for Gerard to finish with the men in the courtyard."

"Has everyone else turned in for the night?" Loraine further probed.

"Yes. Mrs. Porter and Meryl retired to their quarters only a short time before you came in." She replied. "So, you and I have the entire room to ourselves, spare a few wandering spirits."

Both women shared a short, pleasant laugh before Loraine became serious again. "I spoke with Eddie tonight, and he gave me some troubling information that you might find interesting."

Sharie sat forward in her chair to listen attentively, as Loraine continued, "He told me about a black woman in the homeless community who claimed she also came here from the 1800s." Loraine sighed with exhausted frustration. "I can't remember the exact year."

"Do you recall if it was 1886?" Sharie asked with keen interest.

"Yes!" she exclaimed. "I do believe that was the year."

Sharie became more focused and impatient. "Did he mention this woman's name?"

"He said her name was Mary."

Sharie stared upward in horror, drawing a deep breath, before clenching her eyes shut with great emotion. After a few moments, she spoke a name aloud, "Mary Wallace!"

Loraine was taken aback by her reaction, "You know of this woman?"

Sharie opened her eyes wide and answered, "Yes." She sighed. "It's reported in the journals that she mysteriously disappeared in that year of 1886." She looked away, still in dazed horror. "She was my great, great grandmother." Loraine reacted with speechless surprise at the news.

A nighthawk landed on the beach, near the point where the lighthouse had stood in future times. It strutted about for a few moments before transforming into a naked woman. Charlotte glanced around in the dark and then clothed herself with a wave of her hand.

She gazed downward at her bare feet, "My feet will thank me for giving them reprieve of those torturous shoes."

She then glanced around again with a perplexed expression, "I think this is Lighthouse Point." She paused. "But the lighthouse obviously doesn't exist yet."

She strolled to the water's edge, just short of where the small choppy waves reached onto the shore. She gazed out with anticipation, over the dark waters of the Atlantic.

It was a scenario she remembered from a distant time in the future when she was in an equally desperate moment, "It worked then." She sighed. "Maybe it'll work again."

She scanned the area, making sure she wasn't being watched, before calling out softly in the night air. "Amphitrite! If you can hear me, please come! I need you!"

She waited, but initially, only heard the gentle crash of the waves making their way to shore. She squinted against the cool breeze that blew in from the ocean and tried again, "Amphitrite!" She waited. "Are you there?"

She listened again, as loud dolphin-like wails could be faintly heard echoing across the expanse of the waters.

The sound brought a smile to her face. The chatter of unseen seagulls mingled with the haunting echoes that seemed closer, and louder.

Charlotte's eyes scanned the darkness with heightened anxiety. She folded her arms tightly in front of her to stave off a sudden, strong wind gust. After a few moments, she finally saw a figure emerge in the waters. Her excitement grew by the second, as she watched the figure strolling toward shore.

As the shapely naked figure sauntered closer, Charlotte's desperation yielded an exuberant smile, "Mermaid! You definitely have a timeless body." She smiled. "I'm quite envious."

Amphitrite quickly blinked, and clothes appeared on her body, "I do love that trick." Charlotte chuckled.

Amphitrite eyed her with wonder, "Let me guess." She paused. "We knew each other in another time."

"Actually, you and I have quite a history." Charlotte grinned and paced closer. "At different times, we were the bitterest of enemies and the closest of allies."

Amphitrite fluffed out her hair and straightened her dress, "How interesting!"

"In fact!" Charlotte continued. "I gave my life defending you in the battle that took place on this beach in the future."

"A man named Steven Spencer told me about that conflict." She eyed Charlotte with suspicion. "Now tell me, who exactly are you?"

"I'm Steven's aunt, Charlotte Locke." She proudly proclaimed. "Poseidon and Zeus sent me from the future to rescue him."

Amphitrite studied her with a raised eyebrow for a quick moment, "Are you by chance a relative of that Satanist cretin, Jonathan Locke?"

"I may regret admitting this." Charlotte rolled her eyes. "But yes, he is one of my direct ancestors."

"You and I have much to talk about, my dear."

"You have no idea." Charlotte glanced toward the cliffs. "I have nowhere to spend the night. Could you possibly take me to the Secret Cave?"

Amphitrite reacted with further surprise, "It appears the Secret Cave isn't much of a secret in future times."

"As I mentioned before, I am one of your most trusted allies in the year 2019." She paused. "I'll assure you that I can still be trusted."

Amphitrite pondered the situation while gazing at Charlotte with calculating eyes, "Very well! Zeus and Poseidon will not be pleased, but I can't leave a time traveler stranded out here alone."

Much later, just before dawn, Zeus, Poseidon, and Amphitrite were involved in a heated conversation within the Secret Cave Room. Zeus tromped about the room like a spoiled child, "How could you dare bring another one of your mortal friends from the future to this cave?" Zeus roared with anger.

"What was I supposed to do?" Amphitrite pleaded. "If I'd have left her alone on the beach, those blasted Puritans would've burned her at the stake by noontime."

Poseidon paced in front of her, "I have to side with Zeus on this one." He stated in a much calmer tone. "It probably wasn't the wisest thing to do."

Charlotte wandered in from an adjacent room with a sassy demeanor, "How do you expect a gal to get any sleep with all this ruckus going on?"

Zeus turned to her with stern eyes, "Quite a bold question from an unwelcome guest."

"Unwelcome!" Charlotte exploded. "I certainly didn't come here to put up with your pompous, god almighty attitude."

Zeus flew into a rage as he stormed down from the altar. "My dear lady!" He angrily exclaimed. "Do you have any idea who you're addressing?"

"I sure do!" She boldly sauntered closer, within inches of Zeus's face. "You're the same immortal god that recalled me from the spirit world, and sent me on this forsaken journey into the past."

Amphitrite and Poseidon attempted to conceal their amusement with her spunky demeanor, "I like her," Poseidon whispered to Amphitrite.

"She definitely has spunk." She responded with a smirk.

Zeus paced away from her rather sheepishly, knowing he had been put in his place. "Now!" Charlotte continued. "I demand to know why Steven is in the crosshairs of danger at the Locke Estate, while the rest of you are fussing over your little secret hideaway."

"At this point, is there any reason for us to be concerned?" Amphitrite inquired. "The only time I ever leave his side is when I go back to the water at night."

Charlotte glanced at all three before continuing. "Meryl Markopolous had visions of what I believe to be the Locke Estate, and of an evil man surrounded by fire." She paused with emphasis as they all listened. "She also strongly sensed Steven was in grave danger."

"Who is this, Meryl Markopolous?" Poseidon asked.

"My bad!" Charlotte glanced upward with frustration. "You would all know her better as Metis?"

"My first wife?" Zeus asked with great surprise.

"Your one and only," Charlotte replied with a grin.

"Well, dear brother!" Poseidon chuckled. "It appears true love is indeed timeless."

Zeus only answered his comment with a sour, hardened glare, while Charlotte noticed an anxious, and troubled Amphitrite. "Is there something wrong, Amphitrite?"

"That vision of a man surrounded by fire." She began, while nervously pacing. "When Steven and I were on our way to the cave last evening, we stumbled upon a Satanic ceremony on the beach with an enormous bonfire." She eyed all three before continuing. "When the man closest to the fire pulled back his mask, it was none other than Jonathan Locke."

Charlotte reacted with surprise, and enlightenment, while Zeus continued to pace in deep thought. "Metis is known to be quite accurate with her prophecies." He revealed. With all the other knowledge I have of this situation, I would agree that we need to take extra measures to keep Steven out of harm's way."

"Finally!" Charlotte exclaimed. "You and I are on the same page about something."

Poseidon looked to Zeus and Amphitrite, "So, what should we do?"

Amphitrite continued to ponder as she paced as well, "As I mentioned earlier." She began. "I'm posing as Steven's wife, and the first cousin of the King of England." She turned to Charlotte. "We'll have you arrive at the Locke Estate tomorrow morning, posing as Steven's sister who lives here in the New World."

"I think I should mention I'm from the Virginia Colonies," Charlotte added. "It's far enough away that Jonathan can't snoop on whether my story is authentic."

"Excellent idea, Charlotte!" Poseidon commanded her with a keen eye. "And I will pose as your husband. We must also take measures to protect you."

Amphitrite reacted with an indignant raised eyebrow to his comment, which Charlotte took notice of with subtle amusement. "That's an arrangement I won't argue with," Charlotte replied, with a sly grin toward Philip. "We'll be known as Mr. and Mrs. Philip Sheridan."

Zeus exploded with frustration toward Poseidon, "Have you forgotten we have a major conflict in the Middle East that we must tend to?"

"That conflict has been going on for centuries, brother." He huffed. "They can wait a bit longer for us to intervene."

Charlotte let loose with a scornful laugh, as she turned to directly address Zeus. "I'll cue you in on something, handsome." She grinned. "Those fools are still fighting each other in 2019."

Zeus sighed, then thoughtfully glanced at all three. "Very well! We have a little over two weeks before the next full moon. We must all work together to ensure things go smoothly."

"The sun is probably over the horizon by now," Amphitrite stated. "I should be getting back to my beloved husband."

She gave Poseidon a long, hard glare as she sauntered by, and he countered with a grumbling glare of his own, while securely slipping his muscular arm around Charlotte's tiny waist, "Charlotte and I will be seeing you and Steven shortly."

Amphitrite departed in a jealous huff, "I could've cut the tension of that moment with a knife," Charlotte commented in a loud whisper.

"That's a common scenario between those two," Zeus remarked while holding an unrelenting stare on his brother.

Charlotte attempted to escape the awkward moment. "Perhaps I should go ready myself to meet my Satanic ancestor, Mr. Locke."

"Wait!" Poseidon exclaimed. He walked over to a large jewelry box that sat on a stand in the corner of the room and opened it. "If someone as beautiful as you will be playing the role of my wife, she needs to be adorned in the finest of jewels."

He first chose an enormous ruby necklace, and carefully placed it around Charlotte's neck, while Zeus watched with utter disdain. He then chose a matching ring, and placed it on her outstretched finger, as she breathlessly reacted.

"It fits perfectly!" She breathlessly exclaimed.

Poseidon lightly brushed her raven hair from her face and gazed admirably into her eyes, while Zeus grunted his disapproval. "Perhaps I should leave the room." He sarcastically commented.

Still flabbergasted by Poseidon's actions, Charlotte quickly replied, "There'll be no need for that, Zeus."

She nervously rushed from the room, and Zeus sauntered up next to Poseidon, who still gazed in the direction she exited, "Amphitrite will not be pleased you chose jewels from her coveted collection," Zeus warned.

"She'll just have to get over it. Won't she?" Poseidon replied with little concern.

In another time period, the morning light fell again upon the world of Branchview, and the town of Lockeport. Gray, dreary skies ushered in the day, along with the heavy rains that followed. Loraine and Eddie started their day early with a visit to a large church dining hall, where a capacity crowd of homeless people were being served breakfast. As they stood at the entrance and observed, Eddie reacted with much-repressed anxiety.

"Being in this place certainly stirs up significant unpleasant memories." He remarked.

Loraine caught the attention of Reverend Moreland, who was busy managing the food line. The Reverend, a youthful-looking man in his early 30s, moved quickly to greet them. "Mrs. Spencer!" He proclaimed with exuberance. "I am so glad you stopped by, so I could personally thank you for the generous donations you, and your family, have made."

"Thank you, Reverend, for all the good you do for these people," Loraine replied.

The Reverend looked toward Eddie, who was scanning the crowd with a sad, sympathetic expression. "It's also good to see you, Eddie. It's been a long time."

"I apologize I haven't been around to help serve meals, Reverend. He reacted with slight guilt. "I've been working a bit of overtime since the tsunami.

"That's fine." He assured. "I believe we have all been working a bit over our normal limits." He smiled. "How can I help you two?"

"We're looking for a particular person," Loraine stated. "A middle-aged black woman by the name of Mary Wallace."

"Everyone either called her Crazy Mary or the Queen of the Gilded Age," Eddie added.

The Reverend's clueless expression gave way to one of all-knowing. "I remember her." He stated with careful thought. "But unfortunately, I haven't seen her around here for some time."

A homeless man in a stocking cap, and few teeth, listened to the conversation from a nearby table. He spoke up with his mouth full of food. "I might know where you can find her."

Everyone turned their attention to the man, who vigorously chewed his food as some spilled out onto his face. "If you know where she is, please tell us, Vincent." The Reverend requested with authority.

The man glanced at all of them with suspicion and paranoia. "You're not going to take her off to the nuthouse, are you?"

"No Vincent!" The Reverend assured as he gazed toward his guests with wide eyes. "I would imagine her family truly wants her to come home."

"I move around a lot." Vincent fidgeted. "I saw her over in New Haven a few weeks back. There's an enormous camp near the waterfront."

"Is there anything else you can tell us about her?" Eddie asked.

"She's an odd one. Stays to herself a lot." He shook his head. "I doubt if you can get her to talk."

Loraine pulled a twenty-dollar bill from her purse and handed it to the homeless man. "Thank you, Vincent." She sweetly smiled. "We certainly appreciate your help."

Vincent held the bill up and glanced at it with wide eyes, and a toothless smile. "Sure! Anytime, lady!

In another century, the early morning sun shined brightly on the Locke Estate, as Abigail quietly entered the house. She glanced into the Parlor where she surprisingly found Steven and Jonathan calmly sitting, and watching her.

They both rose from their seats, and bid her a courteous bow. "Mrs. Spencer!" Jonathan announced. "I assumed you were upstairs sleeping, as your husband told me."

Steven reacted awkwardly and glared at her as she tried to cover for herself. "I snuck out early to take a stroll along the seashore."

"Is that so?" Jonathan saluted her with his glass of brandy. "It must've been quite early, being that we've all been up for most of the night."

He chugged down his drink and turned to Steven. "I find it hard to believe that you'd allow such a lovely lady to escape your side for such a long time, Mr. Spencer."

"I had a lot on my mind, Mr. Locke." She spoke in her defense as she strolled the rest of the way into the room. "I needed to be alone for a while."

Jonathan smirked. "For Mr. Spencer's sake, I certainly hope you were alone."

Abigail took offense and became irritable, "Are you assuming that I?"

"With all due respect, Mr. Locke." Steven interrupted sternly. "I fully trust the devotion of my wife, and I grant her the freedom to get off to herself from time to time."

"Very well!" Jonathan adjusted his demeanor. "I should warn you though, that drunken hooligans frequent the beach during the night. It's no place for a lady to be by herself."

Steven cleared his throat, and abruptly changed the subject. "It's been an eventful night, darling." He stated, his eyes locking firmly on her. "Mrs. Locke tragically passed away during the early morning hours."

Abigail reacted with a mix of emotions, "I am truly sorry for your loss, Mr. Locke."

The conversation was interrupted when Sherriff Morton, a gruff, weathered-looking man with a long scruffy mustache, entered from another portion of the house. He dragged Jenny into the room by the arm with a book of witchcraft in his other hand. Deputy Doren, a short skinny man with a slight limp, and a high-pitched voice followed closely behind.

He forcibly dragged a resistant Liddy along, as Morton held up the book. "Look what I found in her room, inside a drawer." He announced. "It appears you were right,

Mr. Locke." He grinned in a sinister manner. "We're dealing with one of them there witches."

"That book belonged to my husband." Jenny protested.

Jonathan strolled over arrogantly, "Well now! Coupled with the fact that we found the poison hidden in the back of one of the pantry shelves, I'd say we have a solid case against her."

"You bastard!" Jenny exclaimed as she spit on Jonathan's face. "You know you hid that poison in the pantry, and I can prove you're a Warlock with the Secret Society.

Steven and Abigail exchanged a concerned glance, as Morton pulled hard on Jenny's arm. "That'll be enough, Ms. McPherson. Come along!"

He hauled her toward the door, while Doren paused with the struggling Liddy. "What do you want us to do with the kid?"

"I don't care." Jonathan angrily replied as he wiped the spit from his face with a handkerchief. "Just get the little brat out of my sight."

Doren tugged her forcibly by the arm. "It's off to the orphanage with you, little lady."

"I hate you!" Liddy yelled as Doren dragged her away. "You know, my mommy didn't do this." She struggled to look back at Jonathan. "Someday you'll pay for being a liar."

Morton laughed mockingly as he grabbed hold of the front doorknob. "It appears her mommy is grooming her to be a little witch as well."

Steven and Abigail glanced at each other uncomfortably, while Morton swung the door open, and was confronted by a surprised Charlotte and Philip as they stood ready to knock. "Excuse Us!" Charlotte exclaimed. "We were just preparing to knock."

"Pardon us, folks." Morton tipped his hat. "We were just leaving."

Morton and Doren breezed by the couple as they hauled the mother and child away. Charlotte and Philip awkwardly continued into the foyer, while Steven stepped forward with astonishment and disbelief. "Charlotte?"

Charlotte immediately moved to greet him with a peck on the cheek, while Jonathan observed with keen interest. "Yes, dear brother!" She exuberantly greeted him. "It is truly I." She leaned in close, whispering in his ear. "Just go along with it."

Jonathan eyed Charlotte admirably and greeted her with a cordial nod. "I'm Jonathan Locke!" His eyes wandered to the beautiful ruby necklace that dangled near her alluring cleavage, "Mr. Spencer never mentioned he had such a beautiful sister."

Philip stepped forward with assertion. "He must not have mentioned she had a husband either." He stated indignantly, as he extended his hand. "I'm Philip Sheridan."

Jonathan reacted rather sheepishly to Philip's masculine appearance, and irritable demeanor, as he accepted his handshake. Through it all, Steven stood back, trying to make sense of the situation. "I'm delighted to meet you, Mr. and Mrs. Sheridan." He motioned them to the Parlor. "Welcome to my home."

"We merely arrived last evening from Williamsburg," Charlotte stated. "We hope to help my brother and his lovely new bride settle here in the New World."

Steven glanced at Abigail with a puzzled expression that she only responded to with a subtle shrug. "I should apologize for all the chaos." Jonathan declared with uneasiness. "We're in the midst of a severe domestic situation." He paused to muster up a display of fake emotion. "My wife passed away last night, and the sheriff recently departed with the woman responsible for her death."

Charlotte casts an enlightened glance at Steven, as Philip stepped again to the forefront. "Please accept our deepest condolences, Mr. Locke." He implored. "We're sorry that we arrived at such an inconvenient time."

"Thank you, Mr. Sheridan!" He nodded. "Please come in, and make yourselves comfortable. I'm certain you all have plenty to discuss among yourselves." He gestured toward an adjacent room. "If you would all be so kind to excuse me. I must retreat to my study, and prepare arrangements for my wife's funeral."

"Of course, Mr. Locke," Steven replied as he turned a puzzled stare toward Charlotte. "My family and I certainly have a lot to catch up on."

Abigail stepped close to Charlotte, eyeing the jewelry with disdain, before casting a resentful glare toward Philip. "What beautiful jewels your husband has adorned you with, my dear."

It was nearly noon by the time Loraine and Sharie made their way to the homeless camp in New Haven. They wandered through the menagerie of make-shift tents, and recklessly strewn garbage, looking quite out of place in their nice, clean clothes. They garnered hard, curious stares from the inhabitants as they slowly strolled along.

"This is impossible!" Loraine exclaimed. "Finding her here would be like trying to find a needle in a haystack."

"Good Lord!" Sharie commented. "Seeing all this makes me so thankful that I have a comfortable life."

A bold young woman with braided ponytails, and wearing a backpack, brashly approached them.

"Hey! You two don't belong here." She squinted. "What do you want?"

"We're looking for someone," Loraine answered.

"Most of these people don't want to be found, lady." She eyed her with suspicion. "Who are you anyway? Some type of social worker?" She grunted. "I know you ain't cops."

"We're nothing of the sort," Loraine replied. "I can assure you."

She stared awkwardly at Loraine, "You talk funny! Are you British, or something?"

Sharie cannot hold her patience any longer, "You certainly have many rude questions, young lady." She balked. "We happen to be looking for a middle-aged black woman named Mary."

"Tons of people in this camp could fit that description." She laughed. "Got any other info?"

"Please!" Loraine pleaded impatiently. "Perhaps you've heard of someone with that description who may have mentioned she came here from the 19th century."

"Why didn't you say so in the first place?" She quipped sarcastically. "You must be talking about Crazy Mary."

"You know her?" Sharie asked with exuberant hope.

"Oh yeah!" she exclaimed in a matter-of-fact tone. "She rarely talks to anyone though."

"Do you know where we can find her?" Loraine asked with urgency.

The girl gazed over her shoulder, then back toward the women. "Maybe!" She pondered. "Gonna cost you though!"

Loraine sighed with impatience, before digging into her purse, and pulling out a twenty-dollar bill. The girl grabbed the bill, and squinted back toward the women, sporting a sly grin. "I know you can do better than that."

Sharie dug into her purse out of frustration and handed the girl a ten-dollar bill. "That's all we're giving you." She sternly peered at the girl. "Now please! Take us to Mary, if you know where she is."

The girl shoved the bills recklessly into the back pocket of her jeans and motioned to them. "Follow me."

The two women followed cautiously down an aisle of lean-to structures, made of cardboard and wood, and passed many shopping carts filled with junk that were people's only belongings. Along the way, mournful eyes embedded in tired, weathered faces watched the women's every move. They arrived at a small makeshift tent, consisting of two worn blankets clipped together with clothespins.

The young girl flipped the flimsy entrance sheet aside and peeked in. "Hey, Crazy Mary!" She yelled. "You got some visitors."

The girl ushered the women in but did not enter herself. "Good luck!" She sarcastically remarked as she held the sheet back for them.

Both women entered and immediately cringed from the smell of urine, and extreme body odor. In the corner was a weathered black woman with dirty clothes, and matted, disheveled hair.

She sat on the ground looking rather worn down, and defeated, with her knees to her chin, and rocking back and forth. "Mary? Mary Wallace?" Sharie inquired.

The woman glared at both her and Loraine through sad, tired eyes. "Who you?" She asked. "Ain't nobody called me that name for years."

"My name is Lori, and this is Sharie." Loraine started. "We heard the story of how you walked into a room at the Branchview Estate in 1886, and somehow found your way to this time."

Mary's eyes widened for a moment, then she emotionally glanced away. "You don't believe all that. Do you?" She asked.

"Yes, we do!" Sharie replied. "We know all about that room."

"We've come here to finally take you home, Mary," Loraine added.

"You two are just as crazy as I am." Mary laughed. "There ain't no going back." She defiantly stated. "That was 133 years ago."

Mary then broke down emotionally and began to weep. "We can't send you back to your time, Mary." Loraine reasoned. "But we can take you back home to Branchview to be with your family."

Mary glared at the two women and shook her head in further defiance. "There ain't no family there for me no more. They are all dead, and gone."

"You're oh so wrong about that, my dear." Sharie's eyes filled with tears. "I'm there. I'm your…great, great-granddaughter."

Mary looked up at the woman with astonishment. She struggled to her feet and placed her weathered hand on Sharie's cheek. "Lord have mercy!" She cried. "I don't believe it!"

"Believe it, grandma!"

Mary glanced around her with heightened anxiety, "I gots to get my things." She nervously fussed. "I can't leave without my things."

"No! No! Sweetheart!" Sharie tried to calm her. "We're going to buy you all new things. You won't need any of this anymore."

Mary began to weep, and Loraine winced as she wandered closer. "Whew!" She exclaimed. "The first thing we desperately have to do is get you a hot shower, and tidy you up."

"Baby!" She replied with wide-eyed exuberance. "If you two find me some hot water and soap, I'll wash as high as possible, as low as possible, and anywhere else possible."

Chapter Nine:

The Evil Lie Grows Larger

At the ocean overlook, near the Locke Estate, Steven, Abigail, Charlotte, and Philp sat on stone benches within a quaint grove of trees. There they caught up on events surrounding Charlotte's arrival and discussed a plan moving forward.

"So, you're basically telling me that I have to wait until the next full moon to get out of this God-forsaken time?" Steven inquired with frustration.

"I'm afraid that's the only option we have," Philip responded.

"It may as well be an eternity," Steven added.

"It's a pity that we're stuck in the stone age," Charlotte commented. "If they only had electric lights, we might be able to leave here sooner."

"What can we do until then?" Abigail asked. "Jonathan Locke seems to have a pulse on everything that goes on in this town."

"We'll just have to play the roles we've created," Philip answered. "I'll secure a room for Charlotte at the hotel in Lockeport, and I'll spend my nights at the cave."

"Hmm! How decent of you!" Abigail quipped with sarcasm.

The two immortals exchanged a hardened glance, charged with tension. It drew raised eyebrows from both Steven and Charlotte, who noticed the friction between the two. "I have to speak up, and say I don't think it's a good idea for Steven to remain at the Locke Estate," Charlotte stated with great concern. "It's only a matter of time before Jonathan figures out that he and Abigail aren't who they say they are."

"I have to agree with you on that," Abigail said. "He's already suspicious about where I was last night."

"Perhaps you could use the death of his wife as an excuse to secure other accommodations," Philip suggested.

"We'd have to be delicate with that situation," Steven warned. "We wouldn't want to bruise his enormous ego."

Everyone pondered the situation, and Steven glanced toward Charlotte with an enlightened thought. "In your family journals, do you recall what happened to Jonathan Locke?" He asked.

"I know he was murdered, but I can't recall when or why." She responded. "It's been a long time since I read those journals."

"I've only just met the man, but I can fully understand why someone would want to kill the arrogant bloke," Philip grunted.

"Indeed!" Abigail nodded. "It appears he finds it acceptable to destroy anything that gets in the way of his desires."

Charlotte looked to Abigail with a smirk. "Considering the manner, he ogled you and me, Steven and Philip should watch their backs."

Steven smiled, and moved the conversation forward, addressing Philip and Charlotte directly. "While you two check in at the hotel, I suppose I'll visit Jenny at the jail."

Everyone glared at him with disbelief that he would suggest such a thing. "Have you lost your mind?" Philip sarcastically quipped.

"There's a method to my madness," Steven assured. "Perhaps she can shed some light on how this scenario grew into a monster of a problem in the future."

"He may be right," Charlotte commented. "If we're stuck here for the next few weeks, we may as well compile some knowledge that we can take back to the future." She looked to all three. "Errors need to be stricken from the journals, and replaced with truth."

"Very well!" Abigail sighed as she looked at Steven. "But I'm going with you." She implored. "Even though Jenny may be innocent, it's obvious that we're still dealing with a witch."

Loraine and Sharie continued their efforts to bring Mary Wallace out of the shadows of forgotten obscurity, and into the mainstream of modern-day life. Sandy Benson, worked patiently to transform the matron into a twentieth-century woman.

"I'm so glad the YMCA was kind enough to let us use their shower." Sharie sighed. "I don't think I could've endured that horrible stench all the way back to Lockeport."

"I simply can't wait to see what our girl looks like when Sandy finishes with her."

"I know." Sharie agreed. "It was a stroke of luck that Eddie's wife worked here, and was able to fit her in."

Just then, Sandy gracefully led Mary from the salon area, and Sharie and Loraine both stood with awe-stricken, breathless surprise.

"Ladies!" Sandy enthusiastically announced. "Let me introduce you to the beautiful new Mary Wallace."

Now sporting a shorter, stylish haircut, a fashionable green dress, matching shoes, and a faux pearl necklace, Mary glanced into the surrounding mirrors with proud, but humble amazement. She turned to Sharie and Loraine with tears of joy.

"I feel like a queen."

"And you look like one, my dear," Loraine replied.

"You do look absolutely gorgeous, grandma," Sharie added.

"I don't wanna hear no more of this grandma stuff." Mary scolded. "You know I can't be no more than a few years older than you, child."

All the women shared a hearty laugh as Sharie emotionally embraced Mary.

"From now on, you'll be known as my beautiful older sister," Sharie stated with assurance.

"You performed an absolute miracle, Sandy." Loraine declared. "She doesn't even look like the same person we brought in here."

"Knowing the circumstances, I did everything I could to ensure she got the best attention possible."

Mary motioned toward Sandy, "That child has magic in them hands." She commented as she further admired herself in the mirror. "She helped me say goodbye to crazy old Mary, and I ain't never going back to being that person again." All the women reacted with joyful laughter.

Chapter Ten:

A Flurry of Revelations

In a darker and more primitive time, Deputy Doren escorted Steven and Abigail to Jenny's dank, dirty cell in the Lockeport jail.

He glared at the couple with squinted eyes as they reached the cell. "You sure you two gonna be alright?" Doren asked. "She's a mean one."

"I'm sure we'll be just fine, deputy," Steven replied.

Doren opened the heavy wood cell door, motioned them in with a grunt, and then closed it behind them. Jenny sat in a dark corner of the cell, staring straight ahead at the floor. "What do you two want?" Jenny asked without eye contact.

"We just want to talk," Steven replied. "We want to hear your side of the story."

"What difference does it make?" she grunted. "It won't save me from these blood-hungry fools."

"We don't believe you killed Mrs. Locke," Abigail stated.

Jenny soberly eyed the couple with disbelief. "We know Jonathan killed his wife." Steven continued. "We were hoping you could tell us why."

Abigail brushed the heavy dust off a wood bench, and daintily sat down, while Jenny glanced longingly at the barred window above her. You're right!" Jenny remarked. "I didn't kill Mrs. Locke, but I am a non-practicing witch as they accuse."

Steven and Abigail exchanged a fleeting, wide-eyed glance, as Jenny continued. "My husband brought Liddy and me here from Scotland to seek a better life." She shook her head. "All seemed well until we met Jonathan Locke."

Steven paced closer to Jenny and urged her to continue, "He found out that my husband was a student of sorcery, and wanted to recruit him to his Secret Society."

She paused. "Jonathan then hired him to work on one of his shipping vessels, and while he was out to sea, he'd come around, and force me to bed with him."

"I'm sorry that happened to you," Steven commented with sympathy.

"He's lower than disgusting vermin!" She exclaimed, glancing away in anguish.

"What happened to your husband, Jenny?" Abigail asked.

"They said there was an accident at sea." She sighed. "That he fell overboard, and was never recovered." She turned to face the couple. "I believe Jonathan had him killed." She gazed off in a corner and shook her head as she continued. "Jonathan's bank sold our house out from under us when we could no longer pay the mortgage. Liddy and I had nowhere to go."

"So, Jonathan hired you as his live-in housekeeper," Steven stated in an assuming way.

"More like a live-in slave." Jenny vented with anger. "He had the twisted notion that I would be his wife, once he disposed of the present Mrs. Locke."

"And of course, you refused to go along with his dastardly plan," Abigail added, and Jenny responded with an obvious nod.

"You mentioned you're a non-practicing witch." Steven curiously inquired. "Did you actually study the dark arts?"

Jenny shook her head no, and again, stared upward as the afternoon light filtered through the barred window, and shined down upon her life-hardened face. "I studied natural medicine and White Magic." She continued. "Folks around here, in their perpetual ignorance, would label that as Satanic witchery."

"But we know it isn't," Steven assured.

Jenny stood and began to pace, back and forth.

"However!" She smirked while shifting her demeanor. "Thanks to my husband, I also have a limited knowledge of the dark arts." She halted in thought. "And while I still have breath in my body, I intend to use it to destroy Jonathan Locke." She wickedly laughed. "If the people of this town wish to paint me as evil, then evil I shall be."

"The dark arts can be a dangerous tool in the hands of a novice," Steven warned. "Just what do you plan to do?"

Jenny turned with a vengeful grin, "I will recall the spirits of all his victims, and they will bring torment, and tragedy on him, and his household."

Steven and Abigail both drew a deep breath of shock as Jenny continued to reveal her plot, "The two of you seem like decent folk. I suggest you both leave the Locke Estate before the curse takes hold." She warned. "Lest you be caught up in the turbulent, and unfortunate happenings."

Jenny then paced closer and boldly addressed Steven, "Mr. Spencer! Do you know what they've done with my Liddy?" She asked. "The bastards won't tell me."

"I believe they may have sent her to an orphanage," Steven answered. "If you'd like, I can inquire if Mr. and Mrs. Branch may be interested in adopting her. They also appear to be fine people."

Jenny laughed out loud, "That just shows how little you actually know." She smirked. "Malcolm Branch is a meek manipulated fool, and though his wife hides behind her religion, she's as much a witch as she accuses me of being."

Steven is taken aback by her comments, and she continued on her ramble, while also continuing to pace with the rage of a caged tiger, "I had hoped perhaps you and Mrs. Spencer would take her." She suggested.

Abigail remembered quickly as she stood up, and paced closer, "I'm afraid that wouldn't be possible under present law. We are not official citizens of this country."

"I'm sorry, Jenny," Steven added.

"I should've guessed you'd have a valid excuse," Jenny replied with a weak, forced smile. "I'm sure you wouldn't want people to think that respected royals including yourselves would ever be associated with a lowly, murderous witch like me."

"That's not true." Steven countered. "We're not concerned with what others think.

Jenny emotionally turned her back to them. "I think you should both leave now."

Steven shot a disappointing glance at Abigail, who replied with a sigh, and a rapid nod. "I'll summon the deputy to open the door."

A short time later, Steven and Abigail left the prison and proceeded down the street, arm in arm, "I think we should at least try to secure a room at the hotel tomorrow evening," Abigail suggested. "We certainly don't want to be anywhere near that house when Jenny unleashes that curse."

"You're right!" Steven agreed. "I hate to even imagine this, but that curse will only be the beginning of what will grow into a monster, and eventually affect all our lives."

"I realize that." Abigail affectionately gripped his arm tighter. "But we must steer clear of the storm, even though we know of its impending damage,"

Steven came to a complete halt as he pondered the situation. "I think we should shift our attention to Branchview, and attempt to become friendly with Malcolm and Beatrice before all hell breaks loose."

"Are you suggesting we pay them a social call?"

"Why not?" Steven replied. "I don't think we have anything better to do this afternoon."

Loraine, Sharie, and Mary arrived back at the present-day Branchview for a memorable homecoming. Mary glanced around with much emotional excitement as they entered the door into the spacious foyer area, "I've finally returned home." She proclaimed.

She paused to take inventory of all the sights, while Loraine and Sharie happily watched, "Welcome back to Branchview, Mary!" Loraine joyfully exclaimed.

"You know!" Mary recanted. "For a few weeks after I arrived in this time, I stood outside the front gate, gazing in. I tried to work up the nerve to go to the front door, and knock. But I was so afraid." She trembled as Sharie moved quickly to comfort her.

"All that's behind you now, Mary."

She continued to look around in wonder, "Oh! How I enjoyed cleaning up this old place. I was so proud of my job."

She paused to reminisce for a moment, then eagerly pleaded with Sharie and Loraine, "Would it be too much to ask for my old job back?"

Loraine looked to Sharie with a sly grin, "With all the new people in this house, I'm sure we could use some extra help."

"I couldn't agree more." Sharie winked. "She probably knows every inch of this house as well as I do." She tried to conceal a smirk as she continued. "Of course, we'll have to schedule your work around your classes."

"Classes? Mary questioned.

"Yes," Sharie replied. "I read in Elizabeth Branch's journal that she had taught you and your husband how to read and write." She shrugged. "I think it's important that we continue those lessons."

Mary is flabbergasted and moved to tears. "This is all beyond my wildest dreams. How can I ever thank you?" She embraced Sharie.

"It's the least I can do for the woman who blazed a trail for me."

"It's been a long day for all of us." Loraine sighed. "I think we should move to the Sitting Room, and continue this chat there."

"That's a marvelous idea." Sharie proclaimed. "I'll see if Mrs. Porter can prepare us some tea."

At the old original Branchview home of 1697, Steven and Abigail sat in the Parlor as guests of Malcolm and Beatrice Branch. Steven was amazed by the humble surroundings of the old home. He tried to steer toward a conversation that might shed light on the history of the family, and the estate itself.

"You certainly have a beautiful piece of land here, Mr. Branch," he commented. "What can you tell me about the history of this place?"

"It was deeded to us by Jonathan shortly after we merged our business interests," Malcolm replied. "Beatrice and I loved the fact that on one side we had a vast forest and a brilliant view of the Atlantic on the other."

"There were many locals who warned us not to settle here," Beatrice added.

Steven's interest suddenly peaked by her comment. "What was the reason for that, Mrs. Branch?"

Malcolm quickly answered for her, "It's said this was once the sacred burial ground for the Wangunk Indians. People believed anyone who settled on this land would be cursed."

Abigail nearly choked on her drink of water, and exchanged a foreboding glance at Steven, as Beatrice contributed to the subject. "We never believed all that heathen hearsay" She glanced upward with a raised hand. "We claimed this land for the glory of God. No demons dare to intercede here."

A tall, gangly-looking girl in her early teens entered from an adjacent room to correct her parents' story. "It wasn't a burial ground." She declared. "It was a sacred gathering place."

"Maureen!" Malcolm scolded. "You should know better than to intrude when we're entertaining company."

"I'm sorry father." She replied. I overheard you talking about the Wangunk Indians, and was interested in hearing what you had to say."

"I wish that girl was as interested in her other studies as she is in history," Beatrice commented in an attempt to dismiss and belittle her daughter.

"Mother!" Maureen quipped with mild embarrassment. "If we don't know our history, we flounder like a ship without a compass."

"That's an intelligent statement from a girl of your age." Abigail interceded.

"You can come in, and sit, Maureen." Her father motioned. "This is Mr. and Mrs. Spencer. They're royals visiting from England."

"I'm so pleased to meet you." Her eyes widened with excitement. "I hope to someday visit England."

"Well!" Steven exclaimed. "I do not doubt that someday you will." Steven shifted his attention back to Malcolm. "Is Maureen your only child?"

"We have two older sons who attend boarding schools in Boston." He answered.

The young girl sat politely, with her hands in front of her, but seemed eager to continue the original conversation, "There's an enormous stone in the field behind our house with all sorts of carved symbols on it." She mentioned, before quickly continuing. "That's where the Wangunk held their religious ceremonies."

"Satanic rituals, no doubt," Beatrice grunted, while Steven discounted her remark, and gave Maureen his full attention.

"I'd be interested in seeing it sometime, and learning more about it."

Maureen reacted with a pleased smile, but her mother again interceded, "One should seek the wisdom of the Lord, and forsake all that's paganism, Mr. Spencer.

Everyone reacted uncomfortably with the exchange, as Beatrice glared at Steven with an emboldened expression. Maureen tried to shift the conversation to something less controversial.

"I saw you, and Mrs. Spencer, in town today." She stated. "You were walking out of the jailhouse."

"The jail!" Malcolm exclaimed with alarm. "I hope there wasn't a problem."

"Nothing like that, Mr. Branch," Steven assured. "We were simply paying a visit to Jenny McPherson."

"What sort of business would you have with that evil witch?" Beatrice asked with indignance.

"Beatrice!" Malcolm sternly spoke up, while casting an angry glance at his wife. "It's not proper to ask personal questions."

"It's alright, Mr. Branch." Steven interceded. "We simply hoped to get an account of what had actually taken place." He paused briefly. "It's quite puzzling why she would want to kill Mrs. Locke."

"Do you honestly believe you'd get an ounce of truth from the lips of that demon?" Beatrice responded, while Abigail squirmed in her seat, and was unable to remain silent for one more minute.

"Mrs. Branch!" She firmly exclaimed. "As a religious woman, you should understand the importance of ministering to the downtrodden. After all, we worship a God of mercy and forgiveness."

"She murdered poor Mrs. Locke with no remorse, and she deserves to burn in hell for it." Beatrice venomously fired back.

"If she killed Mrs. Locke, then I'm certain the legal system will determine her guilt or innocence," Abigail stated confidently. "As far as her fate in the afterworld, that will be determined by God, not us."

"The evidence in this case undeniably points toward her, Mrs. Spencer," Malcolm remarked. "I certainly hope you're not insinuating that Jonathan may have killed his own wife."

Steven shot a quick glance of warning toward the simmering Abigail, but she ignored him and persisted in her case. "I'm simply stating that Jenny has a right to a fair trial, just as anyone else would."

Beatrice was visibly miffed with her remarks, and the tension continued to grow between the two women. "Anyone who would align themselves with that Jezebel is surely an agent of Beelzebub." She proclaimed.

Abigail rose from her seat with fire in her eyes, as Maureen and the two men nervously anticipated the impending conflict. "Mrs. Branch!" Abigail exclaimed with ever-brewing anger. "I am certainly not an agent of Satan." She scolded. "But for someone like yourself, who claims to be a woman of God, you certainly enjoy talking a lot about the devil."

Beatrice rose from her seat with an explosion of anger, while the fact mildly amused Maureen that someone actually countered her mothers' bullying. "How dare you, you…royal hussy!" Beatrice exclaimed with frustration and outrage.

Steven immediately subdued Abigail by the arm before any further escalation could occur. "I think it would be a good idea to leave now, darling." He suggested.

The two women exchanged fiery glares, and Malcolm took a firm stance between them. "I'd have to agree with your husband, Mrs. Spencer." He stated. "I'm afraid your welcome in this house has surely expired."

Abigail stormed from the room ahead of Steven.

Moments later, Steven struggled to catch up, as Abigail marched away from the house in a huff. He tried to keep up with her determined stride as they proceeded along the pathway toward the deep woods. "Thanks to your little catfight, I'll probably never get any more information about the Branch family," Steven stated with frustration.

Abigail never broke her rapid stride, as she boiled over with anger. "I loathe that bloated, despicable, self-righteous woman."

Steven attempted to calm down the angry goddess in any way he possibly could. "Abigail!" He commanded in an authoritative tone. "Please! You need to settle yourself!

She came to an abrupt halt and surprisingly turned her anger toward Steven. "Since when do you have the right to give me orders?" She trembled. "You're beginning to sound like Poseidon."

"Abigail!" He pleaded to no avail, as she continued her rant.

"You men are all alike." She continued.

Steven rolled his eyes with frustration and mumbled to himself. "I know I'll regret doing this. But…"

He quickly grabbed Abigail squarely by the shoulders and pulled her in for a long, passionate kiss that caused her to swoon as he slowly released her. "Now! He exclaimed. "Hopefully that will settle you down, and somewhat change your demeanor to a more amicable one."

Maureen's voice interrupted the romantic moment. "Mr. and Mrs. Spencer! Wait!"

They turned to see the young girl running down the pathway after them. She caught up, and leaned over, pausing to catch her breath. Still breathing heavily, she looked up at Steven with serious eyes. "Mr. Spencer! I think you know more about that stone than you'd like to admit." She sighed. "I could tell by the look in your eyes when I mentioned it."

Steven tried to dissuade the young girls' insistence. "I simply have a keen interest in history." He proclaimed. "That's all, and nothing more."

The diversion didn't work, and the girl defiantly shook her head. "No! I know there's something more." She maintained with a bold stare. "You're from a different time than ours, and you two are definitely not married."

"What would make you think that?" Abigail asked with visible offense.

Maureen looked away for a moment before answering, "I'm not as close-minded as my parents. I can perceive things that other people can't see."

"So, you're saying that you're a seer?" Abigail asked with great curiosity. "I too have those same abilities."

Maureen nodded in an all-knowing way and held Abigail's attention with her serious blue eyes.

"I can tell you're deeply in love with Mr. Spencer, but he's in love with someone from his own time."

Abigail rolled her eyes in surrender and glanced away with slight embarrassment for a quick moment. "Oh!" She chuckled. "The girl definitely has the gift."

Steven gazed back nervously toward the house. "Let's walk along further down the path. I wouldn't want your mother to release the hounds on us."

The young girl laughed, and the three began to stroll along as they conversed. Maureen wasted no time in getting back to her assumption of Steven.

"I actually know you're from a different time because I saw you appear in the field behind our house."

"What exactly did you see?" Steven asked with cautious surprise.

"There was a flash of light, and I jumped out of bed to see what it was." She replied. "I saw you stand up near the rock, and you were carrying some sort of strange fire stick."

"That's what we call a flashlight in the future."

Maureen reacted with a puzzled expression that quickly turned to curiosity. "Where exactly are you from, Mr. Spencer? I somehow feel like we're connected."

Steven and Abigail exchanged a cautious glance, and they all came to an abrupt halt. "This may be hard to believe." Steven cautiously began. "But in the future, your ancestors will build a large mansion on the site where your present house and that stone now rest." He paused, while Maureen soberly listened. "I entered a room near the same spot you saw me appear, and was somehow transported to this time." He paused again. "I am a relative of yours from the year 2019.

Maureen was flabbergasted and abruptly turned to Abigail. "Then who exactly are you?" She questioned. "Every time I look at you, I think about the ocean."

Abigail looked away in careful thought before answering. "I'm sorry, Maureen, but I can't reveal that to you." She sighed, before continuing. "I will say that myself and a few others are working together on a plan to get Steven back to his own time."

"Then you need to know all about the full moon cycle and the secret of that stone." Maureen eagerly suggested, while Steven and Abigail exchanged a surprised, serious glance.

"You know those things?" Steven urgently asked.

"I know an old Wangunk Indian Shaman that does." She replied with a nod. "His name is Stargazer, and he can tell you everything you need to know about that stone and the gateway of time."

Steven and Abigail were totally flabbergasted. "Does this Stargazer live here in Lockeport?" Abigail further probed.

"He lives in Deer Island, but I can arrange for you to meet with him in a few days."

Abigail placed her hand on the girls' shoulder and looked seriously into her eyes. "That would be good for us. We'll be staying at the hotel in town by that time." She paused with slight anxiety. "You have to promise you won't tell anyone about us, or what we told you."

"I promise," Maureen assured. "I'm the only other person who knows about the secret of that gateway, and I swore an oath to Stargazer that I would never tell another soul." She smiled. "Of course, in your case, I'm making an exception."

"I hope we can trust you, Maureen," Steven replied. "My life and future depend on all this."

She took hold of Steven's hand and stared seriously into his eyes. "I know it does."

Simultaneously, a pleasant conversation took place between Charlotte and Philip in a Lockeport hotel room. While they waited for Steven and Abigail to arrive, Charlotte grew anxious as the long shadows of late-day fell upon the room. "I was hoping they would've shown up by now." She sighed. "It's getting on near sunset."

Philip strolled to the window and parted the flimsy drapes to glance out. "I seriously doubt they'll make the trip into town this late in the day." He commented. "The town streets aren't the safest place to be after dark."

"I agree." She laughed. "I think I'd rather venture into the deep woods at night, than to stroll anywhere down there in that jungle."

Philip sauntered away from the window and sat in a chair opposite Charlotte. He leaned in close and amicably. "I've thoroughly enjoyed spending time with you today, Charlotte." His eyes hypnotically locked onto her. "I find you to be very enchanting."

"Yes! She breathlessly exclaimed. "I've enjoyed being with you as well." She replied in a hesitating, timid fashion.

He leaned in closer and gently engaged in a passionate kiss with her. She submitted for a few moments of sensual bliss, before pushing him away, and quickly standing up in frustration. Philip reacted with disappointment, and also stood rather frazzled. "Have I done something wrong, Charlotte?"

Charlotte nervously fidgeted, trying to regain her composure and resisted the temptation of embracing him again. "I'm sorry, but I haven't had a man kiss me like that for some time."

"I consider it a pity that men have refrained from doing so." He cupped his hand delicately against her trembling cheek.

Charlotte nervously turned away, fighting her inner desires for a moment, before turning back toward him for a lingering glance. Instinctively, and with a surrendering sigh, she pulled him in by the collar of his overcoat, and passionately kissed him again. Almost as quickly, she pulled away, turning her back on him, as she began to hyperventilate with sensual exhilaration. Philip was baffled by her fickle behavior.

He twirled her around, embracing her with his strong arms, and she melted from her contained passion.

"No! This isn't right!" She exclaimed with insistence, as she pulled away again. "Perhaps you should leave now, Philip."

"But it is right, and you know it, Charlotte." He pleaded with his eyes. "Stay with me in this time, and we'll have a wonderful life together."

Charlotte forced a smile at the thought, but quickly looked away. "I'm sorry, Philip, but I simply can't."

"I don't understand!" He exclaimed with borderline anger and frustration.

Charlotte took hold of both his hands and attempted to calm his somewhat bruised ego. "In my future life, I did some unpleasant things that I now deeply regret." He kept a firm, patient hold on her hands, but gently coaxed her to sit down on the loveseat with him, as she continued. "I was fortunate enough to earn a chance at redemption from the Council of Elders." She sighed, which garnered a wide-eyed response from Philip. "In another time, my spirit is serving its sentence, in solitude on the Island of Avalon."

"But I can ensure your present soul energy is pure." He commented with puzzlement. "Forgiveness is a major staple of our faith. Surely I could speak to the Elders on your behalf."

Charlotte shook her head defiantly and continued. "You already have done that in the future." She smiled sadly. "There's more to the story." She smiled through her tears. "In that future time, you fall in love with a wonderful woman. She'll be the key to the happiness you've sought for centuries."

"But I'm in love with you, Charlotte." He reasoned. "Can't you understand that?"

"No, you're not, Philip." She shook her head defiantly. "You're simply infatuated with me." She gently squeezed his hands. "This woman I speak of in the future will capture your heart, as no other woman has since Amphitrite." Philip listened with astonishment as she continued. "Like me, she has raven black hair, and eyes as blue as the Atlantic on a sunny day." She fondly, but sadly stared upward. "Unlike me, she has a soul pure with goodness, and it further illuminates her sparkling personality."

"But I know you have feelings for me." Philip declared with frustration. "Why would you sacrifice your own desires, and happiness for the sake of this woman?"

She sighed with deep emotion. "Because I created that woman out of evil intent, and she blossomed into something more beautiful than I could ever hope to be." She paused while Philip processed the statement with utter astonishment. "She is your true soul mate, and I would never do anything to jeopardize her happiness, or yours."

"This woman must surely be worth the centuries-long wait." He commented with a thoughtful nod.

"Oh! I can assure you of that, my friend." She forced a smile.

Philip let loose of her hands, and an emotional smile graced his face. "You are truly a beautiful soul, Charlotte. I heartily believe you will find the redemption you seek."

At that, Philip stood, and slowly strolled to the door, while Charlotte followed. "Goodnight, fine lady! I'll see you in the morning." He cordially nodded, before departing.

Charlotte closed the door and leaned against it with a sigh. She clasped her hands close to her heart and sadly whispered. "Goodnight, Poseidon!"

At the Locke Estate, Steven and Abigail were merely returning for the evening. As they entered, they saw Jonathan and his three sons who had recently returned from boarding school earlier that day, conversing in the Parlor. The three boys were still neatly dressed in their school uniforms, and politely stood when they saw the couple.

Bartholomew and Cameron were the eldest twins, who were seventeen. Although they appeared indistinguishable, one could surely understand Bartholomew was the subdued type, while Cameron brimmed with mischievousness. Their younger brother Theodore looked nothing like them. He was an energetic boy of fourteen with long wavy hair and thick spectacles.

"Steven, Abigail!" Jonathan announced. "Please come in, and meet my sons."

The three boys lined up like proper gentlemen to meet the Spencer's as they entered the Parlor, and Jonathan handled the introductions. "These two handsome gents are my eldest, Bartholomew and Cameron." Jonathan then jokingly mussed his other son's curly hair with his hand. "And this scruffy-haired lad is my youngest, Theodore."

"We're delighted to meet you, boys," Steven stated.

"We're so sorry about your mother," Abigail added.

The two older boys gestured a nod of gratefulness, while Theodore stared at her with wonder. "You're very pretty." He commented.

"Theodore!" Bartholomew scolded with visible embarrassment. "It's not proper to address a married woman in that fashion."

"That's quite alright!" Abigail interrupted. "I'll accept it as a compliment."

"Abigail and I will attend the funeral in the morning," Steven strolled closer to Jonathan, "But we've decided that under the circumstances, it might be better if we sought accommodations elsewhere after tonight."

"You're welcome to stay beyond that," Jonathan assured.

"We appreciate the hospitality. But being newlyweds, we'd prefer a little time alone."

Steven gave a sly wink to Jonathan, who knowingly acknowledged. "I can fully understand that." He smirked.

"It's been a long day." Steven sighed. "I believe my lovely wife and I will be turning in for the night." He took hold of her hand and smiled. "It was good to meet everyone. I hope you all have a pleasant evening."

Jonathan pleasantly nodded and then watched as the handsome couple ascended the stairs. Cameron and Bartholomew sauntered closer to their father, while Theodore tagged timidly behind. "Snooty, filthy royals!"

Cameron exclaimed. "We should hang them along with that woman that killed our mother."

"You have much to learn about business, and life, my good son." He slyly smirked. "We need to pose as allies to the royals to gain our own power over these lowly colonists, and Puritans." He let out a sinister chuckle as he turned to address all his sons. "Yes, you all have a lot to learn."

Later that night, Abigail silently snuck down the stairs in the dark. She quietly opened the front door and exited the house. Simultaneously, Jonathan emerged from his study beneath the stairs and entered the foyer with his eyes fixed on the now closing front door. He waited, and listened to the soft sound of her footsteps, as she made her way across the wood plank landing of the front porch. He hurried to the side window to peek out, then turned with an enlightened grin.

At the beach below the Locke Estate, a now barefooted Abigail strolled to the water's edge. As she gazed out over the dark ocean and shed her human clothes, she was unaware that she was being watched from a distance. As she began her stroll into the water, the curious eyes of Jonathan Locke watched from a squatted perch, amidst a patch of wild seagrass.

A chorus of Mermaid calls and chatters echoed hauntingly across the dark waters. Jonathan gasped, and his eyes grew wide as he watched the naked beauty dive below the waves as she transformed, kicking her tail above the surface as she swam away. He was stricken with awe at the sight he had just witnessed.

"The goddess of the sea!" He whispered out loud to himself.

"It's all true! He proclaimed with amazement. "She really does exist."

Chapter Eleven:

The Witches Curse Begins

While circumstances were deteriorating in Colonial-era Lockeport, the present-day town experienced a grand revitalization. A bird's eye view of Main Street revealed an active restoration process virtually everywhere. On this particular late summer morning, Loraine strolled along the sidewalk thoroughfare, taking in the sights, amid the sounds of hammering, and heavy equipment. She paused momentarily to take careful inventory of her thoughts, as though she entered them in a page of one of her novels.

The resilience of human nature never ceases to amaze me. For a small town nearly wiped off the map by an earthquake and tsunami, it would have been easy to accept defeat, and simply fade into oblivion. But within just a few short months, the proud citizens have nearly rebuilt it, and life is finally returning to a more normal state of affairs.

Loraine glanced across the street toward the City Diner, and a smile graced her face. A few moments later, she breezed in from the street and sat down on a stool at the nearly refurbished counter. Several workers maneuvered around the small diner, and Suzie busied herself preparing things behind the counter.

She looked up and enthusiastically greeted Loraine with a smile. "Hey!" She called out over the noise. "What do you think?"

Loraine scanned the room with a sweep of her eyes and reacted with excitement. "It's beginning to look like the grand old diner that I remember." She smiled. "How soon before you think you can reopen?"

Suzy leaned on the counter and sighed., "Considering the workers can only be here a few days a week, and the fact that some old diner components are hard to find, I'm guessing at least another month."

"I'm sure Steven and Philip will be one of your first customers when that time comes." She assured with hopeful intent, before breaking with emotion over her own statement. Suzy hustled around the counter and slipped a comforting, sympathetic arm around Loraine's shoulder.

"I miss Steven too." She stated. "But I just know he'll make it back home." She gave an assuring wink. "Believe me."

Loraine responded with a warm smile, while Suzy glanced out the window with stoic optimism. "Soon our little town will be back to normal, and all this tragedy will be a distant memory."

Two carpenters worked nearby, and casually observed the two women. Tre, a clean-cut, young black man in his early 20s stayed steady with his work. While Josh, a tough, muscular, and heavily tattooed white man in his early 30s paused with his eyes glued on Loraine.

"Who's the fox with the British accent?" He asked.

"I can tell you're not from around here." Tre answered with a shake of his head, and a chuckle.

"What's that supposed to mean?" Josh replied with offense.

"That's Steven Spencer's wife." He answered with an assured nod.

"So, who's this Steven Spencer?" He grunted.

Tre gazed up at him with disbelief. "Man! You don't know much. Do you?" He lowered his voice and continued. "He's a well-known fiction writer and the heir to the Branchview Estate."

Josh glanced toward Loraine and grinned.

"Is that so?" He asked, never taking his eyes off of her. "I noticed she's looking a bit distressed. Maybe things aren't so perfect in paradise."

"I'd leave that one alone if I were you." Tre chuckled.

"Yeah! Maybe you would." He boldly glanced at Tre, before glancing back toward Loraine with a confident grin. "But you're definitely not me."

Back in time at the old Locke Estate, Steven and Abigail entered from the stairs to find a sharply dressed Jonathan, staring out the Parlor window, and cradling a glass of bourbon in his hand. "Good morning, Mr. Locke!" Steven announced. "Where are the boys?"

Jonathan turned around and slowly strolled in their direction with an arrogant smirk on his face. "I sent Bartholomew and Theodore into town ahead of me." He replied as he twirled his drink in his glass. "I have no idea where Cameron might be." He chugged down the remainder of his drink and strolled closer to address Abigail.

"How was your little dip in the ocean last night, Mrs. Spencer?" He laughed. "Or should I call you by your Mermaid name?"

"I beg your pardon?" Abigail reacted with great offense.

"You must truly be mistaken, Mr. Locke," Steven added. "Abigail was with me for the entire night."

"No!" Jonathan arrogantly chuckled. "I'm afraid you're mistaken, Mr. Spencer." He set his empty glass down. "You know, I followed her to the beach last night."

"He's right, Steven." Abigail quickly spoke up. "I did sneak out for a late-night swim." She turned to Jonathan with a stern glare. "But I had no idea I was being watched."

"But you were." He countered as he paced in front of the couple with intimidation. "In fact, I found it curious that you went into the ocean, and never came back out."

"On that, I'm convinced you're mistaken," Abigail grunted indignantly. "Perhaps you had a few too many bourbon drinks, Mr. Locke."

"Really, Mrs. Spencer?" He stepped a bit too close for comfort, and Steven defensively placed his arm between them, as Jonathan carried on with his rant.

"Perhaps the tales about a beautiful red-haired Mermaid that I hear from the sailors are true."

"That'll be quite enough, Mr. Locke," Steven replied with rising anger. "I will not stand by idly while you continue to insult my wife."

Jonathan retreated a few steps, then drew a long, squiggly edged dagger from under his overcoat, and Steven immediately placed himself between him and Abigail. "I wonder if I would disembowel your wife, would she have the innards of a woman or a fish?" He laughed.

"You'd have to go through me first, Jonathan." Steven sneered. "And I'm certain you won't have the same success as you had with that pig at the bonfire."

Jonathan's eyes grew wide with enlightenment. "So, you two have been spying on me as well."

"Enough to know that you're a pitiful excuse of a man who killed his wife, and blamed it on an innocent woman." Abigail venomously replied.

Jonathan boiled over with anger and raised his dagger to strike. Steven forcibly blocked the progress of Jonathan's hand with a swift, martial arts move, sending the dagger sailing across the room. Jonathan set to fight back, while Steven's eyes glowed red with anger, and he roared with the ferocity of an angry lion.

He picked a surprised Jonathan off his feet by the neck with little effort and dangled him in the air. "Steven! No!" Abigail desperately interceded.

Steven roared again, before tossing him like a rag doll across the Parlor. Jonathan crashed into a side table, and crumpled to the floor, trembling in fear. "Who the hell are you people?" He demanded. "You're not human."

Cameron quickly entered from the stairway and ran to Jonathan's aid.

"Father!" He cried. "Are you alright? I heard roars that sounded like a lion."

He helped his father up, and Jonathan set a hardened glare on the couple. "I'm fine, son." He replied. "Mr. and Mrs. Spencer were just leaving."

"And with pleasure!" Abigail sneered, while she took a firm hold on Steven's arm. She grunted with anger toward Jonathan as they quickly exited the house.

Moments later, as Steven and Abigail fled the house, they held hands as they made their way down the rough jagged rock stairway to the beach.

"What in the blazing devil happened to you in there?" Abigail frantically asked.

"It was a display of the superhuman powers that the three of you gave me in the future," Steven replied. "I can't contain those powers when myself, or someone I care about is threatened."

"That beast!" Abigail cried. "It was like a half-man and half-lion." She breathed heavily as they hurried along. "You could've killed Jonathan, and then we would've had a real problem on our hands."

"I just instinctively wanted to protect you." He responded with frustration.

Abigail came to an abrupt halt as they reached the beach, and she turned to look seriously into Steven's eyes. "You do love me! Don't you?"

"Yes!" Steven blurted out before correcting himself. "Actually, it was my uncle who loved you very much. So much in fact, that he came back within the soul of my father, and then myself." Steven paused with emotion. "He had promised somehow he would return to you."

"But it didn't work?" She curiously inquired, and Steven shook his head in response.

"My father and I were both in love with someone else when we met you." Steven emotionally recanted. "You had to go to him instead."

"In spirit?" Steven reluctantly nodded yes, and she looked away with much emotion.

"We must never mention this again." She trembled with anxiety. "Once you're gone, Zeus, Poseidon, and I must erase our memories to preserve the future as it is."

She turned to continue forward on the beach, but Steven halted her again. "Amphitrite! He waited until she turned around. "For what it's worth, I now know why Matthew loved you so much."

She glanced upward toward the house and struggled to hide her emotions. "Come along!" She ordered. "We have to get away from here, and keep a low profile since Jonathan now knows our secrets."

Under gray, late summer skies, Sharie and Mary strolled along in the old servant section of the Branchview family cemetery. They searched among a row of generic markers, carefully looking at each name engraved on it.

"All these grave markers," Sharie remarked sadly. "I wonder when the last time was that someone paid respects to the poor souls buried here."

Mary walked a few paces ahead of her. "I knew many of these people." She commented. "As long as I'm here, they ain't never gonna be forgotten."

"Now that you're here, you can help me update the history so that they're surely not forgotten." Sharie proudly stated.

Mary continued to search and suddenly dropped to one knee in front of a marker. She placed her hand above the engraved name ELIJAH WALLACE.

"Lord have mercy! I found him." She glanced back up at Sharie with tears in her eyes. "My Eli lived to be ninety-six years old."

"And those were ninety-six fruitful years," Sharie added, as she helped Mary back up to her feet.

"What happened in those years after I was gone?" Mary asked.

"According to the journals, he never remarried, and he never gave up hope he would one day find you."

"That's my Eli!" She replied in fond remembrance. "He was a wonderful man."

Sharie continued, "Although he had help in his later years, he remained Mr. Branch's personal butler right up until the day he died." She smiled. "In fact, it's written that he died in the huge chair in the foyer, with a peaceful smile on his face."

"I don't doubt that for a minute!" She exclaimed. "He loved his position in the house, and he was so handsome in that butler suit."

Sharie was amused by her comments and continued with the story. Mary clung tightly to every word being said. "He continued as Branchview's resident artist. He sold many of his works to the richest citizens of this region."

"He was so full of talent, and well-liked too."

"That's not all." Sharie continued. "Eventually, when he learned how to read and write, he wrote several essays on human rights and was involved in local politics. He was a highly respected citizen in this community."

Mary is overcome with emotion, "I'm so proud of what he did with his life."

Sharie stared down at the stone with a reverent nod and an assuring smile, "I'm proud of you too, grandpa." She spoke. "And I promise you'll never be forgotten." The women huddled close, as a single ray of sunshine broke through the thick, dark clouds.

In another time, a tense scene unfolded within the Secret Cave Room. Steven sat, leaning forward in one of the ornate, gilded chairs, while Amphitrite paced nervously. "I telepathically summoned Zeus." She announced. "He should arrive at any moment."

Steven glanced around the large cavernous room with wonder. "I'm curious, Amphitrite. How did the gods set up such a place in the new world?"

"This place has been here for much longer than the colonies." She replied with a smile. "It's just one of many elaborate hideaways throughout the world that are in the god's possession."

Zeus had entered without either noticing and quickly joined the conversation. "It's also one regretfully ignored for many years before this." He paced further into the room and continued. "I found this location while on an expedition with my good friend Leif Erickson, right around the year 1000 AD."

He continued as he strolled closer to Amphitrite and Steven, and motioned to the high ceilings and walls. "The crystals that adorn this cavernous room were formed at the inception of this earth, holding incredible power, and healing energies." Myself and the other gods have come here for centuries to renew themselves from the rigors of life." He turned to Steven and concluded. "Outside of Leif Erickson, you and Charlotte are the only mortals to have ever laid eyes on it."

"And for that, I'm grateful. Steven replied.

Zeus then turned his full attention to Amphitrite. "I sensed your urgency in my summons." He began with a stern, unrelenting stare. "What sort of crisis have you, Poseidon, and the mortals caused?"

"Jonathan Locke has learned my true identity." Amphitrite timidly answered.

Zeus exploded with such ferocious anger that even Amphitrite cringed. "How could you be so careless as to allow such a thing to happen?"

"He followed me to the water last night, and saw me transform." She explained. "When he confronted me about it this morning, Steven intervened on my behalf, and displayed the powers we granted him in the future."

Zeus looked angrily toward Steven, then pointed to Amphitrite. "Your love for this man has truly dulled your extrasensory power. You should have known you were being watched."

She shrugged with shame, as Zeus continued too relentlessly pace. "Where are Poseidon and Charlotte?" He inquired. "Surely this Mr. Locke is wise enough to assume they aren't who they appear to be as well."

"I summoned Poseidon at the same time as you." She answered. "I would've thought he'd be here by now."

Zeus erupted with further rage but quickly calmed himself to logical thought. "I don't have a good feeling about all this." He pondered. "If Poseidon is forced to use any of his powers, his identity could also be compromised."

"Surely, we have to come up with an alternative plan," Steven suggested.

"Silence, mortal!" Zeus commanded with renewed rage. "All this complication is of your doing."

"I will not be silent!" Steven protested defiantly. "And I've had enough of your lofty arrogance."

Zeus marched aggressively to within inches of Steven's face, but he failed to intimidate him. "Need I remind you that I could turn you to dust with a wave of my hand?" He threatened.

"Then do it!" Steven sneered. What do I have to lose?" He countered angrily. "If you don't destroy me, Jonathan Locke and the people of this God-forsaken town surely will."

At that moment, Poseidon entered the room with authority. "What's going on here?"

"It appears Jonathan Locke has discovered their secrets," Zeus grunted. "Where's Charlotte?"

"I left her back at the hotel." He answered with heightened anxiety. "I must go back. If what you say is true, she could be in grave danger."

"You'll do no such thing," Zeus commanded, before pondering further. "No one in town has ever seen me." He reasoned. "I'll bring her back here, and if anyone tries to hinder my efforts, I'll wipe this entire town, and its' people from the face of the earth."

The other two immortals and Steven stayed silent, only exchanging anxious, worried expressions.

At the Lockeport Hotel, Sheriff Morton and Deputy Doren pulled a struggling, resistant Charlotte out of the building to where Jonathan Locke waited. "Where is your husband, Mrs. Sheridan?" Jonathan asked.

"I don't know," Charlotte answered with frustration. "He left a short time ago with Steven and Abigail, and only said he'd be back by sunset."

"Sounds like we have a pack of spies among us, Jonathan." The sheriff quipped.

"Spies!" Charlotte defiantly pulled her arms free. "I demand to know what this is all about."

Jonathan got within inches of her face and eyed the ruby pendant in her cleavage. "I've discovered your dear brother and his wife are not who they say they are." He paused. "And that leaves me to question the true identity of you and Mr. Sheridan, and what business you may have in my town."

Charlotte backed away in disgust and anger.
"Has anyone ever mentioned how horrid your breath is, Mr. Locke?"

Jonathan glared at her with disdain and reached for the pendant. He grasped it within his hand, with the intent of ripping it from around her neck.

But instead, he quickly released it, screaming in agony. "That stone! It burned my damn hand!" He cried as he turned to Morton and Doren.

Even Charlotte was taken off guard by the incident. She glanced down at the pendant, then back toward Jonathan with a perplexed expression.

"She's a witch!" He charged. "Throw her in the cell with Jenny McPherson, and I'll deal with her later." He huffed in anger, still cradling his hand in pain as he turned away. "I have a damn funeral to attend."

Another intense situation began to develop in the future. Loraine waited in the check-out line at the Stop n' Shop, placing the items from her cart onto the belt. Josh lingered nearby, in front of a magazine rack, secretly observing her.

As Loraine busied herself, she also failed to notice Bob Hartley standing in the line in front of her. "Mrs. Spencer!" He exclaimed. "How good to see you."

"It's good to see you as well, Mr. Hartley," Loraine replied with surprise. "Congratulations on your grand re-opening of the Mermaid Inn."

Josh listened with interest as the two conversed. "Thank you so much!" He smiled. "I hope to see you there tonight for the ribbon-cutting ceremony. I know your mother, and everyone else in the household is coming."

"I'm afraid I'll have to decline and take a rain check, Mr. Hartley." She sighed. "My husband is still out of town, and I really don't feel much like celebrating."

"Well! If you change your mind, come on down. It should be quite a festive party."

"I'm sure it will be." She pleasantly replied.

Bob departed with his groceries, while Josh continued to observe as Loraine retrieved her bagged items, and prepared to leave. He quickly, and intentionally, walked in her path, lightly bumping her, and causing a few items to spill from the bag. "I'm so sorry, ma'am! Josh exclaimed. "I should've been watching where I was going."

"Yes! You should've!" Loraine reacted with annoyance.

Josh went down to one knee to retrieve the items and then stood to block her progress again. "My name is Josh Tennant, and I'm sure you must be an earth angel."

"Really, Mr. Tennant!" She rolled her eyes. "Would you please step aside, and let me be about my business?"

"Wait!" He pleaded. "Perhaps I could make up for my clumsiness by buying you a cup of coffee sometime."

Loraine sighed and shook her head as she held her hand up to display her wedding ring. "In case you failed to notice Mr. Tenant, I am already spoken for, and I am pleased with my marriage."

"Such a pity for me, and every other man." He replied with a smirk. Loraine grunted with disdain as she abruptly walked away. A spurned Josh watched with a stern, angry expression.

In another spectrum, tensions also continued to mount by the minute. Inside the Lockeport jail, Sheriff Morton opened the cell door, and pushed Charlotte in, while Jenny passively observed from the corner. "This is outrageous!" Charlotte protested. "You'll be sorry when my husband and brother return."

"We'll just throw them in there with you." Morton laughed as he slammed the door shut.

Morton turned to Doren and gestured toward the cell. "Keep an eye on those two. I'm going to the funeral."

"Those two ain't going nowhere, sheriff," Doren replied as they walked into the outer office.

Jenny strolled up to Charlotte shaking her head sarcastically. "I suppose those knuckleheads accused you of being a witch for wearing a black dress." She extended her hand. "I'm Jenny McPherson."

"Yes, I know who you are!" she accepted the handshake. "I'm Charlotte Sheridan." She paused. "I'm so sorry you've been falsely accused."

"It's nice to know I have supporters, but save your pity." She paced away with a smirk. "There's no doubt that you and your friends will be falsely accused of some ridiculous crime, and probably will meet the same fate as me." She turned with a foreboding expression. "At the end of a rope."

"It should be that despicable Jonathan Locke that gets a noose around his neck" Charlotte fumed.

"Don't worry! She answered with a carefree chuckle. "Jonathan's punishment will be much more severe, and before this day is through, he will feel the full effects of my wrath."

"What exactly are you talking about?" Charlotte urgently probed.

"You'll understand, my dear." Jenny smiled. "Simply sit back, and enjoy the show."

Charlotte slunk back, and took a seat on a dusty bench, staying silent. Her eyes never wandered far from

Jenny, as she observed her with deep concern, and equal foreboding.

Josh returned to the City Diner, late from his lunch break. He stomped in with a foul attitude, and Tre immediately confronted him. "Hey!" He whispered loudly. "Where have you been, man? I had to cover for you with the boss man."

"It's none of your business." Josh quipped. I just had a few things I needed to tend to."

"That's cool!" Tre returned to his carpentry chores and tried to change the subject. "You going to that big party at the Mermaid tonight?" He asked. "The whole damn town's gonna be there."

"So, I heard!" Josh grunted as he grabbed a large piece of wood, and pulled out his measuring tape. "I'm not going." He paused. "I got some unfinished business with that Mrs. Spencer."

"Don't tell me she agreed to go out with you." He laughed.

"You think that's funny?" Josh aggressively grabbed Tre by the collar of his shirt.

"Hey! Cool it, man!" Tre pulled away. "I don't want to lose my job."

Josh settled down a bit and continued with his work. "That uppity bitch turned me down."

"What did you expect?" Tre rolled his eyes. "She's married to the richest guy in town." He sighed. "Just let it go, Josh."

"Let me tell you." He scolded with his finger. "If you like that face of yours, you'll refrain from trying to tell me what I should, or should not do."

He tossed the piece of lumber aside, and stormed away in a huff, leaving Tre with disturbing thoughts.

Ezekiel slowly, and calmly strolled into the Lockeport jail, where Doren sat behind the desk with his feet comfortably propped up.

"What can I do for you, mister?" Doren asked, barely moving a muscle.

Ezekiel confidently strode forward with a stern demeanor. "The gentleman at the front desk of the hotel mentioned that you brought Charlotte Sheridan here." He struggled to keep his cool. "I demand you release her immediately."

Doren put his feet down, stood up, and took on the meanest expression he could muster. It was more comical to Ezekiel than it was threatening. "Who the hell are you?" He asked.

"That's no concern of yours." Ezekiel countered with a sober face. "Now, do as I say, and let her go."

Doren tried to pull his gun from a drawer, but Ezekiel grabbed him by the neck and suspended him in the air. "That wasn't a request you pitiful, squiggly little runt! That was an order."

Doren's eyes bugged out, and he gestured downward to the open drawer, where the keys to the cell were kept. Ezekiel grabbed hold of them with one hand while tossing Doren against the wall like a discarded rag doll with the other.

He glanced at Doren, who laid against the wall in a crumpled heap and let out an arrogant grunt. He then grabbed the gun from the drawer. He bent the barrel with his enormous strength, and smashes its handle grip into pieces, before proceeding on to the cell.

Charlotte was amazed when Ezekiel opened the door, and casually stepped in. "Come on, Charlotte! It's time for us to go."

"I have to admit." She commented. "You're the last person I expected to see."

She sauntered ahead of Ezekiel, and he turned to Jenny. "Are you coming too?"

"I have nowhere else to go, mister." She answered with a hopeless chuckle.

"I'll leave the door open in case you change your mind."

A few moments later, Ezekiel and Charlotte strolled from the jail without further incident, and proceeded cautiously, but rapidly along the street. "I must get you out of town without anyone noticing." Ezekiel urgently stated.

"You want to clue me in on what's going on?" She inquired, while trying to keep up with his rapid stride.

"Jonathan Locke has learned Steven and Amphitrite's secret." He replied with disdain in his tone. "He was no doubt holding you in jail with hopes of learning more."

"Oh no!" Charlotte tugged his arm with urgency. "Here comes Sheriff Morton now." She gazed toward an alley between two buildings and pulled him along. "Hurry! Before he sees us."

Once they were in the shadows of the buildings, she quickly pulled Ezekiel close, embracing him with a passionate kiss. All the while, watching over his shoulder until the sheriff had passed from view. She then pulled away, but Ezekiel remained visibly stunned by the occurrence.

"I must admit! That was quite nice." He remarked before Charlotte spoke with anxious urgency.

"Jenny McPherson has some sort of retaliation planned against Jonathan." She stated. "Believe me! I know first-hand that when a witch makes a threat, it should always be taken seriously."

"What do you think she intends to do?" He inquired.

"I have no idea." She nervously replied. "But right now, I need to fly out of this two-bit town." She removed the ruby necklace and ring and handed them to Ezekiel. "Take these, and return them to their rightful owner." She secured them into his hand. "I'll meet you at the entrance to the cave, handsome."

Without further word, Charlotte swiftly waved her hands down the length of her body, transformed into a hawk, and soared away into the sky. Ezekiel stood startled, and surprised, as he watched the bird quickly disappear.

He strode from the alley, muttering to himself, and shaking his head with amazement. "I have to agree with Poseidon. She is quite a fascinating woman."

Moments later, Sheriff Morton entered the jail and discovered Doren still crumpled in a corner, stunned and moaning. "Doren!" He hurried over to help him. "What happened here?"

"I think I broke my back." He gestured to the open cell. "Some feller I never saw before, came in here, and took Mrs. Sheridan." He groaned in pain. "This guy had the strength of an ox." He said as Morton helped him to his feet. "He picked me up, and threw me against this here wall like I was nothing."

Morton looked down at the bent and smashed gun lying on the floor. "I'd say he had superhuman strength if he did that to your gun."

"Mr. Locke isn't going to be happy about this," Doren whined.

"I agree with you there," Morton replied.

"I wonder what's going on between him and these people?" Doren inquired.

Knowing him, and the fact that she was such a pretty woman, he probably fancied killing her husband, so that he could take her as his new wife." Morton answered sarcastically, as he strolled over to the open door of the cell.

He peeked in with surprise at Jenny, who stood calmly with her arms crossed in front of her. "Why didn't you run when you had the chance, woman?"

"Where could I have gone where you wouldn't have found me?" She grunted and paced closer. "Besides, I want to be around when all hell breaks loose in this town."

"What's that supposed to mean?" Morton sneered.

"Just wait until sundown, Sheriff." She laughed and calmly turned away. "You'll know at that time what I'm talking about."

The evening eventually fell on the Locke Estate, while Jonathan and his three sons sat casually in the Parlor, and solemnly reflected on the day.

"I think your mother would've been satisfied with the service and wake." Jonathan proudly proclaimed. "I spared no expense."

At that moment, there was a loud clap of thunder outside, and all took notice. Jonathan strolled over to the large picture window and peered out over the ocean. "It looks like there's a substantial storm rumbling in from the Atlantic." He turned to the boys. "Perhaps we should light the lamps."

Bartholomew stretched and yawned. "I'll light the ones in the upstairs hallway, then I reckon I'll turn in for the evening."

"It's rather early for that. Don't you think?" Jonathan inquired.

"I'm very tired father," Bartholomew replied. "Besides, I have some reading that I need to catch up on."

Jonathan nodded to his son. "If you should need anything, just ring the bell by your bedside."

"Goodnight, everyone." He said before ascending the stairs.

Another loud rumble of thunder ushered in a steady rain that pounded against the roofing tiles, and a loud, howling wind prompted the other two boys to quickly rise to their feet with alarm. "It sounds like a bad one, father," Cameron commented. "I'll light the lamps in the other part of the house."

"Very well!" Jonathan replied as he grabbed a box of wooden matches from the table. "Theodore and I will take care of the others, and I'll also place another log in the fireplace."

Before he could make another move, the front door flew open and the wrath of the storm entered, knocking over anything in its path. He hurried, bracing himself against the strong wind, and with considerable effort, was able to push the door closed again. He then bolted the lock for good measure.

He took a deep, anxious breath, and proceeded to light the oil lamp in the Parlor. Suddenly, a host of apparitions appeared in the room and swirled down upon him from the high vaulted ceiling.

They surrounded him and a terrified Theodore, screeching with eerie, ungodly cries. "Father!" Theodore screamed. "What's happening?"

Jonathan looked around with anxious fear, as Cameron entered from the other portion of the house. "I…have no idea." He trembled.

He held the oil lamp toward the apparitions, while they taunted him with remarks that could not be easily interpreted. The boys placed their hands over their ears and watched with horror. The apparition of Meredith Locke descended from the stairway in the long flowing black dress she was buried in.

She leapt from the bottom landing and floated through the air toward Jonathan. "Jonathan! Jonathan! Why did you poison me?" She cried.

Cameron and Theodore were terror-stricken at the sight of their mother's spirit, while Jonathan glanced to his boys with speechless panic. "Mother!" Cameron cried. "What are you talking about?"

She floated closer to the boys, pointing an accusing finger at Jonathan. "He's a murderer!" She proclaimed. "He killed me, and blamed it on that poor Jenny McPherson."

"That's a lie!" Jonathan yelled. "That's not your mother! That's a demon!"

"It's all true!" Meredith maintained. "He's responsible for the deaths of all the spirits in this room." The other spirits responded with a chorus of deafening shrieks and unworldly moans.

Theodore grabbed his father's twisted edge dagger from a nearby table and gripped it tightly. "You killed my mother!" He cried.

"No! No!" Jonathan yelled in denial. "You don't understand, Theodore."

In a burst of anger, Theodore bolted toward his father. "I hate you!"

Before anyone could react, he plunged the dagger into his father's stomach. "Theodore" Cameron cried in horror. "What have you done?"

Cameron immediately ran to his father's side, and Theodore stood trembling in shock, suddenly realizing his action. The spirits abruptly fled the room, laughing maniacally as they disappeared through the vaulted ceiling. Within seconds, the only sound that remained was the wake of the rapidly dissipating storm outside. One last rumble of thunder sounded in the distance before everything fell silent.

Jonathan collapsed to his knees with a shocked expression and muttered his last words. "The curse has begun."

As his eyes rolled back, and he crumpled to the floor, the blaze within the fireplace exploded outward, and into the house. All the oil lamps exploded, engulfing the wood floors, nearby furniture, and everything else in flames.

Theodore looked to his brother in desperation, then tried to revive his father by shaking him. The flames quickly closed around them, and Cameron grabbed hold of his brothers' arm. "He's dead!" he cried. "We need to save ourselves."

Theodore looked to his brother with panic. "Bartholomew! He's upstairs in his room."

Cameron pulled his younger brother to the door, and they heard the sound of a ringing handbell upstairs, along with the desperate, terrified cries for help. "Get out of here!" Cameron yelled. "I'll get Bartholomew."

Theodore fled the house, and the incoming oxygen fanned the flames, creating a wall that drove Cameron back from the stairs.

His only hope diminished when a part of the flaming ceiling fell into his path. "Bartholomew!" He cried against the furious rage, and heat of the flames that caused him to retreat back toward the door. In tears, he reluctantly ran from the house to save himself, simply as a considerable portion of the main beam crashed behind him.

Down on the beach, Amphitrite rested upon the rocks, longingly watching out over the darkening waters of the Atlantic.

Charlotte wandered up and sat nearby. "I love the way the air at the beach smells after a storm," Charlotte commented.

"There's nothing quite like it," Amphitrite replied.

Charlotte leaned back against a rock. "You're thinking about Steven. Aren't you?" She smiled. "I do know how you feel about him."

Amphitrite sighed and continued gazing off in the distance. "Certainly, you must know that Poseidon has feelings for you as well."

"Oh yes!" Charlotte exclaimed. "I know that all too well."

"That fact would flatter most women," Amphitrite added.

"And I am indeed flattered." She replied with frustration. "I have feelings for him as well." She paused with much regret. "But due to circumstances beyond my control, we can never be together."

Amphitrite glanced at her with a raised brow and laughed. "How ironic!" She smiled. "Perhaps like me, you have a habit of falling in love with men you can't have."

"Sister! You are so right about that." Charlotte laughed heartily. "In fact, you and I were both in love with Steven's father in a future time."

Amphitrite sat straight with sparked interest. "Tell me about that."

"Jack Branch and my twin sister Penelope were very much in love." She started. "But she was married to his brother."

"That must've been quite a quandary."

"Tell me about it." She continued. "I knew I could never begin to compete for his affections with my perfect sister, and a beautiful goddess such as yourself."

"So, what happened?"

"I killed him," Charlotte answered remorsefully.

Amphitrite reacted with wide-eyed surprise and moved to change the subject. "Zeus returned my jewelry. He mentioned you were anxious to rid yourself of it."

"The jewels are surely cursed." She replied. "The pendant burned Jonathan's hand when he tried to pluck it from my neck."

Amphitrite gave an all-knowing nod. "The ruby will do that when handled by one with an evil soul."

"If that's the case, I'm surprised it didn't incinerate in my hands."

"You're far too hard on yourself, my dear." Amphitrite craned her neck to look at something over

Charlotte's shoulder. "Speaking of fire. There's some sort of orange glow in the sky, over near the point."

Both women swiftly walked further out onto the beach to get a better look. From that vantage point, they could see a large structure burning atop the cliffs. "Oh my God!" Charlotte exclaimed. "That's the Locke Estate!"

Chapter Twelve:

The Guardians of Branchview

After a long day of running errands, Loraine returned to Branchview after dark. She turned from the main road in her SUV and was surprised to find the front gate open.

"Oh goodness!" She complained out loud. "Either that gate is broken again, or someone neglected to close it." She continued through, stopping on the other side, trying to close it with her remote device. She waited a few moments, "Oh, nuts!" She sighed. "I need Tony to check that out as soon as possible." She placed the car into gear and continued up the long driveway toward the grand old house.

Moments later, she made her way up the front walkway, carrying several shopping bags, and dangling her keys from one hand. While she struggled to unlock the door, a dark figure with a ski mask emerged from the bushes. The intruder covered her mouth with one hand while jabbing a syringe into her arm with the other.

She let loose with a cry of pain before dropping the bags to the sidewalk. She struggled and tried to fight back, but the man was far too strong. The drug quickly took effect, and her body fell limp into his arms. The intruder pulled his mask off and revealed himself as none other than Josh Tennant. He glanced around with caution, before opening the door himself, and dragging a semi-conscious Loraine inside.

Upstairs, in the Branchview Nursery, Mrs. Porter sat with the babies, watching a television show, unaware of the events unfolding downstairs. She glanced at the babies who calmly rocked back and forth in their swing chairs, "Ahh!" She complained, switching off the remote. "These TV shows get more ridiculous by the day. I should just sit here, and read a good book."

She glanced at the table clock next to her, then to the babies who watched her every move with wonderment. "I believe it's time for your little ones to have your bottles."

Downstairs in the foyer, Josh tied Loraine's hands and feet with thin rope, while she sat semi-comatose in a chair. He paused and stood back to admire his accomplishment, before pulling a folded cloth sack from his backpack, "Stay silent little fox, while I gather some goodies from this grand palace." He chuckled while flashing an evil grin. "Then, my dear, we can have a little fun of our own before I leave."

The foyer clock chimed at 8 PM, and it initially startled Josh. His attention was then further diverted by a baby's crying, which could be faintly heard from upstairs.

He turned back toward Loraine, "I thought you were supposed to be home alone, sweetheart."

He pulled a gun, and some more rope from his backpack, before heading upstairs. As he entered the North Wing, he heard Mrs. Porter humming loudly to the babies from behind the closed door of the nursery. He quietly, and carefully opened the door.

He entered and snuck up behind Mrs. Porter, who was still humming and casually paging through a Better Homes and Gardens magazine.

He swiftly cupped his hand over her mouth and shoved the gun against her temple, "This is the deal, old lady." He sneered in a creepy voice. "You don't yell, and I won't snap your neck. Understood?"

Mrs. Porter nodded rapidly with wide-eyed fear, and Josh removed his hand. "Do what you want with me, but do not hurt these babies."

He glanced over at the toddlers who were both suckling on their bottles, contently observing him with big eyes. "I may be mean, but I certainly ain't no monster." He replied. "Now, I want you to tell me if there's anyone else in this house."

Before Mrs. Porter could answer, the lights in the room flickered, and they both paused to take alert notice. Within the open doorway to the room, the spirit of Maggie appeared. "I'm here, and you need to leave!" She demanded.

Josh turned, with his gun aimed at the door, "Where did you come from, kid?" He laughed. "Did you get those weird clothes from Granny's attic?"

"That's not funny, and I told you to leave."

"Ooh!" He joked. "You're pretty brave for such a little squirt."

"Don't say I didn't warn you."

Josh became annoyed, while Mrs. Porter nervously watched the drama unfold. "Get over here, you little brat!"

"Come get me, stupid!"

Josh lunged at her but found himself grasping for air. He looked around the room with confusion. "Where'd you go, you little runt?"

"Over here, dummy!"

Maggie reappeared on the opposite side of the room, and Josh became further frustrated. "How did you do that, you little rug rat?"

The ghost of Daphne Branch then appeared near the center of the room, stern-faced, and dressed in her elegant 1940s attire. "I'll take it from here, Maggie."

Josh is somewhat startled at first, but then chuckled in a sinister fashion. "Well! Well! Welcome to the party sweetheart. You look like you just stepped out of a Turner Classic movie."

Daphne boldly paced closer. "This isn't your party, and I'm definitely not your sweetheart.

With that comment, Josh lost all patience and pointed the gun in her direction. "Get over here next to the old lady, you entitled bitch!"

Daphne disappeared and reappeared directly behind him. "Is this where you'd like the entitled bitch to be?"

He turned around, startled. "Who the hell are you people?" He trembled with anxiety. "Some kind of circus freaks?"

At the outside entryway to the house, Tre cautiously snuck up onto the main walkway and saw the discarded shopping bags at the front door. "Oh no!" He exclaimed, "I hope I'm not too late."

He entered the partially open door and immediately spotted an unconscious Loraine in the chair. He quickly ran to her aid, checking her pulse, and then the pupils of her eyes.

Loraine lightly moaned, and Tre tried his best to calm her, as he alertly glanced around for any sign of impending danger. "It's okay, Mrs. Spencer! I'm going to get you out of here."

He pulled a cell phone from his pocket and quickly dialed 911. He propped the phone between his ear and shoulder and talked as he untied her. "Yeah! 911!" He spouted with urgency. "This is Trevane Russell. I need the police and an ambulance at the Branchview Estate as soon as possible. Please hurry!"

Upstairs in the nursery, Josh was growing frustrated with the spirits' shenanigans. He pointed his gun, first at the somber-faced Maggie, then at Daphne, while Mrs. Porter observed with wide-eyed anxiety.

"Listen to me!" He stated nervously. "I've had enough, and I ain't messing around."

"Neither am I!" Maggie teased.

"Nor am I!" Daphne echoed with a sly smirk.

Maggie turned toward the babies. "Olivia! London! Do just like I taught you."

Josh looked first to Maggie, then Daphne, and then the babies with a bewildered expression. The babies reached their little hands outward towards Josh, while Maggie and Daphne did the same. The gun immediately flew from his grip, landing clear across the room. Just as quickly, the lights flickered, then went out, leaving the room in total darkness.

Josh immediately cringed in pain and cuffed his ears from a sound no one else could hear. He fell to his knees in agonizing pain, as a terrified Mrs. Porter fled the room.

Josh's eyes searched the darkened room in fear. Suddenly, Daphne and Maggie's faces appeared within inches of his face. They both transformed into hideous, bug-eyed beasts that roared. Josh retreated to a corner, and hunkered in fear, as the laughter of the spirits echoed throughout the room in a loud, taunting way.

Downstairs, Sheriff Albertson, and Officers Petty, and Liebel stormed through the front door with their guns drawn.

Tre held Lorain's head steady within his hands and tried to keep her from losing total consciousness. "Hands up where I can see them," Albertson commanded.

Tre frantically raised one hand, while continuing to hold Lorain's head up with the other. "Don't shoot! I'm the one who called you." Tre pleaded. "She's been drugged, and needs medical attention immediately."

Just then, a hysterical Mrs. Porter ambled down the stairs in a panic, gripping tight to the banister rails as she descended. "There's a crazy man upstairs with a gun." She cried.

Officer Petty intercepted her at the bottom of the stairs, and tried to calm her down, while Officer Liebel hurried past them and up the stairs. "We'll get him, ma'am!" Petty assured. "Just get out of the house, and keep a safe distance."

Mrs. Porter nervously nodded and continued out the front door. Albertson turned to Tre, who was still holding his one hand up. "Get Mrs. Spencer out of the house as well." He commanded. "An ambulance is already on the way." Tre hoisted her into his arms, and carried her from the house, while Albertson hurried up the stairs.

The officers cautiously charged into the Nursery with their guns drawn and discovered a terrified Josh, crouched in the corner with his hands covering his face, and trembling in fear.

They all inched closer, and Albertson cautiously shook him, "Come on you! Get up!"

Josh looked up at them with terror-filled eyes, and the officers were shocked at what they saw. His hair had turned snow-white from the ordeal, and his mouth remained agape, but he was unable to speak. "What in the hell happened to him?" Liebel quipped.

Josh tried desperately to speak, but couldn't. He fearfully pointed toward the babies, who calmly observed from their swing chairs. The officers looked cluelessly toward the babies, who both responded with joyful laughs.

"I don't know what the hell happened up here," Albertson stated. "But whatever it was, it must've literally scared the devil out of him."

"Knowing the history of this place, and some rumors surrounding it, I wouldn't be surprised," Petty remarked.

Albertson pulled an unsteady, trembling Josh to his feet, and slapped the handcuffs on him, before handing him off to Liebel. "Take him downstairs, and read him his rights." He turned to the other officer. "Petty! You can help me with these babies." Josh stared in horror as he passed by the giggling, smiling babies, and was led from the room.

The rest of the house inhabitants were gathered around a large table at the Mermaid Inn, while music, dancing, and celebration took place around them. Tony and Suzy returned from the dance floor and joined them.

"Suzy!" Tony joked. "You're going to dance the legs right off of every man in this place."

"Just wait until after I have this baby." An unhappy Andrea chimed in. "I'll be dancing out there with the best of you."

Just then, a panicked Millie hurried up to the table, holding her cell phone. "Mrs. Porter just called me." She breathed heavily. "There's been an incident at Branchview, and they had to rush Lori to the hospital."

"Are the babies alright?" Ezekiel inquired with great concern.

"Yes!" She answered. "But poor Mrs. Porter is shaken. I promised her I would leave for the hospital immediately." She fidgeted nervously. "Bill is bringing the car around to the front right now."

"I'll go with you." Philip offered.

"So will I," Gerard added.

"Mary and I will return to Branchview, and tend to Mrs. Porter and the babies," Sharie stated with urgency.

"Ohh! No!" Andrea moaned as she began to hyperventilate, and panic.

"Andrea!" Tony cried out with concern. "What's wrong, sweetheart?"

"The baby!" She pointed desperately to her bulging belly. "I think it's time!"

Back at Branchview, Sharie and Mary rushed in to find a small gathering in the Sitting Room. Sheriff Albertson was holding baby Olivia, and Tre was holding baby London, while a visibly exhausted Mrs. Porter sat nearby, sprawled out in a chair.

"We hurried as fast as possible," Sharie announced. "Is everyone all right?"

"Everyone's fine, Mrs. LeRoux." The sheriff assured. "Mrs. Spencer was injected with a large dose of morphine, but they expect her to be okay."

"Tre Russell!" Sharie exclaimed with surprise. "I haven't seen you since you played high school football with my Marcus."

"Mr. Russell here is a hero," Albertson announced. "He saved Mrs. Spencer and the others."

"How did that happen?" Sharie inquired.

"I work with Josh, and I knew he had eyes for Mrs. Spencer." Tre recanted, "I surmised he was up to no good, so I followed him here."

"It could've gone the other way easily," Albertson remarked with a stern glance toward Tre. "You really should've called us first."

"Let's just thank the good Lord that this young man was here in the first place." Mary proclaimed, with one hand raised to the heavens.

"I'll second that," Sharie added.

The sheriff stared toward Mrs. Porter, who sat wearily with her hand to her head. "Mrs. Porter and the babies were very fortunate." He stated. "Josh Tennant is a career criminal with a turbulent history." He paused with emphasis. "Somehow, he was released from the state penitentiary a few months back on good behavior. He won't be so lucky this time."

"I hope that beast of a man spends the rest of his life behind bars." Mrs. Porter finally spoke up.

"That might just be the bars of an asylum, Mrs. Porter." Albertson sarcastically quipped. "The man was half out of his mind when we apprehended him."

"In what way?" Sharie curiously inquired.

"Well!" Albertson continued. "I was hoping Mrs. Porter could shed some light on what happened."

"Sheriff!" Mrs. Porter exclaimed with much distress. "If I told you what happened in that room, you'd put me into an asylum."

Everyone looked wide-eyed toward Mrs. Porter, and the Sheriff suddenly held baby Olivia away from him at arm's length. "I do believe this little one has had an accident."

Sharie pinched her nose and winced at the stink. "I believe you're right about that, Sheriff."

Mary boldly stepped forward, taking the child from the sheriff's grip. "I've changed me more babies in my time than I'd care to mention." She grunted. "I'll go ahead, and take care of this little lady."

Mrs. Porter finally stood up as Mary departed with baby Olivia. "If you all don't mind, I'd like to call it a night."

"That's fine, Mrs. Porter." Albertson nodded. "If I have any other questions, I'll notify you."

Mrs. Porter took baby London from Tre's arms. "I'll take this little one upstairs, and put him to bed."

Mrs. Porter departed with the baby, as Albertson gazed down at the stains on his uniform. "I suppose I should go back to the station, and get a change of clothes."

He chuckled, "My deputies will never let me live this one down." Sharie and Tre reacted with subtle amusement.

In the hospital waiting room, all the other inhabitants of Branchview anxiously waited on word of both Andrea and Loraine. Dr. Opperman, a portly, and balding man with wire-framed glasses, entered the room first, and looked around. "Is there a Mrs. Sandstrom here?"

Much to his surprise, practically the entire population of the room stood with anticipation, as Millie nervously stepped forward. "Please tell me my daughter will be alright, doctor."

"She'll be fine." He assured. "She's sleeping soundly now, but she should be able to go home in the morning."

"Thank heavens!" She sighed with relief.

Everyone else drew a collective sigh, and Dr. Scotnicki strolled in next. Tony stepped to the front in anxious anticipation. "Mr. Freeman, and the Branchview clan!" The doctor called out with a grin. "I'm pleased to announce Andrea has given birth to a beautiful, healthy baby boy."

Congratulations and cheers went up throughout the room, as they all surrounded Tony with good wishes. Philip bear-hugged his son and whispered in his ear. "Your mother would've been as happy, and proud as I am."

"Thank you, father." He replied with a grateful smile.

Later that night, in the Branchview Nursery, the antique table clock ticked loudly, and read 2:35 AM. The ghosts of Daphne and Maggie emerged from the dark shadows of the room and sauntered up to the babies' cribs.

They stood watching the sleeping children with joyful admiration. "We do make a fine team. Don't we, Maggie?" Daphne declared.

Maggie looked up to her with serious eyes and nodded. "The children will always be safe with us watching over them."

Daphne sighed and smiled down at the child. "That's true for the others in this household as well, my dear."

Chapter Thirteen:

After The Fire

As the sun rose in another spectrum of time, the citizens of Colonial Lockeport were attempting to process the tragic events surrounding the fire at the Locke Estate. Ezekiel went into town early to find out what he could from the locals.

Late into the morning Steven, Charlotte, Amphitrite, and Poseidon were waiting for him to return. "I wonder what's taking him so long?" Amphitrite impatiently fidgeted.

"If he doesn't get back here soon, I'll have to go looking for him," Poseidon warned.

"There'll be no need for that, brother," Zeus announced as he sauntered from the shadows, and took a seat at the table with them. "The news in town is that

Jonathan Locke and his son Bartholomew perished in the fire."

"And the others?" Amphitrite inquired.

"The other two boys are fine, and staying at the Branch residence." He replied.

"I can't believe Jonathan is actually dead." Steven proclaimed with surprise, as he turned to Charlotte. "I thought you said someone killed him."

"That's what was written in the journals," Charlotte answered with equal surprise. "It also was recorded that Bartholomew had died in an accident, but it never said what type." She took a deep breath. "I certainly hope our being here hasn't somewhat altered the course of history."

"That full moon can't arrive soon enough." Steven quipped with frustration.

Poseidon looked to Steven in all seriousness. "You must meet with this Stargazer, and find out all you can about that rock behind the Branch house."

Steven put his hand to his head and sighed. "I know! I have no other choice than to go back into Lockeport. Maureen Branch has already set up a meeting with him today."

"You can't go by yourself. I'll go with you." Amphitrite suggested, but Zeus immediately rebuked her.

"I forbid you to go, Amphitrite. If you were forced to use your magic, the townspeople would surely know your true identity."

"He's right!" Steven stated with a caring glance.

"Then I'll just have to go with him." Charlotte maintained. "If I'm forced to use my magic, the worst they could do is accuse me of being who I am." She definitively nodded. "Then I'll simply incinerate this town, and fly away from this stone-aged place."

The tension in the room finally lifted, as everyone found humor in her statement.

Inside the entranceway of the old Branch home, Malcolm prepared to leave, and Beatrice was present to see him off. "Did the boys finally get to sleep?" He asked.

"They're resting, but I don't think they'll get any sleep," she replied. "They're still quite shaken."

"Understandably so!"

"I know the witch had something to do with that fire." Beatrice seethed. "The sooner she hangs, the better."

Maureen entered from the other room and interrupted. "Father! Can I ride into town with you?" She asked. "I want to see if Stargazer is at the General Store."

"I don't like you talking to that old Indian, young lady." Her mother lectured. "He's nothing but a heathen."

"Now Beatrice!" Malcolm scolded. "It doesn't hurt for Maureen to just talk with him. He is knowledgeable about local history."

"I simply wish that child would educate herself a little more on the bible, and a lot less on history." She grunted indignantly.

Malcolm shrugged off his wife's comment and turned to his anxious daughter. "I'll bring the horse and carriage around, Maureen. Run and grab your sunbonnet, and I'll wait for you."

In the town of Lockeport, Steven and Charlotte boldly strolled along the main thoroughfare, hoping to find Maureen and Stargazer. Sheriff Morton swiftly moved toward them, not noticing them right away. Unable to avoid them, he reacted awkwardly as they encountered each other.

"Sheriff Morton!" Steven called out.

"Now before you two start in on me, I was only acting on orders from Mr. Locke when I put your sister in my prison." Morton innocently pleaded, while Steven stood firm.

"And he gave you no reason for it?" Steven quipped.

"None whatsoever."

"That's a lie, and you know it." Charlotte charged. "You all accused me of being a witch."

Morton stammered in a cowering way. "But ma'am…you're pendant…

"I'll accept no excuses for a comment like that." Steven asserted. "I'm certain the King of England would not be pleased with the way your town has treated a member of his royal family."

"I was certain Jonathan had a valid purpose." He turned to Charlotte. "Please accept my deepest apologies, Mrs. Sheridan."

"I suppose under the present circumstances, I'd be willing to forgive, and forget," Charlotte stated with an extensive, critical glare at him. "I hope our bodyguard didn't rough up your deputy too much. He is quite protective of me."

"He's a bit bruised and shaken up, but he'll live," Morton replied with slight amusement, before looking ahead down the street with determination. "If you'll both excuse me, I have to meet with the judge about getting Ms. McPherson's trial moved up" He continued with a slightly raised brow. "I believe she may have had something to do with that fire at the Locke Estate."

"How could she do that from a jail cell?" Charlotte sarcastically asked.

"That little witch told me that all hell would break loose last night after sundown, and she was right," Morton grunted. "I have to make sure that woman hangs before she curses all of us."

Steven and Charlotte shared a quick, enlightened glance as a horse and carriage carrying Malcolm and Maureen Branch came to a halt in front of the three. "Good morning, Mr. Branch, Maureen." Steven cordially greeted them.

"Good morning Mr. Spencer, Morton, Ma'am!" Malcolm nodded to all three, before turning to Steven.

"I suppose I should apologize for my wife's behavior the other evening." He sighed. "She can be rather abrasive at times."

"Believe me!" Steven chuckled. "As you witnessed, my wife can be just as bad.

Malcolm looked first to Charlotte, then back to Steven. "Where is your wife, Mr. Spencer?"

"She went ahead to Hartford without me," Steven answered in quick thought. "This is my sister, Charlotte Sheridan. We'll be staying here in town until her husband can rejoin us."

Malcolm tipped his hat, and acknowledged her again, while Morton impatiently cut in. "Do you suppose I could come out to your place later and talk to the boys?" He asked. "I hope they can shed some light on what exactly happened last night."

"I'd prefer you waited a day or so," Malcolm answered. "They're still quite shaken over all this."

"Father!" Maureen interrupted. "Can I go on over to the General Store?"

"Very well, Maureen." He nodded. "Just stay away from that back room. That's no place for a young lady to be."

"Yes, father!" Steven helped her down from the carriage, and she gave him an assured wink, before turning back toward her father. "Perhaps Mr. Spencer and his sister could stop by the house later, and I could show them the Indian rock in the back yard."

"I suppose that would be alright, as long as it fits into their schedule." The young girl smiled at her father and ran off toward the General Store. "Mr. Spencer, Mrs. Sheridan! Please excuse me if you will. I need to have a few words with Sheriff Morton in private."

"Of course, Mr. Branch," Steven replied. "Perhaps Charlotte and I will stop by to see Maureen later this afternoon."

Both Malcolm and Morton tipped their hats to Charlotte, and she and Steven strolled away toward the General Store."

Moments later, inside the store, Maureen spotted Stargazer sitting among a group of men at the entrance to the back room. He was a man in his mid-seventies, with long locks of white hair, and weathered skin. He puffed enthusiastically on a rolled cigarette, as he listened to the other men talk about the fire at the Locke Estate.

Maureen wandered over, and whispered in his ear, just as Steven and Charlotte entered the store. The two casually glanced their way, and Maureen subtly motioned for them to meet outside.

Back at modern-day Branchview, a weary-looking Loraine returned home from the hospital with Millie and Suzy. Sharie and Mary enthusiastically greeted them in the foyer.

Loraine only replied to the well-wishers with a weak smile. "How are you feeling, dear?" Sharie asked with great concern.

Loraine distressfully put her hand to her head, and slowly paced closer, while Suzy steadied her. "I…I feel like I have the worst hangover ever."

"Let me get you settled in the Sitting Room, and then I'll fix you a cup of coffee." Suzy offered.

Loraine turned to her, looking as though she were ready to faint. "No thank you, Suzy." She sighed. "I just want to go rest, and be alone for a while."

With that, Loraine slowly, and with help from her mother, ascended the stairs. She held tight to the banister railing, while the remaining trio watched with sympathetic concern. The stresses of everyday life without her beloved Steven were beginning to show. When she reached the top landing, she set her eyes on the open doors of the East Wing. She broke away from Millie's arm and slowly wandered toward it.

Loraine continued into the wing, with Millie following her at a comfortable distance. She mustered all her strength, and sauntered up to the double doors of the imaginary room, staring sternly at them. Suddenly she thought she heard voices coming from the other side, and with anger and frustration, she swung the doors open.

She stared at the solid brick wall on the other side and became overcome with emotion. "Steven!" She cried out loud. "Please come back to me."

Simultaneously, in the alleyway just outside the General Store, Steven and Charlotte had barely begun conversing with Maureen and Stargazer, when suddenly, Steven heard Loraine's voice carrying in on the sea breeze.

He immediately reacted with much surprise. "Did you hear that?"

Maureen and Charlotte reacted with a baffled expression, while Stargazer remained calm and serious. "I heard it." He replied. "It was your loved one calling to you through the portal." He laid a weathered hand on Steven's shoulder. "I'll meet you and Charlotte after sunset in the extensive clearing of the woods between Branchview and the Locke Estate." He continued. "There, we'll discuss what you must do to get back to your own time."

Maureen then looked to Steven and Charlotte assuredly. "Come to my house this afternoon as well, but you must avoid my mother and Cameron Locke. I sense they both could be a major problem for us."

"Whatever the case may be with Cameron Locke, we must handle him in a delicate manner," Charlotte warned.

"Do you know something that we don't know?" Steven asked with great curiosity.

"I know that if Cameron died due to our actions, my sister Penelope and I, as well as many of our preceding relatives, would cease to exist in the future."

"If that were the case, it would include me," Steven remarked. "But how would that affect us in this spectrum of time?"

"We'd simply cease to exist altogether." Charlotte sadly stated. "That might be a blessing for me, but it would be very unfortunate for you, and our beloved Branchview family.

Chapter Fourteen:

The Eternal Wait

For a long while that day, Loraine sat on a folding chair in front of the double doors in the East Wing. Millie had respectfully left her daughter to sort things out. She was lost within the words streaming through her mind like well-rehearsed lines from a play.

As the days dwindle closer to the next full moon, I find myself growing anxious and weary. I can't help thinking about how many other lives were crushed and forever altered by the cursed secret of that room. I also wonder what caused it to exist. Perhaps Steven and Charlotte would hold the answers to those questions when they return. If in fact, they do return at all.

The thoughts caused Loraine to emotionally break, and she placed her head in her hands. Bumpers wandered into the room, and faithfully settled at her feet. She glanced down at the little dog with a subtle, heartfelt smile, before setting a determined focus back on the now-closed doors.

At Lockeport General Hospital, Tony and Philip approached each other from opposite ends of the hallway. The father and son enthusiastically greeted each other with a handshake. "I was just heading to visit with you, Andrea, and my new grandson," Philip stated.

"Andrea and the baby finally fell asleep." Tony wearily replied. "Let's go over to the Mermaid Inn, and have a burger and ale." He smiled. "We can stop back later when they're both awake."

They both turned and started strolling back toward the elevators at the end of the hallway. "I'll have to take a rain check on that," Philip replied. "I should get back to Branchview, and check on Lori."

"It was all my fault that the gate was opened last night," Tony stated with much regret. "I thought for sure that I'd fixed it earlier in the day."

Philip came to a complete halt and grabbed his son firmly by the shoulders. "Listen to me!" He commanded. "The motor on that gate dates back to the 1930s. It's certainly seen its better days."

"What can we do about it?" Tony asked with frustration. "We can't risk another nut case coming onto the property, and harming a member of the family."

"I agree, but the budget is stressed from all the damage that the tsunami caused." He paused in thought. "I'll make it a point to speak with Gerard about replacing it. Perhaps I can fund it."

"I'm trying so hard to make the transition to the mortal world," Tony grunted. "It isn't as easy as I thought."

"Believe me!" Philip smiled. "Don't believe for a minute that being a father in the real world will be any easier either."

At the old Branchview home, Steven and Charlotte paid Maureen a late afternoon visit. As they curiously surveyed the rock in the backyard, Malcolm held back a curtain from within the house and watched, while Beatrice strolled up behind with her usual stern demeanor. "What are those royals doing here?" She quipped indignantly.

"Mr. Spencer, like Maureen, has a fascination with history and archaeology." He turned to his wife. "Maureen is simply showing him the etchings on the rock."

"We should have that rock removed from the property." She grunted with disdain. "Those etchings are no doubt pagan symbolism used in some sort of Satanic ceremony."

"That rock has been there for centuries, and it will remain there for many more." He paused with major emphasis before concluding. "End of discussion!" Beatrice strutted away, irked by her husband's rebuke.

Meanwhile outside, the trio hovered over the rock, studying its etchings. "I'm guessing this large X here signifies where the rocks' position is," Steven commented.

"That's correct," Maureen stated. "That's what Stargazer told me."

Charlotte then pointed to a winged figure, surrounded by several smaller stick figures, situated in the upper right corner of the rock. "Does that winged figure signify an angel?"

"Stargazer said it signifies the queen of the forest faeries, and the smaller figures are the woods people," Maureen replied to the baffled and stunning couple. "He mentioned the average human eye cannot see them."

"I've heard that statement before," Steven replied. "Only those that are pure in heart can witness the unseen."

"Or the evil enemies," Charlotte added.

"But forest faeries, and woods people?" He questioned with disbelief.

"Is it any more unbelievable than mermaids, immortal gods, or even witches?" Charlotte countered with a clever grin.

"You do have a point there, Charlotte." He then turned to Maureen. "Did he explain what their significance is?"

"He never totally explained that to me." She replied, before pointing to the left corner where there was a circle, with a spectrum of lines radiating from it. "That signifies the full moon and its rays upon the earth." She stated before pointing toward a stick figure within the lines radiating from it. "That figure signifies someone being transported through time."

Steven studied the etching closer. "This broken line that leads from the rock to the center point in either direction, consists of seven dashes, ending with arrows pointing in that direction."

Charlotte studied the other parts in the etching with serious thought. "What are those other smaller circles that go outward, and surround where the rock is located?"

Maureen shrugged cluelessly. "He said he would tell me when he felt it was time for me to know."

After a few pondering moments, Steven marched off seven paces from the actual rock and stood in that spot. "I suppose this spot signifies where we currently are in time." He theorized. "The further out you go from that spot, determines where you will end up in the spectrum of time when the full moon is shining on that particular spot."

"I believe I entered somewhere over there to the left." Charlotte pointed just beyond where Steven was standing. "I remember glancing to my right, and feeling grateful that I didn't fall onto that rock."

"Both positions are to the left, signifying a backward journey in time." Steven theorized. "That would mean we need to exit to the exact spot on the right side of the rock to go forward in the spectrum."

"That makes sense," Maureen added. "Where you end up in time would depend on where you're standing within the spectrum of light."

"So, our main task is finding that proper spot," Steven strolled over to further study the rock, "I'm sure Stargazer will fill us in on much more tomorrow evening."

"Hopefully so!" Charlotte replied. "I'm also eager to learn more about the forest faeries and woods people, and what their connection is to all this."

Simultaneously, Cameron and Theodore stood surveying the still-smoldering ashes of the Locke Estate.

"I can't believe our family and home are all gone, Teddy."

Theodore became emotional. "I never meant to kill our father. I was so angry when I learned he killed our mother."

Cameron rested his arm across the back of his brother's shoulder and pulled him closer. "I have little concern over my father now," Cameron replied. "But I'll never quit hearing Bartholomew's cries, and that damn bell. It's something that will haunt me for the rest of my life."

"It'll be alright, Cam. We still have each other."

"That's right, Teddy. But we must never tell anyone what happened."

"But Sheriff Morton is bound to suspect something," Theodore remarked.

"You heard what father said before he died." Cameron sneered. "It was the curse of the witch that caused all of this."

"We have to recover that knife in the ruins before anyone else finds it," Theodore remarked with considerable anxiety. "Surely they'll think it's foul play if it's found near our father's body."

Cameron pondered the situation, then had a sudden moment of enlightenment. "That might work in our favor." He suggested with a smirk. "We can always blame his murder on those bloody royals."

"But that would be a blatant lie, Cam."

"Would it now?" He questioned, before continuing. "I overheard he and Mr. Spencer having words the other morning, and when I entered the room, our father had been knocked to the floor."

"That's still not enough proof he actually did it."

Cameron chuckled arrogantly, then displayed a clever grin. "There's also no solid proof he didn't."

In the present, after a long afternoon nap, a re-energized Loraine strolled briskly through the door to the nursery, where Millie and Mrs. Porter were caring for babies London and Olivia. "How are my little angels this afternoon?"

"Rambunctious, and full of energy." Mrs. Porter quipped as she struggled to handle a squirming baby London.

"And they haven't even had their midday naps yet," Millie added.

"I'll sit with her for a bit. Mother." She took baby Olivia from Millie's arms. "Would you mind if I had a word in private with Mrs. Porter?"

"Not at all, my dear!" She smiled. "It's nearly my tea time. Could I prepare some Tetley for you, and Mrs. Porter as well?"

"Oh yes, mother! That would be absolutely marvelous."

Loraine waited until her mother left the room, and a nervous Mrs. Porter gazed toward her with worried eyes. "Is everything alright, Mrs. Spencer?"

"Everything is fine," Loraine assured. "You've been a trooper through this whole crazy ordeal." She sat down in the rocking chair and clutched the baby close. "I am rather curious in finding out what happened in this room the other night." She paused with serious eyes focused on Mrs. Porter. "The sheriff mentioned the intruder was so terrified his hair turned white, and he lost the ability to talk."

Mrs. Porter continued the conversation as she set baby London into a playpen. "I can't seem to wrap my head around it." She sat back down. "You'll think I'm insane when I tell you what I saw."

"Try me!" Loraine rolled her eyes. "With all the bizarre things I've seen in this house over the past year, there's little that would come as a shock."

Mrs. Porter took a deep breath and then proceeded.

"While that terrible man held me at gunpoint, Maggie's ghost appeared in the room, along with an apparition of a woman I've never seen before."

"What did she look like?" Loraine inquired.

"She was adorable." She glanced off to a corner of the room as she recalled. "She was a brunette and wore fashionable 1940s era clothes. The type with those shoulder pads."

Loraine immediately took on an enlightened expression as she listened. "That sounds like Daphne Branch."

Mrs. Porter shifted in her chair, while baby London watched everyone with keen interest from the playpen.

"Wasn't she the woman whose remains were found in the window box of the East Wing?"

"Yes!" Loraine replied. "She was Steven's grandmother." Mrs. Porter gazed upward, blessing herself with the sign of the cross, as Loraine continued. "She had assured Steven that she would watch over our children."

"Bless her soul."

Loraine lifted Olivia into the playpen with her brother, and both babies curiously watched as though listening to every word of the conversation.

"What happened next, Mrs. Porter?"

"That's when things took a peculiar turn." She placed her hand distressfully to her head and continued. "Maggie told the babies to do what she taught them. Then she, the babies, and Mrs. Branch all reached their hands out toward that despicable man." She paused with anxiety, and Loraine urged her on with a nod. "What happened next was like nothing I could ever imagine." She trembled. "The man fell to his knees, holding his ears as though he heard some sort of high-pitched noise no one else could hear."

Loraine shook her head with amazement. "I have heard of cases where spirits emit a sonic wave to ward off evil people, and unclean spirits who have entered their domain."

"The real kicker is the babies did it too." She commented with wide eyes. "Your mother said this wasn't the first time that strange events have happened involving the children."

Loraine reacted with alarm. "Did she mention what the other strange events were?"

Mrs. Porter nodded and continued. "She said on several occasions, she'd witnessed stuffed animals, baby bottles, and other items floating across the room, and into their waiting grip."

"I wonder why she never told me."

Loraine glanced at her children with a mixture of wonder and disbelief, while the babies responded with a joyful burst of laughter.

As the sun went down in a time long forgotten time, Steven and Charlotte journeyed deep into the heart of the woods near Branchview. Darkness quickly fell under the thick canopy of trees as they made their way along a worn, trodden path. "I feel exactly like a child on an adventure." Charlotte giggled.

Steven halted her progress when he heard a rustling in the nearby brush. A deer stepped out onto the path, and curiously looked their way before moving on. Steven glanced all around, trying to remember how the surroundings looked in the future. "Do you remember where the clearing is?" He asked. "Everything looks so different."

"I went there several times in the future to meditate." She replied. "If memory serves me right, we should be coming across the creek soon, and the clearing is just beyond that."

They continued through the dark woods until they came to a gently flowing stream. They both paused to watch the shallow, peaceful flow of the water across the rocks, then glanced toward the bank on the other side.

"In the future, we had a footbridge instead of stepping stones," Charlotte commented. "I'm afraid these awkward shoes won't carry me gracefully to the other side."

"Then I'll just have to carry you."

Before she could respond, he scooped her off her feet, and into his arms effortlessly. He then proceeded to carefully step over the rocks to the other side. "Oh my!" She exclaimed breathlessly. "I totally understand why women swoon in your presence."

"Behave yourself, aunt Charlotte!" Steven joked.

A few moments later, they arrived at the clearing and walked to the center. There, an enormous fire pit was flaming, brightly lighting the surrounding area. "It looks as though we've arrived before Stargazer." Steven proclaimed.

Charlotte cluelessly glanced toward the fire. "I'm sure that fire pit didn't ignite by itself."

There was a loud growl, and they turned to see a huge black bear stalking them from the edge of the clearing. It sniffed at the air and began to pace closer. "Stand absolutely still, Steven." Charlotte warned. "I may have to use my magic if it gets any closer."

"Trust me!" He assured. "I am not going to move a muscle."

The bear growled again, and curiously stalked closer, while Charlotte spoke under her breath. "Okay there, Mr. Bear!" She sighed. "I regret having to do this, but we refuse to be an item on your menu this evening."

She began to raise her hand toward the ever-encroaching bear just as a quick, loud whistle echoed throughout the clearing, and Stargazer stepped forth, virtually out of nowhere.

"Benjamin! No! No!" He stepped past the couple with one hand raised toward the now halted bear.

The bear shook his head from side to side, and groaned, almost in disappointment, while Steven and Charlotte watched with amazement. Stargazer vigorously, but affectionately scratched the bear on both sides of its' enormous head as though it were a pet dog.

"Be on your way, my friend." He commanded.

With a final pat of his hand on the side of the bear's head, it turned and ran back into the deep woods. "He's just protecting his territory." Stargazer smiled as he paced back toward the couple.

Steven and Charlotte breathed a sigh of relief as Stargazer came to a halt before them, sporting a wide grin.

"Where did you come from?" Steven cluelessly asked. "It's like you just stepped out of thin air."

"When you spend as much time with nature as I have, you learn to glide through the woods like a silent, gentle breeze." Stargazer chuckled.

"I'd have to say you've mastered that method well," Charlotte commented.

Stargazer then glanced all around the clearing, as though searching the darkness. "You can all come out now, Nebriana." He called out.

A glowing light enveloped the trio, and they turned to see a beautiful winged fairy with pointed ears highlighting the delicate features of her face. From behind her, a host of dwarf-sized gnomes, all carrying tiny lanterns, stepped out from the deep woods. At least two dozen male and female faeries followed them, with the same glowing aura as Nebriana. They all peacefully assembled around the trio, as Nebriana stepped forward to join them.

"I'd like to introduce you to Nebriana, the queen of the forest faeries." Stargazer announced as he gestured toward the others." These beings are her entourage, and the seldom-seen woods people." He turned to Steven and Charlotte with a grin. "They already know everything they need to know about you.

Steven and Charlotte observed with awe-stricken surprise, and Charlotte set her eyes firmly on Nebriana. "I know you!" She proclaimed with amazement. "In future times, you would often watch me from the edge of the woods. I don't expect you knew I could see you."

"I knew!" Nebriana nodded assuredly as she stepped closer, and gently placed her hand over Charlotte's heart. "I know you were once a dark soul, but now you're of the light." She stepped back and looked into her eyes with fascination. "It is seldom that I see a human who has truly made an effort to redeem themselves."

Charlotte exchanged a quick, astonished glance with Steven, who answered with an assured wink. Nebriana smiled and set her eyes on Steven next.

"The infamous Steven Spencer!" She announced with an all-knowing nod.

"You know about me?" Steven inquired with astonishment.

"I know of you." She confidently stated. "The wind has whispered your name, and I've observed you with the Mermaid Amphitrite, and the gods, Zeus and Poseidon."

"Are you acquainted with them as well?" Steven further probed.

"Like them, I'm an immortal." She smiled sweetly. "And yes, we have worked together."

"We will all work together to help you find your way back to your time." Stargazer intervened. "It's of much importance to us as it is for you."

His statement went over the head of a still astonished Steven but didn't escape the alert attention of Charlotte, who saw something more. "We read the etchings on the rock." Steven began to explain. "We understand most everything, except for the proper spot we must stand, and the exact time we must be there to be transported back to our time."

"I will speak the time and coordinates, and imprint them in your mind's eye." Stargazer laid his hands at the middle of both Charlotte and Steven's foreheads, before closing his own eyes for a short pause of concentration. "Between the moments of 12:37 and 12:45 AM, at approximately 343 degrees North, 28 degrees 3'6" North, and 82 degrees 42' 44" West." He lifted his hands away and opened his eyes. "I will have Maureen mark the exact spot with lime, but if the rain should wash it away, you'll have to use a compass, and pace it off yourselves."

"Speaking of rain!" Charlotte inquired. "What will we do if the clouds obscure the moonbeams? Will we have to wait another whole month?"

"If that is the case, I, along with Zeus, will part the clouds, and clear the sky near the moment you ascend," Nebriana assured.

"Have you spoken with him about this?" Steven asked.

"Not yet, but I will summon him in the coming days."

"How will we know the exact time?" Steven further probed. "Portable timepieces don't exist yet, and neither of us brought one."

Stargazer handed them both a pocket watch on a chain. "These are set to universal time." He commented. 'You mustn't let anyone see you with these." He warned. "They would surely accuse you of wizardry."

"How did you get possession of these?" Steven further queried.

Stargazer and Nebriana exchanged a fleeting glance. "As I mentioned before, there was another important reason to make sure you get back to the future," Stargazer stated in all seriousness. "We need to secure the help of you, and your family in the future."

Steven and Charlotte exchanged a perplexed expression, as Stargazer continued.

"I've traveled into the future on many occasions, and once beyond the time you're returning to." He looked away with sadness. "There will be greed-driven people who will attempt to gain control of the beautiful land surrounding Branchview."

They will demolish the Branchview house, and plow under these beautiful woods that we call our home." Nebriana sadly added. "They will develop this land with ugly structures that will escalate their monetary wealth."

Steven and Charlotte reacted with wide-eyed surprise and astonishment. Then, Steven humbly nodded to them both. "I promise you that my descendants and I will do everything in our power to ensure that atrocity never takes place." He stated.

"I believe, and trust your words, Steven Spencer." Stargazer also nodded with respect. "I know that you have already done many good things to shift an otherwise dismal fate for the Branchview Estate."

Nebriana signaled to the other faeries and woods people, and comforting magic settled upon the clearing.

"Now we shall all eat, drink, and celebrate with our honorable guests on this enchanted late summer eve." She proclaimed.

A male fairy placed a crown of flowers on Charlotte's head and kissed her on the cheek before scampering away. Stargazer then pulled a thick-rolled cigarette from the medicine pouch hanging around his neck and held it up in front of Steven and Charlotte.

"Natures wild herb." He quipped. "It works well to free the mind of all worries." He smiled. "Would you both care to join me?"

"I'm guessing that must be marijuana," Steven commented.

"I do believe that's what you call it in your time?"

"Oh yes!" Charlotte giggled. "I smoked a good bit of that in the 1970s."

"I briefly visited the 1970s." Stargazer exuberantly stated. "There was a band called the Grateful Dead whose music I greatly enjoyed."

Charlotte rolled her eyes and laughed. "Why am I not surprised?"

The woods people surrounded them, and offered wooden cups, brimming with a sweet-smelling elixir. Nebriana raised her cup to her guests. "May we all drink the precious nectar of the forest."

Charlotte eagerly took a sip, and her eyes brightened with delight. "This is delicious!"

Stargazer lit the joint, and took a satisfying drag, before handing it off to Steven, who reluctantly accepted it. He examined it for a moment, before deciding to partake.

"Ah! What the heck!"

Music and laughter were prevalent in the dreamlike, magic atmosphere. In the gnomish woods, the mystical creatures played small concertinas, wood flutes, and tom-tom drums, while joyfully dancing around the fire pit. They all celebrated long into the pleasant summer night.

When morning arrived in the deep woods, the bright sun peeked over the canopy of trees and shone upon the clearing. It found Steven and Charlotte huddled closely at the base of an enormous elm tree, in a deep sleep. Charlotte opened her eyes, squinting against the light and warmth of the late morning sun. She swatted at a menacing fly buzzing about her face, and she knocked her flowery crown from the top of her head. She quickly pulled away when she realized she had been using Steven's firm chest as her pillow.

Steven then slowly awakened, squinting his eyes in discomfort, and placing his fingers to his temples, where he discovered a crown of now withering flowers anchored atop his head as well. "That was quite a party." He declared.

"I'd have to say that was an understatement." She replied. "Although I don't remember much beyond my second sip of the forest nectar. It was all bright colors, and blur beyond that."

Steven chuckled, and stretched his arms. "Not to mention that heavy-duty pot Stargazer had." He shook his head. "I haven't parted like that since my college years."

"Now I know why they call him Stargazer." She quipped with amusement as she sat up, and straightened her wrinkled clothes. "I certainly hope you and I didn't do anything foolish that we should regret."

"We both still have our clothes on," Steven stated with sarcastic humor. "So, I think we're safe."

They both shared a hearty laugh, and Charlotte looked away in thought. "Had you been Poseidon, I think the situation may have been drastically different," Charlotte stated.

"Since we're being dreadfully honest," Steven added. "I'm not sure I could've fended off the temptation, had you been Amphitrite."

They chuckled with amusement as Charlotte assured. "That shall always remain our little secret. Cross my heart." She stared at Steven thoughtfully and continued. "You are so much like your father. He was a dandy."

Steven leaned forward with keen interest. "On that subject, what happened to cause my mother to marry Daniel II instead of my father? My mother never gave me the full story before she died."

Charlotte took a deep breath and proceeded to recant. "My father was a wheeler-dealer. He did whatever he could to support my sister and me after our mother died, and many times, he was involved in some questionable dealings." She paused while Steven listened attentively.

"He instigated an illegal investment scheme in which an associate of Daniel II lost a lot of money." She sighed. "Daniel hated my father anyway, and threatened to expose him to the authorities."

"Why didn't he?" Steven asked.

"Daniel struck a deal with him." She replied. "He demanded that either my sister, or I marry him, and in exchange, he would make the scandal go away."

Steven shook his head in disbelief. "So, why didn't he marry you?"

"Daniel was extremely jealous of your father, and he wanted everything he possessed, including Penelope's love." She grunted with disdain. "He didn't want me, and I certainly didn't want him." She glanced downward, closing her eyes with much emotion. "Penelope married Daniel to save my father from prosecution." She looked away with pain and continued. "I had hoped so much that Jack would've then fallen in love with me."

"But he didn't," Steven concluded.

"And the bitterness from that drove me into being insanely evil," Charlotte added with regret.

Steven took hold of her hand with much sympathy. "I'm sorry, Charlotte!"

"Perhaps we should continue this conversation at a more appropriate time." She sighed, as she remembered the pocket watch in the pouch around her waist. She quickly took it out to check the time. "Good grief! It's already a quarter until noon. We need to be getting back to the entrance of the cave."

"I agree!" Steven added with much alarm. "We should've checked in with Amphitrite and the gods long before now."

Meanwhile, Malcolm ushered Sheriff Morton into his parlor where Cameron and Theodore sat, nervously waiting. "Hello, boys!" The sheriff greeted them. "I was hoping you might be ready to give me insight into the events leading up to the fire."

"Just tell them everything you know." Malcolm urged.

As Morton and Malcolm proceeded to sit down, Theodore shot a desperate glance at Cameron, prompting him to speak first. "Theodore and I had gone down to the beach to watch the sunset, but a sudden storm drove us to seek shelter below the cliffs."

"That's odd!" Morton quipped. "It never even stormed in Lockeport. In fact, it was a magnificent sunset at the harbor."

"You should know as well as anyone that isolated storms sometimes strike out here on the point." Malcolm interrupted. "We had a storm here as well."

Morton nodded to Malcolm and continued. "Very well! What happened next?"

"When we emerged from beneath the cliffs, we discovered our house was fully involved in flames." Cameron continued. "I could hear my brother's cries for help. I entered the house, but the flames were too intense, and drove me back." He placed his head in his hands with great emotional distress.

"Really, sheriff!" Malcolm protested. "Is this absolutely necessary? The boys have been through so much."

Morton shot a quick, searing glance at Malcolm and continued anyway.

"We recovered your father, and brothers' remains this morning." He pauses with a raised brow. "We also found a large dagger near what we believed to be your father's body."

"Surely you aren't insinuating that the boys killed their father?" Malcolm inquired in a quick outburst.

Morton only glanced at Malcolm with annoyance, and again proceeded. "Do you know anyone who might've wanted to kill your father?"

"Sheriff!" Malcolm interceded again. "You know as well as I do that there are several people who are resentful of Jonathan's success, and power in this community. He's bound to have at least a few enemies."

Cameron nervously bit at his lower lip, as the conversation escalated. "I also know that there are certain people who would benefit greatly from his death, Mr. Branch." The sheriff sharply commented.

"Are you insinuating that I...?"

Cameron interrupted before it escalated further. "I did overhear a heated argument between our father, and Mr. Spencer that morning."

Both Morton and Malcolm paused and listened with keen interest. "Do you recall what the argument was about?" Morton inquired.

"All I know is it got physical, and Mr. Spencer pushed my father to the floor."

Morton eyed both boys with serious thought. "Do you have anything to add to that, Theodore?"

"No sir!" He nervously responded. "I wasn't home at that time."

"Very Well!" Morton concluded. "You two boys can leave the room now. Mr. Branch and I need to discuss this further."

The boys got up, and politely left the room, while Morton turned his full attention to Malcolm.

"Perhaps all this had something to do with Jonathan wanting me to incarcerate Mr. Spencer's sister and her husband." Morton theorized.

"Why wasn't I aware of this issue?" Malcolm protested.

"I didn't think it was necessary at the time."

"It's urgent now. They've become friendly with my daughter Maureen. I fear for her well-being." Malcolm nervously fidgeted. "What do you intend to do?"

Morton shrugged, "Perhaps, I'll begin by checking the passenger lists of all the ships that have entered our port over the past several months. That way, I can find out if the Spencer's, in fact, arrived from England, and if they are actually who they claim to be."

"Do you suspect they might be spies?" Malcolm inquired.

"Until there's solid proof, one can only assume."

Behind a wall partition that separated the Parlor from the entranceway, Maureen hid, and quietly listened while Morton continued. "By the way, I'll need you and Beatrice at the courthouse by 10 am tomorrow. I was able to convince Judge Pearson to proceed with Jenny's trial earlier."

"My wife should be pleased to hear that."

Morton cracked a smirk, "By dusk tomorrow, Jenny should be hanging from the gallows pole."

The two men stood up to conclude.

"Concerning Mr. Spencer." Malcolm inquired. "If he or his sister should drop by, what should I do?"

"Absolutely nothing!" Morton commanded. "We do not want them to know we suspect anything."

With wide-eyed anxiety, Maureen reached over, quietly opened the front door, and snuck out well ahead of Morton and her father.

At the Secret Cave Room, Steven and Charlotte exhaustingly entered, escorted by Amphitrite, who removed their blindfolds.

Poseidon rose from the table where he was patiently waiting. "It's about time you two showed up." He stated with authority.

"I apologize for our tardiness," Stephen replied, as his eyes scanned the room. "Where's Zeus?"

"He had business to tend to in Athens," Poseidon answered. "He should be back by day's end."

Amphitrite directly addressed both of them, appearing quite angry. "So, what have you two been doing all night?"

"Good grief, Amphitrite!" Charlotte exclaimed. "I feel like a teenager being grilled by my parents."

Steven shook his head with initial amusement and answered, "We met with Stargazer in the clearing of the woods last night to discuss the etchings on the rock."

"Did that take up the entire night, and most of this morning as well?" Amphitrite grumbled.

Poseidon rebuked Amphitrite with a quick glance, then gestured for more information. "What were you able to find out?"

"We found out that, aside from Stargazer being a Shaman, he's also a stoner." Charlotte quipped jokingly.

Amphitrite and Poseidon both cast a perplexed look toward Charlotte. "A stoner?" Poseidon replied cluelessly.

"Oh! Never mind!" Charlotte remarked with annoyance. "I keep forgetting not to use common expressions from the future that you two obviously wouldn't understand."

Steven tried to get back on point, "Stargazer introduced us to Nebriana and the other inhabitants of the woods." He explained. "They invited us to stay, and join them in their late-summer celebration."

Amphitrite stomped closer in a huff before he could elaborate any further. "That explains it!" She raged. "I'm guessing you both experienced the infamous forest nectar as well."

"Oh yes!" Charlotte distressfully put her hand to her forehead. "And we're certainly feeling the after-effects."

Amphitrite looked to Steven, fuming with jealousy. "Did Nebriana try to seduce you while you were under the influence?" She questioned, touching an obvious raw nerve with Steven. "I know for a fact that she can be an alluring little nymph."

"Nothing happened, Amphitrite!" Steven snapped back with a rising annoyance that surprised her. "We simply partied with a bunch of fairies and dwarfs, and had quite a grand time in the process." Poseidon busted out laughing hysterically, as Steven paused in pondering thought. "And I can't believe I just made that statement."

"We may have gotten a bit high, and inebriated," Charlotte added. "But I assure you, no unsavory activity took place."

Amphitrite turned to Charlotte with a bold smirk. "So says the woman with the shady reputation."

"You should talk!" She exclaimed, igniting like a live wire. "You aren't exactly an innocent little Mermaid. You tend to forget that I know a bit of your history as well."

Poseidon stepped between the two raging women, hoping to calm them. "Enough! You two women need to step back, and reign in your emotions."

"Emotions!" Amphitrite exploded. "You're the one who's been jealous of Steven and me while making a play for Charlotte's affections."

Poseidon and Steven rolled their eyes at each other as Charlotte continued to fuel the fire. "Oh hush, Amphitrite!" She dismissed her with a wave of her hand. "You're just jealous that you weren't there at the party. It's fortunate for Steven that you weren't."

"What's that supposed to mean?" Amphitrite snapped back.

"Oh, really dear!" She sarcastically exclaimed. "Everyone in this room knows you have the hots for him."

Amphitrite fumed with anger, and Steven interjected himself into the argument, waving his hands. "Ladies!" He paused with emphasis. "I'm still in the room, and I don't appreciate being the object of your bickering."

Poseidon threw his hands upward in frustration. "I concede to this ridiculous conversation."

"I'm going for a swim!" Amphitrite defiantly grunted as she moved quickly to exit the Cave Room.

"I'm going to sleep off the rest of this hangover," Charlotte mumbled as she swiftly exited to an adjoining room.

"Women!" Poseidon vented with raging frustration.

Steven sighed, and gave a friendly slap to the back of Poseidon's shoulder, "Well, look at it this way." He grinned. "Now that they're gone, we can finally discuss the important issues at hand."

Chapter Fifteen:

Another Mystery Unravels

In the 21st century, Loraine enjoys afternoon tea time with Eddie and his family in the Sitting Room. She hoped to find more clues and answers to the mystery of the double doors in the East Wing.

Mary entered from the foyer and stood humbly in the doorway with her hands cupped in front of her. "Excuse me!" She announced. "You wanted to see me, Ms. Loraine?"

"Yes, Mary!" She got up and quickly escorted her the rest of the way into the room. "Please do have a seat, and join us."

Mary immediately noticed Sandy Benson, and her face lit up with delight. "There's that young lady that worked her magic on me." She smiled. "How are you, Ms. Sandy?"

"I'm fine, Mary," Sandy replied pleasantly. "And you're looking as lovely as ever.

Mary appeared flattered by her comment, as she and Loraine took a seat. "Mary!" Loraine gestured toward everyone. "This is Sandy's husband Eddie Benson, and their daughter Tricia."

Little Tricia stood and respectfully nodded toward Mary. "It's a pleasure to meet you, Ms. Wallace."

"It's so good to meet you too, young lady." Mary acknowledged. "You're just as pretty as your momma."

The little girl appeared delighted as she sat back down, and Mary's eyes wandered to Eddie, who greeted her with a cordial nod.

"I already know that you're the fine gentleman responsible for me being here," Mary remarked. "I can't thank you enough."

"I'm truly sorry it didn't happen sooner." He responded. "I know what an awful experience it was for you."

Loraine picked up the conversation from there. "As you know, Eddie entered through the portal eleven years after you, Mary." She paused. "I was hoping the two of you might help solve the mystery surrounding that imaginary room."

Mary turned to Eddie with curiosity, "You said your name is Benson. I don't recall a family by that name."

"Actually, my real name is Edward Branch. My father was Daniel's cousin, Nicholas Branch."

Mary's face lit up with enlightenment, "I faintly remember you when you were just a little boy. You visited occasionally with your parents."

"Those visits were few and far between." Eddie chuckled. "My father and Daniel didn't exactly get along too well."

"Such a shame too," Mary responded. "I know your momma and daddy were good Christian folk, just like your Aunt Elizabeth."

Loraine leaned forward on the edge of her seat and addressed Mary directly. "Do you recall anything strange that may have happened around the same time you disappeared?"

"Oh Lord, yes!" She responded with much exuberance. "Things were never the same after Daniel had that big rock dug up in the courtyard."

"The rock that's still there, that's overgrown with ivy?" Loraine further questioned.

"Yes ma'am!" She answered with an assured nod. "Mr. Daniel was mystified with the etchings on that rock, and so was his secretary, that Miss McPherson."

Loraine and Eddie glanced at each other with complete surprise. "Was her name Liddy McPherson? Loraine asked.

"Yes ma'am! She and Daniel spent a lot of time studying that old rock, and talking serious like." She shook her head as she remembered more. "All us servants figured them two were having an affair or something."

Eddie glanced to her with piqued interest, "This Liddy McPherson. How old would you say she was?

"I'd have to guess she was in her early twenties. She definitely caught the eye of the menfolk." Mary paused in thought. "It's funny how that girl suddenly quit coming around though." She shrugged. "We all figured Mrs. Branch got wise to their happenings and put an end to it."

"Mary!" Eddie exclaimed with disbelief. "This Liddy McPherson showed up at Branchview shortly after I did, eleven years later. She wasn't any older than you just described."

Mary, Eddie, and Loraine quickly exchanged desperate glances, filled with thoughts of unthinkable horror. Feeling awkward, and left out of the conversation, Sandy rose from her seat and grabbed Tricia by the hand.

"I suppose Tricia and I will go on ahead, and let the three of you sort this out, Lori." She paused. "We'll meet you and Eddie at the graveyard."

"I apologize for leaving you out of the conversation, Sandy," Loraine replied with slight embarrassment.

"That's alright, Lori. I really think this might be a bit too much for Tricia to comprehend."

"I understand." She acknowledged. "I promise we'll be along shortly."

Sandy responded with a polite, and subtle nod to everyone as she and Tricia departed the room. "Liddy must've traveled back and forth through that portal." Eddie proclaimed.

"I agree" Loraine added. "She and Daniel must've mastered the secrets in those etchings."

"I remember now, how strange the servants and all the others reacted when she returned." He pondered for a moment, then pointed to Mary. "I remember your husband, Elijah, warning me to stay away from her."

"He and all the others must've known something wasn't right about her," Mary responded with wide-eyed seriousness.

The revelations totally flabbergasted Loraine, "That might also explain how she was able to grant Daniel twenty extra years of youth."

"Say what?" Mary replied with a perplexed expression.

"Remind me to explain that later, Mary." She sighed. "I guess we're definitely onto something here, but we mustn't keep Sandy and Tricia waiting."

"I have one more question." Eddie nervously cut in. "Why did Daniel have that old rock dug up in the first place?"

"Daniel's young brother, Matthew, had just returned from college, and wanted to take the East Wing as his personal quarters," Mary explained. "They had plans of extending that Wing into where the courtyard is, and that old rock was in their way."

Loraine and Eddie shared another enlightened glance, "That explains the double doors that lead to nowhere." Loraine proclaimed.

While the future residents of Branchview tried to piece together clues to solve the mystery of the time portal, Steven and Charlotte were about to discover a new obstacle in their efforts to return from the distant past.

After a few hours of napping, Charlotte had wandered out to the beach and found a perch atop one of the rocks beneath the cliffs. She gazed out at the peaceful, serene waters of the Atlantic, as Steven approached, and sat down next to her.

"How are you feeling?" He asked.

"Much better!" She laughed. "And you?'

"Coming around."

They both chuckled and continued gazing outward, lost in their daydreams. Charlotte broke the silence first. "I suppose you want to pick up where we left off this morning in our conversation."

"If you feel like it." He smiled. "I know it's a distasteful subject for you."

"True! But I think you deserve to know the truth." She drew in a deep breath of sea air and continued. "Daniel Branch II knew Penelope planned to leave him for Jack, and it drove him insane." She paused hesitantly as she shot a lingering glance at Steven. "After I killed Jack, Daniel approached me about killing Penelope. In return, he promised to marry me, and make me the sole heiress to his fortune."

Steven knowingly attempted to finish the story for her. "And when he found out my mother was pregnant with me, he changed his mind, and killed you instead."

Charlotte defiantly shook her head.

"That's what you, and everyone else were led to believe." She sighed with despair. "When he realized it wasn't his baby, he was more determined than ever to kill her. But as evil, as I was at that time, I couldn't let that happen for the sake of Penelope, and the baby."

"Your conscience made you reconsider."

Charlotte nodded and continued.

"He and I argued about it, and I drew him into the cellar with the intent of killing him." She grunted with disdain. "With that despicable man out of the way, my sister and her baby could live the rest of their lives wealthy, and happy."

"What happened next?"

"I was foolish enough to let my guard down, and when my back was turned, he hit me on the head with a shovel." She emotionally sighed and continued. "The bastard doused me with lighter fluid and set me on fire. He stood over me, and watched as I burned to death." She sadly turned to Steven. "You know the rest of the story."

"In truth, you basically gave your life so that my mother and I could live." His eyes welled with tears. "He spared my mother, but sent me to the orphanage."

Charlotte sadly, and emotionally nodded, "I never wanted to be evil Steven. I wished I could've used my magic for good"

"I know you had a good heart like my mother, but I suppose circumstances in life caused you to be dark."

Charlotte cringed at the reality of his statement. "Now that I know how this whole lie got started, I feel even more foolish to have ever been taken in by it."

Steven slipped a sympathetic arm around her and pulled her close, "I know."

They heard a faint voice calling out to them, and looked up the beach to see Maureen running toward them, frantically waving her hands.

By the time she reached them, the young girl was totally out of breath, "Maureen! What's wrong?" Steven asked with great concern.

She struggled to catch her breath, "My premonitions were right." She replied. "You can't go into town, or go anywhere near my parents' house."

Steven and Charlotte exchanged a clueless glance.

"How did you know where to find us?" Charlotte asked.

"I concentrated hard on both of you, and I kept getting a vision of the beach and the water."

Charlotte turned to Steven with astonishment, "You were right. She is a clever child."

"I overheard my father, and the sheriff talking." Maureen continued. "Cameron convinced them that you killed his father and brother, and they also suspect that you're all British spies.

Both Steven and Charlotte are flabbergasted and taken aback by the unexpected news, "Precisely what we didn't need." Charlotte sighed. "Another wrench thrown into our plans."

In the future, Loraine tied up another of the many loose ends she had been dealing with in Steven's absence. She, Eddie, Sandy, and Tricia stood respectfully in front of Emma's refurbished headstone, and gravesite. Her eyes swept the area surrounding it, and she gave an approving nod.

"I think the maintenance crew did a fine job of cleaning this place up" She stated. "It was a total disaster before."

"It's beautiful, and peaceful here now," Sandy replied.

"I have no idea what her headstone looked like before," Eddie added. "But I think it's an appropriate tribute to her now."

"I like the little birdie they carved next to her name," Tricia remarked.

Loraine leaned over, putting her arm across the little girls' shoulders, and recanted, "Emma told us how much she enjoyed sitting in the garden and watching the bluebirds. I thought it would be a pretty thing to add." Tricia smiled, then Loraine took a deep emotional breath, and continued. "Should we all do this?"

Everyone agreed, and beginning with Tricia, each of them laid a fresh arrangement of flowers on Emma's grave, then paused for a moment of silent meditation. Loraine went last, and she whispered as she placed her hand over the newly carved words NEVER FORGOTTEN just above her name.

"I'll always keep my promise, Emma. You shall never be forgotten."

They all solemnly began to stroll away, while Tricia turned to look one last time, and pointed with wide-eyed excitement.

"Look! It's Emma!"

They all turned and gasped at the sight of a beautiful bluebird perched proudly atop Emma's headstone.

Through tear-filled eyes, and emotional smile, Loraine exclaimed, "Yes, Tricia! It most certainly is!"

Another day came to an end for a homesick Steven, as he still sat on the same rock on an all too familiar beach, in another time. As he watched, the sun sunk below the horizon, casting its' amber glow on the calm waters of the Atlantic.

Poseidon quietly approached and sat on a nearby rock, "Charlotte told me you might be here."

"Where else would I be?" He laughed sarcastically. "I have nowhere else to go."

"I heard all about the accusations against you." He sighed. "Witch-hunting seems the sport of choice in this part of the world." He stared at the horizon. "We'll consult with Zeus about all this when he returns."

"Has Amphitrite returned yet?"

"That'll take a bit of time." Poseidon chuckled. "My guess is she's sitting on some faraway beach, trying to deal with her own penned-up frustrations."

"She's a strong-willed woman," Steven commented.

"As is Charlotte, Poseidon added with a smirk. "When two women like that come together, it's best to expect a violent storm."

Both men laughed, and then noticed the figure of Zeus emerging from beneath the water. He continued to walk toward them, and within moments, he stood before them, showing no signs of having been in the water. "Greetings, brother!" Poseidon nodded to him. "I trust everything went well in Athens."

"As well as possible," Zeus answered bluntly.

Steven curiously stared at Zeus, which earned him an indignant glare in return, "I was just wondering." Steven pondered. "If all of you can appear, and reappear at any time, and at any place you wish, can you also travel through time in the same manner?"

"Why should we?" Zeus grunted. "We're immortal gods. "What benefit would it be of ours?"

"I suppose you have a point there."

"Besides, it would be against our oath," Poseidon added. "It would not be in the best interest of humanity to use our powers to alter fate."

"Which is the exact reason I'm cautious in aiding you and Charlotte." Zeus quipped.

Poseidon stood, and took in a deep breath of the salt air, "Concerning that subject, a new complication has arisen."

"Why am I not surprised?" Zeus replied, casting a disgruntled expression at both men. "Come along! We'll discuss this further over a goblet of wine in the Cave Room."

Across the spectrum of time, the haunting sound of the huge grandfather clock chimed at 1 AM in the Branchview foyer. The single chime reverberated and echoed through the dark, quiet house. Loraine entered the upstairs hallway from the double doors of the North Wing, barefoot, and dressed only in her nightgown. She sauntered near the top of the stairs, and gazed all around her, and upward into the dark corners of the ceiling.

"Daphne!" She loudly whispered. "I know you're here somewhere. We need to talk."

She waited a few moments in anticipated silence, and finally, the unmistakable apparition of Daphne Branch appeared on the landing just below her.

"Hello, Darling!" She gestured to her surroundings. "How fitting that you should beckon me at the location where I took my last living breath."

"I need to speak with you about the babies, among other things."

"Ahh! My beautiful grandchildren!" She grinned. "Such a favorite subject of mine."

Daphne turned for a quick glance at the portrait painting of the stern-faced woman on the landing and gave an indignant grunt.

"I understand you've repaired that deplorable picture." She sighed. "How unfortunate for me that it was the last face I saw before I tumbled to my death." She trembled, "It still gives me the creeps just looking at it."

"I would've rather retired it to the attic," Loraine stated in a tone of agreement. "I feel the same way every time I have to wander by it."

Daphne chuckled, and gracefully ascended the stairs to join Loraine at the top landing, "Do you have any clue who that horrid-looking woman might have been?" Loraine asked. "Unlike all the other paintings, it has no nameplate."

"That would be Beatrice Branch." She declared as she took the last step up to the landing. "She was the original mistress of what would've been the original Branchview homestead that stood on this location."

"That would be the period Steven is trapped in as we speak," Loraine replied. "The thought of that gives me the chills."

Daphne gave a saddened nod and glanced down the stairs, "What gives me the chills is standing at the top of these stairs." She shivered. "Would you mind if we moved away from here?"

"Not at all" They strolled closer to the North Wing doors. "Can you tell me anything about that rock in the courtyard?"

"Like the closed-off East Wing, that was one of the many mysteries about this place Daniel was reluctant to discuss." She replied. "I do know that he had a fascination with it, as did Liddy McPherson."

"So, it is conceivable that she may have known the secret that surrounded it."

"Obviously!" Daphne grunted. "That little trollop would sneak around here in the middle of the night, and she and Daniel would meet at that rock. Is it any wonder they had planned to meet there on the night I was killed?"

"It's all beginning to make sense now." Loraine pondered with enlightenment. "You knew they were meeting there, and you never approached Daniel about it."

"I could've cared less if the two of them were carrying on." Daphne declared with utter disdain. "Daniel and I slept in separate beds, and on those rare occasions he forced himself on me, I would simply cringe, and close my eyes until he was through."

"I'm sorry that such a fine woman as yourself had to deal with that." Loraine put her hands to her hips and pondered further. "Daphne! Was there a full moon on that night you died?"

"Oh yes!" She recalled. "It was a beautiful night that you could only imagine in your dreams." She swooned. "The moon was full, with a beautiful aura surrounding it, and the sweet smell of lilacs lingered in the night air." She sighed. "I only wished I could've been with the one I truly loved on a night such as that."

"Was there someone else?" Loraine inquired with a sly grin.

Daphne gracefully paced about the landing, and Loraine followed her with her eyes.

"This is digging a bit deep emotionally. But yes, there was someone else." She halted and held a firm stance in front of Loraine. "His name was Darren Branch." She smiled fondly. "He was the family attorney and Daniel's nephew." She emotionally sighed. "He was the real father of Jack, which explains why he was always my favored son."

Loraine gasped at the revelation. "Whatever happened to Darren? He wasn't mentioned in any of the journals."

"He made the tragic mistake of loving someone that was a possession of the almighty Daniel Branch the first." She looked away emotionally. "They found his body floating in Lockeport Harbor." Loraine was shocked as

Daphne continued. "Now, with that out of the way, I believe you wanted to discuss something about our wonderful babies."

"Have you been instilling magic in those babies?" Loraine narrowed her eyes and grinned.

"I'm afraid I wouldn't have the abilities for that." She laughed. "But I do know that Maggie has been nurturing the magical abilities they inherited from you, my dear." Daphne beamed with a clever smile, while Loraine was silenced, and somewhat baffled over the revelation.

The following morning, at the break of dawn, Philip and Ezekiel led a procession to the beach at Lighthouse Point, with Tony, Andrea carrying their newborn baby, and Tina following close behind. They strolled to the waterline, where Ezekiel bent down and captured a bit of water in the palm of his hand. He then walked over to where Andrea eagerly presented the baby boy.

With a smile, he pinched a smatter of the water with his fingers and traced the sign of the cross on the baby's forehead. "May the waters of our ancestors bless, and cleanse this precious child Michael, and may it always serve as a symbol of his heritage."

Andrea then handed the baby to Philip, who walked ankle-deep into the ocean and held the child high over his head. "Amphitrite! Behold, your grandson!" His voice echoed out. "Civilizations of the Nereides, and the Oceanides, rejoice! For I present to you this child, Michael, son of Triton and Andrea."

All clapped and cheered, while a haunting chorus of Siren wails, and clicks echoed loudly from the depths of the Atlantic.

At that same moment, in a distant time, Amphitrite stood at the edge of the water near that very spot. She listened attentively as the echoes traversed across the spectrum of time to reach her ears.

Charlotte curiously approached her from behind. "Amphitrite! Is everything alright?"

She turned to Charlotte with great wonder. "Did you just hear that?"

"Hear what?" She replied with a perplexed expression.

"Poseidon's voice calling to me from the ocean."

"That's impossible! Poseidon is in the cave with Steven and Zeus. I just left them."

Amphitrite raised her chin with further wonder, and glanced one more time toward the water, before abruptly changing the subject. "I'm sorry you and I had words, Charlotte." She turned, "I said some things…. it was wrong of me to say."

"I came down here intending to apologize to you as well." Charlotte giggled. "I was obviously suffering the after-effects of that delectable forest nectar, and reacted a bit nasty."

Amphitrite smiled and shook her head. "You and I have grown to be just like sisters. Haven't we?"

"Yes, we have. And believe me!" Charlotte added. "Sisters do have squabbles from time to time."

Both women laughed, then cordially draped their arms across each other's back as they strolled away, along the serene beach.

Chapter Sixteen:

Judgement Day

Zeus, under the guise of Ezekiel Sphere, casually entered the rustic Lockeport Courthouse where Jenny was to stand trial. The courtroom was filled, and he had to lean against the back wall to observe the proceedings. Deputy Doren, who was several feet away, caught eye of him and began to move his way with determination. Ezekiel shot a hard, stone-cold glare at him, and calmly shook his head to warn him off. Doren immediately had second thoughts about another encounter with this bull of a man. He halted his progress, backed off, and cowered away. Ezekiel couldn't help but find humor at the moment.

Albert Marshall, a distinguished, but cocky lawyer, paced impatiently in the front of the room. Judge Pearson, a gruff old gentleman with bushy, snow-white eyebrows, started the proceedings and ordered Jenny to the witness stand in an authoritarian manner. She casually strolled to the front, took a seat, and stared stone-faced sober towards the attendees.

"Mrs. McPherson!" Marshall began. "Am I correct in understanding that you're pleading not guilty to the charge of murdering Meredith Locke, but you agree to the charge of being a witch?"

Marshall got within an intimidating distance from her face, but she hardly flinched. "That would be correct." She replied.

A buzz of conversation erupted in the courtroom but quickly quieted, as Marshall arrogantly strutted away. He then quickly swung around dramatically and pointed a threatening finger her way. "You understand the accusation of witchcraft still carries the sentence of hanging?"

"Yes, I'm well aware of that." Jenny quipped.

Marshall strolled away again with a satisfied smirk and gestured to the judge. "I rest my case, your honor."

Judge Pearson leaned forward in his seat and spoke directly to Jenny. "Mrs. McPherson. Since you have no one to speak in your defense, is there anything you'd like to say to this court in your defense?"

"I'd like to reinforce my claim that it was indeed not I, but Jonathan Locke, who poisoned his wife, and ordered the murder of my husband at sea." She boldly proclaimed. "That loathsome scoundrel of a man was, in fact, the grand wizard of The Society of Satan."

Marshall jumped up from his seat with both panic and anger. "I object!"

The courtroom erupted, and Beatrice Branch shot up from her seat, pointing at Jenny. "She speaks with the lying, foul-mouthed tongue of the devil himself."

"And you should know better than anyone of the way he speaks, Mrs. Branch!" Jenny fired back.

Judge Pearson repeatedly slammed his gavel down. "Order in the court!"

Several men, including Sheriff Morton and Marshall himself, exchanged anxious glances over her accusations. Ezekiel took alert notice and reacted with an enlightened expression. As the courtroom settled down, the judge turned his attention back to Jenny.

"Mrs. McPherson! I'll abruptly strike that last statement from the records, being that Mr. Locke is now deceased, and cannot defend himself to the charges you make." He paused with a disdainful expression. "Would you like to add anything else?"

"Only that I'm glad that thieving, lying bastard is dead." She venomously responded. "I will go willingly to the gallows, cursing this pitiful town until I breathe my last dying breath, and finally see Jonathan Locke once again as he burns in the fiery flames of hell."

The courtroom erupted in chaos again, and Beatrice Branch stood up with vigor, pointing an accusing finger toward Jenny. "Kill the murderous witch now!" She yelled out.

Pearson slammed his gavel down with a vengeance until all order was again restored in the room. "I will not allow such unrest in my courtroom." He screamed with anger. "I'll therefore call an end to this debacle of a hearing by declaring the sentence." He turned his full attention to Jenny and continued. "Jenny McPherson! On the charge of murder, I declare not guilty, due to insufficient sufficient evidence."

Moans and grumblings erupted in the crowd, and the judge peered a warning at the gathering with his thick eyebrows raised until all was silent again.

"On the charge of practicing witchcraft." He continued. "I declare guilty."

Cheers erupted in the crowd, and again, the judge waited for a calm, with his gavel poised to strike if needed. "I sentence you, Jenny McPherson, to be hung by the neck until death, at sunset on this 10th day of September 1697. May God have mercy on your soul." He glanced at her with slight pity, before striking his gavel for the last time. "This court is hereby adjourned."

Jenny sat still, staring straight ahead, and waited for the sheriff. Attorney Marshall could not resist taunting her for one last time. "I'll be in the first row, watching with keen pleasure as you take your last breath, witch."

"Will you now?" Jenny responded with a clever grin, as she raised two fingers, and pointed them directly at his glaring eyes. "May the light permanently cease in your world, Mr. Marshall."

Marshall backed away, and his expression turned to one of horror, as he clutched at his eyes. "Ahhh! My eyes are burning!"

Blood emerged from between his fingers, and trickled down the sides of his face, as he screamed in agony. Jenny laughed maniacally as Marshall fell to his knees, and several men rushed to his aid.

Beatrice blessed herself with the sign of the cross, then fainted into her husband's arms. The crowd observed in stunned, silent terror, as Sheriff Morton and Deputy Doran quickly ushered Jenny from the room. Even Ezekiel was disturbed over the sight he had just witnessed.

"These pitiful fools! They brought this curse upon themselves." He whispered to himself.

Moments later, Ezekiel lingered among the angry, chaotic crowd outside the Lockeport courthouse, as Sheriff

Morton and Deputy Doren roughly lead a convicted Jenny down the dusty street toward the jail. Her hands were tightly tied, and a black hood now covered her head. People pushed, jeered, and taunted her as a rope leash dragged her along. Little children also picked up rocks and stones, and hurled them at her as she went by.

Ezekiel watched the dismal state of affairs with much remorse. In his mind, he recited the thoughts streaming through it.

Even after centuries of immortal life, I still have not grown callous to the ignorance and cruelty of the human race. I've seen countless talented people turn evil by the lies and selfish ambitions of others, which have inevitably destroyed their lives. I can't help but wonder what sort of life Jenny McPherson would've had if she had never come to this town, or met Jonathan Locke. I also wonder what alternative fate may have been for the future ancestors of both the Locke and the Branch families. It's beyond pity that so many lives were destroyed by the actions of one devious man.

Ezekiel's thoughts were momentarily interrupted when Malcolm Branch was seen fighting his way through the crowd. "Sheriff!" He yelled. "I need to have a word with you.

Morton acknowledged the request with a nod and turned to Doren. "Can I trust you to get this prisoner back to her cell?"

"You can count on me, sheriff." He assured. "Besides, if she tries to get away, this crowd will tear her apart."

Morton motioned Malcolm off to the side, and Ezekiel moved closer to eavesdrop. "I did a little checking on the Spencer's." Morton grinned.

"And...?" Malcolm added with anticipation.

"They weren't listed as passengers on any of the incoming ships from Great Britain over the past six months, and my contact with the British delegation never heard of them."

"So, it appears they're frauds." Malcolm theorized. What do you suppose is their purpose for being here?"

"I don't know." He shrugged. "But I'd be willing to bet Jonathan Locke found out, and that's the reason he's dead."

Ezekiel was further startled when Maureen strolled up and tugged on his arm. "I know you're with the Spencer's. I can read it in your aura."

Ezekiel was perplexed by the statement of the young girl. "I'll explain later." She impatiently remarked. "You and I need to talk."

She motioned for him to follow, as Ezekiel glanced back one more time at the sheriff and Malcolm before following her.

Doren led Jenny back to her cell at the Lockeport jail, and shoved her inside before slamming the door shut. The push caused Jenny to tumble to the floor, and Doren laughed as he watched her struggle to get back to her feet.

"Well, Missy! Just a few more hours, and you'll be stoking the fires of hell."

Jenny, with the hood, still covering her head, and her hands still firmly bound, struggled to pull herself up onto a wood bench. "I'll be sure to save you a warm place, Mr. Doran."

"Say what you want." He scoffed. "But you ain't gonna do to me what you did to that attorney fella." He shook his head defiantly. "Not with your eyes covered, and your hands tied." He shook his head. "No ma'am!"

"You greatly underestimate my abilities." She laughed.

Doren scoffed again at her remark before stomping away, taking a seat behind the desk, and then swiveling to watch her with pent-up anxiety.

He then leaned back in his seat and studied her as she sat silently on the cell bench, weaving forward and back. "You listen to me, witch!" He pointed with heightened anxiety. "You try any foolishness, and I'll shoot you right where you sit." He paused with definitive emphasis. "You hear me?"

"I don't need to make a move, Mr. Doran." She calmly stated. "I can destroy you, and this entire town with a simple thought. I can also accomplish it as much from the grave as I can from here."

Doran grew nervous as Jenny began to chant in a foreign tongue, and he swatted at a cockroach crawling up his arm. He jumped back with fear, as several other roaches poured out from the desk drawers in front of him. He stood, and yelled as several more appeared on the floor, and began to crawl up his pant legs.

He screamed in horror and tried to run, but the roaches came at him quickly from all directions, and soon covered half his body. As the roaches devoured his flesh, he screamed and cried in agony, while Jenny maniacally laughed beneath her dark hood.

Chapter Seventeen:

The Guardian of The Caribbean

On the beach near the cliffs, Amphitrite, Charlotte, and Steven laid resting in the midday sun. A cool, late summer breeze blew in from the Atlantic, signaling that the warm season was quickly winding down. Charlotte opened her eyes and gazed out over the ocean, squinting fiercely against the reflecting light on the water. She quickly jumped to her feet when she spotted a figure emerging from the depths.

"Amphitrite!" She cried. "Wake up! Someone is approaching from the water."

She woke with a yawn, and focused her attention on where Charlotte was pointing. Steven was startled from his napping, and also looked in the same direction. "It can't be!" Amphitrite exclaimed with surprise.

She ran out to the water's edge, while Charlotte and Steven curiously followed. A stunningly beautiful black woman strolled in from the water. Her unblemished coffee-colored skin, moist from the sea mist, shined brightly in the sun. Her wavy hair fell past her shoulders like ebony silk, and her mesmerizing eyes sparkled like black diamonds. "Lindiwi! Guardian of the Caribbean!" Amphitrite announced. "How long has it been?"

Lindiwi laughed and answered with a strong Jamaican accent. "Far too long, my redhead sista!"

The two women embraced, while Steven and Charlotte looked on with wonder. Steven's muscular chest and abs were exposed from his opened shirt, and Lindiwi took full notice. "Mmmm! Dat is a right handsome man." She playfully wide-eyed Amphitrite. "He belongs to you?"

"Unfortunately, not." Amphitrite sighed. "His heart belongs to someone in a distant place." She gestured toward Steven and Charlotte. "This is Steven Spencer, and his sister Charlotte." She paused with a grin. "Poseidon, Zeus, and I are helping them with a troublesome dilemma."

Lindiwi gracefully extended her hand, accompanied by an accentuated nod to greet both of them. She then turned her attention to Charlotte and gently brushed the back of her hand against her cheek. "I can tell dey be kin." She proclaimed. "She is a very pretty woman indeed."

Charlotte reacted with a pleasant smile, and a grateful bow of her head, while Amphitrite grew anxious. "Tell me!" Amphitrite impatiently interrupted. "What brings you to this part of the Atlantic?"

"Ah! I will be needin help from you and Poseidon." She proclaimed seriously. "Da bloody pirates been snatchin dose in my clan, and kill dem for dey amusement. De dirty sea dogs hang dem from de main sail ta dry in de hot sun."

Amphitrite reacted with open disgust, and blessed herself with the sign of the cross, while Steven and Charlotte listened with keen interest. "Who are these nasty bilge rats, and for what reason are they doing this?" Amphitrite inquired.

"Dat be none udder dan Cap'n Nathan Walsh and da crew of da Black Onyx." She spat in the sand and continued. "De call us evil sea witches, but de is da evil ones. De do da deeds of da devil hisself."

"But you possess immortal powers!" Amphitrite exclaimed. "Is there nothing you can do to stop them?"

"Me clan has not de power as I to defend demselves. Dey snare da schools in unsuspecting traps. I've never met with dem face to face."

Amphitrite paced as she pondered the situation, then took a firm stance. "Then the three of us will have to hunt them down, and give them an ultimatum." She huffed. "Either they cease this dastardly action immediately, or we'll send them all to the depths of Davey Jones's locker, where the sharks can feed on their miserable carcasses."

"Yah! Dat be me fiery sista! She laughed.

Steven and Charlotte stood at a comfortable distance and commented under their breath. "I'd like to see that confrontation," Steven whispered.

"I pity those clueless pirates. I doubt these feisty Mermaids will even need Poseidon's help." Charlotte added.

"Come!" Amphitrite invited. "I'll take you to the cave where we can rest, and leave tomorrow at dawn."

Lindiwi paused to fill her lungs with sea air. "Nah! We shud leave right quick. Der is a nasty storm a-brewin'. I can feel it in me bones."

Amphitrite closed her eyes and faced the open sea for a moment. "You're right, Lindiwi. Foul weather is but a few short hours away." She turned back to further address her. "We'll gather Poseidon, and hasten our journey."

At the Lockeport jail, Sheriff Morton returned to find the office area empty, and quiet. "Doren!" He yelled. "Where in the blazes are you?"

He wandered further into the room and halted in shock as he discovered what remained of Doren, on the floor behind the desk. He immediately cupped his hand over his mouth and vomited.

"Dear God!" He exclaimed in horror, as he glanced toward Jenny's cell, where she sat pensively. "Witch!" He screamed. "What in the hell have you done?"

She turned her hooded face in the direction of Morton's voice. "I have my head covered, and my hands tied. What could I possibly have done?"

"You know damn well." He stomped over and gripped the bars to the cell door in anger. "What sort of hellish vermin did you call upon that did this to poor Doren?"

"I always complained you had a roach problem here in the jail." She calmly stated. "Mr. Doren was perhaps the biggest cockroach of all, and as my late husband used to say, Vermin eventually devour their own" She laughed. "I'm sure you remember my husband, sheriff. His name was Roger McPherson. Jonathan had him killed when he refused to be part of your little Secret Society club."

"What do you know about the Secret Society?" Morton sneered.

"I know that aside from Jonathan Locke and Mr. Marshall, you, the now-departed Mr. Doran, and several other of your low-life associates are members."

"You can't prove that." He trembled with anger. "There are many good, moral people in this town. The Secret Society is merely a myth."

"I'm afraid not!" She replied with anger. "Most of the movers and shakers in this town are devout members, and the rest are sniveling Puritans who bask in their self-righteousness, and wait on you hand and foot."

Morton gripped the bars with nervous desperation.
"So, tell me now! You did these horrid things to Doran and Marshall. Exactly what sort of fate do you have planned for me?"

"You pitiful coward!" She laughed mockingly. "I won't raise a finger to you, for you've already sealed your own fate."

"What are you saying?"

"I'm saying those who have passed false judgment on the innocent, when they are truly unrighteous, shall suffer a fate much worse than Mr. Doran, or Mr. Marshall." She snickered. "And that, dear sheriff, is something beyond my control."

Morton sneered in anger and stormed away. "Sunset can't come soon enough, witch."

Inside the secure confines of the Secret Cave, Steven and Charlotte sat silently across in the candle-lit room. They listened as thunder and furious winds howled outside the caverns. They could also hear the waves violently crash against the base of the cliffs.

The sounds made them both shudder with anxiety. "Amphitrite and Lindiwi were right about that storm," Steven stated.

"It's lucky Zeus is a god." She answered. "Otherwise, I'd be concerned about his well-being." She checked the timepiece stashed in her waist satchel. "He is running a bit late."

"Charlotte!" He pondered. "What else can you tell me about the Locke family journals? Was there anything from this period that stands out in your memory?"

"It was a long time ago when I read them, and it had been rewritten from memory by my grandfather." She sighed. "The original journals perished when the second Locke Estate was destroyed by fire." She pondered in thought for a moment. "From what I recall, there was mention of a pox epidemic that wiped out over half the population of Lockeport in the winter of 1698." She glanced to Steven. "Unfortunately, Theodore was a victim, but Cameron survived."

"Was there any mention of the Branch family's fate?" He asked. "I never had the chance to read that far back into their journals."

"None that I recall." She replied with a sigh. "By that time, the Branch family would've been excluded from our journals."

"It's obvious by our existence that Cameron indeed survived." He sighed.

"But I wonder what became of Maureen."

"She's a strong-willed girl." She smiled. "I have to believe she survived as well."

At that moment, Zeus quietly, and somberly emerged from the shadows. He dropped down into another chair at the table and stared straight ahead in silence. "Is it over?" Steven cautiously asked.

"Yes!" Zeus shut his eyes and sadly nodded. "But yet, in another sense, it's only just begun." Charlotte and Steven exchanged sorrowful glances as he continued to recant the events of the day. "I couldn't believe the ignorance, and callousness of the mob as they cheered on her death." The anger ebbed and flowed in his voice as he continued. "Then, at the exact moment she died, the skies grew black, and a raging storm swept in from the Atlantic. One such as not even I had the power to control." His eyes widened as he continued. "A massive bolt of lightning struck down from the sky, and took down at least ten people that I counted." He looked away with remorse. "It reminded me of the tragic day that Jesus Christ was crucified."

Steven and Charlotte exchanged looks of disbelief. "You were present when Jesus died on the cross?" Steven asked.

"Oh yes!" Zeus replied in a matter-of-fact tone. "As was Poseidon, and many other gods. We all knew, and dearly loved our brother Jesus. We spent much time with He and his disciples." He nodded with much certainty. "He was truly everything He claimed to be." He looked away with uncharacteristic tears welling in his eyes. "None of us could ever fathom being as glorious, and perfect as Him." He blessed himself with the sign of the cross, then glanced around the room. "Where are Poseidon and Amphitrite?"

"They were called away to the Caribbean to help Lindiwi," Charlotte explained. "Something about a problem with pirates."

"Ahh! Lindiwi!" Zeus laughed and shook his head. "The woman with curves, and a swagger that could lead even the most righteous man astray."

Steven gave an accentuated nod of agreement, while Charlotte shook her head with annoyance. "You men!" She exclaimed. "All you can think about is one thing."

"And I imagine you women never think of it at all." Steven scoffed.

All three shared a quick, hearty laugh, then Zeus returned to a more serious subject again. "I overheard the sheriff talking to Malcolm Branch." He began. "As expected, they've confirmed you aren't who you claim to be." An anxious glance passed between the three. "I also met with Maureen Branch." He paused with a sigh. "She surprisingly sought me out in the crowd, and she seems to be a gifted young intuitive,"

"Yes!" Steven replied. "We were already aware of her abilities."

"From what she foretold; many troubles lie ahead for the town of Lockeport." Zeus looked to Steven with much concern. "We have to make sure we don't fail in getting you two back to your own time."

Charlotte answered in an all-knowing matter.

"I think we already established that fact, handsome."

Meanwhile, somewhere over the dark, and much calmer waters of the Caribbean Sea, three heads popped up from the depths, on the starboard side of a large barque cruising through only slightly choppy waters. Poseidon pointed to the bow of the ship, where the name Black Onyx was boldly lettered on the side.

The trio submerged again, only to re-emerge moments later near the front of the ship. They began to scale up the outer framing of the bow, grabbing onto the figurehead carving of a large-breasted woman, then shimmying up toward the bowsprit.

Poseidon paused at eye level with the protruding breasts, and humorously whispered to himself. "A bit top-heavy for my taste, I must say."

The main deck of the ship was alive with the loud banter of drunken sailors celebrating the pleasant night. The keen eyes of Mr. Ward, the tall lanky Quartermaster, caught sight of Amphitrite as she snagged one of the fore ropes with her foot, and tumbled onto the deck. "Hoy there!" He yelled. "Intruders!"

Within seconds, the three were surrounded by pirates with their swords drawn. The trio held firm, however, ready to battle with their powerful gold swords.

Captain Nathan Walsh, a regal-looking chap with dark features, long curly hair below a tricorn hat, and a long doublet coat, maneuvered to the front of his men. He aimed his sword within inches of the trio. "Who are ye that dares to trespass upon me ship?"

Poseidon held one hand up, "We come in peace to make a truce."

"Liars they are!" Ward cried. "They are demons from the depths, Cap'n!" He gestured. "There be no boat from whence they came."

Walsh raised one hand, never taking his eyes off the trio. "Silence, Mr. Ward! Let em speak their purpose, before we slice out their gizzards, and feed em to the sharks." He gestured for Poseidon to continue.

"You and your crew have been killing harmless Mermaids who guard these waters."

"We are doing the will of the Almighty." Walsh arrogantly laughed. "They are nuthin, but demons of the sea that bring ill fortune to those who sail these waters. They deserve to rot til death in the hot sun."

Filled with rage, Lindiwi stepped forward and raised her sword. "Liars they are!" She charged. "De sirens are peaceful inhabitants of dese waters. Let me cut da dirty sea dog's head from his body."

Poseidon stepped up to halt and calm her. "There will be no bloodshed on this deck if you agree to leave these peaceful creatures alone."

"Aye!" Walsh chuckled. "And just what do the three of ye think ye're gonna do to a ship full of pirates if we fail to agree?"

Poseidon pointed his sword toward the foresails, and a bolt of electricity flew from the tip, and immediately incinerated them. Several pirates hopped about, blessed themselves, and dropped their swords to the deck. "There now!" Poseidon accentuated. "Do we negotiate, or do I send this entire ship to the depths?"

Walsh arrogantly raised his head and sneered. "I shan't negotiate with lowly sea demons."

"So be it!" Poseidon aimed his sword at the mainmast.

Abel, a pot-bellied pirate with a large gold earring, fought his way to the front. "Wait!" He yelled. "They are not demons, Cap'n." He bowed. "They be gods!" He gave an assured nod and continued. "I hear tell of the legend. He would be Poseidon, emperor of de sea. De red-haired beauty be his wife, Amphitrite, and de seductive dark one be Lindiwi, guardian of da Caribbean."

Abel laid down his sword, and bowed again, in reference to the trio, while Walsh exploded with anger. "Hogwash, I say! Gods be only tall tales, and here say."

Would you be willing to test that theory, Captain Walsh?" Amphitrite taunted. "If so, we'll destroy this ship from bow to stern."

Walsh cowered a bit, while another rugged-looking pirate with weathered skin, piercing gray eyes, and a thick mop of brown hair pushed his way to the front and spoke in a heavy Scottish brogue. "If ye're truly who ye claim ta be, then so liberate those of us that serve against their will."

"Are you a prisoner, sir?" Poseidon asked.

"Me services were sold to the Captain." He sneered. "I be his slave!"

Poseidon gazed out to the open waters. "I estimate that we're a mere one hundred nautical miles off the coast of Antigua." He glanced up at the foremast. "You'll need repairs on that mast." He paused with emphasis. "Once ashore, if there is any man who wishes to be liberated, he shall be free to go his own way."

"Do dat sound like an offer from a demon, Cap'n?" Lindiwi asked.

With a sigh, Walsh lowered his blade in surrender. "Very well!" He replied. "I'll leave da damn sea nymphs be. Just spare me ship."

"Just so you keep your word, I'll stay on board for the duration of the journey." Poseidon firmly stated. "The ladies will swim alongside to stay the course." He extended his hand to Walsh. "Do we have a deal, Captain?"

Walsh reluctantly shook hands to seal the agreement. "Aye!" Will I be permitted to recruit new seamen in port?"

"Only if they're recruited of their own free will."

One pirate continued to persist with his own pleas. "If it be fit, sir. Might you ensure me passage to the American Colonies so that I can kill the scoundrel who separated me family and I, and sold me onto this boat to rot?"

"I'm sure there will be ships in port heading to that destination. I'll do what I can." Poseidon assured.

He gave a respectful bow of gratitude, while Amphitrite paced closer, and eyed him with curiosity. "May I ask who this man would be that did this to you.? She asked.

The pirate spat on the deck with pent-up anger. "He be the man who owns this bloody barque, and profits most from its' plunders."

Walsh intervened, and spat upon the deck with disgust. "The man he speaketh of be none udder than Jonathan Locke." He ranted. "Da scoundrel pays us for disrupping the bizness of his shippin foes."

"I know of this man, Locke." Poseidon proclaimed. "I can say with certainty that he is already dead."

"It be a right shame the devil took em before I had my chance at em." The pirate sneered.

"Captain!" Poseidon curiously exclaimed. "Was Mr. Locke's business partner aware of his actions?"

Walsh shook his head with a definite certainty.

"Malcolm Branch be a fair n' honest man." He stated. "He had no idea what Locke was doing."

Poseidon pondered the situation, then turned his attention back toward the young pirate. "Can I ask what your name would be sailor?"

"Aye, sir!" He nodded. "Me name be Roger! Roger McPherson! Poseidon and Amphitrite exchanged a long, enlightened glance, tinged with both surprise and foreboding.

In a different spectrum of time, Loraine and Sharie called a special meeting in the Branchview Dining Room for the resident staff, special guests, and inhabitants.

They both stood at the head of the table and motioned for everyone's attention. "We have some announcements we'd like to make that concern all within our inner circle." Loraine began.

"I've arranged a separate meeting with nonresident personnel," Sharie added. "There are certain things we must say that shouldn't be heard by anyone outside the household."

Loraine took a deep breath and continued. "In light of my recent experience, we've found it necessary to reinforce our security here at the estate." She motioned to Gerard. "Gerard was able to secure the funds to install a new, state-of-the-art, front gate mechanism to replace the old one."

Gerard stood, and commented. "The gate will be closed at all times to ensure safety from intruders. All of you will be issued a security code for entry."

Sharie picked it up from there. "I'll train the staff on gate procedures, and on using the new security system for the house."

"I was under the impression that the ghosts were our security system," Millie remarked with straight-faced humor that garnered a hearty laugh from all in attendance.

Loraine quieted them all again. "We also received some troubling news from the state of Connecticut regarding the lighthouse. It appears they've decided to make it totally automated, and will not rebuild the residence portion." She gestured sadly toward Bill. "That leaves our good friend, Mr. Crawford, without a job, or a place to live."

Everyone else glanced his way with sympathy, but Loraine swiftly continued. "But I believe I might have a positive solution for him." She was unable to conceal a clever grin. "This house has been without a resident butler for nearly a century, and I think that tradition needs to be continued." She again glanced toward Bill. "With that in mind, I'd like to offer that position to Mr. Crawford, if he would be gracious enough to accept it."

The offer flabbergasted Bill, "I...I'm just so overwhelmed." He stuttered. "I don't know what to say."

"I believe the proper word you need to say is yes" Millie quipped.

Everyone in attendance unanimously agreed, and Bill bowed gentlemanly toward Loraine. "In that case, my dear lady, I graciously accept your offer."

Congratulations erupted throughout the room, and Loraine motioned to quiet the gathering again. "Oh! There's more." She smiled. "As you all know, Mr. Crawford is an exceptional artist and photographer." She motioned for him to stand next to her. "There's a large art room in the West Wing that hasn't been used in at least a hundred years. I plan to have that room refurbished for Mr. Crawford, and he will also be an official in-house artist.

Bill was emotionally moved, as Loraine hugged him, and Millie stood up and planted a firm kiss on his cheek.

Loraine then conceded the floor to Sharie, and she motioned one last time for silence. "There's yet, one last issue I'd like to mention." Sharie smiled toward Mary and Mrs. Porter, who sat nearby in traditional black and white maid uniforms with Branchview Staff embroidered on the left front breast portion of the outfit. "Our Mary thought we should revert to the more traditional uniforms once standard for the household staff, and I whole heartily agree." She motioned for them both to stand up. "I think these uniforms restore a sense of pride, and dignity, well deserved within this house."

Mary and Mrs. Porter proudly displayed their new uniforms, while everyone clapped, and Ezekiel responded with a loud whistle, that ushered in another round of laughter. Loraine stood one last time to address everyone.

"Before we conclude, I have some other things I'd like to say" She paused and glanced at everyone. "I consider everyone in this room a part of my family." She emotionally stated. "We are aware of the secret lives of each other, as well as the hidden mysteries that exist within these walls." She paused. "With this in mind, we must continue to uphold that knowledge as sacred, and protect it." Everyone nodded in agreement. "In two days, there will be a full moon, and we all hope for Steven and Charlotte's safe return." She choked up and paused to regain her composure. "But should fate deal with us an alternative outcome, rest assured that life will go on, and we will always remain strong as a family unit."

All stood in a rousing, and respectful ovation. Loraine turned to Sharie with an assured wink. "I believe we've turned a page, and started a new chapter here at Branchview."

"I couldn't agree with you more, Lori."

On the Caribbean Island of Antigua, Poseidon, under the guise of Philip Sheridan, finished his business with the pirates. He sat at a small side table in a pub with Roger McPherson. The two men conversed, drinking mugs of rum, while rowdy, drunken pirates and sailors carried on around them.

Roger reacted sadly to the grim news of his wife's fate. "So, the bastards killed me, Jenny." He remarked, staring down at the hardwood table with stewing anger. "What be the fate of me daughter, Liddy?"

"The last I heard, she was in foster care, and under the custody of a Mrs. Barrow." He curiously gazed at Roger. "I must ask. Do you plan on going back for her?"

Roger stared back, while pondering the question, and tapping his fingers on the tabletop. "Aye! I'll be claiming me daughter, and I'll also be certain to make that bloody town of Lockeport suffer for what they did."

Philip took a large slug from his rum, without taking his eyes off Roger. "I understand you're a practitioner of the dark arts, Mr. McPherson."

"Aye! It always be a fascination to me, Mr. Sheridan." He paused. "However, after marrying Jenny, and starting a family, I'd no intention of ever using it."

"Why didn't you use those powers to escape the ship?"

"Pirates be a superstitious lot. Had I shown even an inkling of my powers, they'd have hung me from the yardarm with them sirens."

"I'd have to guess that under the present circumstances, you might revert back to using those dark powers."

"On that account, you'd be right." Roger sneered. "If it's evil they want, it's evil they'll get."

Philip took a final gulp of rum and abruptly changed the subject, "I've secured passage for you on a

British merchant ship named The Elizabeth Anne. It leaves port at first light."

"I'm much obliged to ye, sir." He nodded. "And the secret ye all have is secure with me."

Philip looked him firmly in the eyes and offered a handshake across the table. As soon as Roger accepted it, he fell into a trance, frozen still in his seat. Without breaking contact with Roger's glassy stare, Philip spoke in a calm, low voice. "When I walk away from this table, you and the others on that ship will not remember me nor the Mermaid goddesses. You personally, will only remember the information I passed onto you about your passage."

With that, Philip let loose of his handgrip and strolled away. Shortly after he departed, Roger snapped from his trance, staring around the pub with confusion. "Aye! The Rum be doing some wicked things to me mind."

He proceeded to hoist an extra-large slug from his mug, before planting it with authority on the table-top.

In the Secret Cave Room, Steven laid resting on a sleigh couch, and staring up at the crystals in the ceiling, as Zeus entered. "So, tell me what's happening in the world above us." Steven chuckled. "I'm dying of boredom down here."

Zeus settled into a nearby seat, "Feel lucky you're below ground, and dry." He sharply commented. "There's been steady rain for two days straight. The Connecticut River has crested, and the swells from the ocean have caused flooding in the streets of Lockeport."

"It appears Jenny's threat was much more serious than anyone may have initially anticipated."

"Perhaps the Council of Elders sided with her on this occasion." Zeus sighed. "Not even my powers can command this vigorous storm." He glanced around the room. "Where's Charlotte?"

"Napping in her room," Steven replied. "Did you hear any further discussion about us in town?"

"I heard talk at the pub about forming a posse to track you down once the weather breaks." He paused with emphasis. "Hopefully we can get you two out of this hellhole of a town before then."

A moment of silent thought passed between the two men. "Do you think Amphitrite and Poseidon will make it back before tomorrow night?" Steven further probed.

"I'd have to say they will. They both can swim long distances at a depth well below the storm." Zeus gave a confident smile and continued. "If not, we'll manage well without them. Maureen will hide you in the stables until the time of departure, while Charlotte remains with Nebriana and Myself. The two of us will do everything in our powers to part the clouds, and enable the moon to shine down at the right moment." Steven only responded with a thought-filled, and worried nod.

Chapter Eighteen:

Into The Spectrum

In the Branchview Study, Loraine attempted to get caught up on some of her work. Reading glasses perched near the tip of her nose, she sat behind the large cherry wood desk and busily typed away on her Apple laptop. The black cat napped atop a cat tree close by, and Bumpers rested loyally at her feet.

Mary entered the open doorway and waited respectfully for Loraine to notice her. Loraine glanced up and removed her glasses. "Hello, Mary! Is everything alright?"

Mary paced toward the desk with her hands humbly cuffed in front of her. "I was hoping I might have a word with you, Ms. Lori."

"Of course!" she gestured to a chair next to the desk. "Please sit down."

Mary took a moment to tickle the purring cat beneath its chin, before sitting down, and Loraine turned her full attention to her. "I meant to say this before, but I had to make sure I was right about it." Mary began.

"Right about what?" Loraine asked with a perplexed expression.

Mary hesitated, then gestured toward the cat. "How long you had that cat here at Branchview?"

"Since shortly after the ordeal." She answered with heightened interest. "She wandered onto the garden terrace while Steven and I were out there one night." She laughed. "I might add she took an immediate shine to Steven."

Mary narrowed her eyes with suspicion. "Was there a full moon that night?"

"As a matter of fact, there was. I fondly remember it was a beautiful night."

Mary gave an enlightened nod and glanced toward the cat, who appeared to be listening attentively from its' perch. She then turned to Loraine and began to recant. "Shortly before that portal took me away, Matthew Branch took in a stray that looked like this one. He called it Midnight."

The cat perked alertly at the mention of the name, and both women took notice. Mary shook her head and continued her story. "That cat was a special one. It had six toes on its' front paw, and a single white spot on its' rear leg." She gestured to the cat again with wide eyes. "That cat has the same markings, Ms. Lori."

Loraine also looked at the cat and appeared stunned. "Are you saying this cat is the same one that Matthew Branch had?"

"Uh-huh!" Mary answered with a slow, sure nod. "I think that portal done took her just as it did me."

Loraine stood up, and approached the cat with curiosity, while Bumpers raised his head in interest.

"Steven and I named her Charlotte." She leaned in toward the cat and addressed it affectionately. "Sweetheart! Is your real name Midnight?"

The cat meowed loudly in response, while Bumpers barked once. The two women exchanged surprised, wide-eyed glances. "That must be why she spends so much time in the East Wing," Loraine commented. "Obviously, that's where Matthew kept her."

"I think that confirms it," Mary responded with certainty.

"I do believe you're right, Mary." She shrugged. "It's obvious that we have a cat that's over one hundred and forty years old."

A chuckling Mary stood up, and once again tickled the cats' chin as she prepared to depart. "Uh-huh!" She nodded. "That old cat and me have a lot in common."

Later that day, as the foyer clock chimed at 7 pm, Loraine slipped on her raincoat and sauntered toward the door.

Bill Crawford, dressed in his spiffy butlers' outfit, entered precisely as she prepared to leave. "Will you be gone for the evening, Mrs. Spencer?"

"No, Bill!" She smiled. "Since the rain finally let up, I've decided to go down by the water for a stroll."

"Perhaps you should let Mr. Sphere or Mr. Seagraves accompany you." He stated with concern. "It'll be dark soon."

"Oh, tit tat! I'll be fine." She grinned with amusement. "And there's no need to address me formally as Mrs. Spencer. You and I are on a first-name basis."

"But I insist!" He exclaimed. "While I'm on duty, it should be the proper way to address the lady of the house."

"Very well! If that's what you prefer, then I shall also address you as Mr. Crawford." She turned to leave but glanced back with a grin. "By the way, you do look quite dignified in your new uniform, Mr. Crawford."

Moments later, Loraine strolled along the pathway through the woods and glanced up at the dark gray, foreboding skies that peeked through the canopy of trees. A sudden, slight breeze shifted the leaves in the treetops, and she paused to take cautious notice.

As she continued, a female voice carried on the breeze in a loud whisper. "Loraine! Loraine Spencer!"

She came to an abrupt halt, and her eyes searched the dense woods that surrounded her. "Who is it addressing me, and what do you want?" She firmly asked, before pausing to wait for an answer.

"Take the footpath to your left, and go to the clearing." The voice instructed. With much apprehension and excessive curiosity, she followed the voices' command.

Back at the Branchview house, Ezekiel, Meryl, Philip, and Tina were all gathered in the Sitting Room for a post-supper conversation. As they all chuckled with amusement, Ezekiel's attention suddenly shifted.

He immediately stood, and listened for a moment, while everyone else became silent. "Darling!" Meryl exclaimed. "Is there something wrong?"

He turned with a baffled expression. "I believe someone is telepathically beckoning me that I haven't spoken to in almost two centuries."

"What part of the world do they need you to traipse off to now?" Meryl inquired with a distressful sigh.

He paused to listen a bit more, then took on a puzzled expression. "It's here! She wants to meet me right here on the Branchview grounds."

"She?" Tina questioned. "Who on earth would that be?"

"It's Nebriana! The queen of the forest fairies!" He exclaimed with surprise. "She's waiting at the clearing in the woods."

Philip quickly stood up, and the women followed suit.

"Do you want me to go with you, Ezekiel?" Philip asked.

"No! I'll go alone." He stated. "She specifically requested to see only me."

"Oh!" Meryl reacted with a haughty grin. "Do I need to be jealous?"

Ezekiel responded with an amused glance. "Keep your jealousy in check, sweetheart. I promise I'll be back shortly."

"If I only had a gold piece for every time you told me that." He kissed her on the cheek and departed with a wink.

As darkness fell swiftly on the clearing of the woods, Loraine arrived, glancing around, and then upward with anxiety at the ever-darkening sky.

"Where are you?" She called out in a trembling voice. "I can feel your presence."

"Look behind you." The voice calmly whispered.

She quickly turned around to find a beautiful apparition in front of her, shrouded in luminescent light. Her fragile wings fluttered as she became more visible, and Loraine was breathless with surprise. "Who, or what exactly are you?" She asked. "A ghost?"

"You have nothing to fear, Loraine. I haven't called you here to harm you." She smiled. "I am Nebriana, immortal queen of the forest faeries."

Loraine immediately broke into nervous laughter. "Faeries? You have to be kidding me."

Nebriana responded boldly with equal amusement. "You've encountered Mermaids, immortal gods, and countless spirits in your life experience, and yet you'd deny the existence of fairies?"

"You do have a valid point." She struggled to keep a straight face. "But how are you aware of who I am?"

"I've observed you from a distance, along with all the other inhabitants of Branchview." She motioned with her hand to everything surrounding them. "I'm the eternal guardian of these woods."

Before another word could be said between them, Ezekiel stepped into the clearing with the beam of his flashlight leading the way.

He immediately shifted to assuming his true identity. "Loraine!" He called out. "You shouldn't be out in these woods after dark."

"Oh! Cool your masculinity, Zeus." Nebriana joked. "She's fine, as long as she's with me."

He moved closer and greeted her with a bow. "You're just as radiant as I remember."

"I believe the last time we spoke was at Gettysburg, during the American Civil War."

"Yes, you were a volunteer field nurse." He sighed. "That was a time I can regretfully never forget."

Loraine listened attentively, while Nebriana handed him an old tattered, and fragile document, tied with a faded red ribbon.

"I've been holding this letter within my care for 323 years."

Zeus accepted it with a clueless expression. He carefully removed the ribbon, and began to read, while Loraine curiously observed. "This is my handwriting." He stated with surprise. "I obviously wrote it, but I don't remember doing so."

"That's because you and the others had to purge your memories to avoid altering the future," Nebriana explained. "As you can see, it concerns the events that will take place tomorrow night and our role in ensuring the successful return of Steven and Charlotte."

Loraine's eyes widened with excitement. "May I read that document?"

Zeus handed the fragile paper to her, and she leaned into the beam of his flashlight, and the glow of Nebriana's aura, to anxiously read it.

"This only says Steven and Charlotte are well at this writing.... you are all working together to help him." She looked up with disappointment. "It says nothing of whether you succeeded."

"That's because neither of us could carry that information into the future," Zeus explained further. "But it mentions the rock in the courtyard as a vital component.

We should clear away the weeds and brush so it's exposed to tomorrow's full moon."

Loraine glanced from one to the other, pleading for more information. "I wish we had more." Nebriana sympathetically added. "That letter has never been read until this moment. I can surely say I only have memory of Zeus asking me to secure it in a safe place until this date."

Zeus laid an assuring hand on Loraine's shoulder. "We can only have faith that we indeed succeeded."

Loraine struggled to hold back tears, and looked to Zeus with extreme disappointment. "I'd like to go back to the house now."

Nebriana expressed great sympathy as they turned to walk away. "Zeus! Wait!" She called out. "May I have a moment alone with Loraine?"

Zeus responded with a nod of approval, and Nebiana moved close to her and lowered her voice to a loud whisper. "Not all my memory from that time was purged." She began. "I can say with absolute certainty that

Steven loves you and the children more than anything in this world."

"He told you that?" Loraine inquired with a renewed sparkle in her eyes.

Nebriana responded with amusement. "He may have been under the influence of the forest nectar, but you are all he could talk about."

"Excuse me! The forest, what?" She responded with a perplexed expression. "Steven doesn't even drink."

"It doesn't matter now." Nebriana chuckled. "Just know that I'm jealous. Myself and Amphitrite both had hoped to capture his heart, but neither of us had a chance against you."

"I shan't be surprised." She replied with a grin. "Amphitrite was deeply in love with him in the future as well."

Nebriana gently cradled her hand. "You must have faith that he will return to you." She assured. "I'm certain we all did everything within our powers to make that a reality."

"Thank you so much," Loraine replied with a warm smile.

"Now that you know I dwell here, I hope you'll come by to visit again."

"I promise I will." She nodded. "I have a feeling that we'll become very good friends."

"And allies," Nebriana added.

Loraine took hold of Zeus' arm and addressed him with a grin. "I'm pleased to be escorted by you, sir."

On a stormy night in 1697, Maureen nervously paced in the old Branch homestead, stopping only to peer out the window into the darkness of the backyard. The rain cascaded down the window-pane in a constant flow, and intermittent lightning flashes lit up the night sky.

Malcolm, who was working by candlelight at his desk across the room, paused to take notice of his daughters' behavior.

"Are you looking for something outside that window, my dear?"

"No father." She calmly answered. "I'm just watching the lightning."

"Be careful!" He chuckled. "St. Elmo's fire can pack a nasty punch."

Beatrice entered from an adjacent room and joined in on the conversation. "This nasty weather is the doing of that witch." She complained. "The river has already crested, and flooded the lowlands, and parts of the town."

"Oh really, Beatrice!" Malcolm snapped. "The poor woman is dead. She cannot harm us from her grave."

Beatrice waved off his comment with a huff and sternly turned her attention to Maureen.

"Young lady! Have you done your evening Bible study?"

"Yes ma'am! Maureen timidly answered, never breaking her stare to the outside.

"Good!" She folded her arms in front of her and stood firm. "I'll expect you to recite the passages to me in the morning before breakfast." She paused to observe her smug daughter. "You should be getting along to bed now. It's getting rather late."

Maureen answered with a simple nod, and promptly departed the room without another word. Malcolm watched until his daughter had trudged completely up the stairs.

"You shouldn't be so hard on that child, Beatrice."

"She needs to be indoctrinated with discipline, lest she fall into the devil's grasp." She proclaimed. "I think you spoil her far too much, Malcolm."

"The devil! The devil!" He exclaimed with much agitation. "You speak so much of the devil that I'd swear he was the master of this household, and not me."

Beatrice flashed a sober glance of warning as the room lit up, and lightning rattled the house.

"Mind your tongue, Malcolm. Lest the Lord strike you dead where you sit."

Malcolm only responded with a frustrated eye roll, and continued with his work while Beatrice marched from the room.

Inside the Secret Cave Room, the countdown had begun for Steven and Charlotte. They impatiently checked the timepieces given to them by Stargazer, while Zeus paced with high anxiety.

"The time is drawing near," Steven announced. "I don't expect Poseidon and Amphitrite will make it back in time."

"You're right, Steven." Zeus agreed. "We can't wait any longer. We must leave now."

Just then, Poseidon and Amphitrite stepped out of the shadows of the room.

"You're not going anywhere without us." Amphitrite proclaimed.

All breathed a sigh of relief and gathered around the returning immortals.

"I trust the pirate issue has been contained?" Zeus inquired.

"For the time being," Poseidon stated. "However, there is another revelation that came to light during our ordeal that should be of great interest to our time-traveling friends." He locked his eyes on Steven and Charlotte before continuing. "We learned that Jenny's husband, Roger McPherson, is alive and well, and on his way to Lockeport as we speak, to collect his daughter." He paused. "I'm sure he'll use his black magic to carry out vengeance for his wife's death."

"That explains how Liddy obtained the powers to carry out her vengeance in the future," Steven commented.

"The plot thickens," Charlotte added with a smirk.

Amphitrite then strolled forward to address them. "It appears you two will be lucky to escape the wrath about to befall this town."

"I wouldn't be so confident yet," Zeus warned. It will take all our combined efforts to part the clouds brought about by Jenny's curse. We have ample time, but we should jump on things."

"Zeus is right!" Poseidon stared in all seriousness. "We should leave now."

Meanwhile, Loraine entered the courtyard in heavy rain gear in 2019. She anxiously looked up at the dark sky, as the rain continued to steadily fall. Ezekiel, also wearing a hooded raincoat, joined her, and lightly rested his hand on her shoulder.

"Tonight, out of all nights. Why should it have to rain?" She turned to Ezekiel with utter frustration. "Is there nothing you can do? You're supposed to be the god who has earthly control over these matters."

"I promise you. We will do everything in our power to clear the weather." He assured. "You must have faith."

A flash of lightning illuminated the courtyard, and they both paused to observe its light show against the dark clouds above.

"The time is drawing near. You should go inside, and wait with the others." He advised. "We can't chance you getting caught up within the portal should it open."

"Thank you for everything, Ezekiel." Loraine lightly kissed him on his cheek.

She then turned, and sadly strolled back toward the house, while Ezekiel sighed, and continued gazing upward in desperation. "May the heavens not forsake us in this hour of need." He murmured.

In a more primitive time, Steven calmed the restless horses within the Branch stables, as Maureen entered. She stood at the large sliding door in her nightclothes, soaking wet, and shivering. "Steven!" She called out in a loud whisper. "Are you here?"

Steven stepped out from the dark shadows of one of the horse stalls and looked toward the shivering young girl with concern. "You should've worn a coat, Maureen. You'll catch pneumonia in this damp weather."

"I had to sneak from the house. I didn't have time."

He quickly removed his somewhat dry overcoat, wrapping it around her, "I must be sure that you live in order to carry the Branch legacy into the future."

As the two conversed, Cameron Locke sauntered in through the partially open door, brandishing an enormous dueling sword. Theodore timidly followed behind him.

"And what future do you speak of, Mr. Spencer?" Cameron inquired in a sarcastic tone.

"This is no concern of yours, Cameron." Maureen interrupted.

Cameron arrogantly strolled closer, while Theodore remained at a safe distance. "Oh! But it is my concern, Maureen." He subtly gestured to Steven. "You're harboring the man who killed my father, and who is also a British spy." He grinned. "If you haven't noticed, he's somehow lost his British accent."

"I didn't kill your father, and I'm certainly not a spy." Steven sincerely responded.

"Then, who exactly are you, Mr. Spencer." He laughed. "I'm just dying to know."

Steven reluctantly glanced at Maureen, then back toward Cameron. "That future that you heard me speak of concerns both our families." He hesitates. "I am the offspring of both the Branch and Locke lineage. I've mistakenly traveled here from the year 2019, and I'm trying desperately to get back to my own time."

"And what about that beautiful wife of yours, and your sister?" He curiously inquired. "Are they also time travelers?"

"That's another story," Steven stated with impatience. "Maureen can fill you in on the details later, but right now, I'm very short on time."

Cameron blurted out laughing, then just as quickly, he turned serious, and aimed his sword within an inch of Steven's throat.

"There's one thing I hate more than the bloody Brits, and that's a liar." He sneered. "You are right about being short on time. I have the mind to run you through right now, and be over with it."

"He's telling the truth, Cameron!" Maureen pleaded. "He truly is my blood relative, and a direct offspring of you." She emotionally continued. "If you kill him, you kill the future of our families."

Cameron's eyes nervously darted between Maureen and Steven. "He's brainwashed you!" He exclaimed. "It's all lies!" He steadied his sword, and the tip touched Steven's throat. "Prepare to die, you lousy Brit!"

Steven's eyes suddenly flared red, and he roared ferociously at Cameron. The young man reeled backward in fear, and Theodore took refuge behind a nearby pile of straw. At the same moment, Malcolm Branch stood in the entrance, pointing his flintlock pistol directly at Steven. Beatrice stood behind him with an expression of horror on her face.

"My eyes truly do not deceive what I've just witnessed," Malcolm stated. "Who, or what are you, Steven Spencer?"

Beatrice abruptly chimed in, pointing an accusing finger. "He's an agent of Satan, who works in concert with the witch. That's why he and his wife visited her in prison."

"No!" Maureen emotionally exclaimed. "He's our relative from 2019, if you don't allow him to leave right now, he'll never return to his time."

"Stay out of this, Maureen!" Malcolm commanded.

Suddenly, the driving rain ceased, and all paused to take notice of the silence outside.

"She's telling the truth!" Steven proclaimed. "The rains have stopped, and the clouds will make way for the full moon. If I'm not near that rock when the portal opens, I'll be left behind."

"He speaketh of the cursed rock." Beatrice trembled with contempt. "He's surely a demon! Kill him!"

"Wait!" Cameron tossed his sword aside. "I believe he might be telling the truth." His eyes darted between the two men. "Let him go, Mr. Branch."

"How can you say such a thing?" Malcolm questioned. "This man killed your father."

"No! He didn't!" Theodore nervously spoke up as he stepped from behind the straw pile. "I killed him! It was an accident!"

Malcolm glanced toward him with disbelief. "What about the fire?"

"That must've been the curse of the witch." He anxiously shrugged. "Spirits of the dead ascended on the house, and the fire exploded all around us. We were lucky to escape with our own lives."

Malcolm's eyes shifted to Cameron, while still aiming the flintlock at Steven. "Is this the truth?"

"Yes!" Cameron stated with exuberance. "I lied to protect Theodore."

"All this is nonsense!" Beatrice charged. "He's put the children under his spell." She forcibly reached for her husband's gun. "Allow me to do the Lord's will, and let me kill this demon myself."

Malcolm pulled away, but she still struggled for the gun. Suddenly it discharged wildly and struck Theodore in the stomach. Cameron ran to his brother's side, and looked up with anger at Beatrice, while everyone else looked on with shock.

"Look what you've done, you fanatical lunatic!" Cameron screamed. "I'll personally make sure you pay dearly for this."

Steven also rushed to the boys' side, "Let me help."

"No, Steven!" Maureen warned. "You have to go now, or the portal will close."

"She's right, Mr. Spencer!" Cameron agreed. "Run now, before it's too late."

Both Malcolm and Beatrice held a firm stance at the entrance to the barn.

"You aren't going anywhere tonight, Mr. Spencer." Malcolm boldly declared.

Steven stood, and countered with rising anger. "You need time to reload that flintlock, Mr. Branch." He sneered, "Just try to stop me." He bolted directly toward them, tossing them both aside as if they were nothing.

Outside, he ran swiftly past the house and set his sight on the field, and the rock behind it. He desperately glanced upward, as the moon began to peep through the clouds.

His heart pounded heavily with anxiety. "Oh, Lord! Don't let me be late."

His foot caught a hole, and he quickly tumbled forward to the ground, awkwardly twisting his knee. He screamed and writhed in pain as he grabbed hold of his injured body part. He then glanced ahead with determination to where the portal had just started to open. Light beams now showered down on the spot where Charlotte was standing.

"Hurry, Steven!" She cried out.

He struggled to his feet and began painfully hobbling toward the portal, while Charlotte anxiously watched. "He's not going to make it." She commented to herself as she gazed upward. "Almighty God, please grant me the power to make this work."

Without another moment of hesitation, she raised her hands toward Steven, who was still several feet away, when the portal began to close in on her. "Fly like a bird!" She commanded. Steven shape-shifted into a nighthawk and soared directly into the portal just as it closed.

The closing left a momentary flash of blinding light in its' wake, followed by dead silence. Malcolm and Beatrice arrived on the scene just in time to witness it and stood shell shocked by the occurrence.

"God in heaven!" Beatrice blessed herself. "What did we just witness?"

"I don't know." Malcolm stared cluelessly into the now dark field. "But there is one thing for certain." He paused with emphasis. "None of us are to ever speak of this night's events again."

Maureen hurried onto the scene, seething with anger as she confronted her parents. From the dark shadows of the tree line, the gods, Amphitrite, Nebriana, and the Woods People all silently observed. "That was too close for comfort." Amphitrite sighed. "Without Charlotte, Steven would've never made it."

Zeus also distressfully sighed, while the clouds once more enveloped the moon, and sprinkles of rain began to fall again. "And, so it begins." He stated. "The events of this night will eventually touch the lives of us all."

"I wish there was something more we could've done," Nebriana replied with frustration.

"It's not within our duties to alter fate, Nebriana," Poseidon advised. "We must purge our memories of all these things as soon as possible."

"The sooner we all do that, the better," Zeus added as he turned to Nebriana. "I trust you secured that letter in a safe place."

"The Woods People and the Green Man have placed it in a secret place." She assured.

"Very well!" Zeus concluded with a firm nod. "We shall all proceed to the clearing, and perform what must be done."

In the present Branchview courtyard, the darkness was shattered with a blinding light. In its' wake, a dazed Charlotte laid on her back on the grassy portion, near the fountain.

As her eyes were still closed, an energetic Irish Setter dog ran to her side and licked her face. "Eww!" She reacted with displeasure as she came to her senses. "Where did that dog come from?"

The dog took off, and raced around the courtyard with excitement, while Philip and Ezekiel ran to Charlotte's aid.

Charlotte sat up and desperately searched the surrounding area. "Where's Steven? I know he made it before the portal closed."

The dog ran to the edge of the fountain pond and started to bark. All three noticed and hurried over, where they found Steven face down, at the bottom of the pond. "I'll get him!" Philip yelled, as he quickly jumped in.

He retrieved Steven's limp body and carried him to the edge, where Ezekiel immediately began CPR. They all worked frantically to revive him, while Loraine and the others hurried to the scene from inside the house. "No! No! No!" She cried as she knelt next to him. "Oh, please! Don't let him be dead."

Finally, Steven began to revive, and cough uncontrollably. Ezekiel turned him on his side so he could spit the water out from his lungs.

He began breathing heavily as he slowly came around. "He's back among the living once again," Ezekiel announced with a relieved smile.

"Oh! Thank God!" Loraine exclaimed as she stared upward.

Steven blinked his eyes at Loraine as she hovered over him, and he struggled to talk. "You're the person I'd hoped to see when I opened my eyes." He weakly commented.

"Yes, sweetheart!" Loraine emotionally stated. "You're finally back home."

"I love you so much." He said with a weak smile.

"Oh, Steven! I love you more than you'll ever know."

Charlotte turned away with tears in her eyes, while Philip and Ezekiel intervened on the couple's reunion. "We need to get him inside, and into some dry clothes." Philip directed with urgency.

They tried to help him to his feet, but his injured knee gave out, and he let out an agonizing groan that caused everyone to cringe. "I suppose I blew my knee out before I went into the portal." Steven painfully explained.

The men anchored him on each side and helped him along, and into the house. A young man, around the age of 19, dressed in casual gentlemen's attire from the late 1800s, wandered over to Charlotte and appeared somewhat puzzled. "Is the other gentleman going to be alright?" He asked with great concern.

"He's a bit roughed up, but he should be fine," Charlotte replied, looking at him with clueless curiosity. "Who are you, and how exactly did you, and that dog get on the grounds?"

"I should be asking you the same thing." He remarked indignantly, before glancing around with confusion. "Who are all these people, and why are they wearing such strange clothes?"

"My name is Charlotte Locke, and I think you need to answer me before I tell you anything else."

"Very well!" He settled his demeanor a bit. "My name is Frederick Ainsworth." His expression turned awkward. "As I recall, the Locke's were no longer welcome here at Branchview."

The dog ran up to him, and he went down to one knee to attend to it. "There, there, boy! You need to settle yourself."

"Now, please tell me how you and that dog got here." Charlotte impatiently requested.

"It was rather strange, actually." Frederick recanted. "I chased Finn here into a room in the East Wing. There was a sudden flash of light, and I woke up moments later on the ground over there."

Charlotte sighed, and looked upward with enlightenment. "I do believe you need to come inside with me, young man. You and I have quite a bit to discuss."

Chapter Nineteen:

Emotional Scars

A short time later, the foyer clock struck at 1 am, and the household was still alive, and bustling with excitement as they celebrated the long-anticipated return of Steven and Charlotte from 1697. Everyone pitched in to help as they carried extra chairs to the Sitting Room. Unfortunately, rest would not come soon enough for the returning heir of the estate. For he now faced a new challenge with the unexpected arrival of a young man and his dog, who were among the ever-growing list of innocent victims claimed by the portal of time.

In the Branchview Study, Philip and Ezekiel helped a visibly worn Steven onto his comfortable desk chair. He had since changed from his wet, archaic clothes of 1697, and was now comfortably dressed in his pajamas and robe. Ironically, the same type of attire he wore when he disappeared.

Loraine and Mrs. Porter observed with great concern as Ezekiel examined Steven's injured knee. "I'm certainly no physician, but I believe you may have damaged the ligaments." He declared. "It is quite inflamed."

"I think there's a pair of crutches in the attic." Mrs. Porter stated. "I can bring them down if you'd like."

"That would be fine, Mrs. Porter," Loraine replied.

Philip pushed an ottoman from an adjacent chair, and carefully propped Steven's leg onto it. "You should keep that elevated as much as possible."

"I'll hurry, and prepare an ice bag for that swelling, and I'll grab those crutches as well." Mrs. Porter further stated. "Can I get you anything else, Steven?"

"Yes, Mrs. Porter! You can!" Steven answered with desperation. "I'm dying for a good cup of coffee. Could you have Suzy prepare a pot of her infamous City Diner brew?"

"I'm sure that girl is a step ahead on that already." She laughed. "I'll hurry back."

"Suffering from a caffeine deficiency?" Philip inquired with a chuckle.

"Totally!" Steven replied. "Imagine my shock in finding that coffee didn't exist in 17th century America."

"I'm surprised you survived." Loraine joked.

Steven glanced anxiously around the room and went into a sudden panic. "Where's Charlotte?"

"She's fine!" Loraine assured. "She being attended to in the Sitting Room. You've both been through an arduous ordeal."

Just then, Charlotte hurried into the room as Loraine spoke. "If you only knew the half of it, Lori." She commented before turning her attention to Steven. "Thank God, you're alright, Steven."

She rushed to his side and took hold of his hand. "You saved my life, Charlotte." He emotionally stated. "Without you, I would've been left behind in that terrible period of time."

"I could've never abandoned my precious nephew." She smiled.

They embraced emotionally, while the others in the room savored the moment. "I'm certain you two have a few stories to tell," Ezekiel stated.

"Indeed!" Charlotte replied. "I can't wait for you to hear what a troublesome pain in the butt you were in that century."

All reacted with an amused smile, while Ezekiel was visibly less enthused. "There'll be ample time for stories later." Philip proclaimed. "Right now, I think Steven and Lori deserve a bit of private time."

"First, I think I should give you all a heads up," Charlotte announced. "We have an unexpected visitor who's in the Sitting Room as we speak. It appears he and his dog arrived through the portal along with us. He claims he's from 1885, and has no clue he's in 2019."

"Someone needs to break the sobering news to him," Loraine commented.

"Oh, I tried!" Charlotte answered, "He's a strong-headed young man that isn't easily persuaded."

"There's one thing for certain," Ezekiel added. "We must not let him leave this house until he is convinced of the truth."

While chairs were positioned in the Sitting Room for the meeting, Frederick curiously examined a table lamp, as Sharie stood, and observed close by. "Astounding!" He exclaimed while gesturing to Sharie. "Edison's theory of electric current worked."

"Apparently!" Sharie answered in a matter-of-fact tone.

"The Branch's must have the prototypes." He continued with much excitement, while his eyes scanned the room. "As well as many other interesting things that I strangely can't remember seeing."

"I wanted to make you aware that I placed your dog in the mudroom for the time being," Sharie mentioned. "I also gave him some food and fresh water."

He gave a bow of respect toward her. "I'll make certain to tip you for that service as soon as I can retrieve my money clip from my room in the East Wing."

"I'm afraid that won't be possible." She rolled her eyes. "We've had to arrange temporary accommodations for you in the West Wing."

"With the servants?" He responded indignantly.

"It's no longer the Servants' Wing." She uneasily responded. "I'm sorry, but I'll need to escort you there now. The family is preparing for a meeting."

"At this hour?" He blurted out in a loud voice that made everyone take notice. "This is outrageous! I demand to see Caroline and her father immediately."

Mary casually entered the room, and Frederick immediately took notice of her. "I recognize that servant." He lowered his voice. "Why is it that I don't know anyone else?" He stared intently at Sharie. "I demand some sort of explanation!"

He impatiently turned his attention back to Mary. "You there!" He commanded. "Come hither!" He waited as Mary sauntered over without urgency. "I remember you served tea and cookies to Lady Caroline and me earlier today. I demand you tell me where the Branch family has gone."

"I see you're still the same uppity, and demanding young man I remember." She grunted.

"I beg your pardon!" He defiantly stated. "It's highly inappropriate for a Negro servant to speak to someone of my stature in such a manner. I'll see to it that Mr. Branch is immediately made aware of this."

Mary and Sharie rolled their eyes and exchanged a long glance. "It's obvious that this young man doesn't share the same political views as the rest of us," Sharie responded with a withering tolerance that set Frederick into a mild rage.

"How dare you insult my politics!" He angrily charged. "I come from a family of proud Connecticut Democrats."

"Why am I not surprised?" Sharie quipped with amusement. "I have a feeling this will be quite a challenge."

"It's okay, Sharie!" Mary intervened. "I'll try to explain everything to him the best I can."

"Explain what?" He demanded.

Mary soberly looked him square in the eyes.

"You may not want to believe this, but you and I have lots in common, and it must do with that room in the East Wing."

Frederick was visibly taken aback by her statement. "I don't understand what you're trying to say."

Mary motioned for him to follow. "Come along! I'll show you to your quarters, and attempt to explain on the way."

"And I'll bring the dog to your room shortly," Sharie added.

As Mary escorted a bewildered Frederick from the room, the black cat strolled in from the foyer, and Frederick enthusiastically pointed to it. "That cat!" He cried out. It belongs to Matthew Branch." He stared at the two women with desperate eyes. "Its' name is Midnight."

Both Mary and Sharie paused to listen with keen interest. "Finn chased it into that room in the East Wing, and I followed." Both women shared an enlightened gaze as they watched the cat saunter comfortably about the room.

A short time later, everyone was finally congregated in the Sitting Room, as Steven hobbled in on crutches, accompanied by Loraine. Everyone clapped and cheered as he made his way to a seat in the front.

Bill, dressed in his uniform, took the crutches, then helped him settle into the chair, while Loraine set a fresh cup of coffee on the end table next to him. "I'll set these crutches aside for right now, sir."

"There's no need to be so formal, Bill." Steven laughed. "We're all on a first-name basis here."

"Not while I'm on duty, sir." He nodded with a grin.

"Nice threads, by the way," Steven commented while looking him up and down. "I hope you didn't get all dressed up for me."

"It's my uniform." He stated with pride. "I'm now the butler here at Branchview."

Steven looked to Loraine with a perplexed expression. "You weren't fooling when you said a lot has happened here since I've been gone."

"You don't even know the half of it." Loraine sighed.

Gerard stood up to address the gathering first. "I know it's a late hour, but we've waited a long time for this moment." He motioned to Steven and continued. "With great pleasure, I wholeheartedly welcome Steven and Charlotte back to our beloved Branchview family."

All applauded as Gerard yielded attention to Steven, who sat casually, with his knee propped up. "Thank you all." He paused to scan the gathering. "I can't begin to tell you how good it is to be back home in the 21st Century." He began. "And how good it is to enjoy a pleasant cup of coffee." Everyone laughed. "I'd like to say with certainty that this moment would've never been possible had it not been for Charlotte." He glanced toward her with great admiration and tipped his coffee cup toward her. "I'll be forever indebted to her."

Steven glanced toward the door, where Mary and Sharie quietly entered, and took a seat next to Mrs. Porter. All three women were dressed in their spiffy new uniforms. He smiled toward them and continued.

"I noticed the changes that have taken place in the short time I've been gone." He looked to Loraine with a wink. "It seems my wonderful wife has transformed the house into a modern-day version of Downton Abbey."

All laughed, while Steven searched each face in attendance, and paused at Tony and Andrea. "I'd like to congratulate the Freeman's on the birth of baby Michael, and for contributing yet another baby to our Branchview Nursery." He smiled and gave the couple an assuring wink. "If this onslaught of newcomers continues, we may have to expand the present Nursery room."

Tina timidly raised her hand and stood. "I'm afraid, perhaps we may need to make that a reality very soon, Steven."

Philip glanced at her with great surprise. "Tina! Are you telling us that you're?"

She rapidly, and joyfully nodded. "I just found out this morning. We're going to have a baby."

Philip lovingly kissed, and embraced his wife, as everyone cheered, and applauded.

Millie nudged Meryl's arm and whispered,

"Perhaps you and Ezekiel will be next." Ezekiel overheard and looked to Meryl with wide eyes. A stern, sober stare met his glance, which caused him to quickly look away.

Charlotte sat silently, with a forced smile, in the aftermath of the joyous announcement. Her emotions eventually overcame her, and she had to flee the room. Loraine watched with much concern as she swiftly departed.

She pondered the reason for her departure, as Steven continued. "I must say!" That joyous announcement is a tough act to follow." He glanced around the room inquisitively. "Before I continue, does anyone else have anything they'd like to contribute?"

Suzy raised her hand and stood. "I'd like to announce the City Diner will have its' grand reopening this coming Monday morning. I hope all of you will stop in."

"I can assure you Steven and I will be there when you open the door." Philip proclaimed.

"Count me in as well," Ezekiel added.

"I'd also like to announce that repairs are complete on my house." She continued. "I should be moving back in by the end of next week." She looked to Steven and Loraine with much gratitude. "I'd like to thank you, and everyone else, for letting me stay here at Branchview, and for treating me like a member of the family."

"You are part of our family, Suzy," Loraine spoke enthusiastically. "Don't ever forget that."

Steven agreed as he tipped his coffee cup toward her with a mischievous grin. "Of course, you could pay me back with a lifetime of free coffee at the Diner."

"That would drive me into the poor house." She jokingly replied as she sat back down.

All were amused, and Steven drew a weary sigh as he moved the meeting along. "It's a late hour for all of us, and we should be turning in for the night." He paused. "We'll have more than enough time to catch up in the coming days. I'm certain of that."

Before he could conclude, Frederick barged back into the room and interrupted. "Enough of this little masquerade." He announced. "I demand someone tell me where Caroline, her mother, father, and all the others have gone."

"Good grief!" Steven muttered to Loraine under his breath. "Keep the bed warm. This may take a while."

"That's alright." She answered. "There's someone else I need to check in on."

Steven reluctantly motioned to Frederick. "Mr. Ainsworth! I think you and I need to have a serious talk." He glared at him with intensity. "Meet me in the Main Study."

Loraine wandered onto the veranda garden and spotted Charlotte sitting in the gazebo, sadly weeping.

She swiftly strolled over to console her, "There, there, my dear!" She exclaimed with great sympathy, as she lovingly embraced her. "Tell me what's troubling you."

"I can't!" She protested with much embarrassment. "I don't think you'd understand."

"Oh, Charlotte! You and I have been through so much in this past year." She paused. "Both good and bad." She rolled her eyes and grinned with amusement. "You can talk to me about anything."

Charlotte wiped away her tears and tried to regain her composure. "I feel so foolish." She paused with emphasis. "I fell in love with someone dear to both of us while I was in 1697." She shook her head. "I never saw it coming."

"It wasn't Steven? Was it?"

Charlotte managed a chuckle, and shook her head, while Loraine further pondered cluelessly. "The only other people we know existed in 1697 were..." She took on an enlightened expression. "Was it Poseidon?"

Charlotte reluctantly nodded yes, and began to cry again, prompting Loraine to pull her closer into her embrace. "How in the world could you have let that happen?"

Charlotte gently pulled away, hyperventilating as she talked. "He fell in love with me first, but knowing the future, I discouraged anything from happening."

"And, when he and Tina shared their joyful news, you realized you were still in love with him."

"I think I actually knew long before that," Charlotte added.

"Well! You did the right thing." Loraine reasoned with a caring smile. "Even if Tina weren't in the picture, it would never work out. You must return to the spirit world, while Philip continues to live among us."

Charlotte glanced up at the full moon that now shined through the parting clouds and reflected sadly. "Throughout my life, and beyond, I've watched others fall in love, and find happiness." She paused emotionally. "But somehow, that same love and happiness has always had a way of eluding me." She distressfully shook her head. "It truly doesn't seem fair."

Loraine stroked a comforting hand through Charlotte's raven locks, while tears emotionally welled in her own eyes. "Oh, sweetheart!" She exclaimed. "You must know that I love you dearly, just as I do the others in this household." She looked her straight in the eyes and gave an assuring nod. "You earned that love, and I'm confident that in your next lifetime, you will find that romance you seek, and more happiness than you could ever imagine."

"After all the evil I've done in my life, do you believe I'll have a chance at another lifetime?" Charlotte sighed.

"I do not doubt it for one minute." She emotionally stated. "We have a merciful creator that knows your heart even more than you do."

Charlotte forced a sad smile. "Steven is so lucky to have you."

"Just be sure to remind him of that as many times as possible before you leave."

They both laughed and emotionally embraced. "You and I need to get some rest, my dear," Loraine advised. "We can talk much more tomorrow."

In the Branchview Study, Frederick patiently sat, and waited as Steven hobbled in on his crutches. Bill followed him in, carrying a fresh cup of coffee, and set it on the coaster of his desk.

"Can I get anything else for you before I turn in for the night?"

Steven waved him off and wearily shook his head. "It's been a long day for all of us, Bill...er Mr. Crawford." He corrected himself with a sigh. "Please! Go get some sleep. I can manage on my own."

Bill answered with a caring nod and departed. Steven then hobbled over to the bookcase and chose a journal from the shelf. With a pained effort, he then settled into the comfort of his desk chair, glancing at Frederick before opening the journal.

"What I'm about to reveal to you might come as a rather sobering shock." He stated. "But you need to take it as truth, and accept it."

"All I'm asking for is answers." Frederick wearily replied.

Steven ran his finger over the pages until he reached the spot he was searching for, then paused to go over it before reading it out loud. "Caroline Branch married Charles Dewhurst in the summer of 1890." He glanced up with a raised eyebrow before continuing. "Mr. Dewhurst was a wealthy industrialist from Detroit. They had three children, and Caroline died in February 1943 at the age of 76. She's buried in the Dewhurst family plot in Bay City, Michigan.

Steven closed the book, and looked up with a sigh, while Frederick could only react with confusion and anxiety.

"How can that be true? I was just with her earlier this evening." He shook his head with frustration.

"I know," Steven replied with sympathy. "Obviously just before you chased the dog into that room in the East Wing." He glanced downward in a moment of thought. "At that moment, you died." He paused. "Or to put it more clearly, you ceased to exist in that time."

Frederick looked away in horror. "Then that servant, Mary, was telling the truth."

Steven gave an assured nod and took a sip of his coffee.

"Let me explain this the best I can." He leaned forward. "You entered into a time portal that brought you here at the moment that Charlotte and I returned from the year 1697."

"Pray, tell me then! What year are we actually in now, Mr. Spencer?"

"Believe it or not. Just as Charlotte told you. It's the year 2019."

The revelation devastated Frederick. But after a moment of deep thought, he looked to Steven with a glimmer of hope.

"You and Ms. Charlotte traveled through time and came back. "Why can't I do the same?"

Steven took a deep breath before answering. "Charlotte and I traveled back to a time before we existed, and we were careful not to alter history." He reasoned. "You, however, traveled to the future." He locked his eyes seriously onto Frederick and continued. "For you to go back from where you came, would only disrupt everything that has naturally occurred in the years since"

Frederick cast his eyes downward in a disappointing stare. "I know Ms. Charlotte tried to tell me all this." He paused. "I truly didn't want to believe it." He shut his eyes as he digested the truth. "This is beyond the worst nightmare anyone could ever have."

"I know," Steven answered with a sigh, "But I promise I'll do everything I can to help you out." He offered a sympathetic smile and tapped Frederick lightly on the shoulder. "We'll talk more about this in the coming days." He concluded with an assured nod." Just be patient."

Frederick reluctantly answered with a quick nod, and rose from his seat with a befuddled, and defeated expression. "I guess I'll go back to my room now, Mr. Spencer."

"Mrs. Porter will ring the bell for breakfast, and she'll keep it warm until around 10 am," Steven stated. "And just so you know. In this century, we don't refer to our help as servants."

The table clock nearby chimed at 3:30 AM, and they both paused to take notice. "I'm afraid we won't get much sleep tonight," Frederick remarked.

"Unfortunately, not," Steven concluded.

Frederick turned before exiting the room. "Time is certainly a mysterious, and cruel part of our lives." He paused. "Isn't it, Mr. Spencer?"

"Yes, Mr. Ainsworth. It most certainly is."

A short time later, Steven arrived at the base of the stairs and switched off the foyer light.

He gazes upward at his impending climb and whispered to himself. "This should be a challenge."

He tucked the crutches under one arm, and leaned heavily on the railing with the other. He then began hopping painfully on one leg, one step at a time.

When he finally arrived at the first landing, he paused to catch his breath and glanced up at the stern-faced portrait of Beatrice Branch that hung on the wall. He recalled all too well, her intimidating glare. In an uncharacteristic display of anger and frustration, he pulled the picture from the wall and smashed it to pieces on the knob of the banister.

He stood breathing heavily, as he stared down at the now destroyed painting that seemed to still stare back at him through a single intimidating eye. He collapsed with exhaustion onto the ascending stairs and emotionally wept.

Chapter Twenty:

New Beginnings

It was a short night's sleep for the inhabitants of the Great House. Frederick was the first to answer the breakfast bell and now sat at the large dining table by himself. While he stared into the cup of tea he cradled in his hand, his dog Finn kept loyal vigil at his feet.

Steven hobbled into the room on his crutches, with both Bumpers and the black cat following. The unexpected showdown between the pets set off a loud flurry of barking, while the cat humped its' back, and hissed.

Frederick held Finn back by his collar, and attempted to settle the dog down, while Mrs. Porter quickly ambled in from the kitchen, covering her ears, with Mary close behind her. "Good grief!" She yelled. "This house is turning into a kennel."

She hurried over and helped Frederick calm his dog, while Mary tried to help Steven control Bumpers and the cat. "I'll take this rascal out to the mudroom." Mrs. Porter scowled, shaking her head as they exited.

"I'll try to round up these two critters, and take em to another part of the house," Mary added.

Bill hurried in from another room when he heard all the ruckus. "Well! If there was anyone else in the house that wanted to sleep in, I can guarantee they're awake now."

He scooped up the cat, while Mary grabbed Bumpers, and they swiftly departed. Steven waited for things to settle, then turned to Frederick with an eye roll. "There's never a dull moment around here."

"Some things never change." Frederick chuckled.

Steven hobbled the rest of the way to the table and plopped down in a chair at the head of the table. "Good morning, Mr. Ainsworth." He propped his injured leg up on another chair. "I didn't expect to see you up and around this early."

"I'm sure you understand that I didn't sleep well," Frederick replied with visible self-pity.

"Believe me!" He gestured toward his knee. "I didn't sleep well myself."

An awkward silence fell between the two men as Frederick pondered what to say next. "How long have you had that cat, Mr. Spencer?"

"At least a few months." He shrugged. "She just wandered up to me in the garden one night."

"Two months!" He exclaimed. "How can that be?" He questioned. "She entered the portal at the same moment as Finn and I."

The situation equally baffled Steven, "Perhaps it had something to do with where the cat was situated in the room when the portal opened. Were you and Finn at the same spot?"

"I had just grabbed hold of his collar when the light flashed."

Steven shrugged again, "I guess that partially solves the mystery."

Mrs. Porter returned from the kitchen with a fresh carafe of coffee, and Steven eagerly raised his empty cup. "I'll explain that later when I understand it better myself."

"I certainly hope that's the last outburst we get today from those rascals." Mrs. Porter grumbled. "The scrambled eggs, hash browns, and fruit salad will be out shortly."

"Bless you, Mrs. Porter! This will be heaven compared to what I had to eat and drink in 1697."

She looked Steven up and down as she topped off Frederick's teacup. "We'll definitely need to fatten you up a bit."

Both men shared a chuckle as she scampered back to the kitchen again. "She's a gruff old girl," Frederick commented.

"With a heart of gold." Steven gestured with his coffee cup.

Frederick settled back in his seat with great ponderance. "I wondered if the help could prepare me a horse and carriage?" He inquired. "I'd like to travel up to Springfield to see what's become of my homestead, and my father's textile mill."

"I don't think you want to go anywhere on your own until you're used to this modern world." Steven cautiously replied.

"I can't just sit around this house." He stated indignantly.

"I can take you up to Springfield sometime tomorrow." Steven sighed. "Today, I need to have a doctor look at this knee."

Philip casually strolled in on the conversation with a newspaper tucked underneath his arm. "I couldn't agree more, Steven." He took a seat at the table. "I'll drive you over there after breakfast."

Frederick continued to cast a puzzling glare toward Steven. "Surely, you're aware that Springfield is nearly a half-day trip from here, Mr. Spencer."

Steven shared an amused glance with Philip before he answered. "Actually, in today's world, it's only about an hour and a half drive." He chuckled. "We haven't traveled by horse and carriage for quite some time."

His statement befuddled Frederick. "I don't understand what you're saying."

"Trust me, and prepare yourself." Steven smiled. "You're in for an awakening."

Steven's cell phone rang, causing Frederick to jump in his seat. Steven set it on the tabletop and switched it to the speaker. Frederick was completely baffled when he saw Steven speak into it. "Yes, sweetheart!"

Frederick was even more taken aback when the device answered him. "Steven!" Loraine shouted from the other end. "Where in the world are you?"

"I'm down at the breakfast table, dear."

"Oh, thank heavens!" She replied. "You weren't here when I woke up, and I went into a complete panic." Her loud sigh brought a grin to Steven's face. "I'll be down shortly, dear. I love you!"

"I love you too!"

Philip found amusement in the call, while Frederick stared at the cell phone with baffled curiosity.

"What in the blazes is that device?"

"That, my friend, is what we call a cell phone," Steven replied. "It's a wireless version of the telephone."

"Brilliant!" Frederick proclaimed with wonderment. "The telephone had only recently been invented in the period I came from. This advanced version is hard for me to comprehend."

"Hang onto your seat." Philip joked. "There's plenty more strange surprises to come."

Loraine hurried into the room and immediately rushed to Steven. She draped her arms around his neck and planted a solid kiss on his lips that even raised the eyebrows of the other men at the table. "Don't you ever leave our bed without telling me where you're going?" She commanded. "I was a total rack of nerves."

"The boss hath spoken, Steven." Philip jokingly remarked.

Just then, Bill re-entered the room again, and approached with politeness and candor. "Excuse me, everyone! I noticed the picture on the stair landing suffered an unfortunate mishap sometime during the night. I could attempt to repair it if you'd wish."

Stevens' face grew flush with rising anger and frustration. "I'd rather wish you'd burn the damn thing." He declared. "I don't ever want to see that horrid witch's face in this house ever again."

Everyone was taken aback and silently exchanged concerned, baffled expressions at his unusual outburst. Just as quickly, Steven reacted with embarrassment over his explosive tirade.

"I'm sorry everyone." He stammered. "Especially to you, Bill. I know you meant well." He paused. "I'm afraid I'm still a bit on edge and emotionally drained." He rose from his seat and retrieved his crutches. "Could you please ask Mrs. Porter to bring my breakfast to the study?"

Without another word, he hobbled from the room. After he was out of earshot, Bill turned to Loraine with a bewildered expression. "Did I say something wrong, Mrs. Spencer?"

"Not at all, Mr. Crawford." She replied with distress. "I'm afraid he may still be fighting some demons he battled in 1697." She forced a sad, worried smile. "We just have to be patient while he mentally heals."

Inside the Main Study, Charlotte sat at the desk looking through an enormous old journal with yellowed, and brittle pages. Steven entered, and was surprised to see her there. "It appears curious minds think alike." He stated as he hobbled over to sit in a side chair.

"I saw what was left of Beatrice Branch's picture when I came downstairs this morning." She commented with a scolding glance. "I helped Mr. Crawford clean up the mess."

Steven gestured toward the book, hoping to dismiss the unpleasant subject of the picture. "What became of that witch of a woman?"

"She died of the smallpox epidemic that struck Lockeport in the winter of 1698," Charlotte replied.

"That was too good of a death for her." He scoffed. "She should've hung from the gallows like Jenny McPherson."

Charlotte stared back at him with much sympathy for an interminable moment. "This behavior is unusual of you Steven, and I must say it troubles me."

"You know what that woman did." He maintained. "She killed poor, innocent Theodore."

"Yes, I know." She placed a caring hand over his. "But please, don't allow hate and vengeance to tarnish your soul as it did mine."

Steven reluctantly nodded, and motioned again to the book. "What about the others?" He inquired. "What became of them?"

Charlotte set her attention back toward the book and recanted what she had previously read. "Malcolm Branch died five years later of natural causes, and his sons joined forces with Cameron Locke to build a thriving business. Cameron died in 1768 at the age of 88." She leaned back in her chair and grinned before continuing. "As for our girl Maureen, she did quite well for herself." She beamed. "She moved to New York City, married a rich entrepreneur, wrote novels, had 5 children, and died in 1777 at the ripe old age of 93.

A smile broke on Steven's face. "She lived to see this country gain its' independence."

Charlotte closed the book and tilted her chin confidently. "And knowing that, I think we need to close this painful chapter and move on."

In the now crowded Dining Room, all the inhabitants of the house had now made their way to the breakfast table. As everyone conversed, Frederick found himself left out of the daily conversation among his new acquaintances.

"If you'll all be kind enough to excuse me." He announced as he stood up. "I reckon I'll retrieve Finn, and retire to my room for a while."

As he departed, Charlotte sauntered in, clutching an empty coffee cup. She and Frederick paused to cordially acknowledge each other as they passed. She then continued to the table, where she took a seat between Suzy and Meryl. As everyone exchanged greetings with her, she refilled her cup from the carafe that sat in front of her.

Loraine looked toward her with deep thought before speaking. "Charlotte!" She called from her end of the table.

"There appears to be something that's greatly troubling Steven. Would you have any clue what it might be?"

"To be straightforward." She paused to take a deep breath. "We discovered a disheartening truth while we were in 1697."

Everyone quit eating and turned their attention toward her while she continued. "Jenny McPherson was hung for a crime she didn't commit." She paused with emphasis. "It was our own relative, Jonathan Locke, who falsely accused her, and set the curse in motion that continued to touch our lives all these centuries later."

"How does Beatrice Branch fit into all this?" Loraine further probed. "He seemed to be quite bothered by her."

"Beatrice waved the Christian flag valiantly." She rolled her eyes. "But in reality, she was more of a miserable witch than Jenny, Liddy, or even I was in my heyday." She glanced around the table before continuing. "She actually accused Steven of being a demon, and attempted to kill him on the night of our return." She clenched her eyes shut as she painfully continued. "During her attempt, she accidentally killed Jonathan's son, Theodore."

All were taken aback by surprise, and Loraine maintained her focus on Charlotte. "I'd like to get a more detailed account of what actually took place." She stated. "Would you mind telling us everything?"

Almost on cue, the clock in the corner of the room chimed at 11 am. Charlotte paused to listen to it, before answering. "I'm willing to tell the whole story in detail if you're all willing to sit here for a while to listen."

"Whatever it takes for us all to understand," Philip stated with utter seriousness. "You must remember that Ezekiel and I were there. But because our memories were purged, we have no account of what took place."

Ezekiel grew uncomfortable with the conversation and promptly stood up. "I'm not sure it's wise for us to even hear it now." He stated. "Perhaps I should take Steven to a doctor to get that knee checked."

"Afraid of hearing something that you don't want to hear, darling?" Meryl teased.

He shot a stern glance at her, then looked to Philip with bewilderment. "If you wish to stay, you can fill me in on any important details later."

"Wait!" Charlotte halted him. "I don't think there'll be any need to take Steven to a doctor." She grinned. "Instead, tell him to meet Loraine and I in the Grand Corridor in about an hour. We should be finished here by then."

Charlotte looked to Loraine with a confident grin, and an assured wink, while everyone else at the table appeared rather befuddled. "I performed my share of destructive acts in a previous time. Now it's time to perform a positive act." She smiled. "Surely, Loraine and I can conjure up enough loving, positive energy to heal Steven's knee." She glanced toward Suzy. "I understand you've got a bit of the gift as well, my dear." She paused. "You can come along, and help."

While the Branchview family strived to regain a sense of normalcy in the future, the gods continued with their immortal lives in the 17th century.

Together they stood on the beach now known as Lighthouse Point and stared out over the vast Atlantic waters. "I have no memory of what brought us all here," Zeus stated. "But I only hope our mission was successful."

"Shall we go now?" Poseidon suggested.

Without further word, Zeus led the way as he strode into the ocean. Poseidon followed suit, but Amphitrite paused, as though listening to some distant sound carrying from somewhere over the waters.

Poseidon turned to see what was delaying her. "Are you coming, Amphitrite."

She snapped out of her deep trance for a moment. "Go ahead without me." She urged. "I believe I'm being summoned elsewhere."

"Hopefully, we'll see you soon."

Poseidon then regretfully turned away and waded to where Zeus waited in waist-deep waters. She watched as they sauntered a few steps further, before disappearing into thin air.

She then whispered to the wind, "I can hear your thoughts from over the spectrum of time. No matter how long it may take, I will find you again, my darling." With that, she continued into the waters and made her wondrous transformation.

Across the estate, on the other side of the great woods, Cameron pulled his horse and carriage to a halt next to Maureen. "Couldn't you just stay for the funeral, Cameron?" She pleaded.

He glanced toward the house with rising anger, "I couldn't bear to be around that despicable woman for even one more day."

Maureen responded with a weak smile, "Where will you go?"

"I'll return for the duration of my schooling, and then I'll come back to claim my share of the business when I become of age."

"Will we remain friends?"

"Always." He smiled. "I'll write when I can." He gazed off into the distance. "Do you think Steven and Charlotte will be alright in the future?"

"I have no doubt, they will," she answered. She then shimmied herself up on the carriage footstep and quickly gave him an affectionate peck on the cheek. "Good luck, Cameron!" She bid to him before hopping back down to the ground.

With a grin and a final nod, Cameron shook the reins, and the horses set to a trot, as he rode off into his future. Maureen stood in his wake and waved vigorously until he was completely out of sight.

Back at the 21st-century Branchview residence, a young time-traveler laid atop his bed in a guest room and pondered his uncertain future.

He affectionately scratched his dog behind its' ear, as it contently rested its' head on his chest. "Oh, Finn!" He sighed. "How will we ever adapt to this modern world?"

In the Grand Corridor, the early afternoon sun streamed through the skylight ceiling, casting calming beams onto the open area where Loraine, Charlotte, and Suzy waited near positioned chairs.

After a few moments, the sound of crutches against the marble flooring echoed through the room, as Steven hobbled toward them. "What sort of important meeting have you women summoned me here to attend?" He grinned with amusement.

"We're going to call upon our White Magic to heal that knee." Charlotte proclaimed.

"I'm so foolish," Loraine admitted. "I should've thought of it long before Charlotte even suggested it."

"It's inevitable," Charlotte replied. "Everything has been like a whirlwind in these past several hours."

Loraine observed the aquamarine pendant Steven was now wearing around his neck. "I haven't seen you wear that since…"

"I know." Steven interrupted. "With everything that's happened, I thought it might be wise to start wearing it again." He then looked to Suzy, who quietly waited a few steps behind the other women. "And what part are you playing in all this?"

"I've been Lori's apprentice while you've been gone."

Steven looked to Loraine for a further answer. "I discovered Suzy possesses an enormous abundance of supernatural gifts." She smiled. "She's learning the craft well."

Steven gave the young woman a nod of approval. "There can never be too much White Magic in this world. That's for certain."

Charlotte took him by the arm and helped him over to a chair. "Enough with the chatter for now." She commanded. "Get positioned in this chair, and prop your leg up on the other."

"Yes ma'am!" Steven replied with a nod.

"Okay!" Charlotte continued with a busy sigh. "You take hold of his foot, Loraine. I'll cradle his head. And Suzy, you just stand with the palms of your hands hovering over that knee."

"With three beautiful women fussing over me, I'm surely the envy of every man in this house." Steven chuckled.

"Good grief!" Loraine exclaimed. "The man with the golden tongue hath spoken."

From out of the shadows, Maggie and Daphne appeared, and Suzy was startled with surprise."

"It's okay, Suzy," Loraine assured. "They're part of our spirit family."

"May we join in?" Daphne asked.

"The more, the merrier!" Charlotte chuckled.

"When I realized my precious grandson returned with an injured knee, I told Maggie that we must contribute a bit of our spiritual magic to help."

On a beam of sunlight, two other figures appeared from the dust as illuminated apparitions. They slowly took human form as Amanda Green and Matthew Branch dressed in their Victorian-style clothes. Suzy stood breathless, watching as the couple stepped forward.

"Amphitrite!" Steven exclaimed with surprise.

"You can refer to me as Amanda now." She smirked. "But don't ever call me Aunt Amanda."

"Fine!" Steven countered. "But I'll always refer to this gentleman as uncle Matthew."

All laughed, except for Suzy, who glanced back and forth between Matthew and Steven with amazement.

"I know what you're thinking," Matthew told her. "The resemblance is remarkable."

"Totally uncanny!" She replied.

Amanda nodded to Charlotte.

"Hello, my dear!"

"You're a sight for sore eyes, Mermaid," Charlotte replied as she eyed her green, silk Victorian dress with a clever smirk. "That dress suits you well. It reminds me of the color of your tail."

Amanda stood back and admired the modern white dress Charlotte was wearing. "And look at you, all dressed in white. I don't believe I've ever seen you wear anything other than black or red." Her eyes swept to Loraine next. "And Lori! Need I say you're just as beautiful as ever?"

"Really now, ladies!" Matthew intervened. "We're not here for a tea party. Let's set about getting this poor gentleman healed."

"Thank you, uncle!" Steven jokingly exclaimed.

Suzy looked around the room as the spirits moved closer.

"Is anyone else showing up to this party?"

"Perhaps we should get on with it before every spirit in the household decides to make an appearance." Amanda mused.

All laughed, then assumed their places around Steven, gently hovering their hands over him.

Charlotte then glanced toward the high ceiling and closed her eyes. "Concentrate on the powerful energy of the love we all share." Everyone meditated for a moment before Charlotte continued. "May the divine energy of love and light enter through our beings, and transmit healing into our dear Steven Spencer."

Beams of white light streamed down onto their heads, and they all trembled under its' power. The light traveled through their being, transmitting out of their hands, and enveloped Steven's entire body in a warm aura of light. The light traveled throughout his insides, like a bolt of electricity, and he surrendered to its' gentle pulse. The auras' light lingered for a short while, then suddenly shot upward, and exited with a loud whoosh sound.

All took a deep breath in the aftermath. While Charlotte continued to cradle his head, Steven opened his eyes, like waking from a peaceful sleep. "Wow! That was amazing!" He remarked with much zest.

"Did it work?" Loraine asked with urgency. "Does your knee feel better?"

Steven carefully rose to his feet, and tested his weight on it, as Charlotte and Loraine steadied him.

"Yes!" He exclaimed with amazement. "I think it's healed.

"Never underestimate the healing power of love," Charlotte stated with tears welling in her eyes.

Steven embraced, and kissed Loraine, while everyone else applauded. He gave a grateful nod to Charlotte, then turned to the others. "Thank you." He emotionally proclaimed. "Could you all possibly linger just a bit longer?"

The spirit apparitions began to fade, and flicker a bit.

"We used up a considerable portion of our energy in the healing process," Matthew replied. "I'm afraid we need to return to the light to recharge."

"Please come back, and visit soon." Steven requested. "I look forward to conversing with all of you."

Amanda strolled closer and kissed Steven on the cheek. "Just call on us, Steven," Amanda spoke loudly as her eyes wandered to the aquamarine pendant. "Our souls will forever be entwined with yours." She gently touched the pendant and smiled. "Whenever you need us, you know what to do."

Amanda then looked to Charlotte with a grin. "You have evolved so much from what you once were, my dear. I'm so proud of you."

Charlotte responded with an emotional nod, while Daphne stepped up next, and kissed Steven on the cheek. "My handsome boy." She remarked while cradling his face with her apparition hands. "You can always count on Maggie and I being around." She glanced upward, and around the room. "We're permanently attached to this old house."

Maggie soberly waved to Steven, before taking hold of Daphne's hand. Then in a silent procession, the spirits stepped off again into the shadows and disappeared with the all too familiar whoosh sound.

"Well!" Suzy exclaimed while struggling to regain her composure. "That was all fascinating."

"You'll need to get used to that sort of thing around here, my dear." Loraine chuckled as she lightly patted her on the arm.

"How do you feel, Steven?" Charlotte asked.

"More energetic than I've felt in some time." He answered with vigor. "I suppose I'll take a stroll down by the water." He announced. "Would you ladies care to join me?"

Charlotte picked up the crutches. "I'm a bit spent." She sighed. "I think I'll stay behind, and put these torturous things in the attic."

"Count me out too," Suzy replied. "I have to drive into town to check on the house, and the Diner."

Loraine flashed a sly grin, took hold of his hand, and moved in close. "I guess that just leaves you and me for that romantic stroll."

A short time later, Charlotte entered the attic and placed the crutches in a corner. She heard footsteps and turned quickly. "Is there someone up here?"

From out of the shadows stepped a dignified, gray-haired man in a suit, and Charlotte's eyes narrowed with disdain. "You!" She grunted. "What are you doing here, Morningstar?"

"You should know as well as anyone, my dear." He chuckled. "I'm always lurking somewhere in the shadows."

"What do you want from me?"

He paced closer, with a perverted grin. "That's the wrong question for a lovely woman like yourself to ask a gentleman like me."

"Don't flatter yourself." She fumed.

"I must ask this." He laughed. "Do you actually believe all these good deeds you are performing will win you favor in the spirit world?"

"That's not for me to decide."

Morningstar strolled closer in an intimidating fashion. "The only thing those deeds will buy you is the same desolation that you've always had." He sneered. "Your so-called God will never forgive you for the evil you've done in your past."

"You lie!" She yelled with anger. "I rebuke you in the name of the true God, and command you to leave my presence, Satan."

Morningstar cowered back and growled. "I'll be seeing you again, Charlotte." He sneered. "You should know I don't give up easily."

He faded into the darkness, and she turned away, trembling with anxiety as she collapsed to her knees with tears streaming down her face.

In the Foyer, Suzy carried some personal items down the stairs and prepared to leave the house, just as Frederick entered from another room. "Excuse me, Ma'am." He hurried over to her. "Would you happen to know where I can find Mr. Spencer?"

"I'm sorry!" She set her items down. "You just missed him. He went down to the beach with his wife."

"On his injured knee?"

"That's something you'll have to ask him about." She shrugged and rolled her eyes.

"I was hoping I could talk to him about going over to Springfield." He fretted. "I'm anxious to find out what became of my family."

"Be patient with him." She reasoned. "He hasn't seen his family in over a month."

"Remarkably, it's been 132 years for me."

"I know." She replied with sympathy. "It must be hard for you." She extended her hand to him. "We were never formally introduced. My name is Suzy."

"Short for Susan, I presume." He seized her hand and gently kissed it. "I'm Frederick Ainsworth, and it's a pleasure to meet you."

"Oh my!" She blushed. "I've never had a man do that."

"That's quite a pity." He grinned. "You are a very pretty young woman."

"Could I call you something a little less formal, like Freddy, or Ricky?" She asked.

"Freddy! Ricky!" He reacted indignantly. They sound like names for some homeless vagabond."

"Excuse me, your highness." She quipped sarcastically. "I certainly didn't mean to insult you."

"Forgive me, please. I truly feel like an alien in a foreign land." He stated with obvious frustration. "I have no idea what I'll do for employment or further education. I'm sure my completed studies at Yale would be long outdated by now." He vented.

"I understand." She stated with a calmer demeanor. "I could offer you a job at my Diner. I'm heading over there after I drop these things off at my house." She subtly gestured to the door. "You can ride along if you'd like."

Frederick appeared confused. "You own a business and a house?"

She shrugged matter-of-factly, "Yeah! Is there something wrong with that?"

He's flabbergasted, "But you're a woman, and you couldn't be any older than me."

Suzy laughed and assumed a firm, proud stance. "For your information, women are permitted to own things in this century." She paused with emphasis. "Both places were left to me after my uncle passed away. Mr. Spencer has been kind enough to let me stay here while repairs were made from the earthquake and tidal wave."

"Earthquake? A tidal wave?" He responded with further shock. "Oh my! I have much news to catch up on." He pondered for a moment. "What is this Diner that you speak about? They don't exist in my time."

"It's what you would've called a public eatery that serves prepared food to customers." She explained.

"You'd expect a young man of my stature to accept such a lowly position as a servant?" He indignantly asked.

"You are impossible!" Suzy exclaimed with frustration. "I can't tolerate another minute of your snobbery."

She picked up her belongings and opened the door just as Charlotte came down the stairs. Suzy turned before leaving, "Look me up if you ever get your head out of the 19th century."

She slammed the door with such force that both Charlotte and Frederick reacted with startled surprise.

"What in the world lit her fuse?" Charlotte asked.

"Obviously, I must've said something that offended her." He regretfully sighed.

"You have a lot to learn about modern women, young man."

Frederick noticed that Charlotte's eyes were swollen, and her cheeks were flushed. "Have you been crying, Ms. Charlotte?"

"Oh! It's nothing." She declared. "Just a little bout with my emotions." She nervously gestured for him to follow. "Come with me to the Sitting Room, and I'll try my best to school you in the proper way to treat a woman in the 21st century."

On the beach at Lighthouse Point, Loraine and Steven were huddled closely atop a large rock. The cool, brisk winds of late summer were a stark reminder that Autumn was drawing near at the Connecticut shore. They both daydreamed as they stared out at the choppy, white-capped waves that rolled to shore.

Loraine glanced down at the aquamarine pendant around Steven's neck, and a comforting smile graced her face. "I can almost feel her presence." She stated. "Can you?"

"Her spirit will always be here, and somewhere out there." He smiled as he recanted. "This rock was her favorite spot."

"You miss her. Don't you?"

"I'm delighted she's finally reunited with Matthew."

"I only wish there was a happy ending for Charlotte." She snuggled her head closer to his chest. I know that she fell in love with Poseidon in 1697."

"She told you that?" He shook his head. "I swore secrecy to it."

Loraine looked up and gave a subtle nod, "She also said Amphitrite fell in love with you."

Steven rolled his eyes, and let out a frustrated sigh. "You can never trust a woman to keep a secret." He stared down at Loraine. "Did she also mention she offered me immortality if I would stay with her?"

"She didn't mention that."

"You should know that she did, and I turned her down." He stated matter-of-factly. "I did so because I love you, and our children more than anything in this world."

Loraine couldn't hide the enthusiasm she felt at hearing him say that. "There you go again with that golden tongue of yours." She giggled. "You always say the words that a woman wants to hear." They snuggled ever closer and passionately kissed.

On the edge of the cliffs above them, Nebriana secretly watched. She smiled with contentment and shimmied impulsively. She then spoke to herself in a muffled whisper. "Welcome home, Steven Spencer."

After one final glance at the loving couple, she whirled around, fluttered her wings, and magically disappeared.

The next morning, while most of the Branchview household was still sleeping, Steven, Philip, and Ezekiel gathered for breakfast at the grand re-opening of the City Diner. The crowded restaurant was alive with activity, conversation, and excitement. Suzy hurried by and paused to top off the men's coffees and exchange pleasantries.

"I think the whole town showed up this morning." She breathlessly stated. "I called in Andrea to help, and we're still overwhelmed." She paused to catch her breath. "At this rate, I may have to put aprons on you guys, and give you order pads."

They shared a quick chuckle, before she leaned in closer, and lowered her voice. "I can't go into detail right now." She stated. "But I had a troubling dream last night that has me worried."

"Did this dream have something to do with a worldwide epidemic?" Ezekiel seriously inquired.

Suzy gave a serious nod, and Ezekiel reacted with anxious concern. "Meryl had that same dream. She told me about it this morning.

All four exchange nervous glances and Suzy jumped when the order bell in the serving window rang.

"I have to go." She said, "But Meryl and I need to talk as soon as possible."

"I'll have her stop by before noon, Suzy," Ezekiel assured as she hurried away.

"Something isn't right about all this." Steven proclaimed with much stress. "I had planned to take Frederick over to Springfield, but I can postpone it if you need my help."

"No! Go on ahead!" Philip firmly replied. "This is an issue that demands the attention of Ezekiel and me alone."

"He's right, Steven," Ezekiel added. "We can't risk involving you with this until we know more."

Simultaneously, in 1697, an English shipping vessel sailed along smoothly on a stiff breeze. Roger McPherson casually strolled on the upper deck area, breathing in the fresh sea air. He approached the captain, a portly fellow who leaned on the starboard railing, gazing out over the Atlantic.

"It's as though ye can see forever on a day such as this," Roger commented.

The captain half turned with a grin. "That is quite true, Mr. McPherson."

"Could ye tell me if we'll be setting anchor anywhere near Lockeport, Connecticut?"

"We should reach Boston Harbor in a mere 15 days." The captain answered. "What business would you have in Lockeport?"

"Me young daughter, Liddy, be there waiting." A smile broke across his face. "We've not seen each other for some time."

"That should be a grand reunion." The captain proclaimed. "Aye, Captain!" His smile turned to an evil grin, as he gazed out over the vast expanse of water. It'll be one that the town of Lockeport shall not soon forget."

Meanwhile, in the future. Fredrick struggled to comprehend the things he'd observed in this modern era, like the BMW SUV parked outside the Branchview mansion. "This is a beautiful horseless carriage, Mr. Spencer."

"We call it an SUV in this day and time." Steven laughed as he opened the passenger door, and motioned him in. "Hop aboard, Mr. Ainsworth."

Steven closed the door and walked around to his side to climb into the driving seat. He started the engine, and music immediately blared from the radio.

"What sort of music is that, and where is it coming from?" A startled Frederick asked.

"That's what we call Classic Rock, and it's coming from that radio right there in front of you." He pointed.

Frederick was dumbfounded. "Classic Rock? Radio?"

Steven pointed to the dash. "If you turn that dial right there, you can get just about any type of music you want." He gestured toward it. "Try it."

Frederick cautiously pushed the dial button and jumped back when loud Rap music blasted out through the speakers. "What in God's name is that terrible noise?"

"That's what they call Rap music." Steven laughed again and turned the dial back to the Classic Rock station. "It's fashionable among the young people."

"It's dreadful!" He exclaimed. "Does radio not play music like Mozart, Bach, and Wagner?"

"Well, Mr. Ainsworth, I'm afraid you're out of luck." He chuckled. "You'll have to wait until we return to Branchview later. Then I can play that music for you on the piano."

Just before the lunchtime rush at the City Diner, Meryl entered and calmly took a seat at the end of the counter. Suzy immediately hurried over when she saw her and leaned in close. "I heard you and I had a similar dream." She seriously stated.

Meryl nodded and began to recite prophecy under her breath, "In the mid-winter, a dark angel will rise from the east…"

"…And spread its' wings of misery throughout the earth." Suzy finished.

"A pandemic such as this world has never witnessed since the dark plague," Meryl added.

Suzy nervously glanced around to make sure no one nearby is listening. "What can we do, Ms. Markopolous?"

"The only thing we can do is wait." She answered with a sigh. "The gods are consulting with the Council of Elders as we speak."

"Who are the Council of Elders?" Suzy hysterically asked in a loud whisper.

"Now isn't the time," Meryl stated. "I'll meet you in the Branchview Study later this evening, and try to explain it the best way I can."

The day trip to Springfield had turned out to be enlightening, but a disappointing experience for Frederick. He and Steven had just discovered his once sprawling family estate was now the site of a residential subdivision.

As they drove, searching for the site of his family's textile mill, Frederick sadly lamented. "I can't believe our beautiful estate is gone and replaced by rows of ugly little homes."

Steven glanced over with sympathy, "I hate to say it, but I'm afraid that's the fate that most Gilded Age Estates have faced over the past several years."

"How in the world did Branchview ever survive?"

"It hasn't been easy," Steven explained. "But the family has managed to preserve it throughout the years." He glanced over toward Frederick. "It's now my responsibility to keep it precisely as it is."

Frederick anxiously glanced out the window at the landscape along the highway. "I think we're getting close." He craned his neck. "Everything seems so different."

"Just let me know where to go," Steven responded.

"Over there!" He. suddenly exclaimed. "I recognize that hill behind that building."

Steven pulled into the parking lot of a Walmart, and shut off the engine, while Frederick searched desperately in all directions. "Are you sure we're in the right spot?" Steven asked.

"This must be it." He declared with frustration. "But the mill!" He shook his head. "It's no longer here." His eyes fixed on the Walmart store in front of them. "It was right there, where this building is now." He shook his head again with disbelief. "What is this place they call Walmart?"

"It's an immense store where you can buy any type of necessity that you might need."

"In other words, I'm guessing it's like a general store on a much larger scale," Frederick stated.

"I guess that's an excellent way to explain it," Steven replied. "We also have one in Lockeport."

Everything that once existed in my life is now gone." He choked emotionally, as he managed to force a weak smile. "Now I know how Rip Van Winkle must have felt."

"A lot of things have changed over the centuries," Steven remarked. "I guess they call it progress."

"I'd rather call it tragic." He sadly looked away. "Could we please just go back to Branchview now, Mr. Spencer?"

"In a while," Steven replied. "First, I think you deserve some answers on what became of your family, and I'm guessing we'll find that information at a local library."

Back at Branchview, the immortals gathered for an urgent meeting in the main study. They made sure to close and lock the door to the room, in order to maintain the utmost secrecy.

"What were you able to find out from the Council of Elders." Meryl impatiently asked.

Philip and Ezekiel exchanged an anxious glance before motioning for Meryl to take a seat. "They're aware of the coming pandemic." Ezekiel sighed with frustration. "But there's nothing we can do to stop it."

"I don't understand!" Meryl started with frustration. "We're still ahead of this. There must be something we can do."

"It's a fateful prophecy written in the Book of Life," Philip explained. "We may have slowed the mission of the Secret Society, but they're far too large in numbers to contain."

"The SOS has allied with the Communist Bloc Nations to destroy the world economy." Ezekiel further explained. "Their objective is to buy all the stocks, and world debt at bottomed out prices. When they achieve that, they will own everything, and they'll establish a One World Government." He let out a stress-filled breath and added. "Much like our late brother, Hades attempted to do."

Meryl pondered their remarks. "That must be what is meant in the prophecy I received about the dark angel of the East. They were referring to China." She glanced off into a corner of the room with an expression of horror. "Does this mean we've entered the beginning of the end times?"

"I'm afraid so." Philip sadly stated. "But we as believers know it will be a slow process. This will be only one of the many miseries they will inflict upon this world before they finally accomplish their goals."

"But we already know that the good will be spared, and evil will be defeated in the end." Ezekiel quickly added.

Meryl closed her eyes and nervously nodded. "Should we warn Steven and the others?"

"Absolutely not!" Ezekiel exclaimed. "We've been instructed not to interfere." He pondered a moment in thought. "I don't understand why Miss McVea is receiving such prophecy, but if she has any further dreams, you should discourage her from telling anyone."

"These people are our friends!" Meryl erupted with frustration. "Isn't there anything we can do to help them?"

They all continued to ponder in troubled thought for a long moment before Philip looked up with an enlightened expression. "Just maybe there is something we can do."

In a grand mansion, just outside of New York City, Charles Laszlo, a rich hedge fund investor, sat in the darkness of his home office, talking on the phone.

"Yes, General Cho! How are things there in Beijing?"

The overweight man in his 80s leaned back in his plush chair and listened to the inaudible chatter. He drew a puff from his cigar and blew a smoke ring in the air. "Good! Good!" He chuckled. "I'm pleased to announce that my labs in Wuhan are nearly finished developing the virus.

He listened to the loud, belligerent chatter on the other end, and held the receiver away from his ear. "Yes! I know we've fallen short of our expectations." He sternly replied. "But that blasted President has countered our every move." He grunted arrogantly. "Little do they know that my people and I are funding every opposing radical group."

He held the receiver away momentarily, as he laughed and coughed simultaneously.

"We will not fail this time." He grinned. "I'll ignite a civil war between these fools that will divide, and destroy this country forever." He listened and chuckled in a sinister manner.

"Yes, yes, General Cho!" He chuckled in a sinister manner. "By the time we're done spreading this pandemic, we'll seize control of the world monetary system, and the entire earth will be ours for the taking."

He paused to listen once more. "Yes, General." He broke into a wide grin. "I will be in touch very soon."

Laszlo hung up the phone, and spun his chair around, sporting an evil grin. He commented to himself in a loud whisper. "Let the purge begin."

Chapter Twenty-One:

Closure Before the Pending Storm

The clock in the Branchview foyer chimed at 7:30 PM, and Loraine glanced up at it with serious concern, while she impatiently paced the floor.

Her mind raced with anxious thought, as she silently recited what she was thinking.

In the few short days since Stevens' return from 1697, I find myself growing anxious whenever we're apart. Perhaps it's an insecure fear I may lose him again. But it could also be that I simply fear that any return of normalcy might be rudely interrupted by yet another of the many crises that we've faced since coming here to Branchview.

Just then, the door opened, and Steven entered with a visibly downtrodden Frederick.

Loraine breathed a sigh of relief as she kissed her husband.

"I was beginning to worry about you two. It is getting on into the evening hours."

"We decided to grab a bite to eat on the road," Steven replied. "I should've probably called."

"If you'll please excuse me, Mr. and Mrs. Spencer, it's been a long day."

"Of course, Frederick," Loraine answered with a warm smile.

As he exited the room, the couple exchanged sympathetic glances.

"No good news, I take?"

"Let's just say whatever once was, doesn't exist anymore."

"That poor young man," Loraine remarked. "Were you able to trace any of his family lineages?"

"He has merely a few distant relatives scattered here and there." He stated. "They were all offspring of his two sisters, he was the only boy."

"So, there was no one else to carry on the family name?"

Steven shook his head despairingly.

"It's probably for the best he didn't remain in his time." Steven sighed. "His family lost all their wealth in the Great Depression. He certainly would've been cast out of high society."

Mary entered from an adjoining room as they conversed. "Excuse me, Mr. Spencer. A woman just called from the gate looking for Mr. Seagraves." She announced. "Said her name was Linda Sanchez."

"Oh, dear!" Loraine exclaimed. "He and Ezekiel left the house shortly after supper, and never mentioned where they were going."

There was a knock on the door, and all looked in that direction, while Mary hurried to answer it. "That'd be her."

Mary opened the door, and a beautiful, well-dressed Black woman in her late 20s, sauntered across the threshold and glanced at Steven with considerable surprise. "Steven Spencer!" She exclaimed. "You're just as handsome as I remember."

Both Loraine and Mary glanced cluelessly between the woman, and an equally surprised Steven. "Lindiwi?" Steven questioned, much to her amusement.

"I haven't had anyone call me by that name for well over a hundred years." She giggled.

"Lord have mercy!" Mary moaned. "Here we go again."

"Excuse me, please!" Loraine asserted. "I feel a bit out of the loop here. I'm Steven's wife, Loraine."

"Oh!" Linda eyed her up and down. "So, you're the lucky one that holds the key to this guy's heart." She slyly winked. "Amphitrite did mention you were quite beautiful."

At that moment, Charlotte descended the stairs and paused with surprise. "Lindiwi?"

Linda glanced at her with equal surprise, "And there's Steven's beautiful sister, Charlotte."

Mary looked toward a baffled Loraine. "Hmmm! This is getting interesting."

Steven cleared his throat and intervened. "Philip and Ezekiel should be back shortly." He motioned to the adjoining room. "Perhaps we should all make our way to the Sitting Room where we can discuss things, and better clarify how we're all connected."

"Could I bring you something to drink, Ms. Sanchez?" Mary asked.

"A glass of cold water would be marvelous." She answered while eyeing Steven with a clever grin.

"And a cup of coffee, and an aspirin for me, Mary." Steven sighed. "I have a feeling I'm going to need both."

A short while later, a more comfortable conversation ensued, and Steven sat mildly amused, and somewhat left out as the three women chatted among themselves. "I am so amazed at what you've just told us, Linda." Loraine proclaimed. "You mentioned you spend your time on land in Miami. Steven and I own a home in Sarasota."

"Oh yes! I know St. Armand's Circle well!" Linda enthusiastically answered. "There's a lovely little dress boutique there. I believe the name of it is Henrietta's."

"Yes!" Loraine sat forward with excitement. "I frequent that store often. It's marvelous."

Steven flashed a fake smile and blinked his eyes at Charlotte, which prompted her to join the conversation.

"So, Linda!" Charlotte intervened. "I noticed you've lost every bit of that charming Caribbean accent that I remember."

"I guess you can say I've become Americanized over the years." She laughed.

"I must say you're a lovely woman. By chance, are you married?" Loraine asked with a naughty grin.

Linda flashed a pouty expression. "I've been married to three mortals who've had no interest in accepting the immortality I could offer them."

"So, did these men simply grow old, and die?" Loraine further inquired.

"No!" She answered in a matter-of-fact tone. "I simply erased their memory of me when they no longer served my purpose, and then I moved on."

Charlotte and Loraine exchanged an unbelieving expression, while Linda took a long sip from her water, and quickly moved to another subject. "I'm guessing we're all immortals here." She glanced at everyone. "After all, it was over 300 years ago when I first met Steven and Charlotte."

"Actually, we're all mortals." Steven quickly answered. "Charlotte and I entered a portal that transported us back to the time when we first met you."

"We only managed to return from there a few short days ago," Charlotte added.

Just then, Philip, Ezekiel, and Gerard all entered from the foyer, with Mary following close behind. "Linda Sanchez!" Ezekiel enthusiastically exclaimed. "I can't believe it!"

Linda immediately stood, and exchanged cordial hugs with the two gods, and then turned to Gerard.

"It's a pleasure meeting you, Ms. Sanchez." He respectfully nodded. "I'm Gerard LeRoux."

She glared at him admirably. "I detect a bit of a French accent."

"French Canadian, actually." He answered with a smile.

Linda turned to Mary with a sly smirk. "I do declare! Are there any ugly men at the Branchview Estate?"

"Obviously not!" Mary scoffed with sarcasm. "You'd be best to know they're all taken as well." She then quickly shifted her attention to Steven and Loraine. "Should I prepare a guest room for Ms. Sanchez?"

"That won't be necessary, Mary." Linda quickly answered while flashing a clever wink toward Steven and Loraine. "I've already secured a place near the ocean for the night."

Mary sarcastically glanced at Gerard as she departed the room, and muttered to him. "I'm sure all you men are heartbroken."

Philip stepped forward into the conversation.

"Well, Linda!" He grinned. "You and I have had our fair share of adventures in the past. It's been some time since we battled pirates in the Caribbean."

"It's funny you'd mention that." She seriously stated. "That happens to be the reason I'm here." She strolled closer. "There's a modern-day pirate based out of Columbia giving us quite a problem." She paused. "His name is Juan Cardones."

"I've heard of him," Philip replied. "Isn't he a major player in the smuggling of drugs, and human trafficking into this country?"

She intently nodded. "I've gotten word he is accompanying a shipment of high-grade heroin, and kidnapped women and children from South America." She emotionally paused. "They'll be on board a cargo ship scheduled to arrive at the Port of Miami on Friday morning. This may be our only chance to capture him."

"And you need my help."

"We have to stop this bastard, and put him out of business, Philip." She shook her head with frustration before continuing. "We can't trust the Federal Agents. Most of them have been compromised."

Philip pondered seriously for a moment, then gestured toward Charlotte. "I'd be all in, but I've already been instructed to return Charlotte to the island of Avalon on Friday."

"Go with Linda!" Charlotte exclaimed as she stood, and intervened. "Ezekiel can escort me back." She boldly tilted her chin upward as she continued. "This animal, Cordones must be stopped. These innocent women and children must be spared."

"She's right, Philip!" Ezekiel asserted. "Those waters are under your jurisdiction. I'm certain that I'll be permitted to return Charlotte."

Philip looked to Ezekiel, then back to Charlotte with regret. "You do know that I may never be permitted to see you again?"

Tears welled in Charlotte's eyes, though she tried hard to hold them back. "Then I suppose we need to say our goodbyes right now." She kissed Philip on the cheek and whispered in his ear. "Thank you for everything."

She hurried from the room before her emotions completely unraveled, and Loraine quickly followed after her. In the wake of their departure, an awkward state prevailed among the others in the room.

"I take we can leave for the Caribbean first thing in the morning." Linda sighed. "My people have placed a tracer on that ship, so we should locate it easily."

"Yes!" Philip replied with obviously distracting thoughts. "I'll meet you on the beach at first light, Linda."

"I should go now, and get rested." She cordially nodded to Steven and Gerard. "Mr. LeRoux. It was a pleasure meeting you. Steven! Ezekiel! It was good seeing you both again as well." She smiled. "I can let myself out."

All the men remained silent for a moment, as they listened to the sound of Linda's high heels click across the tile floor of the foyer. They continued listening as the door creaked open and then closed again.

"Well! We'd planned on waiting until tomorrow. But under the present circumstances, I suppose we'll have to hold our meeting tonight." Philip stated.

"Another meeting?" Steven cluelessly asked.

"Ezekiel and Philip have presented an ample proposal concerning Branch Consolidated," Gerard replied. "It's essential that we discuss it with you."

Steven glanced at each man with curious thought, just as the foyer clock chimed. "It's 9:30 now," Steven stated. "I'll meet you all in the Study in 15 minutes." He paused with an expression of deep concern. "First, I need to check on Charlotte."

In the dimly lit Branchview Nursery, Millie and Bill casually watch over the three babies as they lay in their side-by-side cribs. "It appears that little Michael and London have drifted off to dreamland," Bill commented.

"And as usual, Princess Olivia is wide awake." Millie quipped with a sigh. "I have a feeling this girl will be a little pistol when she grows up."

"In other words, just like her grandmama." He laughed.

"I'm sorry I won't be around to see them all grow up." She replied with a sad smile. "I'll need to go back to England before long."

Bill became visibly upset by her statement. "You didn't tell me about this before, Millie."

"Surely, you knew my visa would expire, and I'd have to return?"

Bill is saddened even more, "Do you want to go back?"

"Not necessarily! She sighed. "I've grown fond of everyone in this household." She smiled sweetly. "That goes especially for you."

Bill was flattered and pondered her comment for a moment. "There might be a way for you to stay a bit longer." He hinted. "Of course, if that's what you want."

"Bill Crawford!" She exclaimed with a sly grin. "What exactly are you trying to say?" She waited for an answer, as Bill stammered about. "Oh! Get on with it! Spit it out!"

"I'm just saying you could qualify for a green card if you would simply grant this old fool the honor of being his wife."

Millie was flabbergasted, and rendered speechless. She glanced down at baby Olivia, who reached her little hand up and loudly attempted to speak.

"Well?" Bill impatiently prodded.

"I believe this young lady may have trying to answer for me." She laughed, before turning to face him with overwhelming emotion. "Yes, Bill Crawford! I most graciously accept your proposal." She declared, and enthusiastically planted a kiss on his lips.

In a dark corner of the room, the spirits of Daphne and Maggie secretly observed, and expressed their joy and approval.

In the Branchview Study, Ezekiel, Philip, and Gerard positioned their seats, as Steven entered, and sat down in his large desk chair.

"Is Charlotte, okay?" Philip asked with great concern.

"She's fine." Steven calmly assured. "It's a very emotional time for her." He glanced toward the others, quickly changing the subject. "Okay, gentlemen! Let's hear this grand new proposal you've presented."

Gerard leaned in, opened his ledger, and began. "As you and I discussed the other day, we must find ways to run the estate in a more fiscally responsible manner." He paused with emphasis. "Between general maintenance, upkeep, and the damage inflicted by the earthquake and tsunami, we've gone way above this year's projected budget."

"Surely, we have enough money in the corporation reserve fund to make up the difference," Steven suggested.

"True!" Gerard agreed. "But we also have to safeguard ourselves against unforeseen circumstances that have unfortunately become the norm as of late."

Steven answered with a thought-filled shrug. "You're the genius in these matters, Gerard. What do you propose?"

Gerard gestured for Ezekiel to take things from there and leaned into the conversation. "Philip and I would like to become silent partners in the Branch Consolidated Family."

Steven looked to the men with stifled disbelief, and Philip picked up the conversation from there. "As you can imagine, we've amassed an impressive bit of the worlds' hidden fortune over the several centuries of our existence."

Steven listened with ever-increasing interest. "We have a large enough stockpile of gold and silver in the Secret Cave alone, to buy the contents of Fort Knox three times over," Ezekiel stated.

"Not to mention, through our association with the Nereids and Oceanids, we also hold claim to all the shipwrecks in the worlds' waterways," Philip added.

"No mere mortal can reach such depths to claim the valuable cargo they contain." Ezekiel chuckled. "As you can imagine, that accounts for a ton of wealth in itself."

Steven leaned back in his seat and mouthed the word "WOW!" before shifting a glance toward Gerard.

Ezekiel carried on with much enthusiasm.
"We want to merge a good bit of that wealth in your interests, to ensure that Branch Consolidated is stable enough to weather any unforeseen circumstance."

"We want to also ensure the Branchview Estate will endure, and always remain as it is," Philip added.

"I'd still have to make sure we operated within conservative measures, of course," Gerard assured.

Steven was totally flabbergasted and finally spoke up. "I'm still waiting for the catch here." Steven glanced between all the men. "There must be some other basis to this offer."

Ezekiel sighed, "The only thing we would ask in return is that you'd close, and dispose of all your factories, businesses, and investments currently operating in hostile countries."

"I assume you specifically mean China?"

Both men nodded their heads intently. "We're secretly partnered with enough other companies worldwide to ensure the spread of wealth, without further feeding China and the Secret Society's globalist ambitions." Philip further contributed.

"Why would you want to do this?" Steven inquired. "You're immortal gods. I thought you didn't concern yourselves in such human matters."

The two gods looked to each other, and Philip spoke first. "We've grown to consider the people here at Branchview our earthly family, and nothing is more important than family." He paused in a moment of uncharacteristic emotion. "You've shown us that all the wealth in the world cannot buy happiness or true love."

"The Globalists, in their lusty ambition of more wealth and power, will make life unbearable in this world," Ezekiel added. "We've abused our powers as gods throughout the centuries, and become no better than them." He lowered his head in shame. "The end days are near, and we consider this our ultimate chance to erase our wrongs, and find true redemption with our maker."

Both Steven and Gerard took the gods' words to heart, and Steven extended his hand, palm down across the desk. "Gentlemen!" He exclaimed. "We have a deal."

All three men placed their hands on the top of Stevens'.

"As brothers, we endure!" Ezekiel proclaimed.

"As a family, we survive!" Philip added with enthusiasm.

"Where we go one, we go all." Gerard enthusiastically concluded.

They lifted their hands in a lofty cheer and congratulated each other. "Would anyone care to join me in the Sitting Room for a congratulatory nightcap?" Ezekiel eagerly asked.

"Count me in," Gerard replied.

"I'll have to pass on that, brother," Philip answered with a regretful smile. "I have an early morning, and long days' journey ahead of me."

Ezekiel and Gerard then looked to Steven. "Go ahead!" He answered. "I'll be along shortly."

While Ezekiel and Gerard departed the room, Philip hung back and lingered. "It looks as though you have something heavy on your mind, Philip."

He nodded and strolled back toward the desk where Steven remained seated. "Do you suppose Charlotte would object if Tina and I were to build our house on the site of the old Locke Estate?"

"I think that would make her happy," Steven stated. "And, as her closest living relative, I must say I approve of it completely."

"Being that both Tina and I hold no registered identity in this world, would you mind assigning your name to the title of the house?" Philip further asked.

"I think that can be arranged," Steven answered with an assured smile.

"Thank you, Steven." He replied with a grateful nod. "We'll discuss this further when I return."

Steven gestured with an assured wink, and while Philip turned to depart, Steven pondered whether to mention the issue between him and Charlotte.

"Poseidon!" He boldly called out.

Philip turned, astonished that he'd addressed him by his godly name. Steven further pondered the issue for a moment, before looking up at him with a grin.

"Have a safe journey, my friend."

Later that night, Loraine exited the North Wing in her nightgown and prepared to descend the stairs. Her eyes glanced toward the East Wing entrance, where she noticed the door was ajar. She paused for a moment, before deciding to check it out.

She wandered into the darkened wing and noticed a lone figure sitting silently in front of the double doors in the hall. "Who's in here?" She called out.

The figure turned toward her, as she flicked on the light, and she could now see it was Frederick. "Frederick!" She exclaimed. "You gave me quite the fright."

"I'm sorry, Mrs. Spencer. I couldn't sleep, and I had to ah…"

"I know." Loraine interrupted. "You came to the last place where you remember your life being normal."

She pulled up a chair and sat down next to him. "I spent many a night staring at these blasted doors. All the while hoping they would suddenly open, and Steven would return to me."

"But he did come back."

"Thankfully."

Frederick continued staring at the doors with great wonder. "The one thing that baffles me is why those doors were wide open that night. When in reality, nothing existed there but a wall."

"I guess that's one of the many mysteries surrounding that imaginary room we may never know." Loraine looked back toward the doors. "After next week, those doors will be removed, and no one will ever wander through them again."

"But they'll always exist in my nightmares." Frederick trembled with anxiety.

"Just know the portal brought positive aspects as well." She smiled. "You have new family and friends who care dearly about you."

Loraine stood up and placed her hand on the young man's shoulder. "Steven is planning a meeting with you, and the other newcomers in the Sitting Room tomorrow." She offered an assuring smile. "We shall all get through this together."

"Thank you, Mrs. Spencer."

As first light broke on the ocean's horizon, Philip and Tina strolled along the shore at Lighthouse Point. Tina pulled her sweater tight around her neck to ward off the stiff, cold breeze. "I think our summer is over." She sadly stated. "The mornings are getting cold again."

Philip gazed out to sea and searched the rough white caps. He squinted against the wind that tossed his long hair back. "Linda should be here soon."

"I just wish you didn't have to go." She moaned. "It's so lonely when you're gone."

He placed his hands gently on her shoulders and stared into her intense blue eyes. "I'll be back soon, and I promise we'll share many moments." He pointed to the clifftop above them. "We'll build our house up there. Just a stone's throw from where we first met." He beamed with exuberance. "We'll have a grand Sitting Room and Veranda that faces the ocean, and we'll spend our idle time, dreaming the days away."

"That sounds wonderful." She giggled. "I love you so much."

He placed his warm hands gently on her rosy cheeks and cradled her face. "In all the centuries of my life, you were the one true love worth waiting for."

As they kissed, the siren's calls echoed hauntingly from the turbulent ocean. They looked out over the rough waves and saw Linda emerge from the depths, waving her arms toward shore. "It's time to go."

In a glitter of stardust, Nebriana appeared next to the parting couple, and Tina jumped back with fear. "It's okay, Tina!" Philip assured. "This is our friend, Nebriana, she'll escort you safely back to Branchview."

Tina glanced at Nebriana with amazement, and then back to her husband. "Everything about our lives is so magical." She smiled. "Be safe, my love."

They kissed once more, before he moved away, waiting for the last moment to let loose of Tina's hand.

The two women watched as he turned to run into the rough waters, and they continued watching until he and Linda disappeared beneath the rough waves.

Back at Branchview, the staff were gathering around the dining room table, enjoying the final moments before their day shift began. Sharie casually paged through an issue of Better Homes and Gardens, while Mary read her Bible. All the others daydreamed and savored their warm cups of coffee.

Andrea rushed in, and Sharie looked up at her with stern eyes, gesturing to an open button on the front of her uniform. She reacted with awkward embarrassment, and immediately secured it. "I'm sorry about that, Sharie. I just got done feeding the baby."

Everyone else responded with an amused glance, as the clock chimed at 7:30 AM, and Mrs. Porter alerted everyone. "Ladies and gentlemen. It's showtime."

Mary promptly closed her Bible and raised her hand in the air. "Thank the good Lord for another day in this beautiful old house."

"Amen to that," Sharie concluded.

Mrs. Porter smiled and rang the lavish dinner bell before ambling through the swinging door to the kitchen.

Later that morning, Steven sat at his desk in the main study, immersed in a book from the family journals. Bill entered and waited politely at the door until Steven looked up, and saw him. "Mr. Benson and his family have arrived." He announced. "They're waiting with the others in the Sitting Room."

"Thank you, Mr. Crawford. Tell them I'll be right there." As Bill departed, Steven closed the book and stared down at it with pondering thoughts.

In the Sitting Room, Gerard and Loraine conversed with Frederick, Mary, Eddie, and his family, while they waited for Steven.

"As I understand it from Mrs. Spencer here, you were an 1894 graduate of Harvard Business School, Mr. Benson," Gerard stated before shifting his attention to Frederick. "And you had just entered your senior year at Yale when you had your fateful event."

Eddie and Frederick exchanged sad, but proud glances. "I'm afraid our education would prove obsolete in this modern world, Mr. LeRoux."

Frederick replied, "I agree," Eddie added. "My wife has taught me how to use a computer, but even after seven years, I find myself far behind on the learning curve."

"Even still." Gerard pondered. "Both of you are intelligent young men, and surely we can find a position in the company for you."

At that moment, Steven breezed into the room, holding the family journal in one hand. He had heard part of the conversation before entering.

"I couldn't agree with you more, Gerard."

He walked immediately over to where Eddie and his family sat. "Eddie! I'm Steven Spencer." He shook his hand. "My wife here has told me a lot about you, and your family."

"I'm pleased to finally meet you, Mr. Spencer." He gestured with a nod. "This is my wife Sandy, and my daughter Tricia.

Steven politely acknowledged Sandy and went down on one knee to address Tricia. "I heard you're a talented little girl," Steven commented to her.

Tricia blushed with a shy smile and ran to hide her face behind her mother. "I apologize," Sandy stated with embarrassment. "She tends to be cautious around some men."

"That's alright." Loraine joked. "My husband tends to have that sort of effect on a woman." Everyone laughed, while Steven smirked at Loraine, and sat down between her and Gerard.

He then opened the journal and set his full attention on Eddie. "Daniel Branch wrote good things about you in this journal."

"I'm speechless," Eddie said. "Daniel was an austere individual who rarely had a positive word for anyone."

"We know that all too well." Loraine quipped.

"On the contrary, he described you as a valuable asset to the Branch Corporation. He went on to say that he mourned your loss as much as he would've his own son."

Steven closed the book and further focused on Eddie. "You may have changed your identity, but you will always be a Branch." He paused with emphasis. "With that in mind, you should know that you and your family will always be part of our family."

"I'm honored that you feel that way." Eddie humbly remarked while Steven continued.

"I understand your house was destroyed in the disaster this past summer."

Eddie sighed stressfully. "The insurance company has been unyielding in finalizing our settlement. The foundation was damaged, and the city condemned it."

Steven pondered the predicament for a long moment. "We're in the process of rebuilding our Carriage House as a modernized replica of the original." He gestured toward Gerard with a quick wink. "Since Mr. and Mrs. LeRoux will be making the Main House their permanent residence, I'd like you and your family to reside there."

Everyone, including Loraine and Gerard himself, reacted with surprise, while Steven beamed with exuberance. "Mr. Spencer! How could we ever begin to repay you for such generosity?" Sandy asked with astonishment.

"There's no need to pay at all." He stressed. "As I mentioned you're all part of this family, and no family of mine should ever have to live in a government trailer." He grinned. "I'm simply giving you the share you deserve." He paused. "I expect all of you to stay here in the Main House until we get the Carriage House finished."

Sandy turned to Eddie and Tricia with disbelief. "I feel like we just won the lottery."

"Furthermore," Steven added. "We'll need an expert carpenter with the skills to replicate the woodwork in the Carriage House, and on the Estate grounds. I'd like that to be your responsibility, Eddie."

Gerard jumped in. "I'd also like to add that we'll set both you and Frederick up with tutoring sessions, and classes at the Community College to bring you both up to speed with modern business."

Both young men were flabbergasted with surprise. "We don't know how to thank all of you. This is beyond generous." Eddie proclaimed.

Steven, Gerard, and Loraine all exchanged pleased glances, then Steven turned his attention to Frederick.

"Mr. Ainsworth! I've also given much thought to your predicament." He leaned forward. "I have no doubt that had you not met your unfortunate circumstance, you surely would've married into the family. With that in mind, we intend to treat you as family."

Frederick gave him a grateful nod, and Steven continued. "I have a trusted friend at the Federal Bureau of Investigation who can help you secure a new name and identity."

"Why would I need a new identity." He cluelessly asked.

"As Eddie can verify from his experience, a man who lived over a hundred years ago cannot assume his old identity, and start a new life in this century without consequence."

Gerard gestured toward Eddie, "I'm sure Mr. Benson can apply his experience to help you in that capacity."

Frederick looked to Steven with serious concern. "Will I also have a home here for the time being?"

Steven glanced first at the Irish Setter resting at Frederick's feet, then to Bumpers, and the black cat sleeping soundly near the fireplace, and a smile lit up his face. "You're welcome to stay here for as long as you'd like, Mr. Ainsworth."

Steven then turned his attention to Mary. "Last, but certainly not least, our dear Mary." He gave her an assured wink. "I'm sorry you and I haven't had the time to chat since I returned, but I'd like to arrange a lunch date at the Mermaid Inn sometime soon."

"I'll be the envy of every lady in town." Mary joked.

All laughed, and Steven continued on. "I certainly hope you're pleased with your arrangement here, and if you ever need anything, please let me know.

Mary raised one hand in the air with enthusiasm. "Mr. Spencer! I'm just as pleased and grateful as can be."

Gerard gestured toward her with a smile. "If my wife doesn't treat you well, I want you to let me know about it."

Mary laughed heartily. "If that child gives me any lip, you'll be the first to know."

All enjoyed a generous laugh, and then Steven looked to them with all seriousness. "Since all three of you arrived here from the Gilded Age, you can be a great support to each other." He gestured with his hands to all three. "Whatever you do, make sure that no one beyond these walls learns of your true identity."

Loraine stood up next, "With all that settled." She announced. "I think we should all make our way to the Dining Room for lunch.

Mary jumped up like a rocket, "Lord have mercy! I should run, and help the ladies prepare it."

Steven halted her. "Absolutely not, Mary!" He insisted. "Today, you're going to join us, and I want you to sit right next to me at the head of the table."

Steven's offer overwhelmed Mary, while Eddie's family, and Frederick all lined up to thank Steven, Gerard, and Loraine.

Little Tricia glanced up at Steven with a sweet smile and gave him a tight hug that melted his heart, and everyone else's as well.

"I'm afraid I can't top that, Mr. Spencer." Frederick chuckled. "But I can tell you that I'm truly grateful."

Steven shook his hand firmly. "You know, Frederick! I think you should reconsider Ms. McVea's offer."

"To work in the Diner?"

"At least for the time being." He answered. "It'll get you out of the house, and give you a chance to get used to this modern world we live in."

Frederick carefully pondered his suggestion. "Perhaps I will do that."

Gerard stepped up to Steven next with a sly grin. "When did you plan on telling me about the Carriage House?" I always assumed Sharie and I would continue living there."

"I decided someone of your stature deserves much finer quarters," Steven answered.

Gerard continued with a perplexed expression. "But you and Loraine are by rights, the Master and Mistress of

Branchview." He asserted. "We could never be anything but guests here in the main house."

Steven glanced first at Loraine, then negated Gerard's statement with a shake of his head. "That couldn't be further from the truth, Gerard." He grinned. "I've decided to move my family to the larger South Wing, which was my mother's quarters. I'd like you and Sharie to occupy the entire North Wing."

Both Gerard and Loraine were speechless with surprise, and Steven continued with more. "Besides, we'll only be residing here for the summers."

Loraine was totally taken aback by his statement. "We're keeping our estate in Florida?"

"Absolutely!" He responded with a clever smirk. "Every writer needs a retreat. We should rename it though." He paused with amusement. "How does Branchview South sound?"

"I think it sounds marvelous, Steven." Loraine marveled. "My mind is absolutely racing with possibilities right now."

Gerard was just as flabbergasted as Loraine. "I don't know what to say." He chuckled. "You're certainly a man of surprises, Steven Spencer."

"I'm only hoping you'll say we have a deal, Mr. LeRoux."

Gerard shook his hand firmly, and with vigor. "Absolutely! I can't wait to tell Sharie."

"We'll all chat later about this," Loraine suggested. "Let's go eat."

Steven took hold of Loraine's hand as they prepared to depart from the room. "I suppose things are finally falling into place around here." He commented.

Loraine pulled him in close for a kiss. "I'm so proud of you, and so happy to be your wife."

"And I consider myself the luckiest guy in the world to be your husband." He beamed. "I think we make a great team."

As they continued to stroll from the room, Loraine glanced back, feeling as though they were being watched. She smiled when she saw Daphne and Maggie's ghostly figures waving from the other side of the room, and gesturing their overwhelming approval.

As the lunchtime crowd began to thin out at the City Diner, a weary worn Suzy took time to clean and straighten up the counter area. Frederick strolled in, and took a seat, acting rather sheepish.

"Well! Prince Frederick!" Suzy announced. "You're the last person I expected to see in my lowly Diner." She strolled closer and looked him up and down. "Where did you get the modern threads?"

"Mr. Spencer took me to a shopping mall, and bought them for me."

She gave him a critical nod of approval. "So, what brings you in here today?"

"I came to apologize for behaving like a complete horse's ass, and I'd like to ask if your offer of employment still stands."

Suzy was surprised and impressed. "Why the sudden change in attitude?"

Frederick stammered to find the right words, while she waited. "On reflection, I realized your offer came solely from the goodness of your heart, and I was a snobbish fool to criticize your intention."

"In that case, I accept your apology." She smiled. "But if you want to work here, I'll need to call you something other than Frederick. It sounds too much like an old man's name."

He chuckled and made a suggestion, "How about Fred?"

Suzy rolled her eyes and laughed, "Oh no!" She protested. "All I can think of when I hear that name is Fred Flintstone."

Her statement completely perplexed Frederick. "Who in the world is Fred Flintstone?"

"Good grief!" She chuckled. "We do have much ground to cover in getting you up to speed on things." She pondered a moment without breaking eye contact. "How about we call you Rick? That's a masculine-sounding name."

He thought about it for a moment, then nodded with definite approval.

"Very well! Rick, it shall be."

Suzy flashed a pleasing smile, then glanced around the near-empty Diner. "This is a slow part of the day." She stated. "It'll be a convenient time to get you trained."

She reached below the counter area, retrieved an apron, and tossed it to him. "You want me to start now?" He inquired.

"Uh, yeah!" She sarcastically exclaimed. "Put that on, and I'll teach you everything you need to know about working in a Diner.

He held the apron up to look at it, then grinned back at her with mild amusement. "Yes ma'am!"

Later that day, the inhabitants and guests of Branchview conversed at the Dining Room table after their evening meal.

Ezekiel raised his wine glass in the air. "Kudos to the kitchen staff for another delicious meal."

Meryl also raised her glass. "I'll second that."

Ezekiel glanced around the table with emotion. "I regret having to mention this now, but when I leave on Friday morning to take Charlotte back to Avalon, Meryl and I won't be returning."

Loraine placed her hand on top of Charlotte's, and flashed a sympathetic smile, while Meryl picked up the conversation. "I'll be going ahead to our home on the Isle of Rhodes."

"And upon my return there, we've decided to renew our vows," Ezekiel concluded.

Everyone clapped, cheered, and congratulated the smiling couple, and Steven raised his coffee mug. "I'd have to say that's a few centuries overdue." He quipped.

All laughed and commented, while Ezekiel turned his attention to Gerard and Sharie. "Have you two decided what to do with the East Wing, since Steven and Loraine won't be occupying it?" He asked.

"I'm definitely not living in it," Sharie stated with absolute certainty. "There's too much bad history in that place."

Ezekiel's eyes wandered toward Tina. He cleared his throat and gestured for her to speak. She meekly raised a hand and set her attention to Gerard and Steven. "I wondered if Philip and I could occupy a portion of the East Wing until the construction of our house is finished. It would be a great space to have when the baby arrives."

Gerard shrugged and looked to Steven. "I have no problem with it. I think it's an excellent idea."

Steven tipped his mug toward Tina. "I fully approve as well."

Tina smiled humbly, and gave a thankful nod, while Loraine entered the conversation. "The doors will be removed next week, and the last of the renovations should be finished. You and Philip shouldn't have to deal with any more issues in that portion of the house."

Sharie shook her head. "I'm not sure I'm sold on that. I'm still wary about unwelcome souls coming and going"

"I can permanently take care of that problem for you tonight." Ezekiel casually replied.

"What do you mean by that?" Steven asked.

Ezekiel took a sip of his wine and leaned into the conversation. "Both Philip and I can permanently seal any portal of time so that no one can ever pass through it again."

"So, what you're basically saying is absolutely no one, including Jenny or Liddy McPherson, can ever pass through it again?" Loraine inquired.

"Exactly!" Ezekiel assured. "If anyone ever tried, they would be forever trapped somewhere else within the spectrum of time."

Sharie raised her hand in the air. "I'll shout an Alleluia to that!"

Steven's eyes grew wide. "And add in a big amen!" He emphasized. "Let's do it, and be done with it."

"Normally, I'd need Philip to assist me with the ceremony, but I'm convinced Charlotte and Loraine have the abilities to help," Ezekiel stated while giving Charlotte a wink of assurance.

"I'd be honored to do one more good deed before I have to go," Charlotte replied.

Ezekiel then turned to Loraine. "I'll need you to gather some sage that I can burn in the incense pot during the ceremony."

"I'll get right on it," Loraine replied with urgency in her voice.

As Suzy closed down the Diner for the night, Frederick helped her clean up. As he scrubbed down the grill, she stood observing with her hands on her hips. "You surprised me." She stated. "You did well for your first day."

"You worked me like a slave."

"You'll get used to it." She giggled.

He looked into the large stainless container on top of the stove. "There's a bit of soup left in there. Would you wish me to dispose of it?"

"Absolutely not!" She exclaimed. "I need you to fill as many takeout containers as possible, and we'll take it over to the park with the rest of these leftovers."

"The park? Whatever for?" He asked.

"I give it to the homeless people that live there." She casually answered.

Frederick paused with his chores and stared at her with both admiration and astonishment. "You really are extraordinary, you know?"

"I try my best to be." She replied with a shy smile.

The inhabitants of the Branchview Estate were now gathered in the Courtyard for the Ceremony to officially seal the portal of time. Everyone was dressed in heavy jackets and shivered against the brisk night air. Charlotte carried the incense pot, gently swaying it, and spreading the fragrance of sage in the air, while Ezekiel chanted in the ancient Greek language. Loraine followed close behind, sprinkling holy water on the ground.

They all came to a halt in their procession and faced the rock. Ezekiel closed his eyes and raised his hands high in the air. "At this moment, I command the powers of the universe to close, and permanently seal this portal of time."

He turned and nodded to Charlotte. "And may no evil spirits, nor agents of fortune reopen it for all eternity." She added.

Ezekiel clasped his hands tightly, then reopened them wide. "So, shall it be!" He exclaimed.

"By divine intention, it is done." Loraine proclaimed.

All clapped and cheered, while Steven stepped forward, and wrapped his arms around Loraine.

"We can finally put that issue to rest."

"Gladly!" She responded.

Ezekiel approached the couple, and together they gazed at the rock.

"What do you plan to do with it?" He asked.

Steven pondered the question for a moment before answering. "When we cleared the brush away, I noticed how much it had sunk into the ground over the years." He stood back to survey it as if trying to remember the way it looked in 1697. "I suppose I'll have our groundskeepers dig it up, and we'll preserve it here as a memorial to all who fell victim to it throughout the centuries."

Ezekiel patted Steven on the shoulder and gave his nod of approval. "I think that would be a very noble thing to do."

The following day, Steven was back busy at work in the main study. He was excited to finally put other issues aside, and resume with his writing. A knock suddenly interrupted his thoughts.

He paused to stare at the door for a moment before saying anything. "It's open! Come in!" He sighed.

Tony slowly opened the door, and entered, carrying a weathered-looking letter in his hand. His uniform was soiled from working outside on the grounds. "I hate to bother you, Steven. But I thought I should bring this to your attention as soon as possible."

"That's alright, Tony." He looked him up and down. "Hopefully, you removed your dirty boots outside the front door.' He chuckled. "If not, you'll be in a heap of trouble with Mary and Mrs. Porter."

"Believe me! I know that all too well." He laughed, "Our crew excavated that rock from the ground this morning, and we found a box made of pure silver buried near the base of it."

"Did you open it?" Steven curiously asked.

"It was rather corroded from having been in the ground for so long. So, we had to take it back to the shop, and pry it open." He carefully handed a brittle, time worn letter over to Steven. "This was inside, and rather well-preserved, I might add. It had your name on the envelope."

Steven placed the letter on top of the desk in front of him, and examined it with a bewildered expression on his face, while Tony continued talking. "There was something else in that box none of us could figure out."

Steven glanced up at him with further curiosity. "It looked like an old rolled-up cigarette, or…" He paused to find the right word.

"Or what, Tony?" Steven impatiently probed.

"Well, Steven! Some of us seem to think it might be a joint."

Both men shared a hearty laugh over the insinuation. "One can only imagine, I guess," Steven commented, before giving Tony a grateful nod. "Thank you for bringing this letter to me."

Tony promptly departed, and Steven waited a few moments before carefully opening the fragile envelope, and unfolding the letter inside it.

October 8, 1697. He read at the top and shook his head with amazement. As he began reading, he could almost hear an endearing voice reciting its' contents within his mind.

Steven. Here's hoping this letter will one day find its' way to you. Cameron and I often spoke of that night and hoped you and Charlotte had indeed found your way home safely.

I think you should write a novel about Amphitrite, the gods, and your magical adventure. Yes, I knew who they were, and I made a vow to keep their secret for the rest of my life.

If you made it back, and are reading this, I hope that you'll have a wonderful life.

With much love from your distant relative,
Maureen.

P.S. Stargazer left you a present to remember him by.

Steven set the letter down with emotional pondering. "Nature's herb." He laughed. "It was a joint."

He then looked upward in fond remembrance of his friends and family, as tears escaped his eyes, and trickled down the sides of his face.

Chapter Twenty-Two:

Sweet Redemption

Friday morning came quicker than all had hoped. Steven and Loraine rose in the pre-dawn hours and sadly assembled in the Foyer to bid farewell to Charlotte, Ezekiel, and Meryl. "I said my goodbyes to everyone last night, but please give them all my regards nevertheless," Charlotte stated with regret in her voice.

Steven stepped forward to embrace, and kiss her on the cheek. "You and I have shared quite an adventure."

"We certainly have." She smiled.

Loraine stepped forward next, and the two women embraced tightly. "I'll miss you." She tearfully stated.

"I'll miss all those sisterly talks we had. I truly cherished them." Charlotte remarked.

"Are you sure you don't want Steven and I to escort you to the water?"

Charlotte shook her head. "I suppose it's better this way," she sighed. "I'd like to part ways, believing I'll see you all again someday."

"You will," Steven assured.

Meryl stepped forward to embrace Charlotte and whispered to her. "Take care of yourself, my dear." She then turned to Ezekiel and kissed him on the cheek. "I'll swim well ahead, and meet you at Rhodes." Ezekiel gave an acknowledging nod, as Meryl exited.

Ezekiel gestured to Charlotte, "We mustn't keep Pegasus waiting."

Charlotte replied with a sad nod, and without another word, she and Ezekiel also departed into the pre-dawn darkness.

Later that morning, after the other inhabitants of the house were all up and stirring about, Tina lounged in front of the large screen TV in the Sitting Room, watching the late morning news.

She listened attentively to the news anchor as she enjoyed a cup of tea. "We have breaking news to report at this hour. Notorious drug lord Juan Cordones was apprehended and arrested in a joint effort by the U.S. Coastguard and DEA Agents. They acted on a mysterious tip, and found Cordones and his associates bound and gagged in a shipping container. Along with them, they discovered several pounds of heroin, and 53 women and children, believed to all be victims of human trafficking. It's believed at this time the vessel was in route to the Port of Miami."

Tina jumped from her seat and howled with excitement, "Steven! Loraine! Anybody! Hurry!

Mary urgently hurried into the room from the Foyer. "Good heavens, girl! What's all this ruckus about?

She grabbed Mary by the shoulders, trembling with excitement. "Philip and Linda did it!" She proclaimed.

"Did what, child?"

"They captured that devil, Juan Cordones." She announced while pointing toward the TV with excitement.

She hysterically ran from the room to tell all the others, leaving Mary in a confused tizzy.

"Lord have mercy!" She proclaimed. "This is way too much excitement for this old lady."

After a lengthy journey across the Atlantic with Zeus, Charlotte arrived at her Victorian home on the Island of Avalon. After bidding farewell to him and Pegasus, she solemnly entered the kitchen area and leaned against the counter. The silence in the house was deafening, interrupted only by the distant sounds of birds singing outside.

She sighed with despair and whispered out loud to herself. "Welcome back to your solitary confinement, Charlotte."

Her attention shifted to the squawking parrot on her outside veranda, and she heard a loud creaking noise that sounded like something moving across the wood plank floors. She swiftly stepped into the adjoining parlor and shielded her eyes from the afternoon sun that shined directly through the French doors leading to the veranda. "Who's out there?"

She waited for an answer as a figure in a wheelchair entered through the open doorway, but the sun's brightness prevented her from seeing who it was. "Who are you?" She demanded to know. "There isn't supposed to be anyone else here."

The figure wheeled further into the room, and out of the brightness, halting at a comfortable distance. Charlotte gasped when she saw it was a disfigured man, who had obviously been the victim of some sort of fiery accident.

"There must be some sort of misunderstanding." The man said. "I was instructed to come here and ordered not to leave. I assumed I was alone."

Charlotte was perplexed as the man wheeled closer, and saluted her with what remained of his hand. "Corporal Manuel Garcia, U.S. Army, at your service, ma'am." His eyes wandered to his surroundings. "You have a lovely home here."

Charlotte gave him a slow nod of respect, "My name is Charlotte."

"What a beautiful name for such a pretty woman."

Charlotte looked downward with subtle shame, "I'm not so pretty on the inside. That's why they sent me here to be alone, Manuel."

"Please! Call me Manny." He paused to stare at her with serious thought. "Everyone has a dark side, Charlotte. Do you regret the things you've done?"

"Every bit of it." She shook her head with frustration. "I wish I could've done as much good as I did evil."

"If you're truly sorry for the things you did in life, you can find forgiveness." He stated. "All you have to do is ask with your heart."

Charlotte emotionally clenched her eyes shut for a moment. "I want that more than anything." She meekly responded.

Manny tried to lighten the moment with self-directed humor. "Now Charlotte!" He exclaimed. "If you were as hideously ugly as I am, then you really would have a problem."

He chuckled, but Charlotte negated it with a head shake and looked away. "Don't say that about yourself." A moment of awkward silence fell between them, and Charlotte turned her sights to him again. "What happened to you, Manny?"

He wheeled a bit closer, "I was with my platoon on maneuvers in Afghanistan. Our Hummer hit an IED in the road, and when they pulled my dead body from the wreckage, I looked like this."

Charlotte emotionally bit her lower lip. "I'm sorry."

"This is the third life in a row that I've gone off to war, and ended up being killed." He sighed. "I guess it's the fate I'm stuck with."

Manny stared through the narrow slits that were once full eyes. "Have you and I ever met before, Charlotte?" He asked. "There's something so familiar about your energy."

"I've been in spirit since the early 1980s." She shook her head. "I don't understand how that could be possible."

"Surely you know that you had other lifetimes as well." He stated.

She shrugged. "If I did, I have no conscious recall of it."

He wheeled uncomfortably within inches of her, "Would you mind if I touched your hand?"

Charlotte reluctantly offered her hand, and Manny gently rested his disfigured hand in her palm. Immediately, a bolt of energy passed between them, and their bodies convulsed from the power. Their lives unconsciously passed before them in those moments, like a movie in fast-forward.

As it finished, they both settled into a calm trance. Manny looked deep into her eyes with great wonder and gasped. "Judith? Is it really you?"

Charlotte's glassy eyes stared straight ahead as though foreseeing an imaginary scene. She reached out with her other hand, and lightly placed it against Manny's chest. "Harry!" She called out with great wonderment.

"Yes!" He emotionally exclaimed. "It's really me." He shook his head in shocked disbelief. "I vowed I would find your soul, somehow, somewhere." He sighed. "I've searched through so many lifetimes."

"I've also searched for you." She trembled. "I could never understand why I never found you again. I never wanted another."

"For me, there could never be another. You are my only soulmate."

Tears streamed down Charlotte's face as another surge of energy passed between them, causing them both to gasp again. They both calmed and snapped from their trances, reacting awkwardly as they struggled to regain their composures. "What just happened?" Manny asked.

"I think we were soulmates in another lifetime." She replied while trying to catch her breath. "I saw you die at the hands of a warrior, and my soul died along with you."

She glanced down as he withdrew his hand, and her eyes grew wide with amazement as it started to transform. Her eyes wandered up to his face, which had also begun transforming. "Manny!" She exclaimed with nervous anxiety.

Manny looked down at his hands with amazement, then raised them to feel his face. Speechless with shock, he slowly lifted himself from his wheelchair. "My God!" He cried. "It's a miracle."

He took a few steps, and they both trembled with excitement. "I'm the complete man I once was in life."

Charlotte cupped her hands over her mouth and emotionally gasped. "And a handsome man you are." She smiled.

They stood for a long moment, staring endearingly at each other, not knowing what to say or do next. Charlotte stammered as her heart filled with love. Her eyes wandered as a blinding light filled the doorway to the outside porch.

"Manny!" She caught her breath. "Would you like to go out on the veranda for a while, and talk?"

He smiled warmly as he turned to look at the light. He then gently took hold of Charlotte's still trembling hand. "Oh, Charlotte!" He exclaimed with exuberance. "My one wish would be to spend eternity, talking with you on that veranda." With that, they firmly gripped each other's hands and strolled into the bright light of their eternal paradise.

On the Isle of Rhodes, Meryl leaned against the edge of her balcony and gazed out over the scenic Aegean Sea. Ezekiel entered from the inside of the house and wrapped his arms passionately around her. "I almost forgot how beautiful the view was here." He commented.

"Hopefully, you'll stay around long enough to enjoy it." She quipped.

He snuggled romantically closer, "Don't worry! I'm not going anywhere for a while."

"I've heard that line a few times over the years." She laughed.

They paused to watch a sea bird flying overhead, and both pondered in dreamy thought. "Let's do it today, and get it over with." He casually proclaimed.

She turned and faced him with great surprise. "Are you sure this is what you want?"

"It took me all these centuries to come to my senses. But yes, I've never been more certain." He pulled her closer and stared into her eyes with great intensity. "You're the only woman who could ever set my heart to flame."

"You old dog!" She blushed. "I've waited seven centuries to hear the mighty Zeus say those words to me."

"Forgive me for the delay, my lady." They laughed and joyfully kissed.

Back at Branchview, Steven and Loraine sat alone at the breakfast table. Sharie entered from the kitchen and sighed.

"It's been a while since this old dining table has been this empty." She commented.

"Where is everyone this morning?" Steven asked.

"Gerard left for the office earlier, and Frederick is likely at the City Diner." She sat down. "I think that boy's rather keen on Suzy." She added with a grin.

"He could do worse." Steven chuckled. "Suzy's a smart girl, and charming as well."

"What about Tina? Where is she this morning?" Loraine asked.

"She went down to the ocean at the crack of dawn to wait for Philip." She shook her head with amazement. "Those two certainly love each other."

Steven smiled and tipped his coffee cup toward her. "Enjoy the break while you can, Sharie." Eddie and his family are moving into the West Wing later today, and we'll have a full house again."

"I wouldn't want it any other way, Steven." Sharie laughed.

On the beach at Lighthouse Point, Tina anxiously sat on the rocks, staring out over the waves of the Atlantic, hoping to catch sight of the man she loved. She was bundled up in a heavy coat and scarf but still shivered.

She nervously pulled the scarf tighter around her face to ward off the stiff, cold sea breezes. "Oh, Philip! Where are you?" she mumbled to herself.

Suddenly, her eyes caught something in the distance emerging from the water, and her heart jumped. She stood, squinting against the sun's intense glare.

After a few moments of anticipation, a smile broke across her face, and she shrieked with joy. "Philip!"

She ran to the water's edge, and Philip hurried his pace as he trudged through the rough waves to the shore. He ran the last several yards, and they met in a tight, passionate embrace. He joyfully lifted her off her feet and spun her around as they kissed.

"You and Linda did it!" She exclaimed. "Everyone in the real world is baffled about how Cordones and his thugs were captured."

Philip let loose with a hearty laugh. "Are you surprised, my dear?"

"Not in the least."

Philip set a determined look toward the cliffs above the point, then gently cupped Tina's face in his hands. "Let's go home to Branchview, and warm ourselves by the fire."

They kissed again, before slipping their arms around each other, and joyfully strolled away along the beach.

Chapter Twenty-Three:

Season's Change

Day gave way to night, and then another new dawn rose on the world surrounding Branchview. The cycle of life and time progressed, bringing with it new and unexpected experiences. As the sun peeked over the horizon of the Atlantic, Nebriana meditated with her arms outstretched to the air, within the clearing of the woods.

Another sunrise brings with it another change of season to the New England shoreline. The coming winter warns us of turbulent times ahead. Before I usher in another spring, humanity will transform forever in our world. I, as well as my sister, the Frost Queen, and all the gods who secretly strive to maintain the balance of good and evil, can only wait and hope our mission here is still far from being over.

Nebriana gazed upward toward the treetops. She twirled, while her fluttering wings lifted her from the ground. Magic flew from her delicate fingertips and painted the leaves in the golden colors of autumn. She then fluttered back to earth, as the morning sun rose above the treetops, and bathed warm light upon her, and the surrounding area of the clearing.

She admired her artistic mastery with joyful wonder, as Claudiana, the Frost Queen of Winter approached. Like Nebriana, she is a sight to behold, with her snowy white hair, pale skin, and flowing white gown. She stood next to her sister and savored the sight. "You've definitely outdone yourself this year, sister." She beamed. "The colors are outstanding."

"The humans should be delighted," Nebriana stated with a proud smile. "If this should be the last time, we need to make it memorable."

"You will linger a bit longer this year? Won't you?" Claudiana asked.

"As long as we can, I suppose." She replied. "I shouldn't need to remind you that our wings are vulnerable to the cold, and it's a long journey to the Hidden World."

"Don't I know it!" Claudiana chuckled. "The trip between here and the Northland seems to get longer every year."

"We certainly have had a good run. Haven't we?" Nebriana sadly stated.

"Keep your spirits up. We may still have a few seasons left." She replied with subtle encouragement. "I suppose it all depends on the humans' response to this next crisis."

"True." She sighed. "We've seen some desperate times in the past when we all thought it was the final curtain."

Claudiana lifted her hands to the air. "And here we are, for yet another round."

Nebriana responded with a comforting smile. "I trust you will help Poseidon protect the inhabitants of Branchview."

"Of course!" She answered. "I'll especially be keeping a keen eye on that handsome Steven Spencer."

"Too bad for you." Nebriana giggled. "He'll be spending the winter at his home in Florida."

"Oh drat!" She exclaimed with an amused sigh. "Perhaps it is the end of days after all." She paused and flashed an endearing smile toward her sister. "Come, dear!" She eagerly urged. "Let's find a cozy spot where we can chat about men, and perhaps a bit more."

At the City Diner, Steven and Philip were having breakfast. Something that had become somewhat of a normal routine for them. "How are things progressing with the house?" Steven asked.

"I'm glad you mentioned that," Philip said between bites of food. "I'll need to have either you or Gerard secure the permitting so that we can begin to lay the new foundation before the first frost."

Philip took a sip of his coffee and enthusiastically continued, "Once we get started, it shouldn't take too long to complete. We'll be following the pattern of the old house's foundation."

"Great!" Steven replied. "I've seen floor plans, and pictures of the old estate at the library. It was a beautiful old house."

"Of course, we'll be modernizing it a bit," Philip added. "Part of the house will be partitioned off for Tony and Andrea."

Steven gestured his approval with a raised coffee cup. "Good! I can imagine the small room in the West Wing is a bit cramped for them, and the baby."

Suzy breezed by, topping off their coffees, and sliding into the booth next to Philip. "Good morning, Suzy!" Philip said with a pleasant smile. "How are things working out with our boy Frederick?"

"He likes to be called Rick now," Suzy responded with a smirk. "And, you tell me, he cooked your breakfast."

He exchanged an impressed glance with Steven, who commented. "You've taught him well, Suzy. This is delicious!"

Suzy beamed pridefully, but quickly changed to a more serious subject. "I'm still having those same strange dreams, and horrible visions."

"The same ones you spoke of before?" Steven asked with great concern.

Suzy rapidly nodded yes. "I mentioned it to Meryl before she left, but she said it wasn't anything to be alarmed about."

Philip's demeanor turned noticeably blunt. Meryl's probably right. You'd be better off just forgetting about it."

"But everything seemed so real." She responded with much anxiety. "What if it were to actually happen?"

"Just drop it, Suzy!" Philip answered sternly, taking both her and Steven by surprise at his change of attitude. "I'm sure you have other more important things to fuss over." He concluded.

Suzy was offended by his tone and took on an attitude of her own. "Perhaps you're right, Philip. I should ignore everything else, and just run my little Diner."

She rushed away from the table without another word, while Philip soberly turned his attention to his food, and avoided eye contact with Steven. "Was that really necessary, Philip?"

"Some things are better off left alone, Steven." He glanced up with all seriousness. "Trust me on that."

Steven only answered with a concerned stare, and puzzled expression, while deciding it best not to carry the conversation any further.

The entire Branchview staff packed into the nursery for a short meeting. They all surrounded Loraine, who held baby Olivia, and Sharie, who held baby London.

"Thank you all for coming to this spontaneous meeting this morning," Loraine announced. "I promise I won't be too long-winded."

"That'll be a first." Sharie joked. Everyone responded with a quick laugh, and Loraine flashed an endearing smile toward her, before continuing. "As some of you may have heard, our other home in Florida has been refurbished from the fire, and we plan to spend our winter there."

A disappointing groan rose from the assembly, and Loraine then gestured to Mrs. Porter. "I've already spoken to Mrs. Porter, and she'll be going with us."

Loraine gestured for Sharie to take it from there. "We've also decided to take cost-cutting measures for the upcoming winter months." Sharie paused, as a few worried mumbles erupted. "The entire South Wing will be closed in the Spencer's absence. We'll also be cutting back on hours, and unfortunately, laying off a few of our groundskeepers."

As everyone exchanged worried glances, Loraine tried to move things along quickly. "We've also decided if you wish to make the seasonal journey with us, we'd be happy to keep you in our employ." Loraine waited and glanced around the room with a smile. Andrea, holding baby Michael, set a long, peering glance toward her husband Tony, while Loraine continued. "Our estate is only a fraction the size of this place, but we'll still need a small staff to assist Mrs. Porter."

Mary stepped forward first. "I appreciate the offer, Ms. Loraine. But Sharie here tells me that Florida is a place where old folks die, and I'm not about to go meet the Lord yet."

Loraine shot an amused glance toward a somewhat embarrassed Sharie, and chuckles filled the room. "Besides, this is the only true home I've ever known," Mary concluded. "I never want to leave Branchview again."

"And you never will, Mary," Sharie assured.

Andrea impatiently handed the baby off to Tony, and boldly stepped forward. "I'd like you to consider Tony and me, Mrs. Spencer."

Tony looked at his wife with great surprise. "Are you serious?" He whispered.

She only answered him with a definite nod, while Loraine seemed amazed. "I'd be glad to discuss it with you further, Andrea." She replied. "It would be pleasant to keep all the children together."

Sharie raised her hand and interceded. "Just one more issue, and we'll let everyone get back to work."

She gestured for Loraine to continue, "My precious mother, who has been a tremendous help to me over the past several months, will return to London soon."

Millie stepped forward and interrupted, "On that subject, I must say there has been a small change of plans." She glanced back toward Bill and motioned him forward. "Come on, darling! This also concerns you."

Loraine and Sharie exchanged puzzled expressions as Bill timidly stepped forward, and took hold of Millie's hand. "I will return to England." She continued. "But only to relinquish my assets, before I apply for my green card to the States." She glanced admirably at Bill. "Mr. Crawford and I will be married."

Loraine's jaw dropped in disbelief as cheers and claps erupted before Bill interceded. "I'll accompany Millie on her journey back to England, and we'll be returning in the Spring." He added.

"I must say, mother. You always loved to catch me off guard on things." Loraine quipped.

"It's what I do best, my dear." She answered with a sly grin.

Bill also motioned for further attention from those in the room. "I'd also like you to gather in the Foyer area after lunch. I have a special surprise for Mr. and Mrs. Spencer." He winked at Loraine, who countered.

"It would take a lot to top the surprise I just heard." She grinned. "What might this be about?"

"You'll just have to wait, and see." He chuckled.

Loraine exchanged a wary glance with Sharie. "Do the surprises never end?"

"The drama never ceases in this old house, Lori." Sharie laughed.

On this pleasant morning, Philip and Tina strolled hand in hand along the Branchview pathway, beneath a colorful canopy of trees. "The colors are so beautiful." Tina proclaimed

"Indeed!" Philip agreed. "Nebriana has certainly done a fine job this year."

Philip appeared troubled as they continued along, and Tina took notice. "Are you alright?" You seem distracted."

"I'm seriously thinking of sending you to Alfheim for the duration of your pregnancy."

Tina came to a halt and faced him. "But I want to stay here with you." She protested. "I don't wish our baby to be born in a strange land without you being there."

Philip carefully contemplated his next words. "Tina!" He began with hesitation. "We're heading into a harsh winter, and being a mortal, you could be susceptible to various viruses."

"You're wrong about that, Philip." She stated with certainty.

He responded with a perplexed expression as she continued, "There's something that you and I never considered." She smiled. "I may have the functional body of a mortal woman, just as you do a mortal man. But like you, I'm immortal."

"What are you saying?" He asked. "That can't be."

"Think about it." Her eyes sparkled with exuberance. "I was created from plaster, and synthetics by a mannequin artist. I was only given life through the magic of Charlotte Locke." She paused to let her words sink in. "I'll always stay as I was created, and never grow any older than what I am right now." She grabbed hold of his arms and stared directly into his eyes. "No human disease could ever destroy me."

Philip is flabbergasted. "So, if you're an immortal as I am, what will our baby be?"

"I guess we'll know that answer in time." She took hold of Philip's hands firmly. "I can tell you one thing for sure. I have no intention of leaving Branchview, or even more so, leaving your side for any extended period of time.

She pulled him closer, and her piercing blue eyes peered directly into his. "Now, I know that something more has been troubling you." She paused. "If you truly love, and trust me, you'll tell me what it is." Philip emotionally sighed and surrendered with a reluctant nod.

In a hallway of Branchview, away from others who might hear, Tony and Andrea engaged in a serious conversation. "Did you ever consider talking things over with me, before you said that to Loraine?" Tony asked.

"Oh, Tony! I can't imagine spending a long, cold winter in that cramped room in the West Wing."

"I know." He replied in a calm tone. "But my father will be livid. He's insistent on keeping the family close together." He pauses with a sigh. "I showed you the plans for the new house. It will be like two separate residences under one roof."

"But it will be a long time before that house is completed, and ready to move into." She reasoned. "This will give me a chance to see something more than Connecticut in the winter, and it will also give the children a chance to continue growing up together."

Tony contemplated the dilemma for a moment. "Andrea! I love you and baby Michael more than anything in this world." He paused. "If this is what you truly want, then we'll do it." Andrea was ecstatic, and the couple embraced in a loving kiss.

Chapter Twenty-Four:

The Book of Life

During the busy lunch hour rush at the City Diner, Rick, formerly known as Frederick, worked diligently over the short-order grill. Suzy paused to lean into the window, appearing anxious. "Is the order ready for table 3?" She asked.

"Coming right up." He glanced up at her while continuing to work. "Is everything alright?"

"Oh, Rick! I feel like Philip, Ezekiel, and Meryl are withholding information concerning those dreams and visions I've been having."

"Should I speak to Mr. Spencer about it?"

"Thanks! But I don't want to pull you in on this." She gratefully smiled. "I'll call Steven once the lunchtime crowd eases up."

Rick flipped the burgers on the grill. "Hey! I thought of a new last name for myself."

"Really? Tell me!"

"Since I'm originally from Springfield, I could use the name Rick Springfield."

"Good grief!" Suzy put her hand to her forehead. "There's already someone famous with that name."

"Oh!" He glanced up cluelessly. "I guess I'll just have to keep trying."

"We'll come up with something." She giggled.

Rick set a platter in the window in front of her. "Order up!"

After lunch, in the Branchview house, the staff and inhabitants gathered for yet another meeting. This time, they gathered in the main Foyer.

Bill stood above everyone, on the first landing of the stairs, next to a picture with a cloth draped over it. He quieted the gathering, as Millie ushered Steven into the room, and positioned him next to Loraine.

Steven looked up toward the covered picture and whispered to his wife. "Please tell me he didn't restore that horrible picture."

"I haven't the foggiest," Loraine whispered back.

Bill cleared his throat and began. "A few short months ago, I took a portrait picture of Steven and Loraine." He gestured to them with a smile. "When the picture that originally hung here was mysteriously destroyed, I could only vision one other taking its' place." He pulled the draping cloth away. "Ladies and gentlemen, I present you our beloved Master, and Mistress of Branchview."

Claps and cheers erupted, while Steven and Loraine were taken aback with great surprise at the regal picture of them, with Bumpers posed at their feet.

"We're so deeply honored by this," Loraine announced in a burst of enthusiasm.

"I certainly didn't expect this," Steven added, shaking his head with amazement as he gazed up at the picture. "Thank you very much, Bill."

Sharie stepped to the center of the Foyer. "Alright, everybody!" She announced. Fun time is over. We all have work to do."

As everyone moved on their way, Bill approached Steven with a proud grin. "I wondered when we'd ever see that picture," Steven commented.

"Maybe it's fate that it was delayed," Bill answered. "Consider it a departing gift from me."

Steven was perplexed, "Wait a minute! What am I missing here?"

"Millie and I will depart for London next week." He exuberantly announced.

Millie leaned in toward the men with a sly grin. "We're getting married!"

Steven looked to Loraine, who simply shrugged, then back toward Millie and Bill with astonishment. "Knock me down with a ton of bricks!" Steven comically stated. "I sure didn't see that one coming."

Millie jokingly elbowed Steven in the ribs. "To tell you the truth, neither did I."

All laughed, and Steven let out an accentuated sigh, as he eyed the elder couple, "Congratulations to both of you."

Millie grabbed Steven by the sleeve with authority. "Come along, and have your coffee, while Loraine and I have a spot of tea." She commanded. "I'll tell you all about our plans."

As Steven is led toward the Sitting Room, he glanced back at Bill with a raised eyebrow. "Are you sure you're ready to settle with this one?" He joked. "She can be a bit bossy."

"I suppose I'll just have to get used to it" He laughed.

After everyone left the room, the spirits of Daphne and Maggie appeared on the stair landing. They stood, and admired the new portrait, "I must say, this is a superior improvement over what was there before," Daphne stated while glancing down at the child. "Wouldn't you agree, Maggie?"

Maggie soberly looked up at her and nodded in agreement. "It looks like the picture of Jack, Penelope, and Scooter in the Grand Corridor."

Daphne stood back and further admired it with a satisfied grin, "It certainly does, my dear!"

While everyone resumed their lives in the future world of Branchview, a final scenario developed in 1697, setting the stage for the escalating drama that would unfold in the years that bridged the past with the present.

In a dreary household in Lockeport, Mrs. Barrow stood with authority over a young Liddy McPherson. Liddy was on her hands and knees, scrubbing the dirty tile floors in the poorly lit room. "When you get done with that, the kitchen needs to be cleaned." She ordered.

She put her hands on her hips, and stiffened her stance, while Liddy remained silent in resuming her chores.

"Have you forgotten how to speak, you little witch?"

"No ma'am! A weary Liddy looked upward. "I will clean the kitchen as well."

"That's more like it." The woman sneered.

There was an unexpected knock at the door, and Mrs. Barrow stormed off to answer it, "Who could that be at this hour of the afternoon?" She complained.

She swung the door open with vigor, and her eyes grew wide with terror. "What in the hell are you doing here?" she inquired. "You're supposed to be dead."

Roger McPherson laughed, as he kicked the door the rest of the way open, and barged in. "I be very much alive and full of vengeance, Mrs. Barrow."

Her fearful eyes quickly shifted to an adjacent room, where a young boy stood in the doorway, trembling with fear. "Henry! Mrs. Barrow commanded. "Go fetch Sheriff Morton."

"Don't waste your time, boy," Roger warned. "The sheriff be dead." He let loose with a sinister laugh. "I left the bloody bastard hanging from the rafters of the jailhouse, just as he hanged me, beloved Jenny."

The little boy ran from the room in fear, while Liddy caught sight of her long-lost father from her vantage in the adjacent room. She ran, and joyfully hugged him. "Daddy! You're alive!"

He went down to one knee to greet the happy girl. "Yes, me dear Liddy, I have returned for you."

Mrs. Barrow sneered at him with anger and brandished a long dagger from the belt of her dress. "You ain't taking her nowhere. The little witch is my ward."

He mumbled a few words in Gaelic and flicked his wrist in her direction. The hand holding the knife ignited in flame, and in both panic and pain, she tossed the knife away and attempted to extinguish the fire with her dress. Roger quickly moved forward and gripped her neck with one hand. He maniacally squeezed tighter, as she fell to her knees, gasping for air. Blood streamed from the corners of her bulging eyes, and nostrils. With one final gasp, she collapsed to the floor, and her eyes stared vacantly, toward the ceiling.

Liddy paced up to her father's side, "Is she dead, daddy?"

"Aye, Liddy!" He kicked her dead body and spat on it with anger. "The old bitch can no longer harm you."

He affectionately stroked the little girls' hair, while she stared at Mrs. Barrow's dead body.

"Come along now, Liddy!" He coaxed her. "We'll start a new life. Just you and me." He smiled. "And I'll teach ye all ye need to know to reap vengeance on those who did you wrong."

"Where are we going now?"

"As far away from this house, and this cursed town as we can get for now." He sneered with disdain as his eyes surveyed the dingy room around them. "We'll return one day, and seek our own type of justice on the people who did this to us."

"How will we do that?"

Roger went down to one knee again to address his young daughter. "Since they accuse us all of being evil witches and warlocks, then that is what we'll be." He grinned. "I'll teach you the craft, and then we'll take vengeance on both the Locke and Branch families, as well as this bloody town." He looked away with determination and nodded. "They will all pay for what they have done to us."

At the modern-day Branchview Estate, Philip escaped to the Main Study to do some reading. He got comfortable in Steven's plush desk chair, leaned forward, and opened the large book. There was a light knock on the door, and he glanced up with a sigh.

"So much for privacy." He muttered sarcastically.

The door slowly opened, and Steven peeked in. "Loraine told me you might be in here. Do you have a few moments?"

Philip closed the book and motioned to a seat on the other side of the desk. "It's your study, Steven. I simply wanted to get away, and do some reading."

Steven sat down and gestured toward the book. "That's a huge book." He joked. "I hope you hadn't planned on reading it all in one sitting."

Philip leaned forward and placed both hands over the cover to conceal the title. "I brought this here from the Secret Cave. It's quite old." He quickly changed the subject. "I understand Tony and Andrea have decided to go south with you for the winter."

"Are you okay with that?" Steven casually asked.

"They're adults, with their own lives." He shrugged. "It's not my duty to tell them what to do."

Steven was perplexed by Philip's cold demeanor and continued with a shrug of his own. "For what it's worth, I'll do everything I can to provide them a pleasant home, along with their employment."

Philip managed a weak smile, "I have no doubts about that."

Steven took a deep breath and continued, "You and I have become as close as brothers over this past year." He paused. "We've fought battles together, shared our deepest secrets, and forged a special trust between us."

"What are you getting at, Steven?" He asked with impatient anxiety.

Steven stared at him for a long uncomfortable moment, before answering, "I know there's something you're keeping from me, and I'm not leaving this room until you tell me what it is."

Philip sighed, and contemplated for a moment, before lifting his hands off the book, "Have you ever read Revelations in the Christian Bible?"

"Of course!" Steven answered. "It's a tough read to interpret, but I was raised in a strict Christian household."

Philip turned the book so Steven could read the title. "The gods have an unedited version of the Bible." He gestured to the book. "We call it the Book of Life."

"What do you mean by unedited?" Steven curiously asked.

"It has all the truths held in confidence from the human race from the beginning of time."

"In other words, the knowledge that would've proved dangerous in the wrong hands," Steven stated with certainty.

Philip gave a definitive nod as he opened the book, and began to read it out loud. "In the final days, there will rise a red serpent from the east, and it will ally with the agents of Satan stationed throughout the world."

He glanced up from the book, as though to beg a response from Steven. "I do not doubt they're speaking of China, and the Secret Society," Steven responded.

"Or, as I prefer to call them, The Society of Satan." Philip concurred.

He continued to read from the scriptures, following along with his fingers. "In those days, these allies will bring plague and unfathomable atrocities that will bring the mightiest nations to their knees. This will be the beginning of the end days on earth."

He closed the book, and peered at Steven with intense eyes, before continuing.

"Those visions that Suzy and Meryl had been foretelling concern the days ahead of us. We've now entered the beginning of the end times."

Steven reacted with nervous thought. "That can't be right, Philip."

Philip glanced toward him sternly with a raised brow. "What would make you say that?"

Steven leaned forward in his chair, as he began to recant. "When I was in 1697, I met an old Indian Shaman named Stargazer." He paused. "He told me that he traveled through the Branchview portal of time to the year 2052."

Philip reacted with considerable surprise, "You mean to tell me that this world actually endured until that time?"

"Obviously!" Steven answered." Although, he did say the world was in a tumultuous state at that time."

"How so?" Philip inquired further.

"This Estate and this house no longer existed as we know it." He paused. "Greedy developers had destroyed it."

"Everything?" Philip probed further.

Steven answered with a disappointing nod, "I made a promise to him, and Nebriana, that I'd do everything I could to prevent that destruction from actually happening."

Philip nearly leaped across the desk with intensity. "You mean to tell me that Nebriana knew of this?"

"Initially," Steven explained. "But like you and the others, I'm guessing she had her memory purged of it after Charlotte and I left."

Philip sighed, and settled back into his chair with great thought, "So, we know that the world will still exist in 32 years. But how is it that evil men have gained control of this property?" He pondered the question for a moment. "Perhaps there are no good people left."

"Wait a minute!" Steven spoke up. "Doesn't the Book of Life give you an approximate end date?"

Philip shook his head, "No one, but the Divine Creator, knows the exact time."

"Then how can you assume there won't be any good people left on earth 32 years from now?" Steven glared across the desk. "Even if Lori and I are no longer here, I do not doubt that our children will be."

"In both books, it states clearly that all righteous people will be evacuated from the earth before evil completely takes hold, and the planet is eventually destroyed," Philip explained.

"You're speaking of the Rapture!" Steven exclaimed with great intensity.

"Precisely!" Philip stated. "And, I have no doubts that you and your family will be among those who are spared."

Philip stood with excessive anxiety and paced away to the far corner of the room, "China and the Globalists of the Secret Society plan to crash the world economy with a pandemic." He turned and paced back toward Steven.

"We've identified the major player in this country as a man named Charles Laszlo." He stated.

"Charles Laszlo!" Steven bolted from his chair. "That old bastard has been spending his billions to destroy capitalism and democracy while promoting communism in this country for years." He paused with utter frustration. "What can we do to stop him?"

"We can't do anything, Steven!" He answered, before settling back in his chair. "We must have faith, and let everything run its' natural course." He sighed with total frustration. "Ezekiel and I will do all we can to spare Branch Consolidated, and Branchview from falling to ruin during our duration here on earth. But we're not permitted to do much else."

Steven also settled back in his seat and looked to Philip with curiosity. "Surely, you'll be evacuated during the same time we are."

Philip shook his head, "We'll remain here to fight in the battle to end all battles. It's our chosen destiny." He raised a hand to halt the conversation. "I've already said too much. We should just leave it at that."

Steven sighed, and gave a reluctant nod of agreement, "There's just one more thing," Steven stated with emphasis. "There's a young lady in the Dining Room with Lori, who deserves an apology and some sort of explanation."

Philip shamefully replied, "Suzy!"

"You know that there's a reason she's been given those dreams and visions, Philip?" Steven reasoned. "Perhaps she could help us all if you'd just give her a chance."

Philip reluctantly responded with a surrendering nod. "You're right! We can never have too many allies in our fight against evil." He smiled. "I'll talk with her."

In the Sitting Room, the ghost of Maggie Branch lifted the lid of the music box that sat on a side table and watched with enthusiastic joy as the porcelain ballerina slowly turned to the tune of Stardust. A curious Tricia heard the music from the outer Foyer and wandered into the room.

When she saw Maggie, she quickly went over and stood next to her. "That's a pretty music box." She commented.

"It used to belong to Penelope," Maggie replied.

"Who's Penelope?"

"She used to live here. She died." Maggie turned and faced Tricia. "I'm Maggie! What's your name?"

"I'm Tricia!" She replied with much excitement. "I just moved here with my mommy and daddy yesterday."

"I know." Maggie soberly nodded. "I remember your father when he lived here a long time ago."

Tricia's eyes grew wide, "Are you a ghost, Maggie?"

Maggie nodded again, then turned her attention to the door when she heard footsteps on the floor of the Foyer.

She quickly set the music box down, and promptly disappeared, while Tricia reacted with confusion.

Steven casually entered the room, sorting through his mail, "Hi there, Tricia!"

"Hi, Mr. Spencer"

Steven glanced around the room, as the music box winded down on the tabletop, "I could've sworn I heard you talking to someone."

Tricia strolled closer, "I was talking to Maggie."

Steven sat down on the loveseat, "Oh! So, you've met our Maggie?"

Tricia nodded an enthusiastic yes, and scooted onto the love seat next to him, "I don't know where she went." She shrugged. "She just disappeared when you walked into the room."

He glanced around the room again and chuckled. "She comes and goes like that."

He smiled, and turned his attention back to the mail, while Tricia contently dangled her little legs, which were too short to reach the floor. "I understand you've found my mother's music box."

"Was your mother Penelope?" She asked while glancing up at him with wonderment.

"Yes, she was." He set the mail aside. "I miss her very much."

"I'm sorry!" she replied with a sad pout.

Steven curiously glanced around, yet again, "Was she here too."

Tricia soberly shook her head, "Are there other ghosts here, Mr. Spencer?"

"Yes, Tricia." He chuckled. "I'd have to say a few ghosts lurk around this old house."

The black cat sauntered into the room ahead of Loraine and immediately leaped onto Steven's lap. "Can I pet the pretty kitty?" Tricia asked with excitement.

"Yes, you can." He handed the purring cat over to the little girl. "Her name is Midnight. Be gentle with her now."

Loraine stood in the doorway and endearingly watched the scenario, before slowly strolling over, "You and that cat." She said while shaking her head. "Have you decided whether we should take her with us?"

Steven hesitated before answering, as he continued watching Tricia pet the contented cat resting in her lap.

"Somehow, I don't think it would be right." He stared up at Loraine. "I suppose she belongs here at Branchview."

He looks back to the little girl, and the cat. "Tricia! How would you like to take care of Midnight while I'm gone?"

"Really, Mr. Spencer?" Her face lit up with joy. "I promise I'll take good care of her."

"I wouldn't trust her care with anyone else other than you."

"Thank you!" She kissed Steven on the cheek. "I can't wait to tell mommy and daddy."

The cheerful little girl cradled the cat in her arms like a baby, as she hurried from the room. Loraine took her vacated seat and kissed Steven. "You just made that little girl's day." She smiled. "I hope you plan on taking Bumpers with us though."

"Of course!" He answered with assurance. "He can ride in the car with me."

"What about me?"

"I planned on leaving well ahead of you so that I could orchestrate the movers when they brought our belongings from storage." He explained.

His announcement ruffled Loraine, "You are not going ahead without me, Steven Spencer."

"Why not?" He inquired with a shrug. "I thought you and the children would be better off catching a flight with the others, and the house would be ready when you all got there."

She faced Steven in a huff, "You and I, and the babies, have shared little quality time." She vented. "I figured a two-day car trip would be good for precisely that."

"That settles it then." He answered with a mild shrug. "You'll all go with me and Bumpers."

They kissed, and Steven leaned back in deep thought, while Loraine watched him admirably.

"What are you thinking about, darling?"

"I was just thinking about my mother, and how she always talked about the grand parties they used to have in the Ballroom." He pondered a bit longer. "I think we should have a party before we leave. Spare no expense."

"Steven!" She exclaimed with great joy. "That's an excellent idea." She leaped from her seat. "I'll hurry to tell the others, and we can start planning." They kissed again, and Loraine hurried from the room with excitement, while Steven leaned back with a contented smile.

Chapter Twenty-Five:

The Wrath of Poseidon

Early that afternoon, Philip sat at the edge of his bed in a guest room of the West Wing. His eyes wandered upward, as he prayed, and spoke the words in a low tone, "Please forgive me for what I'm about to do. But something must be done to stifle such evil, and I can't tolerate sitting still while it destroys innocent lives." He paused in careful thought and closed his eyes. "I realize I will be fully held accountable when I face my final judgment." He opened his eyes and gazed upward again. "Please know that my heart was in a righteous place"

Philip reverently bowed his head, while Tina breezed into the room. She noticed his somber demeanor and immediately sat down next to him, slipping her arm around his broad back. "Sweetheart! Are you alright?" she asked with great concern. "I heard you talking before I entered the room."

"I'm fine." He smiled. "I was just saying my daily prayers."

She turned toward him with much exuberance. "I'm so excited!" She announced. "I just spoke with Lori, and she told me that we can begin moving into the East Wing."

"That's wonderful news." He smiled weakly. "It'll be good to have our own personal quarters."

They joyfully snuggled closer, "Do you think we could start moving in tonight?" She asked.

"Let's make it tomorrow night." He stated with a wink. "I was just preparing to leave for New York. I have some business to tend to, and won't be home until late."

"Okay!" Tina answered with a frustrated sigh. "Would you mind if I drove up to New Haven to do some shopping?"

"I'd feel much more confident if Lori went with you." He glanced downward with great worry, "There's much evil lurking about, and I'd prefer you don't go anywhere by yourself."

"You're so overly protective." She exhaled a deep breath, and kissed him on the cheek. "You're going to be such a good father."

"I've made a vow to play that role properly this time around." He answered with amusement.

They kissed again, and Tina got up to depart, but turned back. "I almost forgot to tell you. Lori and Steven are holding a formal party in the Ballroom before they leave."

"A party!" Philip's face lit up with a smile. "What a splendid way to send them off."

"I'm going to miss them so much when they're gone." She sadly stated. "I truly love our Branchview family."

"As do I." He added with great enthusiasm and emotion."

After everyone had cleared from the Dining Room following lunch, a weary Mrs. Porter sat down at the empty table. The Irish Setter, Finn wandered in and settled comfortably at her feet. She buried her face in her hands, and began to cry, while the dog looked up at her with sad, caring eyes.

Loraine entered the room, and upon seeing her weeping, she immediately hurried to comfort her. "Mrs. Porter!" She exclaimed with deep concern. "What on earth is wrong, my dear?"

Mrs. Porter reacted with embarrassment and tried to regain her composure, "Oh! It's nothing really." She just shook her head. "Just an old lady feeling rather melancholy."

Loraine slipped a comforting arm around her. "Oh, come now!" She stated. "If you can't confide in me, then who can you trust?" She reasoned. "Please do tell me what's wrong."

"I've been having problems remembering little things lately, and it's starting to affect me in my daily duties." She sighed. "I fear I'm just getting old and losing my functioning capabilities."

"Oh, hogwash!" Loraine quipped. "You're just tired, and could use some rest."

"I just don't want to be put out to pasture." She replied with a weak smile. "You and Steven are the only family I have left."

"That's not true." Loraine countered. "Everyone in this household is your family, and we all love, and care dearly for you." She laid an assuring hand over Mrs. Porter's trembling hand. "We'll always be there for you, my dear."

She gave a warm smile of reassurance before continuing, "Now, I'm going to mix you a tincture of Bacopa, Periwinkle, and Ginkgo." She advised. "I want you to put 10 drops into a purified glass of water, twice a day, and drink it." She paused. "I'm convinced you'll notice a difference within a week or so. I'll even put a bit of my special magic in there for good measure." She winked with assurance.

"What if it doesn't work?" She countered with frustration. "I never want to become a burden to anyone."

"It will work." Loraine confidently placed her hands firmly on her shoulders. "That bit of magic I speak of is love. And there is no greater healer." She nodded assuredly. "Steven and I will hire some extra help to ease some of your burdens. Whatever the future may hold, always know that we'll give you the same special care you've given us for so many years."

Mrs. Porter was overwhelmed, "I'm so grateful to have all of you in my life."

"And we, as well as everyone else here at Branchview, feel the same way about you."

The two women emotionally embraced, while Finn jumped up, nudging his head against them, whimpering, and attempting to join in. The women both laughed, and Mrs. Porter extended her arms out to the dog and embraced it. "Come on, you old pooch!" She chuckled. "You can join in on this love fest too."

After an eventful day, the Foyer clock chimed at 10 pm in the Great House. The front door opened, and a very tired Rick entered. As he shut the door, Steven strode in from the Sitting Room, wearing his robe, and carrying a manilla folder. "Oh good!" Steven exclaimed. "I've been waiting up for you."

"I apologize." He answered. "Suzy gave me a ride home after we closed the Diner."

Steven held up the folder with a grin, "I met with Agent Guitierez earlier today, and he had this to give you."

He handed it over, and Frederick quickly opened it. "That has all the proper paperwork, including a birth certificate, and a social security card you'll need in your new life."

Frederick looked everything over carefully. "I suppose I can now count myself as a member of the modern world."

"Either I or Gerard will have to teach you how to drive a car." He chuckled. "But we'll definitely take our time with that."

"I guess I'll now be known as Frederick Worth."

"Or, Rick Worth, if you prefer," Steven commented with a smile.

He shook his head with amazement, "I think I like the sound of that." He paused. "I can never thank you enough for all this, Mr. Spencer."

Steven waved off the comment and moved the conversation along, "How are things going for you down at the Diner?"

"It's hard work, but I don't mind it."

"You sure spend a lot of time there." He commented with a sly grin. "Would I be wrong in saying you might be a little keen on Ms. McVea?"

Frederick blushes with embarrassment, "I have to admit. I am fond of her."

"Do you happen to know if she has similar feelings for you?"

"I don't know." He responded with visible frustration. "She can be a bit distant at times."

"Well!" Steven sighed. "Just like you, that young lady has been through a lot in a short period." He paused. "Give her some space, and she'll come around."

Frederick responded with a grateful nod. "If you'll excuse me, I think I'll turn in for the night." He concluded with a sigh. "It's been a long day." He paused. "Goodnight, Mr. Spencer."

"Goodnight, Mr. Rick Worth," he turned his head back at hearing the sound of his new name and gave an approving smile and nod.

At his mansion in West Chester, New York, Charles Laszlo sat in his dimly lit home office, browsing the internet. He was a stodgy man, with vacant eyes set deep, with intense circles beneath them. He took a long drag off of his cigar and coughed afterward.

He paused when he heard a noise at the other end of the room, and placed the cigar on the edge of an ashtray next to his desktop, "Martin!" He called out. "Is that you?"

An imposing figure slowly strolled from out of the shadows of the room. The dim light revealed the stern face of Philip Seagraves. "I'm afraid Martin is taking a little catnap, Mr. Laszlo."

Laszlo reached for a hidden button beneath his desk. "That button won't work either." Philip confidently stated. "I took it upon myself to disable your security system ahead of time."

"Impossible!" He grunted. "That system is completely hack-proof." He chortled arrogantly. "State of the art!"

Philip chuckled with equal arrogance. "Not against my supernatural magic, Mr. Laszlo."

"My other security person shows up in around 20 minutes. You'll never make it out of here alive." He sneered. "Nevertheless, what do you want?"

"I thought maybe we could have a drink, and a little chat." Philip held up a wine bottle. "I borrowed this fine Chardonnay from your wine cellar." He glanced at the label and nodded his approval. "1938! I think I made an excellent choice if I can say so myself."

"Very well!" He grunted. You'll find glasses on that mini bar over there."

Laszlo reached into his desk drawer and pulled out a revolver. While Philip had his back turned, he maniacally fired every bullet in the chamber into him. Philip only twitched, and rolled his eyes, as he continued pouring the wine steadily into the glasses. He flipped the heavy stone of his Tiger's eye ring upward and sprinkled a considerable amount of powder into one of the glasses.

He then turned to see the now shocked face of Laszlo, still holding the gun in his trembling hand. "Mr.

Laszlo!" He exclaimed with a chuckle. "Is that any way to treat a distinguished guest?"

He confidently sauntered across the room and set the crystal glass of wine in front of a still stunned Laszlo. The elder man finally set the gun down on the desk and peered with awe-stricken wonder at Philip as he settled comfortably in a chair on the other side. "Who the hell are you?" Laszlo asked in a demanding tone. "You can't be human."

Philip grinned and raised his wine glass toward him, "You're right about that, but let's not talk about me." He stared with intense intimidation. "Let's talk about the plot that you, the Society of Satan, and the Chinese military have for bringing down the world economy."

Laszlo let loose with an evil chuckle, followed by a short coughing attack.

He recovered a bit and took a short sip of wine, "That was a fine choice of wine. I'm impressed Mr…"

"Seagraves! Philip Seagraves."

Laszlo gazed at him with calculating eyes. "What do you know about the Secret Society, Mr. Seagraves?"

"I know it consists of Globalist lunatics like yourself, who want to rule the world, while most of the population serves as your slaves."

"What you perceive as lunacy, I regard as brilliance." He chuckled. "My colleagues and I own, and control everything. That includes the media, politicians, and the justice system, Mr. Seagraves." He paused. "We can't be defeated, because we're too widespread, and the identity of our players is greatly concealed." He continued despite Philip's mocking expressions. "We secretly fund groups that oppose each other to promote civil unrest. We call it to divide, and conquer." He grunted. "The general population is so ignorant that they actually fall for it."

"You are an evil and pitiful excuse for a man. Aren't you, Mr. Laszlo?"

Laszlo tipped his wine glass toward Philip. "Maybe in the view of simple minds." He grinned arrogantly. "The only winners in life are those who have power over others.

Surely, you're smart enough to realize that, Mr. Seagraves."

"I understand that more than you could ever know," Philip stated without a flinch. "I also know that the powerful eventually grow arrogant, and slip up. In such cases, they set themselves up for a great fall."

Laszlo's face grew stern, as he took another larger sip of his wine, nearly emptying the glass. He then went into another coughing spell that was somewhat worse than the others. "Not feeling well, Mr. Laszlo?" He tauntingly asked.

"What did you put in my wine."

Philip shrugged mockingly. "Only a lethal dose of the same rat poison that you sprinkle into every batch of your pharmaceutical products." He glanced upward. "I believe you and your kind refer to it as societal genocide." He then sat forward in his seat. "The fewer mouths there are to feed, the more portions available for the pompous and socially privileged.

Laszlo clutched at his throat as he began to choke, and gasp for air. His eyes widened with desperation, while Philip sat observing in calm amusement. He provided commentary for the benefit of the dying man.

"You're now bleeding internally, and soon your organs will shut down, and cease to function." He grunted. "Lucky for you, it's a much shorter death than the victims of your manufactured virus will suffer." Philip chuckled arrogantly. "Oh yes, I know all about that dastardly plan as well."

Laszlo tried desperately to speak one final word but fell from his chair instead. Philip got up and stood over his crumpled body with intimidation.

"It'll all be over soon." Philip coldly stated. "Such a pity that you won't be able to further contribute to your evil causes."

Laszlo gasped for one last breath of air, and spit blood from his mouth, "When you get to hell, tell your Master that Poseidon sends his regards." He sneered. "Also tell him that I'm well-prepared for battle."

Laszlo's eyes grew wide one final time, before rolling back into a vacant stare. Philip took a business card with only a simple image of a trident on it and placed it into Laszlo's lifeless, open hand.

"Goodbye, Mr. Laszlo."

Philip blessed himself with the sign of the cross, and calmly walked away, disappearing into the shadows of the room.

Chapter Twenty-Six:

Farewell Until Spring

The following morning, all the inhabitants and staff of Branchview gathered in the driveway to say goodbye, as Millie and Bill set to depart for the airport.

Millie and Bill both approached Steven and Loraine, while Tony opened the door of the SUV for them. "I wish we could've stayed for the party," Millie stated with regret.

"There will be other parties, Millie. I promise." Steven answered with assurance.

She kissed him on the cheek and turned to her daughter. "Thank you for everything, my dear." She smiled. "I appreciate, and love you much."

"Oh, mum!" Loraine sadly exclaimed. "I love you too, and I'll miss you so much."

The two women emotionally embraced, "Come on, you two!" Tony impatiently interrupted. "If we don't get going, you'll miss your flight.

Bill and Steven shared a firm handshake, "Have a safe journey, Bill."

"We'll see you in the spring, Steven." They both waved before they entered the SUV. Tears flowed down Loraine's face, and Steven pulled her close as they watched the car drive away.

That night, Philip laid awake in his bed, while Tina slept soundly. He stared off into the darkness in troubled thought. After a few long moments, he carefully crawled out from beneath the covers. He paused to admire his wife in a peaceful slumber, before quietly slipping out the door.

Moments later, he casually strolled along the pathway now stretched with fallen leaves. A cold wind whistled through the dark trees, creating a mournful sound. He heard footsteps on the path behind him and bravely turned to confront them, but nothing was there.

"Nebriana! Is that you?" He called out. "Have you not flown off to the secret world yet?"

He waited a moment for an answer. When he set his sights ahead again, he was confronted by the grotesque figure of Satan. He looked even worse than any book could ever describe, complete with his horns and pointed tail.

He came within an inch of Philip's face with intimidation, "Hello, Poseidon!" He barked with a gravelly voice.

"Back away, Satan!" Philip sternly commanded. "Your breath smells of rot, and putrid sulfur."

Satan backed away a bit and growled with anger, "What business do you have with me?" Philip inquired.

"You left your calling card when you killed one of my prized disciples." He sneered. "That is a mortal sin you must answer to."

"I'll answer to the true God at my judgment, and never to you." He boldly answered.

Satan wickedly laughed and curled his grotesque fingers in front of him. "You can kill as many as you want, but there are many more that will rise to take their place." He grunted. "Our cause is too strong for you to defeat, Poseidon." He paused and paced in front of him. "You realize, I am the master of this world now. I own and control the media, the entertainment industry, world governments, politicians, the justice system, and even the preachers who claim to promote your God." He continued to pace back and forth with a sneering grin. "The days are numbered for your kind. Your God has forsaken this world, and allowed me to cease it." He grunted. "When I've conquered it, I'll then set my sights on the hidden world."

"You're insane!" Philip taunted. "That day will never come, and you know it. Good will triumph over evil, and I plan to fight you all the way to the end."

"You believe a lie, fool!" Satan stared and pointed at him with intimidation. "You should know that I could use a man of your power, and wealth. I could offer so much more than your God, or your life of goodness could ever offer."

Philip exploded with anger, "I will not forsake my God, and I am wise enough not to follow you." He pointed an accusing finger back at Satan. "You're so drunk with insanity, and arrogance that you believe your own lies."

Satan angrily roared in a tone that shook the ground and echoed through the surrounding woods. But Philip continued to stand firm, and unshaken, "Go ahead, Satan!" He taunted. "Destroy me, as I know you can, but know that you'll never have my soul."

Satan let out a wicked grunt and continued to pace the path in front of Philip. "Don't tempt me, Poseidon. You know that I'm not permitted to harm you." He laughed. "You may be strong-willed, but I know of your weaknesses." He laughed again. "Those despicable do-gooders at Branchview, and your lovely little Tina."

"You should know that they're protected by the shield of righteousness. I forbid you from harming them."

Satan paused to savor Philip's angry tone and tried to prod him further, "Have you forgotten Tina and

Charlotte Locke once belonged to me?" He grunted. "That is until you brought light to their souls."

"I intend to enlighten many more souls before my time is done."

Satan cupped his hands near his chin and pondered further, "Speaking of Charlotte Locke. I know of your innermost desires, and lusts for her."

Philip reacted with utter disgust, "You are pervertedly insane!" He charged. "That's an outright lie, and you know it."

"Is it now?" Satan chuckled. "Or, could it be that you simply don't remember?" He shrugged. "Why not ask your best friend, Steven Spencer? He can tell you."

Philip boiled over with anger, "Your sick strategy of divide and conquer will not work on me. I'm finished listening to the garbage that flows from your wicked mouth." He pointed a finger of warning at Satan. "I command you in the name of my Almighty God, be gone from my presence, and this sacred plot of land."

A flash of lightning struck out of nowhere, and Satan recoiled in fear. When it subsided, Satan angrily growled at Philip. "Our paths will cross again, Poseidon."

"I have no doubt they will." He challenged. With a final sneer, Satan disappeared in a cloud of black smoke.

Claudiana strolled up next to Philip in the aftermath. "It looks like we'll have our share of problems with that scoundrel." She commented.

"I'll do everything in my power to prolong the inevitable," Philip answered.

"Know that we'll do everything in our powers to help as well." She added.

Philip turned to the radiant Frost Queen and smiled. "Even though I dislike winter, it's always good to see you again, Claudiana." He sighed. "How long have you been watching?"

"Long enough to know what his intentions are." She grunted. "All the commotion between you two was enough to wake up the entire woods."

Luckily, Nebriana is a deep sleeper." He quipped with humor.

"We both had a bit of the forest nectar with Green Man last evening." She laughed.

Philip glanced upward with amusement. "She'll definitely need much rest for the long journey." He paused in quick thought. "I'm surprised she hasn't left already. It is getting a bit late into the season."

"You and I should discuss how to handle this pending crisis," Claudiana stated with a seriously raised eyebrow.

"If you'd be willing to accompany me to Lighthouse Point, I'll tell you everything I know so far."

"I'd be honored to, Poseidon." She smiled. They cordially entwined arms and continued strolling along the dark pathway.

The dining room clock chimed at 6:30 AM, while Mary and Mrs. Porter enjoyed a cup of coffee and quiet time before their day began. Tina entered the room and appeared to be disturbed. "Good morning ladies!" She announced. "Have you by chance seen my husband this morning?"

"Hasn't been through here yet, baby," Mary replied.

"Is everything alright?" Mrs. Porter asked. "You seem troubled."

Just then, the door to the kitchen swung open, and Philip strolled through, holding a cup of coffee. "Everything's fine, Mrs. Porter." Philip casually answered. "I went for an early morning stroll at Lighthouse Point."

"Is that so?" Tina countered with her hands on her hips. "According to my calculations, you've been gone from our bed since at least 3 o'clock this morning.

Mrs. Porter and Mary rolled their eyes at each other, and awkwardly rose from the table. "We should get an early start on that breakfast, Mary."

"Uh-hmm! I do agree."

The two women evacuated the room, fleeing the impending encounter. "Would you like to tell me where you were?" Tina asked.

Philip made a motion to calm her and spoke in a low voice. "I woke up, and decided to go down to the point to meditate."

"Philip!" She exclaimed with frustration. "I'm your wife, and I'm carrying our child." She reasoned. "I think I deserve a better explanation than that."

"We don't need to inform the entire household of our issues." Philip calmly stated.

"All I know is I'm growing tired of waking up in a cold bed, and wondering where my husband is."

"You're right!" He stressed. "Let's go back to our room, and I'll explain everything to you."

Tina stood with her arms firmly crossed in front of her, staring sternly at her husband. "Okay." She sighed. "If we're going to make a life together, you need to start being more open with me."

Philip gave an agreeing nod, "Yes, dear."

At the clearing in the woods, light began to break on the Autumn colored treetops. Nebriana, and Green Man, a mythical creature with a face of green leaves and ivy, as well as skin like the bark of a tree, met near the fire pit in the center of the clearing. From within the deep woods, other Faires and Woods People also emerged. The leaves fell from the surrounding trees, covering the green grass of the clearing, and they all stared upward to watch.

Claudiana entered from the footpath and marched up to join them. "Well!" Nebriana exclaimed. "Where have you been this morning?"

"I spent a good part of the night at Lighthouse Point with Poseidon."

"Is that something I need to worry about?" Green Man quipped.

"Nothing like that." She rolled her eyes. "He simply informed me on the situation evolving in the outside world." She took a deep breath. "It wasn't reassuring."

"We all knew it was coming." Green Man sadly stated. "The great prophets wrote it."

A single leaf fell onto Nebriana's shoulder, and she brushed it off. "The time has arrived for the changing of the guard."

"The fall went by so quickly this year" She sighed. "I fear it's going to be a long and solitary winter."

"Fear not Claudiana," Nebriana stated. "We have to be optimistic, and look forward to the spring when we'll hopefully gather again, and joyfully drink of the forest nectar."

Claudiana giggled and turned her attention to Green Man. "Ahh! The wonderful forest nectar!" She smiled. "We can thank our good friend here for that."

"I took it upon myself to leave a generous portion in your lair, for those long, cold nights." He replied.

"Bless you, Green Man!" Claudiana said with a wink. "You're such a dear!

Claudiana then glanced all around her with a pleasurable grin. "I do so envy you two. You have so much color in your seasons." She sadly sighs. "For me, there's only white and gray, and I always look forward to those few days when there's a blue sky and a fiery sunset."

"You also have the evergreen trees I created, especially for you." Green Man replied.

"I still sense you carry that lifelong crush for my sister." Nebriana teasingly commented with an eye roll.

"Hope springs eternal." He sighed. "Perhaps one day I'll resemble more the appearance of a man than a beast, and she'll find me irresistible."

Claudiana affectionately laid her fair hand on the bark textured arm of Green Man. "No man could ever possess the goodness you carry within you, my dear."

She leaned in, and gently kissed his green-leafed cheek, and he shivered. "That could be what I needed to get me through a season's long slumber." He stated with exuberance.

All shared a hearty laugh before Nebriana wearily sighed. "I heard they're having a party at Branchview tonight. Perhaps you could stop by, and get a peek in the window."

"If only I could join them." She replied as she glanced around her again. "The first snow will be coming early this year." Nebriana groaned. "Just be sure to keep it contained until we're well on our way to the hidden world."

"And, try to hold off on the frost as well." Green Man added. "At least until the Woods People and I are secure, and warm in our underground places."

Claudiana reached out her hand, and both Nebriana and Green Man gently placed their hands over it. "Farewell, my good friends."

Green Man chuckled and blinked his eye, "I'll see you two cuties next year."

"Until the spring," Nebriana added with a warm smile.

With a wave of his branch-like arm, Green Man and the Woods People slowly retreated into the deep recesses of the surrounding woods. Nebriana turned to her Faires and motioned to them, "Ready yourselves for flight."

A loud buzz echoed loudly throughout the woods, the Faires rapidly flapped their wings and took flight into the early morning skies. Once airborne, they looked like a giant swarm of lightning bugs.

Claudiana watched with delight as they merged to form an arrow-shaped light, and headed northeast across the Atlantic waters, on their long journey to the hidden world. Once they were out of sight, she swept the train of her long white gown across her entire body and disappeared.

The clock in the Branchview Foyer chimed at 7:30 that evening, as Steven strolled in from another portion of the house, dressed in his tux. Concurrently, Philip hurried down the stairs, also wearing a formal tux. "Well! It's a rare occasion for me to see you all dressed up." Steven joked.

Philip paused to check himself in the spacious Foyer mirror. "I could get used to dressing like this."

Philip turned and hesitated as if wanting to say more, and Steven sensed it. "Is there something else on your mind?" He asked.

"Would you have a few moments to talk before we go to the Grand Corridor?"

"Absolutely!" Steven answered. "We can talk in the Sitting Room."

The men entered the room, and Steven closed the doors behind them. He then motioned to two chairs near the fireplace, where they both moved to sit down. "Is everything alright?" Steven further probed.

"Everything's fine," Philip assured. "I had something I needed to ask you."

Steven coaxed him on with a silent gesture, "When you were in 1697, did something happen between me and Charlotte?"

Steven took a deep breath and rolled his eyes, "Well!" He paused. "The two of you fell in love." Philip reacted with surprise, but Steven was quick to continue, "Nothing became of it." He stressed. "Charlotte prevented it from going any further." He sighed. "But I think she returned to the future, still harboring those same feelings for you."

"And, of course, my memory had been purged of it all," Philip replied with an expression of enlightenment. "That would explain her reaction toward me." Steven gave an uncomfortable nod and continued, "Now that you're aware, do you have any regrets?"

"Had anything become of it, it would've drastically changed history." He reasoned, "Many future tragedies may have never taken place." He pondered. "But then, I never would've met Tina either."

"Charlotte was wise enough to realize all that," Steven added. "In a sense, you could say she sacrificed her own happiness for the sake of love."

Philip gave a long sigh of relief, "Thank heavens for that."

Both men pondered and reflected on the situation for a long moment. "For what it's worth." Steven reluctantly continued. "I must admit to you that I also secretly harbored feelings for Amphitrite when I was back in that time."

"I can't blame you." Philip chuckled. "I do not doubt that her feelings ran deep for you as well."

"She did offer me immortality if I'd remain with her in that time." He sighed.

"What made you decide not to?" Philip curiously asked.

"My wonderful wife and babies, who were waiting for me in the future," Steven replied with much emotion. "No beautiful goddess or promise of immortality could ever entice me away from them."

Philip smiled and gave him a friendly pat on the shoulder. "You made the right decision, my friend."

"I know I did." Steven proclaimed. "Besides, I could've never endured staying in that horrid time period without my coffee." Both men shared a hearty laugh as they stood again. "Come on, Steven! We have a party to go to."

Steven halted. "I'm curious, Philip." He paused. "What made you ask me about all this?"

"Oh!" He pondered. "Just something an old devil mentioned to me." Philip moved ahead with a clever grin, while Steven was somewhat baffled by the answer.

Music and magic filled the air in the Branchview Grand Corridor on this splendid night. The room was filled with residents of the house, along with many dear friends, and a sprinkling of past spirits that decided to secretly peek in.

Loraine placed her arm around Steven and pulled him close. "What a marvelous night!" She exclaimed. "I'm so glad we did this."

They kissed, while the band leader stepped to the microphone, "I have a request to have the resident musicians play a tune."

"I think that means us," Steven commented. Ezekiel, Philip, and Meryl emerged from the crowd and proceeded with Steven to the stage.

Steven took a seat at the piano, Philip chose the mandolin, Ezekiel took the hornpipe, and Meryl seized the violin. "I think we should have a little fun." Steven quipped. "Follow my lead."

He started playing the first notes of "The Sailor's Hornpipe" slowly, as the others picked up the tune and joined in.

They all found the rhythm, as the momentum of the music building. Everyone began to clap to the beat and eventually danced, as the tune picked up speed.

As the attendees joyfully danced, Eddie took time from dancing with Sandy, and twirled little Tricia around, picking her up off her feet. Just then, the ghostly figures of Amanda Green and Matthew Branch glided by as they waltzed to the tune. Tricia's eyes grew wide when she saw them.

"Look, daddy! Ghosts!"

"Yes, I know!" Eddie smiled. "They were friends of mine, many years ago."

"Do you think we could talk to them sometime?" The little girl asked.

"I think that could be a possibility," Eddie replied with a smirk. Eddie then pulled Sandy close, and joyfully kissed her, while Tricia joined in on the family embrace.

Frederick and Suzy also casually talked, as they gracefully glided along with their waltz. "I didn't know you could dance so well, Rick." She commented, "There's probably a great bit that you don't know about me." He replied. "Perhaps it's time I learned." She further commented with a grin.

Frederick glanced at her with much surprise, "Could I take that as meaning you'd like to be my steady?"

Suzy laughed heartily at his statement. "You can interpret it any way you'd like, Mr. Worth."

As the four musicians played the last note of the song, and all cheered, Steven glanced off to the side and observed Loraine lovingly admiring him. He let loose with a joyful laugh, and responded with a loving smile, right back at her.

At the end of the night, Steven was the last member of the household to retire to bed. He loosened his tie and turned out the Foyer lights before ascending the stairs. As he reached the first landing, he paused to admire the picture of him and Loraine. Suddenly, he heard distant music echoing from the Grand Corridor. He curiously glanced that way, and decided to check it out.

As he entered the now dark, and deserted room, the piano continued to play the haunting tune of "Stardust". It echoed forebodingly throughout the cavernous room. No one was sitting at the piano as it played, and when Steven got closer, he spotted the keys playing on their own accord. Just then, Daphne Branch appeared on the piano bench, and smiled endearingly at him, as she gracefully played the final notes of the tune.

Steven clapped, and sat down on the bench next to her, "That was my mother's favorite song."

"I know." She winked. "Such a beautiful old standard." She sighed. "The party was wonderful, Steven. It was like the ones I remember from so long ago."

"I never knew you played."

"Where did you think you, and your father, inherited the gift?" She countered with a sly grin. "It was my spirit who always guided your fingers across the keyboard."

Steven glanced upward with an emotional smile. "You watched over me, long before I knew you even existed."

"Oh yes!" She replied. "Just as I watch over your children now."

"Why haven't you gone to the light, grandmother?"

Daphne carefully pondered the question, "You sound like Maggie." She chuckled. "I guess I'm afraid to leave my family, and this old house." She paused. "Maybe it's just fear of what lies beyond that light."

"But Darren…umm…my grandfather, would be there waiting for you."

"And, what would I tell him?" She shot a hopeless glance at Steven. "It was because of me that he was killed."

"He knows the truth." Steven sympathetically stated. "You can always come back here, and visit anytime, just as Maggie does."

She cupped her hand gently on the side of Steven's face, "Perhaps I'll consider it."

"I wish we had had more chance to talk while I was here."

Daphne shrugged and glanced around the room, "I certainly don't have anywhere I need to be right now." They both laughed, and she continued. "We can talk a bit now, and a lot more later, when you return."

Steven gave an assuring nod, "You can count on that, grandmother."

The fateful morning arrived too soon, as the household members lined the circular driveway to bid farewell to Steven and Loraine.

With the babies strapped securely in the back seat, Loraine ushered Bumpers into the car and waved goodbye to everyone. Steven jogged over to where Tony and Andrea, who held baby Michael, and Mrs. Porter stood.

"I'll see you all next Thursday." He stated. "I'll have a shuttle waiting at Tampa airport when your flight arrives.

"I'll make sure we all get there safely," Tony replied with an assuring nod.

The men exchanged a firm handshake, then Mrs. Porter laid a trembling hand on Steven's arm.

"Be safe, Steven." Steven laughed. "I wish I had a nickel for all the times you told me that, Mrs. Porter." He leaned in, and kissed her on the cheek, then waved to everyone else before he hustled back toward the car, and jumped into the drivers' seat.

Philip and Ezekiel conversed as they watched the car drive away. "What shape do you think the world will be in when they return to the Spring?" Ezekiel asked.

Philip took a deep breath, before answering, "We can only hope for the best, brother."

As Steven drove the car down the long driveway, Bumpers propped his paws against the dashboard, and stared out the windshield, while his little tail wagged with excitement. Loraine wiped tears from her eyes as she stared out at the Autumn gray Connecticut skies.

Steven glanced over at her with concern, "Are you okay, sweetheart?"

She forced a smile and gently laid her hand on top of his, "Yes, I'll be alright."

As the car exited the massive gates, and entered onto the main road, Loraine closed her eyes and imagined a bird's eye view of the immense estate they were now leaving. In her mind, she visioned the massive main house, with its' high spired roof, and beautiful gardens. The

Pathway winding through the vast, enchanted woods which led to the cliffs and beach at Lighthouse Point, and the seemingly endless Atlantic Ocean.

As they drove along, she silently recited the thoughts that streamed into her mind.

Life is an amazing journey, filled with unexpected twists and turns that mold our fate. People come and go, and enrich our lives, sometimes changing them forever. One thing for certain about this journey is that it consists of a never-ending battle between good and evil. No matter how dark and hopeless the days may seem, we must always seek the positive, and know beyond a doubt that love conquers all.

FOUR DAYS LATER.
LONG BOAT KEY, FLORIDA

In the office/library of their Florida estate, Steven paused to unpack various items from the many boxes stretched about the room. He was dressed casually in a faded pair of jeans, and a Led Zeppelin T-shirt. He glanced up at the half-filled shelves of the bookcase, then back at the several boxes of books that still needed to be placed.

"There's virtually no end to this." He chuckled.

He wandered over to the huge Angel of Sorrow statue that sat in the middle of the room and placed his hand upon its' smooth surface. He felt the same renewed sense of strength radiate from it, as he had several other times in the now distant past.

Loraine breezed into the room, wearing baggy sweat pants, and a white V-neck T-shirt. Her cheerful presence pleasantly interrupted Steven's deep thoughts.

She glanced around the room, with her hands resting firmly on her hips, "Things are finally beginning to look as I remembered them." She stated with an impressive nod.

"It seems like it's taking forever to reach that point." Steven sighed.

She strolled over and draped her arms around him.

"I've already taken Bumpers out, and put the babies down for their nap."

"Is the new nanny in the Nursery with them?" He asked.

"Yes, she is," Loraine answered with a sly grin. "Perhaps now, you and I can take a romantic stroll around the neighborhood."

Steven stared upward with a grin, then turned, and firmly placed his hands against her hips. "I was thinking maybe a nice flight around the neighborhood might be better." He teased. "We could fly out over the Gulf, and maybe even catch a bird's eye view of some Mermaids frolicking in the water."

"Steven!" Loraine laughed. "Are you just being silly, or are you saying…?"

Steven rapidly nodded yes, "Charlotte taught me that same bird trick."

A wide grin erupted across Loraine's face, "I'll race you to the door, Mr. Spencer." They both hurried from the room, laughing and giggling like children.

On the large cherry wood desk by the window, the monitor on the Apple desktop lit up to a blank writing screen. Letters began to appear on their own until a simple message was completed. It read…

"SEE YOU SOON!"

Author Biography

 Brian was born and raised in Erie Pennsylvania and has been involved in some capacity of writing since a very young age. After graduating from Penn State University, he lived several years in North Carolina and then Florida, where he presently resides. His accomplishments cover a wide spectrum from writing Psychology Textbooks, several essays on Metaphysics, articles on health and fitness, songwriting, and screenplays. He is also the author of The Balanced Journey, a common sense guide to living from a Spiritual and Metaphysical point of view. (Amazon Publishing, 2012).

In 2017, he retired from FedEx after 21 years of service and began a new career as a script doctor for the movie industry. He is also very active in Historic Preservation, causes that support our Military Veterans, a fan of Classic Rock Music, and is an avid fitness enthusiast.

Branchview Series

- The Unexpected Journey
- The Epic Showdown
- The Portal of Time
- The Fall of the Secret Society – *Coming Fall of 2022*

Additional Books

- Stories of the Hidden World
- The Balanced Journey

www.ingramcontent.com/pod-product-compliance
Lightning Source LLC
Chambersburg PA
CBHW070708100726
47907CB00001B/93